To all the Yankee fans who are with them not just in sensational years like '27 but the rest as well.

© 2017, W. G. Braund / Out Of The Park Worldwide.
All rights reserved.

No part of this book may be used or reproduced by any means, graphic, electronic, or mechanical, including photocopying, recordiing, taping or by any information storage retrieval system without the written permission of the author /publisher except in the case of brief quotations embodied in critical articles and reviews.

Contact info
Out of the Park Worldwide
Post Office Box 695 • Marmora, ON K0K 2M0 • Canada

ISBN: 978-0-9977758-0-8 - *Hardcover*
ISBN: 978-0-9977758-1-5 - *Softcover*
ISBN :978-0-9977758-2-2 - *e-book*

Cover photograph courtesy of
Baseball Hall of Fame & Museum

Book Design
timmyroland.com

W.G. **Braund**

1.

THE BABE MAKES A PICTURE SHOW

"Must be like shootin' fish in a barrel out here."

Anna Nilsson sat in front of a makeup mirror dabbing at her perfectly-sculptured cheeks. Ted Wilde, a tall man with salt and pepper hair, stood behind her.

"I'm goink to be verking vit an actual base ball player? I thought you ver getting a real actor to play da guy," said Nilsson when she was told Babe Ruth would be playing the part of Babe Gibson.

"That was the plan," Wilde told her patiently. "But someone told me Ruth was coming out here, so it just seemed natural to get him."

"But, can he act?"

"Better than most ball players. He's got personality to burn … and he's certainly used to having his picture taken."

o o o

"Wilde's directed most of Harold Lloyd's comedies," Marshall Hunt told the Babe as they arrived at the First National lot a few minutes later. Hunt was from the *New York Daily News*. He'd gone west with Ruth. They'd become good friends and Hunt was usually somewhere in the background when photographs were taken of the Bambino. He made a point of learning his schedule and invariably he'd show up - at a charity event or a prizefight or a vaudeville show. Whenever the Babe visited a hospital there was Hunt waiting for him at the front door. A small, round-shouldered man with a mischievous twinkle in his eye, Hunt was always on the lookout for a swell time. He enjoyed a good meal, a cigar, and a few cocktails. He was one of the few reporters who could keep up with the Bambino's all night prowls.

Babe Ruth

Sometimes he and the Babe took a drive out into the countryside for a chicken dinner at a roadside diner in whatever luxury automobile Ruth had just bought. Hunt told a colleague he knew he could trust not to say anything, "Usually the Babe's really after chicken and a daughter."

Hunt was always on hand when Ruth did anything heroic or funny and he got the scoop. But if there was any hint of scandal or wrongdoing Hunt would get his boss to send someone else to cover it so his friendship with the Babe wouldn't be compromised.

When Joe Dugan commented on Hunt being around so much, Ruth bellowed in the cavernous bass tone that made him sound like a bear, "Marsh is okay I guess, but someday I hope the little runt misses a train. A guy has to have some privacy."

"Your co-star's name is Anna Q. Nilsson," Hunt continued. "She's Swedish, a real beauty. She's a former model and a bona fide movie starlet. Nilsson's done more than eighty pictures. She's a bit hard to understand though. She's got a pretty thick accent."

"Who cares?" said the Babe. "It's not like anybody's gonna hear her. Long as she looks good."

o o o

A skinny twenty-year-old guide who took potential investors on studio tours led Ruth and Hunt through the lot to where *Babe Comes Home* was being shot. Along the way they passed an Indian village, a college football field, a jungle, a pirate ship, a one-room schoolhouse, a casino, and a circus tent. Ruth saw a familiar figure. He recognized him even without his pork pie hat.

"Hey! I know him," Ruth blurted. "That's Buster Keaton. What's he makin'?"

"I think it's called Steamboat Bill Junior," the guide told the Babe.

Four enormous fans blew at Keaton as he struggled to walk along a city street. Hats, newspapers, and myriad other wind-blown objects pelted him. He pretended to get knocked out and then stood up, trying to get his bearings in front a two-story house. Keaton stood stock-still and expressionless.

"What's with them?" the Babe asked, pointing at a group of crew members who were huddled together and seemed to be praying.

"Everybody told Keaton this stunt was too dangerous - even for him. That house front he's standing in front of weighs four thousand pounds."

"So what?"

"It's about to fall on him."

"You gotta be kiddin' me!"

The cameraman was a pro. He'd filmed hundreds of two and four-reelers. He kept the camera rolling, but he looked away and cringed as the house front fell on top of Keaton.

"I've seen a lot of stunts being filmed, but I can't watch," said the guide. He covered his eyes.

The house front fell right on top of Keaton. Everyone gasped.

He'd planned it perfectly. There was a tall window on the second floor of the house and there were no panes of glass in it. Keaton now stood, unharmed, in the space occupied by the window. He'd had no more than two inches to spare on either side.

"Holly shit," muttered Ruth. "Keaton sure is a brave son of a bitch."

"Brave or loco," said the guide as he attempted to regain his composure. "He did a lot of crazy stunts in the picture he made a few weeks ago too. It was called The General. It had an exploding bridge scene. I heard it was the most expensive stunt ever done."

"I'm definitely goin' to see *that* picture when it comes out," said Ruth. "This one too."

A trainer walked past with a huge tiger on a leash. Marshall Hunt jumped into the Babe's arms. Ruth laughed and set him back down when the tiger was led into a cage.

"You got the whole goddamn world in here!" yelled the Babe as an acrobat in tights fell into a net sixty feet below a trapeze. A few people turned around but no one needed to worry about noise on a movie set.

"We're cranking out twenty pictures a week," the young man told him.

Babe Ruth

Two men in ten gallon hats and chaps and three shapely belly dancers passed them. Ruth gulped. "Must be like shootin' fish in a barrel out here."

"What is?" asked the guide.

"Gettin' laid."

"It is pretty easy. A lot of the hunkiest actors aren't really … interested."

"What d'ya mean?" asked the Babe. "Who wouldn't wanna screw these dolls?"

"Good to see you, Babe," shouted Ted Wilde from across an Old West saloon. He wore a wide-brimmed hat, an-open-throat shirt, riding breeches, and leather puttees.

The guide shook his head. "They all think they're Cecil Fucking B. De Mille," he muttered as he left Hunt and the Babe and headed back to the front gate. Wilde took them to the commissary, which was full of attractive people dressed as gladiators, ladies-in-waiting, pirates, and pirates' wenches.

"You play Babe Gibson, the star of the Los Angeles Angels, and you meet a washerwoman named Vernie. That's the part your co-star Miss Nilsson plays," explained Wilde as Ruth looked at the commissary's selection. "Normally we'd be done in two weeks, but this picture's going to be a six-reeler, so we may be as much as three weeks shooting it."

Ruth wasn't eating the way he had when he broke into baseball with the Red Sox as an eighteen-year-old, though people still made up stories about him eating a dozen hot dogs and washing them down with a dozen sodas. His stomach couldn't take that anymore. He chose a few slices of ham, a couple of pieces of cheese, some pickles, and two apples.

Wilde looked puzzled. "Is that all you're going to have?"

"Whatever pounds I pack on, I just gotta work off again."

"I see. At any rate, sweet Vernie has to clean Gibson's uniforms and they're always covered in tobacco stains," Wilde continued. "They fall in love and Vernie's only wish is that Babe would quit chewing tobacco. He does, but then he can't hit home runs anymore. In the big game Babe really needs a homer. He looks up in the crowd and spots Vernie. She blows him a kiss and throws him a package of tobacco."

"Sounds like a real winner," said the Babe. "When do we start?"

"Today, as a matter of fact. We're shooting a scene in which you come out of the dugout and you pull a bag of chewing tobacco out of your pocket. You go to stuff a big chaw of it into your mouth but then look up and see Vernie in the crowd. She shakes her head to show she doesn't want you to do it and you look sheepish, shrug, and toss the bag into the dugout. Then you go to the plate and strike out. Be sure not to accidentally hit any of the pitches or we'll have to cut and start over and that costs money."

o o o

The next morning at six Ruth headed out on a five-mile run along Hollywood Boulevard, past the jacaranda trees, peppers, palms, and magnolias. As he jogged he thought back to how he'd run from the cops and truant officers through the back alleys of Pigtown so often when he was a little kid. A pink Packard slowed down as it caught up to and then passed him. Its windows were open and a poodle had its head out of one of them.

"Hazel," Ruth heard the driver say. "You are not going to believe who that runner was."

"Who was it?"

"It was Babe Ruth! Not a word of a lie."

"Edith, you really must stop taking that tonic or elixir or whatever it is. You're positively delusional."

"I am not. That was him!"

"Yes dear. Just as you say. Like last week when you told me we'd passed Tom Mix on horseback."

"We did! That was Tom Mix - on a palomino."

o o o

In addition to his $30,000 salary Ruth'd had the studio build a handball court and exercise room so he could keep in shape and avoid boredom between takes. During lunch breaks Ruth sometimes played tennis with the extras. When he sparred with his phony teammates, many of whom had been boxers, a large crowd of technicians and office workers gathered to watch. The Babe joked with them as if he'd worked on the lot for years. "Take that, ya bald-headed shit!" he yelled as he landed a punch on the

Babe Ruth

chin of a stocky extra. He looked at the audience and blushed. "Sorry. I forgot there were dames here," he called out.

"No need to worry, Babe," said a pretty brunette secretary in a tight skirt. "We hear lots worse from the studio bosses. Lots worse."

o o o

After the first week of filming Wilde threw a party for the cast so they could relax and get to know each other better. He told them to bring as many friends as they liked, as long as they were in the business. He invited some of the old gang as well. The people who'd been in the early Griffith pictures were considered part of the older crowd now, even though they were still in their late twenties or early thirties. They drank martinis off in a corner by themselves and talked about the good old days of the two-reelers when they'd made scenes up as they went along.

"Where's Anna Nilsson?" Ethel Shannon asked Wilde. Ethel was a tiny redhead who played a washerwoman in *Babe Comes Home*. She'd left her press agent, whom she'd just married, at the bar talking to some other publicity people. The *Chicago Tribune* had sent a reporter out to Hollywood to do a piece on Babe Ruth as a film star. He'd written of a day on the set when the cast had sat in box seats while the director paced the diamond explaining to them how he needed to block an upcoming scene. Ethel Shannon had no trouble squeezing into her seat. Behind her, the Babe was having a great deal more difficulty. He ended up touching Shannon's back with the toe of his shoe. She'd wheeled around on him and snapped, "Don't you get fresh with me, playboy."

The Trib reporter had gone on to explain that Ruth had apologized and Shannon had realized it had just been an accident. His shoe had been dirty and it left a spot on her dress. The Babe offered to get it dry-cleaned. She told him not to worry - she'd get her husband to make the studio buy her a new one. Shannon and Ruth laughed about it and they were great pals from then on.

"When she heard the Babe was coming to the party she told me she wasn't feeling well and was going to stay in," Wilde told Ethel.

"Stuck up bitch!" Ethel muttered under her breath.

"What did you say?" Wilde asked.

"Nothing, Ted, nothing. Swell house you've got here. Have you got anything to drink?"

"We have orange blossoms - orange juice and sugar syrup." He hesitated. "And there might be just a hint of gin in them too," he said with a wink. He handed her a drink in a long-stemmed glass. "And this is a Pink Lady. It's grenadine, apple jack, and egg white. Oh, and I forgot, there's gin in it as well."

A blare of saxophones and wild laughter wafted from the next room. Wilde heard someone who'd clearly had more than a couple of Pink Ladies say, "They danced and drank on the lawn until the sun came up and then they fell asleep in the garden. The cops came by but Mickey bought them off with a handful of twenty dollar bills."

Wilde turned around when the butler signalled him that another guest had just arrived.

"Who is it?" Wilde asked.

"Miss Bow," the butler told him.

"Clara Bow's here!" exclaimed Ethel. Everyone turned to look. Bow was absolutely stunning.

She wore a backless, knee-length black dress and patent-leather pumps that made her look a lot taller than she really was. Jet black hair, shiny and cropped just below her ears, framed her heart-shaped face, the ends tapering forward on each side. A smooth curtain of bangs stopped abruptly just above her eyebrows. Her skin was pale but she had high, perfectly-sculpted cheek bones, flirty brown eyes, and crimson, bee-stung lips. Her looks were so dazzling she seemed to give off sparks. A half dozen bangles dangled from her wrists. Around her neck was a tiny gold box.

"What do you think she carries in that little box?" Shannon asked Wilde.

"From what I hear, it's cocaine," he whispered.

"She's certainly come a long way since she won that beauty contest in Brooklyn," said Ethel, "but someone really must convince her to stop chewing Juicy Fruit with that Cupid's bow mouth of hers."

"She positively oozes sex appeal," said Wilde. "I wish we could afford her."

Babe Ruth

"The girl can't act!" said Shannon, a little too loudly.

"The public still lines up to see her. And I hear she gets forty thousand fan letters a week," said Wilde as he headed to talk to Bow. "Too bad there's nothing inside that pretty little head but dollar signs and tuxedos."

"Constance!" called Bow as she swept past Wilde and Shannon. Constance Talmadge, who might have been almost as beautiful as Bow if her high-bridged nose were a touch shorter and her lips a bit fuller, was smoking a cigarette in a pearl holder.

"Dat must be a Lucky Strike yer smokin'. God knows dey pay you enough," said Bow.

They both laughed.

"What is it dey have ya say?"

"Reach for a Lucky instead of a sweet," said Talmadge.

"Ya, dat's it."

"They do help me stay thin. Aren't we all supposed to look as though we haven't seen food in a year?"

"What kinda diet are you on?" asked Bow.

"A delightful medley of tomatoes, parsley, and spinach," answered Talmadge. "What about you?"

"I'm nibblin' a lotta cucumbers," said Bow.

"Or things the same shape and size, I'll bet."

"You hussy!" said Bow, loud enough to make some of the guests spill their drinks.

"Oh, so I'm the hussy. Are there any men in town you haven't bedded?"

"I just happen ta think people oughta have their fun without havin' ta get married," said Bow.

"Did you hear the latest?" whispered Talmadge.

"No, but I'll bet I'm about ta," answered Bow.

"Gloria Swanson's taken up with some banker from Boston who wants to get into the picture business. He's wined and dined her at the Waldorf and Delmonico's and he's putting up close to a million for the picture she's making with Barrymore."

"What's wrawng wit dat?" asked Bow. "Sides the fact she just got hitched lass year?"

"Well, he's a strict Roman Catholic for one thing. And he has a whole flock of kids," Talmadge explained.

"Don't dey all, sweetie? What's dis swell's name?"

"Kennedy. Joseph Kennedy."

"Never hoid a him."

"Apparently he made a bundle on the Yellow Cab Company. There are whispers he's a bootlegger on the side," said Talmadge.

"He can't be all that bad then," said Bow.

"Have you ever been to Gloria's house? It's an absolute palace. King Gillette, the razor blade millionaire, built it. Twenty-two rooms, a private elevator, a movie theater, and five marble baths. Apparently she's screwed the banker in every one of them."

"Enough a da chit chat, I wanna dance," Bow announced. She left Talmadge and went off to look for a partner.

A white-haired judge in an expensive suit stood at the side of the dance floor with a drink in his hand. He was startled when Bow took his glass and set it on the bar. "Come on honey, let's cut a rug," she yelled, pulling him onto the dance floor.

The judge tried not to look foolish as Bow swayed her hips provocatively to the music.

"Relax, yer honor," said Bow. She started to undo his buttons, beginning with the top jacket button. "Rich man, poor man, beggar man," she chanted, undoing another button with each designation. When she got to "Indian chief" she undid the top button of the judge's pants. He turned beet red and fled the dance floor.

"What are ya bein' such a stick in the mud fawr?" she called after him. "I wuz just havin' some fun is all." She shrugged her shoulders and rejoined Talmadge.

Babe Ruth

"There's Ruth," said Talmadge, motioning to the huge foyer.

"It is. I didn't know he was comin'. I hear da Babe's got quite da appetite," said Bow, "and I don't just mean for food and booze."

"I hear he's nailed more women than fastballs. He's not much to look at, but they say he can go all night."

"Hi, Babe," said Wilde as Ruth breezed past the butler.

"Hi, boss," Ruth replied. "Mighty fancy digs ya got here. Got any good whiskey?"

"We might be able to scare some up," said Wilde. "Jives, see what you can find for Mister Ruth."

"Yes sir," answered the butler, hurrying from the room.

"You sure know how ta throw a party," said the Babe. "There's a lotta great lookin' broads here."

o o o

The Babe sipped smooth Scotch and talked baseball with some actors and directors. They wanted to know if the Yankees were going to be able to beat Connie Mack's rebuilt Athletics.

"The Indians nearly caught us last year. This time the Senators and the A's are gonna give us the most trouble," Ruth told them between puffs on a huge cigar.

"Are you ever going to hit fifty homers again, Babe?" asked George Bancroft, who'd just had a heated argument with his director over whether one bullet could possibly stop the character he was playing.

"Maybe," said Ruth. "I'm in better shape than I've been in five years. Go ahead, punch me in the gut. Hard as you can. You'll see."

The men looked awkwardly at one another. They threw plenty of fake punches in four-reel oaters, but punching Babe Ruth was another thing. No one was very anxious to take him up on his invitation.

Finally a tall man with chiselled good looks stepped forward. "The name's Cooper, Babe. Gary Cooper. I just finished a western with Tom Mix. I'm the guy you see getting shot off a horse and falling into a gulley full of sharp rocks."

"Punch away, Cooper," said Ruth.

"Cooper threw what he thought was a pretty hard punch. But all the medicine balls Art McGovern had fired at his stomach had paid off for the Babe. He just laughed. Cooper shook his hand to ease the pain.

◦   ◦   ◦

"I wanna meet him," Clara Bow whispered to Wilde.

"Who?" asked Wilde.

"Who d'ya think? I know all da movie stiffs here. I wanna meet Babe Ruth."

"I thought you went for boxers and football players."

"In the Babe's case I think I could make an exception."

"I'm sure you *could*. Wait here."

Bow took out her compact and powdered her cheeks. Then she put on another layer of lip gloss even though she already had plenty on.

Wilde went over to the group Ruth was in. "Babe, could I borrow you for a minute?"

"Could ya what?" asked the Babe, confused.

"I mean could you come with me? There's someone who'd like to meet you."

"To talk about movies or baseball?"

"Probably something lascivious," said Wilde.

"La what?" asked the Babe.

"Never mind, come with me. I have a feeling the two of you will hit it off."

◦   ◦   ◦

"Clara, I would like to present the Sultan of Swat and a fine film actor, Babe Ruth. Babe, this is Clara Bow, the *It Girl*."

Ruth's eyes nearly popped out if his head.

"I'm real glad ta meet yuz," said Bow, batting her thick eyelashes and toying flirtatiously with a spit curl.

"Me too. I thought you looked swell in pictures. In the flesh you're even sweller."

Babe Ruth

"Ain't ju da sweet tawker. Can I feel your muscles, Babe? Dey must be real big."

Seeing where this was headed Wilde shook his head and left them alone.

Babe held out his arm and flexed.

"I was right, yer real strong, not like dem puny actors I gotta spoon wit on da lot every day. I bet ya got a real big bat too." She waited to see his reaction.

"I haven't had any complaints," said Ruth with a grin.

Bow giggled. "Why don't ya come 'n see me on da set some time?"

"I'd like that just fine," said Ruth. "What picture you makin' now?"

"It's called Rough House Rosie. I play a flapper dat tricks her childhood sweetheart inta marryin' her and den falls fer a rich guy. Say, could you be a babe and get me a drink?" She laughed at her own joke.

"Be glad to. I could use another myself, it's mighty hot in here," said Ruth, pulling his starched collar away from his neck.

"Maybe we could take a nice cool ride up da coast in my new roadster," said Bow. "It goes real fast. Do you like ta go fast, Babe?"

"Whenever I can."

o   o   o

Bow's car was parked on the lawn. It was crimson red, exactly the same color as her lipstick. Ruth guessed it was not a coincidence.

"Is that a Kissel?"

"Ya, it's a Kissel Gold Bug Coupe. Pickford and Fairbanks have one a dem too. Course dey got a lotta caws. I hear dat fighter's got one too, da Mauler guy."

"Jack Dempsey."

"Ya. Dat's the guy. And William S. Hart - da cowboy star - he's got one too."

"He played Wild Bill Hickok didn't he? I loved that picture."

"Hart has Billy the Kid's six shooters."

"He does?"

"And he's met Wyatt Earp and Bat Masterson."

"Earp? And Bat Masterson too!"

"Kinda sad Hart's on his way out. He ain't made nuttin' since *Tumbleweeds* a couple a years back. Now Tom Mix is da star a da oaters."

"Ya. He's good too. I like his pictures a lot."

They got into the car and Bow floored it. Ruth grinned and held on for dear life.

"I never been with a dame that goes as fast as you," said the Babe. Bow's scarf blew straight out behind her as she tore along the coastal highway. Ruth looked down at the rocks below as the car skidded around a hairpin turn.

"Want some?" he asked, handing her a silver flask.

Bow took a gulp. "Dat's good stuff ya got there, Babe."

Ruth stared at Bow. He'd never seen such a beautiful face. Like most flappers she had her breasts flattened with a bandeau brassiere so it was hard to tell how large they were but she had a tiny waist and gorgeous legs. She'd hiked her skirt up so she could operate the pedals. At the speed they were travelling he felt he should be watching the road, but he couldn't keep his eyes off her creamy thighs. Twice she got a bit too close to the edge of the road and sent pebbles cascading into the ocean.

"You like ta gamble, Babe?"

"Sure. Mostly the ponies."

"I was tinking we could go ta dis place I just hoid about."

"Where is it?"

"It's on da Nevada bawder. It's a casino. You can gamble all ya want there."

"Isn't that a long way?"

"It would be kinduva long drive I guess. But if we got some refreshments for da trip it'd be kinda romantic in da desert at night, wit da stars and awl. Don't ya think?"

Ruth thought about what it would be like to spend the night with this amazing-looking creature. "When were you thinkin' a goin'?"

Babe Ruth

"Why not tonight?"

"Tonight?"

"Ya, we can leave right now. I just gotta stop for gas."

"Listen, sweet cheeks, there is nuthin' in the whole world I'd rather do than take off with you into the middle of the desert right now but a lotta people are gonna be waiting for me at the studio in five or six hours."

Bow pouted. "Aw, whata ya gotta be such a spoiled sport for, Babe? I taught we could have ourselves a swell time tonight."

She reached over and put her hand on Ruth's crotch. He was hard in an instant, as hard as he could ever remember. "Damn, you got a big pecker! I'd hate to waste one a dose."

Her eyes returned to the road, but she kept her hand where it was until she had to shift gears.

"How about Saturday night, doll? We aren't shootin' any scenes on Sunday."

"Awl right. We'll go Saturday night. Ya promise?"

"Oh, I promise all right. Wild horses couldn't keep me away."

2.

PICKFAIR AND BREAKAWAY HOUSE

"Honey, I forgot to duck."

"What picture they making next door?" Ruth asked the next morning when he and Hunt arrived on the set. "The one with Sound Stage No Noise No Deliveries in big letters on the door. What the hell's a sound stage anyway?"

"They're making a musical," answered Ted Wilde. "With talking."

"What d'ya mean, *talking?*"

"It's called a dialogue picture. People in the theater will hear the actors speaking."

"How the hell are they gonna do that?"

"I'm not sure, but somebody's figured out a way."

"Who's in it?"

Marshall Hunt interrupted. "It's a singer that went to the same school you did, Babe - St. Mary's Industrial School in Baltimore. Al Jolson."

"The jazz singer?" asked Ruth.

Wilde laughed.

"What's so funny?" asked Ruth.

"You called him the jazz singer."

"So what?"

"That's the name of the picture."

"Oh."

"Warner Brothers couldn't afford Jolson. They're just a small studio and they were thinking of asking him to lend them the money to make his own picture," Wilde chuckled. "Then their Rin Tin Tin movies took off and they made a killing on the pooch. No one really believes dialogue pictures will catch on. It's just a novelty. They're having a hell of a time shooting it. They can't build sets because of the noise of the saws and the hammers. And if anyone whistles or a catering truck arrives they have to start all over again."

o o o

That night the Babe boxed two rounds with Jack Dempsey in a charity event. The referee was the booze-loving, children-loathing W. C. Fields. While Ruth and Dempsey's gloves were being laced up, reporters went to get some quotes from the irascible actor/comedian. They ended up playing straight men.

"A lot of men are joining boxing clubs these days to get into shape. Do you believe in clubs for women, Mister Fields?" asked a reporter from the *Los Angeles Times*.

"Yes, if no other form of persuasion works," Fields deadpanned.

"Fighters have to be in peak physical condition. Do you get any exercise?" a reporter from the *Hollywood Citizen* asked.

"Certainly. I tremble and shake for an hour every morning when I wake up," Fields explained. "And I exercise self-control. I rarely drink anything stronger than gin before breakfast."

"You'll drown in a vat of whiskey some day," harrumphed a journalist from the *Examiner* with thick, horn-rimmed glasses.

"Death, where is thy sting?" cried Fields.

When the bout got under way Ruth fought Dempsey to a draw, though everyone knew the Manassa Mauler had taken it easy on the Babe. His nose was flat enough as it was. The two sports heroes got along famously and Dempsey invited Ruth to his house in Los Angeles.

o o o

He found it easily the next afternoon. It was white stucco and its most dramatic feature was an elaborate heraldic crest emblazoned in bold bas relief above the entrance archway. The house had lush gardens and a spacious patio in the back with a large cooking grill. In the driveway was Dempsey's Kissel Gold Bug roadster. Memories of gorgeous Clara Bow rushed to Ruth's mind and he found himself getting aroused.

A middle-aged Negro housekeeper answered his knock. She told him that Mister and Mrs. Dempsey were on the patio and directed him around the back. Beds of hollyhocks, gladiolas, pink rhododendrons, and violet hydrangeas surrounded the walkway, though Ruth wouldn't have been able to name any of them.

"Hey champ," said the Babe. "Helluva garden you got here, Jack."

Dempsey laid *The Way of all Flesh* down on the table, stood up, and shook Ruth's hand.

"Thanks, George, it's my new hobby. This is my wife Estelle. Estelle Taylor."

Estelle had penetrating brown eyes, high cheekbones, a model's nose, and wavy brown hair. She wore a white blouse and grey slacks.

"I forgot you were married to a movie star, Jack. You're beautiful, if ya don't mind me sayin' so, Mrs. Dempsey, I mean Miss Taylor."

"Not at all, Babe. Can we get you some lemonade? With a gin chaser perhaps?"

"I expect the Babe'd prefer a cold beer," said Dempsey.

"A beer would be great. Two'd be even better."

"Two it is then, and another whiskey for you, Jack," said Estelle, leaving to get the drinks.

Dempsey reached down and pulled a weed from the garden and then stood backup.

"You guys gonna make it two in a row this year, Babe?"

"I dunno, Jack. Connie Mack's really loadin' up with players. They're gonna have a pretty stacked lineup. The White Sox and Senators are gonna be good too."

"How many homers d'ya think the young lad's gonna hit? Your new first baseman. What's his name, Gehrig?"

Babe Ruth

"Ya. The kid's as strong as an ox. He might hit a bunch."

"Is he much of a drinker?"

"If you count milk he is."

Dempsey laughed. "You met any hot lookin' women out here, Babe?"

"A few. Clara Bow's the hottest. She's a real pistol."

Dempsey smiled. "She sure is. I'd love to ..."

Estelle arrived with the drinks on a tray. "What was that you were saying, dear?"

"I ... I was just telling the Babe I'd love to be able to swing a bat like he does."

Estelle gave her husband a menacing look. "You were, were you?" she asked, clearly not believing him.

Ruth took a big swig from one of his beers and wiped his mouth with his sleeve. "I thought you were swell in that picture you did with that Barrymore fella," he told Estelle.

"Don Juan," said Dempsey. "Estelle played Lucretia Borgia."

"Somebody told me you were supposed to make a romance picture with the Sheik guy before he croaked," said Ruth.

"Rudolph Valentino. A terrible shame he was taken from us so soon," sighed Estelle.

"Is it true what Jack said to ya after the Tunney fight?" Ruth asked her. "I don't believe a whole lot a what I read in the papers."

"Oh it's true all right. When I asked Jack how he could lose to Tunney, he said, 'Honey, I forgot to duck'."

"What's this I hear about you not fightin' him again, Jack?" asked the Babe. "That was a close decision last time. You just needed to get in a couple more shots."

"I was rusty. I took too much time off after the Firpo fight and I just wasn't prepared for Tunney's style. The man danced around the canvas like it was a freshly-waxed ballroom."

"What are you doing these days? Besides gardenin'."

"I'm making picture shows now too. And endorsing shit and travelling around. Exhibition bouts here and there."

"You ain't fightin' for real anymore?"

"Nah. I know when I'm through."

The Babe snorted. "All right then sit on your ass and feel sorry for yourself. You know, pal, guys like us can't back off the spotlight. We gotta keep goin' ta bat, trying for home runs until we grind ourselves into the ground."

"It's different for you, Babe. You haven't lost a thing. As for me, I don't know if I still got it."

"Well you sure as hell aren't gonna know until you get back in there and try."

o o o

The Babe was staying at the elegant, ornately decorated Hollywood Plaza, the town's first skyscraper hotel. It was located at Selma and Vine on a beautiful tract of land surrounded by date palms and orange and lemon trees. Art McGovern, who'd come out for a working holiday to see what kind of shape his star pupil was in, timed the Babe as he ran wind sprints up and down the hotel's thickly-carpeted halls on the days he wasn't needed on the set. Some of the guests, unaware that a two hundred and forty pound man was charging up and down the hallways, believed their city was witnessing another one of those annoying earth tremors.

One time, Ruth narrowly avoided smashing into a well-dressed couple coming out of their room.

"Sorry folks," he called back as he disappeared around a corner.

"Snookems, do you know who that big man that nearly trampled us was?" the man asked his wife.

"No, dahling, who was he?"

"It was Babe Ruth, the famous baseball player."

"You really must stop reading those improbable scripts people send you, Niles, your imagination is starting to get the best of you."

o o o

Ruth was surprised to have Friday off. The studio was shooting scenes

Babe Ruth

with Nilsson and Ethel Shannon. He was going to have breakfast sent up to his room but he decided he should go for a run instead. As he passed the front desk the manager called him over.

"Mister Ruth, so good to see you. I hope you are enjoying your stay with us. We have a message for you but we were not sure you had awakened and we did not wish to disturb you. The manager snapped his fingers twice and a young clerk handed him an envelope which the manager gave to the Babe.

Inside was an invitation. It read, "Hope everybody's treating you swell. I hear you're trying to stay in shape while you make your picture. Come on out to my place and we'll play some tennis." It was signed *Doug Fairbanks*.

The Babe had the desk clerk call Marshall Hunt and the Babe told him about the invitation.

"Everybody knows where Fairbanks lives. He and Pickford have a big estate out in the boonies. If you're playing tennis with Fairbanks I gotta warn you, he's pretty damn good. When Bill Tilden played Fairbanks he actually lost a couple of sets."

o o o

Ruth got directions from the hotel manager and arranged to borrow a car - which turned out to be a yellow Hupmobile Eight Touring roadster - so he could drive out to Douglas Fairbanks' estate. It was in Beverly Hills, which Ruth had never heard of.

When he passed the Beverly Hills Hotel several elderly women sat in rocking chairs on the veranda. Ruth slowed down to read a sign on the front of the building. It said NO MOVIE PEOPLE ALLOWED! Oriental waiters in uniforms set tea cups in front of the matrons.

"Husbands must be oilmen or real estate moguls," the Babe said aloud to no one as he hit the gas. He drove on through deserted scrubland.

"Looks like an abandoned real estate development," Ruth muttered to himself as he steered the big car along scarcely traveled dirt roads. "Sidewalks runnin' right inta fields. And lamp posts, but no streets."

A handful of mansions in the style of Spanish haciendas rose between hillocks at the foot of the Santa Monica Mountains. They looked purple and majestic the distance. They were surrounded by acres of terraced gardens and orange groves. After turning onto a shaded driveway and following it for what seemed like a mile the Babe reached a huge set of gates. Above them was a sign that read PICKFAIR. A guard opened the gates and after Ruth had parked the roadster a valet opened his door for him.

The lush interspersed gardens of roses, camellias, and oleander that lined the front of the estate were alive with exotic animals. Douglas Fairbanks bounded out the front door. He was wearing a white sweater, white trousers, and canvas running shoes. A large shaggy dog trotted along beside him. Fairbanks was carrying two rackets. He looked as handsome in real life as he did on the big screen.

"Tennis anyone?" Fairbanks called out.

o o o

"I've invented a new version of tennis, Babe," said Fairbanks as he handed Ruth a racket. "Instead of all the silly thirty and forty love, ad in, ad out nonsense, one player serves four times, then his opponent serves four times, and back and forth until one of them has fifteen points. That's a set. It's best four out of seven sets. Like in the World Series."

"Makes sense to me. What d'ya call it, Doug?"

"I call it 'Doug'."

"Well, that makes sense too I guess. Let's play."

o o o

"You can really smash the ball, Babe," Fairbanks told him when Ruth had won the match four sets to two. "If you worked on your serve and your footwork a bit, you could give Tilden a run for his money."

"You must have money to spare, Doug. This is quite a palace you got here."

"I built it five years ago to use for Robin Hood."

"I loved that picture," Ruth interrupted. "The Thief of Bagdad too."

"Thanks, Babe. At any rate, that's why I have the huge ramparts and the drawbridge. I was the first one to move out here. There wasn't much around then. Not that it's built up much since. You can still hear the coyotes howling at night."

Babe Ruth

"You know how you were talkin' about how they say thirty and forty love in tennis, Doug?"

"Yes, what of it?"

"What's love got to do with it?"

Fairbanks chuckled. "Nothing at all. You know how when your team fails to score in an inning they say you put up a goose egg?"

"Ya, cuz a zero looks an egg. So?"

"Well, tennis was invented by the French and they said l'oeuf - that's French for egg. The English thought they must be saying love for some reason and it stuck. It's the same as May Day, the thing a captain says when his ship's in trouble. Of course he isn't talking about May or day. The French would signal m'aidez, which means help me, and the English misunderstood that too."

"I bet there aren't even too many captains that know that," said Ruth. "Where did you learn all that stuff, Doug?"

"There's always a lot of down time on the set between takes."

"Don't I know it," agreed Ruth.

"Well, instead of flirting with sexy actresses - which Mary would be sure to find out about - I read books. You know - speaking of the English mixing up French words and expressions - the French get a big kick out of it when rich Americans burn themselves in their hotel bathrooms sticking their hands under the cold water tap. The C stands for chaude, which means hot, not cold."

"That exact thing happened to me when I went to Paris a while back."

"Did you like France, Babe?"

"Not really. Nobody recognized me."

"That must have seemed strange after all the attention you get in America."

Ruth got a far off look in his eyes and said, "Nuthin' like I used to, Doug, nuthin' like I used to."

The Babe remembered '25. It would be very hard to forget. First there was the long hospital stay after his intestinal attack, then the struggle to regain his timing and his swing, then the disastrous road trip in which his average fell below his weight of 270, and being fined a whopping five thousand dollars for misconduct off the ball field detrimental to the best interests of the club. Even worse, Miller Huggins hadn't let him rejoin the lineup - even after Ruth apologized for saying the Yankees needed a new manager because he would never play for Huggins again.

One columnist after another had written how Ruth had touched all the bases, letting down his manager, his teammates, Yankee fans, and the kids who idolized him. Even the President had lambasted him for setting a poor example for the nation's youngsters. The Babe would never forget the words of Jimmy Walker, the senator and soon-to-be mayor of New York, when he spoke at a dinner for the city's sportswriters. He'd said, "I'm here at the invitation of Christy Walsh and Marshall Hunt because I continue to have a great fondness for you and believe you to be a terrific athlete. But I also believe you are a great fool."

The room had gone deathly quiet. Walker continued, "We all know that you had a very difficult childhood and deserve to be forgiven some of the excesses of which you have been guilty. But it is time for you to solemnly swear to mend your ways. The cheers of your former greatness are only echoes now, Babe. Do you intend to let down the dirty-faced kids in the streets of America once again as you have this past year, or will you give the youngsters their great idol back?"

Brother Matthias, who knew more about Ruth's difficult childhood and early struggles at St. Mary's Industrial School for Delinquent Boys than anyone, had tried to console the Babe. But he had sobbed for a full five minutes before struggling to the podium to say, "I know as well as anyone here what mistakes I made this season. The Senator's right to call me a fool. I deserve it. I want the sports writers of New York to know that I'm going to work hard this winter, and I'm going to keep on working hard to win back the respect and admiration I've squandered."

As much as Walker's words had stung, far worse had been the looks of disappointment in the eyes of kids. They'd idolized Ruth and followed him

Babe Ruth

everywhere. But in '25, when his hedonistic behavior contributed mightily to the Yankees' freefall to seventh place, and choruses of boos filled the Stadium every time he struck out, there hadn't been many youngsters waiting for him outside the gates.

After his spectacular first two seasons in New York a lot of people had begun saying he was the best player ever. In '25, people were claiming Ty Cobb had regained that distinction. Ruth thought back to a game in Detroit in late September of '16 when Cobb had been desperate to overtake Tris Speaker and capture his tenth consecutive batting title. Ruth had gotten him to ground out his first three trips to the plate and then struck him out to end the game. The Babe smiled at the memory of Cobb flinging his bat in disgust.

Ruth been as good as his word and had worked hard to get back in shape. He looked down and patted his belly, now a shadow of its former self. He'd had a good year in '26, a great one for almost anyone else, but he'd come nowhere near his record of fifty-nine homers and had been soundly criticized for getting thrown out to end the World Series. He still had work to do, things to prove. He was thirty-three now and a lot of folks were saying he was over the hill. More and more people were saying young Lou Gehrig was the next Babe Ruth. "I'm still around, dammit," Ruth said out loud.

"What was that you said?" asked Fairbanks.

"Nuthin, Doug. Is that Mary Pickford?" asked the Babe as a golden-haired, innocent-looking twenty-five-year-old emerged from the house wearing a plain, business-like Bramley dress. Even Ruth knew that Fairbanks was married to Mary Pickford.

"Yes, Babe, that's my Mary."

"The two of you passed me while I was running on Hollywood Boulevard the other day. You were in a sky blue Cadillac and two wolfhounds and a German shepherd had their heads out the windows."

"I *told* you that was the Babe," said Mary, having overheard as she approached. "Welcome to Pickfair."

"Pickfair? I saw the sign. What is it?"

"That's what we call the place," Mary explained. She looked around and sighed. "I've come a long way since I was Gladys Smith from Toronto making fifty dollars a week doing two-reelers." She turned to her husband. "Don't forget, darling, we're going to Charlie's place for lunch. He's going to help us get the academy going."

"What is it we're calling it?"

"Douglas! You've forgotten already? The Academy of Motion Picture Arts and Sciences."

"That's quite a mouthful," said Ruth.

"That's exactly what thought," muttered Fairbanks.

"Say, why don't you come with us, Babe?" asked Pickford. "Charlie loves meeting anyone famous. So long as they aren't in the movie business. People call his place Breakaway House because parts of it are rather fragile. He used studio workmen for some of the construction. They're used to building temporary sets."

Ruth chuckled.

"Charlie's cook is amazing," said Mary. "He brought him over from France. You must be hungry after tennis, I hear you have a bit of an appetite."

"Not so much anymore. The reporters exaggerate everything I do. They sell more newspapers if they write that I eat like a horse."

"I imagine you two are thirsty, we'll take some drinks for the ride. What do you think of Prohibition, Babe?"

"I try not to think of it at all."

○ ○ ○

Chaplin's place was done up in black and white marble. Luxurious vines twisted across its walls. A shining suit of armor stood in the foyer beside an impossibly large urn. Chaplin was reclined on a chaise lounge in the huge salon when they arrived. At first Ruth didn't recognize him without his trademark moustache and thick eyebrows. Huge tapestries hung from the walls between French windows and a vase of roses sat on every table. A baby grand piano dominated the room. Chaplin had a roaring blaze in the enormous fireplace in spite of the heat.

Babe Ruth

He was short - Ruth guessed about five foot four or five - and his head seemed a little too big for his delicate body. His hair was coal black, his skin ivory white, and his eyes were deep blue pools. He looked depressed. When he greeted Ruth and Pickford and Fairbanks the Babe was taken by surprise.

"I didn't know you were British, Charlie."

"Born in Walworth, just outside London, old chap. The studio chooses to downplay it. It's not as if anyone can hear me."

"He seems kinda down in the dumps," the Babe whispered to Fairbanks. "What d'ya suppose is the matter?"

"His wife left him and she took the children."

"Oh. That was a pretty rotten thing to do."

"Maybe it wasn't meant to be, Babe. She got pregnant and Charlie married her to avoid a scandal. She was only sixteen and he's thirty-five."

A butler came in and announced that luncheon was served on the terrace.

"That's rough about your wife leavin' ya, Charlie," said the Babe as he tucked into a Cobb salad. He had to speak up - in the middle of the huge backyard a crew of workmen was noisily building a bridge over a swimming pool the exact shape of the Little Tramp's bowler hat. "You two gettin' a divorce?"

Pickford and Fairbanks looked at one another but Chaplin didn't seem bothered by the question.

"Yes," he sighed, "and it's costing me a king's ransom."

"How much does that cost?"

Chaplin chuckled. "In this case, Babe, a king's ransom costs exactly six hundred thousand dollars."

"Holy shit! No wonder you're down in the dumps."

"I know what might cheer you up a little, Charlie," said Fairbanks. "A fishing trip to Catalina Island. If they'll give the Babe an afternoon off he can join us. I'll have a steer killed and sunk to attract the fish the way I did last time."

"Damn, you movie folks do *everything* big."

"Getting down to business, boys," interrupted Mary, "are we seriously going to name Rin Tin Tin best male actor just because the pooch got the most votes?"

Ruth knew the three needed to talk about their new, awkwardly-named academy, so he thanked everybody and left after the second glass of ten-year-old Scotch the stuffy butler had poured him. As he pulled out of the driveway he was thinking that Chaplin might be a riot on the screen, but he was a real gloomy Gus off it.

o o o

Clara Bow picked up Ruth at his hotel at eight o'clock on Saturday night. It was getting dark. He was happy no one had seen her pull up. Bow reached over and opened the passenger door. She had her already short skirt pulled up so she could work the pedals. Her legs were just as beautiful as Ruth remembered.

"Climb in, loverboy."

"I'm lookin' forward to it," said the Babe.

Bow floored it and they tore out of the parking lot.

"They keep gettin' me chauffeurs and I keep firin' 'em cuz dey won't drive fast enough," she told Ruth. She handed him a bottle. It was half empty already.

"Good hooch," said the Babe after taking a swig.

They drove at high speed out of the city, past countless oil derricks and out into the desert. Ruth watched as she grasped the gear shift with her right hand. He kept wishing it was something else she was holding on to. When they reached Barstow they stopped to find out where they could get some refreshment for the rest of the trip. In this town it was the barber that took care of folks' 'necessary'. His place was closed when they arrived but the porch light was on. They knocked and a weary-eyed woman in an apron came to the screen door.

"We're really thirsty from our drive and we still have quite a ways to go," Ruth told her.

"Just a minute," she told him.

Babe Ruth

"Sam! There's a fella here who looks just like Babe Ruth and he's with a woman that looks like that It Girl in the movie magazines. They say they're thirsty."

Sam came to the door in his undershirt, picking his teeth. His eyes widened. "Lord love a duck, it is Babe Ruth!" He looked at Bow. "And that is Clara Bow!"

"Heavens to Betsy," his wife said. "They really are who they are, I mean …"

"Listen, folks," said the Babe. "We still got a long drive …"

"Certainly, Babe. What'll it be?"

"A bottle a gin for her and a bottle a bourbon for me. Good stuff."

"No problem."

Sam opened a door and went down some stairs. He returned a minute later with two bottles. One read 'London's Finest' and the other was 'Kentucky Gold'.

"How much?" asked Ruth.

"Fifteen for the gin and twenty for the bourbon," answered Sam.

"Pretty steep," said Ruth, handing him a fifty dollar bill.

"Shipping's pretty dear this far out," explained Sam. "And the farther it travels the more cops there are to bribe."

"Keep the change then," said Ruth.

o o o

Bow pulled the roadster over to the side of the deserted highway an hour past Barstow. A coyote scurried into the bushes. An owl perched on a branch eying them suspiciously. The Babe looked around. He didn't think he'd heard the motor make any unusual noises. "Somethin' wrong, dollface?"

"Ya, I bin wantin' ta do dis for a while now." She put her hand on Ruth's crotch. His member swelled instantly. Ruth unbuttoned his fly and his tool popped out. Bow reached down and got her small handbag. She opened it and took out a condom.

"These new latex safes are so much better dan da rubba ones," she said.

"That a Trojan?" asked Ruth, squirming in anticipation.

"Ya, like dey say in dem ads, 'Pleasure you want. Protection you need. You think she's just your gal, but she may just be everyone's pal.'" Then she giggled, "Put it on before you put it in."

Ruth thought of a quip Joe Dugan had come up with, "Don't be a fool, cover that tool."

"Enough a da jokes," said Bow. She kissed the Babe hard on the lips, pulled up her shirt, and climbed on top of him.

It didn't last long, but Ruth counted that Bow had climaxed five times. An hour later they got talking about whether they wore pyjamas at night and about how that Sigmund Freud doctor said the whole world runs on sex or the libido or something and they had to pull over again.

They reached the border just after midnight. The Cal-Nev casino was easy to spot. There was nothing else around for miles except hyenas and tumbleweeds. Inside, roulette wheels, slot machines, and poker and blackjack tables were set up on a cement floor. There were no pictures on the walls and no windows. A man in a tuxedo quickly explained the rules of blackjack to Bow and handed her a pile of blue chips. Ruth headed for the poker tables.

Bow had fun, but she kept on losing. After twenty minutes her pretty blue chips were all gone. Another man in a tuxedo noticed and brought her a pile of a hundred more. They were gone in half an hour. Bow stood up. "I'm bored with this silly game," she announced. She went and tried her luck at roulette. The manager, an oily-looking man with shifty eyes and a day's growth of whiskers, came out and handed her a blank check to sign to cover her losses. Clara looked at the lumbering body-guards with chests that stretched their starched shirt fronts and signed it.

On the way home the Babe drove, fast, but not quite as fast as Bow had. He was in a good mood. Not only had he screwed a beautiful movie star, he'd won fifteen hundred dollars at the casino. Bow looked upset though, very upset.

"What's the matter, Clara?"

Babe Ruth

She started to cry. "Oh, Babe, I messed up. Big time."

"Whad'ya mean?"

"I shoulda listened harder. I thawt dem chips was worth fifty cents each. Turns out dey were fifty dawllars apiece. I was bettin' ten or twenty on every spin!"

"I coulda told ya they'd be worth more than fifty cents, doll," said the Babe.

"I signed a blank check. They said they were gawna make it out for twenty thousand dawllars!"

She sobbed harder.

"They duped you, Clara."

"What am I gawna do, Babe?"

He put his arm around her. "They're nuthin' but a bunch a crooks. You're not gonna honor that check. That's what."

"Oh. Of course, I hadn't thought of that. Yer a real life saver, Babe."

"What do you do when a fella saves your life?"

"I show him how grateful I am."

They stopped and Bow showed Ruth that she was very grateful indeed.

o o o

A few days later the Sultan of Swat accepted the good wishes of close to two hundred actors, cameramen, electricians, stage hands, extras, and messenger boys who'd come to see him off and hopped on The Twentieth Century with a sunburnt but smiling Marshall Hunt in tow to head back to New York. Hunt was lugging a new set of golf clubs Ruth had bought. As the train sped through the mountains the Babe kept thinking about Clara Bow on the desert road. He'd gone to see how Ted Wilde was doing and to ask him if he was going to make a speaking picture of his own. Ted assured the Babe that talking movies were just a fad.

Wilde told him about the latest buzz around the studios. Two tough customers from the Cal-Nev had paid a visit to Clara Bow when her check had bounced. They'd threatened to pour acid on her pretty face if she didn't make good on it. B. P. Schulman, her studio's boss, had immediately called the district attorney, Buron Fitts, who was trying to make a name for himself by cleaning up corruption. Fitts enjoyed earning favours from studio executives. He had a brace of detectives hide behind a curtain in Schulman's office where goons were lured by the promise of payment in full. When they showed up, Schulman's check book lay conspicuously open on his desk.

"Now let me just get this straight, gentlemen," said Schulman, picking up his fountain pen. "You're telling me that, unless I write this check, you are going to throw acid in Miss Bow's face so that she can never work in pictures again? Is that correct?"

"You heard it right, mister," growled the goon who seemed to be the leader. "And we ain't playin' wit yuz. We got the juice right here. So no more a your jaw music. Gimme that check or little Miss Bow won't be worth shit ta anybody."

Out from behind the curtain had burst Fitts' men, brandishing pistols. The Cal-Nev hoods were handcuffed and booked for extortion and several other crimes as well. Fitts promised to provide police protection for Bow, but he was fairly sure the casino owners knew they'd risk losing all their Hollywood clientele if they took things any further. The Babe was glad. He'd have felt awful if anything had happened to the 'It Girl' because of what he'd told her to do.

"Ya know, Marsh, this wild ride I bin on has been pretty damn great," the Babe told Hunt as he puffed away on a cigar in the smoking room, "but I believe I might just cut back a tad, get home before six in the morning the odd time, cut back on the booze and the beer a bit too." He paused. Hunt looked at him expectantly. The Babe punched him in the arm. "Nah. On second thought I'd put too many hard-workin' bootleggers outta business."

Babe Ruth
& the 1927 YANKEES have the BEST SUMMER EVER

3

ENOUGH TO BUY A NEW HOUSE EVERY MONTH

"I feel like an athlete again."

When the Babe had arrived at Grand Central Station after making a picture called Headin' Home in 1920 a sign with "Welcome Home Babe" in huge red letters had greeted him. A squad of private police and railroad security men had been powerless to hold back two hundred adoring, overzealous fans who broke through barriers to get at their idol. Outside the station was a much larger throng. Now there was no crowd at all.

"Do ya think people are still pissed I got caught stealin' to end the Series?" Ruth asked Hunt.

He headed straight to his apartment at the Ansonia, a palatial building on Broadway between 73rd and 74th. It had three restaurants and was really more of a hotel than an apartment building. Ruth's suite had eight huge rooms, maid service, three times a day replenishment of towels and sheets - a good thing given his lifestyle - and several other conveniences.

There was a Swedish masseuse and a Negro concierge, who did his best to keep kids away from the front of the place, especially when Ruth let him know he was going out. Whenever he planned to leave he shot a "Goin' out" message down a pneumatic tube to the front desk.

Ruth was stepping into a cab one morning when he stopped and asked the doorman, whose name he could never remember, if it was true that Arnold Rothstein had met at the Ansonia with the group of gamblers that threw the Series in '19.

"Ya, they met here, Missa Ruth. Course I didn't know who they were at the time. But they were the shadiest bunch a characters I ever laid eyes on."

Babe Ruth

The Babe often went for a swim in the Ansonia's indoor pool, at one time the largest in the world. Florenz Ziegfeld was there sometimes, frolicking in the shallow end with a long-legged brunette. Ruth knew that Ziegfeld lived with his wife in a thirteen-room suite and had a somewhat smaller one a floor above for his mistress.

"I wanna meet him, Flo," Ruth heard her say one morning as he was towelling off and checking out the size of his waist.

Far from thrilled to have to do it, Ziegfeld swam over and asked the Babe if he'd mind terribly.

"Only if ya do me a favour," said Ruth.

"What do you need, Babe? Tickets to a show? Some dancer's telephone number?"

"No. Tell me about the roof farm. I heard this joint's got its own farm on the roof and I think somebody's pullin' my leg."

"It does, Babe. Ask the manager if you can go up and see it."

The Babe could scarcely believe it when the manager led him up a flight of stairs that led from the top floor and took him out onto the roof. A pair of Rhode Island Reds clucked a greeting as they stepped out into the morning sunshine. The man pointed to the cows and chickens that provided the guests with milk and eggs.

"No wonder everything's so fresh," said Ruth. "Now I get why you have that sign in the restaurant, the one that says the eggs you eat tomorrow are still in the hens today." A nearby Holstein nodded and mooed in agreement before returning to chewing her cud.

o o o

Richards Vidmer and James Harrison, the only writers that covered every Yankee game, met for breakfast in a diner across from Harrison's apartment building the day before Ruth returned to New York to compare notes on the off-season. Vidmer was popular with the players. He was a scratch golfer and he'd lettered in baseball and football in college. The son of a highly decorated brigadier general who'd fought at San Juan Hill, Richards had trained as a pilot and barely survived an in-air collision during the war. Vidmer never had a drink until after he'd handed in his copy at

5:30 but he was quite adept at catching up.

Vidmer was a good-looking man and his beautiful, brown-skinned wife was the daughter of an Indian rajah. The Yankees teased him whenever they saw him talking to another woman on the road.

"I don't write about what you guys do with dames, so leave me alone," he'd tell them.

Richards had been in his hotel room one night in '23, his first year on the road with the Yankees. He'd just gotten in and it was around midnight. The phone rang. It was the Babe.

"Come on up ta the suite for a nightcap," bellowed Ruth. Vidmer was sure the Babe must have been drinking but he sounded stone sober. Ruth always could hold his liquor.

The Babe poured him a bourbon on the rocks when he arrived and told him to take a load off. They sat and talked about the team and about the Senators and the A's and the Tigers, and about what a prick Cobb was to Gehrig.

"I could hear the bastard all the way from right field yellin' at Buster, callin' him a big Weiner Schnitzel and a thick-headed Dutch bum and telling him to keep his foot on the bag," Ruth told Vidmer. "Finally Lou'd had enough and he charged into the Tigers' dugout to get the jerk. Cobb hid behind somebody and Gehrig was so flustered he ended up banging his head against a cement post."

He reached for his glass and noticed light coming from under the Babe's bedroom door and a shadow pass by.

"You got a woman in there?"

"Ya."

"Why didn't you say so? Why did you call me to come up? I've been sitting here all this time nattering away and you've got a dame in your room."

"No. No. That's why I called ya. That broad's hotter than a two-dollar pistol on a Saturday night. I figured I could use a rest."

Babe Ruth

It was the sort of thing Vidmer never wrote about.

"Have you kept track of any of the players over the winter?" asked Harrison, spreading jam onto a piece of toast.

"Hoyt made fifteen hundred bucks a week singing at the Palace Theatre and the Babe spent the fall on the Pantages vaudeville circuit doing three shows a day, four on Sundays," said Vidmer.

"I hope he didn't embarrass himself the way Bill Tilden did."

"Who could have guessed a tennis star would look foolish playing Dracula?" chuckled Vidmer.

"At least Tilden got paid well for making a fool of himself. How much did Ruth make?" asked Harrison.

"Eight thousand a week," Vidmer told him.

Harrison whistled.

"Twice as much as Fanny Brice, W.C. Fields, and Al Jolson get," said Vidmer. "I saw his act. He jumped onto the stage through a tissue paper hoop and tooted on a saxophone. No melody, just tooted random notes. Then he tossed a baseball around and told a few lame jokes."

"Doesn't sound too entertaining," said Harrison.

"It was boring as hell."

"I could be boring for eight grand a week."

"He's making a ton of money endorsing cars. Chevrolets, Cadillacs, Chryslers, Packards, Studebakers, I've lost count. And Victrolas and appliances. Even kennels. Everywhere you look, there's that big, moon-shaped puss of his."

"Didn't he make a movie, too?" Harrison asked.

"Yes, a six-reeler called Babe Comes Home."

"How many of those Hollywood hotties do you suppose he slept with? I hear they're pretty easy."

"About a hundred I imagine. Bob Meusel and his brother Irish and Lazzeri were in a stinker called 'Slide, Kelly, Slide'. I've got no idea how much *they* got paid."

Harrison set a dollar bill on the table. "How much is Ruth going to hit Ruppert up for?"

"I heard rumours he's going to ask for a hundred and fifty thousand, but he's said he really just wants a hundred. I think he'd be happy with eighty grand a year. Jacob Ruppert sent him a contract for fifty-two, the same as he's made the past five years. It's what all the owners do - even if a player's had a season for the ages. Of course the Babe sent it back unsigned."

o o o

Wearing his full length raccoon-skin coat, Ruth showed up at Ruppert's brewery at 91st and Third Avenue at 12:15 on Thursday for the negotiations and anticipated signing. Ed Barrow, the Yankee general manager, convinced his boss to keep the Babe cooling his heels for a few minutes. Barrow was a bull of a man, a ex-prize fighter. He'd floored former British heavyweight champ Sandy Ferguson once in a barroom brawl. He had enormous black eyebrows which Ruth thought looked just like two furry caterpillars. Barrow handled the negotiations - if you could call them that - with most of the players and Ruppert dealt with the stars. They were both involved in this, by far the most important deal.

Ruth didn't mind having to wait in the least. A shapely young secretary in a skin-tight skirt invited him to have a seat. He sat down between two paintings of Prussian horsemen. The secretary got up to straighten them - even though they were both perfectly straight - to allow the Babe a chance to assess her curves up close.

Outside, a window washer was enjoying the show. "Who's that dish modeling for, anyway?" he asked himself. When he stretched as far as he dared and saw who the audience was he yelled, "Holy shit! It's Babe Ruth!" and nearly fell off the scaffold.

Ed Barrow came to the door, a look of disapproval spreading across his face. "I see you've been making time instead of killing it," he grunted.

"I hope you get everything you want, Babe," purred the secretary.

Ruth winked and looked her up and down again. "I usually do."

The brewery giant was no giant in stature. Ruppert, who liked to be called the Colonel, was five-foot six but stocky and he carried himself in an imperious manner. He dressed impeccably, his greyish-white hair slicked back and his small moustache perfectly trimmed. He often remarked that it was a shame men didn't dress as well as women. Ruppert had never married. He told everyone that it was too much fun being single, that there were too many beautiful girls in New York to ever allow a man to be lonesome. But he startled Fred Lieb of the *New York Telegram* when he confided to him that he was afraid of getting married. In his German accent he whispered, "Fred, I'm afraid that if a woman marries me for my money, when I grow old she might take on a young lover and then I would have to kill her."

Ruppert lived alone - except for a butler, maid, cook, valet, and laundress - in an enormous Fifth Avenue apartment. A former actress and chorus girl who was thirty years younger than the Colonel hosted parties at Eagle's Rest, his Tudor mansion in Garrison, New York, which was a home for his peacocks, his prize-winning Saint Bernards, and his beloved monkeys.

"A one-year contract, nothing more," Barrow insisted when the meeting got underway in Ruppert's huge, richly carpeted office. Hunting trophies lined each wall. "We don't know that you won't have a relapse like you did in '25."

"I ain't gettin' any younger, Colonel. I gotta have some security. I want two years. At a hundred grand for each."

"Nothing doing," said Barrow.

"Well then I guess you're gonna need some other big name to fill all those seats you got. I made sixty-five thousand for twelve weeks on vaudeville, I'm helpin' sell Cadillacs, Studebakers, Victrolas, and a bunch of other stuff, and I'm in the movies now. Heck, I might just open a chain a gymnasiums with my pal Art McGovern."

"Sounds like you've got it made in the shade," grunted Barrow. "We'll see how long that all lasts if you're not playing ball anymore. I've heard rumors that Connie Mack won't be able to afford Ty Cobb's salary for more than one year. We could get *him* to play right field for us."

Ruppert interrupted Ruth before he could go back at Barrow. "Gentleman, gentlemen, I really must intervene." He turned to the Babe. "Mister Root, I am going to give you *three* years, more security than you've asked for."

Barrow was non-plussed. "But Colonel, what about …"

"However, the salary will be less money than you are asking for. I will pay you two hundred and ten thousand dollars over the next three years. Seventy thousand for each season. That is all."

The Babe thought for a moment. He wished he'd brought Christy Walsh along, but not even he or Cobb or Hornsby or Walter Johnson were allowed to bring a representative into salary negotiations.

"That sounds fair, Colonel, you've always been good to me. I'll sign."

The Colonel took his fifty dollar fountain pen out of its ivory holder and handed it to Ruth. Barrow frowned and then stepped out to tell the secretary to invite the anxious reporters up to Ruppert's office. The Babe was all smiles. Twenty photographers snapped pictures with their new Speed Graphic cameras as he signed his contract and flared his huge nostrils. Joe Dugan had once said you could drive a Ford through them.

"What did you get, Babe?" asked Ford Frick of the *Evening News*.

Ruppert answered for him. "Mister Root will be paid two hundred and ten thousand dollars," he announced.

The reporters gasped.

"Over three years," Ruppert explained. "He will be the highest paid player in baseball. We came to terms without any trouble. Babe will go to camp on Saturday and everything will be fine. He thinks he has five more years of baseball in him and I believe he is right. I'm happy about his work with Mister McGovern and I am sure he will take better care of himself than he has in the past. I have not seen him looking so good at this time of the year since he first arrived from Boston."

"You can tell your readers that I'll earn every cent of my salary, boys," Ruth told the reporters. "There'll be no monkey business for me this year. Huggins won't even recognize me when I get to camp. I've trimmed eight inches off my waist. I put on four pounds on the trip back east but I'll work that off and by the time the exhibitions start I'll be in prime shape."

o o o

Fred Lieb loved to crunch numbers. His wife Mary always teased him about his fascination for stats sheets and numbers. She was glad he didn't

Babe Ruth

apply his obsession to the grocery bill or the way she balanced the check book - or didn't. Lieb calculated that if Ruth played every game and they averaged an hour and forty-five minutes he would make $4.33 per minute.

After the signing the two men went for a celebratory beer at a speakeasy on the patio in back of a brownstone. It was sheltered by trees and bushes and had never been discovered by the police. Lieb told the Babe, "Every day you'll earn four hundred and fifty dollars, enough to pay for a trip to Europe. And every month you'll make twelve thousand bucks. That's enough to buy a real nice house. If you hit forty-seven home runs like you did last year, you'll get fourteen hundred per homer."

"I think I might hit more than that this year," Ruth told Lieb. He paused to admire the ass of the homeowner's daughter, who was waiting tables. "I might just top my own record. A course when I hit fifty-nine in twenty-one more than half of 'em were at the Polo Grounds. God, I sure loved hittin' there with that short porch in right. Only two hundred and fifty-seven feet down the line. It's a lot harder hittin' at the Stadium. I hit five balls more than four hundred and eighty feet to left and center last year and all of 'em were caught or just went for extra bases."

o o o

The next day a tongue-in-cheek story appeared in the *New York Times* under John Kieran's byline. It told of an innocent waif waiting for his hero, the Sultan of Swat, outside the brewery. The youngster had heard that the Babe had signed his new contract and would be forced to play for a measly seventy thousand dollars a year.

"Say it ain't so, Babe, say it ain't so," wailed the imaginary boy.

o o o

Ruth headed to Artie McGowan's eleven thousand square-foot gym for the well-heeled and too well-fed across the street from Grand Central Station that day. After the disastrous 1925 season a lot of people had decided Ruth was washed up. The former flyweight boxer had saved his career.

McGowan, who'd grown up in Hell's Kitchen, had developed theories on exercise and nutrition that were all the rage. His gym had rowing machines, massage rooms, sun lamps, electric-ray cabinets, sitz baths, handball and squash courts, and even golf driving nets. Few could afford the $500 membership though. For the Babe it was well worth the money.

"I love makin' rich guys sweat," McGovern told Rud Rennie of the *Herald Tribune* when he had gone to learn about the Babe's exercise routine in March of '26.

"How d'ya turn the Babe around?" Rennie asked.

"Around the middle of December of '25 Ruth came into the gym a physical wreck," said McGovern. "His blood pressure was low, his pulse was high, and he weighed two hundred and sixty pounds. The slightest exertion left him short of breath and his muscles were soft and flabby."

"What's his routine now?"

"His new diet is poached eggs on one slice of toast for breakfast, salad for lunch, and lamb or chicken with two vegetables for dinner. I have him do leg lifts and crunches, lift weights, ride a stationary bike, hit the rowing machine, spar a few rounds with me, and we play catch with a medicine ball. When he came to me he was bushed after one game of handball. Now he plays five or six games and asks, 'Who's next?'"

"What's his weight?"

"He's lost forty-one pounds and nine inches off his waistline. And his pulse is down from ninety-two to seventy-eight."

Ruth appeared in a bath robe after his massage and a cold shower.

"How ya feelin', Babe?" Rennie asked him.

"Real good. I feel like an athlete again. Only problem is I had to buy a new supply of collars and have all my suits taken in."

○ ○ ○

Art McGovern and his trimmed-down client attended the New York baseball writers' dinner at the Hotel Commodore, the scene of Ruth's earlier humiliation. They staged a mock argument over whether Ruth should have dessert. Then they sparred in their tuxedos. It was great fun. Everyone told the Babe he looked better than they'd seen him in years.

James Harrison sat at his Underwood typewriter the next morning. His editor had told him he wanted a piece on the Yankees' chances of repeating.

Babe Ruth

Harrison took a last drag of his cigarette, butted it out in the ashtray, and began pounding away at the keyboard, consulting his record sheets when he needed to. As always, he said aloud what he was typing.

"The Yankees may have won the pennant last year, but when the forty-two baseball writers were surveyed recently only nine, this reporter being one of them, said the Yanks will go all the way in '27. Most opt for Cornelius McGillicuddy's rebuilt Athletics. Mack went out and paid Jack Dunn, the Orioles' owner who sold George Ruth to Boston, buckets of money for three outstanding minor leaguers, Max 'Camera Eye' Bishop, Joe Boley, and a big southpaw named Robert Moses Grove. Grove, nickname Lefty, went 10-12 and 13-13 his first two years in Philadelphia, but he led the league with 194 strikeouts in '26 and lowered his E.R.A. from 4.75 to 2.51.

Connie has an all-star infield. At first is hard-hitting Jimmy Dykes. His backup is a muscular teenager the Yankees passed on named Jimmie Foxx. At second is slick-fielding Bishop, who made just eight errors in '26. His backup is Eddie Collins, the captain of the 1919 Black Sox. He doesn't steal fifty bases a year anymore, but he hit .355 last season. Sweet-swinging Sammy Hale is at third and Mack has installed Joe Boley at short.

Behind the plate the A's have an outstanding young catcher in Mickey Cochrane, a football star at Boston University. His nickname is Black Mike but it could easily be Jumbo the Elephant considering how far his ears stuck out.

In centerfield is 25-year-old slugger Al Simmons. It's really Aloysius Szymanski, but most reporters can't spell that. He has a habit of putting his left foot "in the bucket" and sliding it away from the pitch and toward the dugout each time he swings. He used the peculiar stance to rack up 253 hits in '25. In his first four years he's averaged .355. Zack Wheat, whose nickname is Buck, plays left field. He has a .317 lifetime average and 1,200 RBIs in eighteen years.

In right is the lovable Ty Cobb. "I know Cobb can still hit," Miller Huggins told me the other day, "but he drove the Tigers nuts. Mark my words, he'll do the same in Philadelphia." If Cobb doesn't ruin the team chemistry it looks to many like the A's will run away with the American League crown."

& THE 1927 YANKEES HAVE THE BEST SUMMER EVER

Harrison lit another Camel, flipped the page of his record book, thought a moment, and went back at his Underwood.

"As for the Yankees, their infield looks promising but hardly remarkable - certainly not on a par with the Athletics. At first is clumsy Lou Gehrig, who has proven he can hit baseballs as hard as anyone, including the Babe. But he's no Hal Chase. At second is smooth-fielding Tony Lazzeri who hits for power but suffers from epileptic seizures. At short is Mark Koenig who made fifty-two errors and batted just .271 in '26. Lazzeri was only a tad better at .275. The American League - including its pitchers - batted .281. At third is sure-handed Joe Dugan whose legs hurt so bad he needs to take a couple of games off every week.

The Yankee outfield is the best in baseball - though Washington's Sam Rice, Goose Goslin, and newly-acquired Tris Speaker are no slouches. Earle Combs is an outstanding leadoff hitter with great range but a sub-par arm, Bob Meusel is a hard hitter and a fine fielder, and the Babe is one of the finest defensive outfielders in the game, even though all anyone ever wants to talk about is his power."

As Harrison tore the full page from his typewriter he noticed the print was getting lighter. He put in a new sheet and decided it would soon be time for a new roller. He looked at the clock. "Time to wrap this up and get some lunch," he thought to himself.

"New York's catching platoon of Collins, Bengough, and Grabowski stacks up as the fifth best in the league behind Philadelphia's Cochrane, Muddy Ruel of the Senators, Cleveland's Luke Sewell, and the Browns' Wally Schang. But it isn't the catchers Miller Huggins is worried about. It's his pitchers.

On August 22 last year the Yanks held a comfortable ten game lead and Hug had fingernails. A month later, after every one of his starters except Shawkey had faded, Hoyt losing five of seven, Pennock three of four, Ruether three of five, and Shocker four out of five, their lead was down to two and Miller's nails were stumps."

Babe Ruth
& the 1927 YANKEES have the BEST SUMMER EVER

4.

BISCUIT PANTS, THE WOP, AND THE BEST OUTFIELD EVER

"Every time I think, it hurts the team."

Early in '23 Paul Krichell boarded a train to New Brunswick, New Jersey. Krichell was in his second year as a scout for the Yankees. His career as a catcher had been literally cut short. His arm had been badly torn when Ty Cobb spiked it with his razor-sharp cleats while sliding into home. Of course Cobb hadn't apologized. Krichell's arm was never the same. He played a while for the Buffalo Bisons in the International League and managed a double and a single off a 19-year-old pitcher named George Ruth when the Bisons played the Baltimore Orioles.

Krichell shared a smoking car with Andy Coakley, who was infamous for having kept Rube Waddell, the best pitcher in baseball, out of the 1905 World Series. Coakley and Waddell had wrestled on the platform of a train station after Rube had tried to knock off Coakley's boater and the eccentric southpaw had injured his arm. Now Coakley was managing Columbia's baseball team.

He told Krichell about one of his left-handed hurlers, a big kid from New York who could hit even better than he pitched. Krichell went to see him at Rutgers and Gehrig belted two home runs in three at bats. After Lou hit one out of South Field onto 115th Street in a game against NYU, Krichell wired Ed Barrow that he'd found the next Babe Ruth. Barrow told the scout to go ahead and sign the kid and Krichell offered him fifteen hundred dollars to play the rest of the year and a two thousand dollar signing bonus. With his mother suffering from pneumonia and his father out of work Lou was very tempted to take the money on the spot but decided to seek the advice of Archibald Stockder, his business professor.

Babe Ruth

"My parents gawt dere hearts set on me graduatin' from cawllege and pursuin' a profession," Lou told Stockder in his thick Brooklyn accent. The professor thought to himself that Lou's enunciation was better in *German* than in English.

Stockder leaned back in his chair and looked Lou square in the eye, "Ludwig, you have been in my business class for almost a year now. I think that ... you should go play baseball."

After his first season with the Yankees, Lou sent Stockder a thank-you card and a box of Coronas, a generous gift - especially for Gehrig.

o o o

Lou's parents went to see him play when he made it to the big leagues, but Wally Pipp played first base. Their son spent the whole game on the bench.

"They pay you all uff dat money to be a bummer?" Pa Gehrig asked his son when it was over. He knew he'd embarrass his son if he spoke in German. "You do nothing duh whole time, Ludwig. What kind off a business is this baseball business?"

"I'm learnin'," said Lou. "I sit beside the manager on da bench and he gives me pointers. I'm stickin' with him so much da fellas are stawtin' to call me teacher's pet."

Gehrig got to play occasionally, but with Pipp hitting close to .300 it wasn't often. Huggins finally wrote him into the lineup for a game at the end of August against the Senators when Bullet Joe Bush was the starter. Bush confronted him before he took the mound. "What are ya doing putting that big klutz in at first? I got a chance to win twenty this year and I ain't gonna do it with him bootin' balls and droppin' easy throws."

In the second inning Joe Judge laid down a bunt. Gehrig stayed at first even though he had a much better chance to make the play than Bush. Bush charged in and fielded the ball but it was too late to get Judge. He stormed up to Lou and yelled, "You stupid college punk, where are your brains?" loud enough for everyone in the park to hear. Lou just stared at the ground, humiliated.

Gehrig finally got into the lineup as a regular, at least for a trial, half way through the '25 season when Huggins realized the Yankees weren't going to catch the Senators. He benched Aaron Ward, Wally Schang, and Wally Pipp, who was batting .242, early in June. Lou hit .341 with six homers and fourteen runs batted in the rest of the month and, though Huggins still had some doubts about him, he became the full-time first baseman for good when Charlie Caldwell hit Wally Pipp in the temple with a pitch during batting practice. Pipp was in the hospital for two weeks and he never got his job back.

Pipp didn't resent Gehrig taking his place - he knew it was the way the game worked - and he could hardly fault Huggins for going with the younger, stronger man. He graciously and patiently worked with Lou, helping him to improve his footwork and teaching him when to reach for a throw and when to let the ball just come to him.

Gehrig belted 47 doubles, 20 triples, and 16 home runs, and drove in 109 runs in '26. His manager had a lot of faith in him but he told reporters that Lou was not a natural by any stretch of the imagination. "Only his willingness to work hard, his grim determination to succeed, and his lack of conceit will make him a complete ball player," said Huggins. Then he grinned. "That and those big muscles of his."

Lou's teammates had taken to calling him Biscuit Pants because he wore his uniform extra baggy to hide his enormous rear end. Gehrig loved putting on the Yankee pinstripes every day. Once Herb Pennock caught him staring at his uniform as it hung in his locker.

"What are you doing, Lou?" he asked.

Gehrig blushed. "Nuttin', just thinking how sharp da uniforms aw."

"Oh, I see," said Pennock.

"Where d'ya suppose dey got de idea ta put the Y over da N like dat, Hoib?"

"Tiffany's," Pennock told him.

"What, da fancy jewellery stawr?"

"That's right. Tiffany's designed it for a medal the New York police were giving out for bravery. Big Bill Devery, the chief of police, was one of the owners of the ball club back then and he decided to put it on the caps."

Babe Ruth

○ ○ ○

Dan Daniels of The *New York Telegram* had sat with James Harrison and Richards Vidmer in the press box one afternoon during a rain delay soon after Gehrig had become a regular. Lou was outside the dugout checking to see how water-logged the infield was.

"Look at the legs on him," said Harrison. "I've seen thinner trunks on redwoods."

"He's a real specimen, terrific hand-eye co-ordination and stupendous power," said Daniels.

"Not a whole lot of fun to be around though," said Vidmer. "Hardly says a word. Just chews tobacco and reads the funny papers."

"And when he craves some *real* excitement, he plays pinochle," added Harrison.

Gehrig lived at home, didn't drink, didn't go on dates, and was too cheap to buy decent clothes, so he didn't need much money. He gave most of his salary to his parents. Several of the Yankee players brought their wives to Florida, Gehrig brought his mom.

Lou liked to go to the movies and he liked to sing. Unfortunately, he couldn't carry a tune in a bucket. He didn't eat out in New York, he preferred his mother's cooking. But when he went out with teammates on the road, usually to a steakhouse, he'd embarrass them by leaving a nickel for a tip, sometimes even less. When Lou wasn't looking they'd sneak back and replace it with a quarter or two. Dugan once said that Lou could squeeze a penny tight enough to make Lincoln's nose bleed.

Gehrig was less clumsy than he'd been as a rookie and he was fielding a lot better, the result of countless hours of practice. But he still hesitated when the ball was hit to him. "Every time I think, it hurts the team," he told George Pipgras.

"You really shouldn't go around saying that," Pipgras advised him.

"When da writers ask me questions dey think I'm rude 'cuz I don't answer right away. They don't know I'm so scared a sayin' da wrong ting I'm nearly shittin' myself."

"Then we'd have to change your name from Biscuit Pants to Crapped His Pants," chuckled Pipgras.

o o o

Tony Lazzeri, whom his teammates good-naturedly called the skinny wop, was born in the tough Cow Hollow district of San Francisco.

"My neighborhood wasn't the kind in which a boy was very likely to grow up a sissy," he told his teammates when he joined the Yankees. "It was fight or get licked. And I never got licked. Matter of fact, I was gonna be a prize fighter."

Lazzeri had powerful forearms from helping his father at the Keystone Broiler Works after being expelled from school at fifteen. "I could toss a rivet with the best of 'em," he told girls he was trying to impress.

Tony swatted sixty homers and drove in 222 runs in '24 during the Pacific Coast League's expanded schedule. To put some weight on him, Tony Roffetti, the owner of an Italian restaurant, treated him to three or more spaghetti dinners a week and coaxed him to "Poosh 'Em Up", meaning hit the baseball long and high. The nickname stuck and New York's Italian fans in the Stadium and next to their radios would urge their native son to do just that.

Other teams had shied away from Tony partly because they thought some of his home runs were aided by the thin air in Salt Lake City but more so because he was epileptic. Ed Barrow was less concerned. He'd done his research and he'd learned that almost all of Tony's attacks occurred in the morning. Bill Essick, the first of the three scouts he sent out to look at him, said he was the best prospect he'd ever seen.

"Isn't the air pretty thin out there?" Barrow asked Essick.

"The air may be thin, but Lazzeri is solid."

"Well then, as long as he doesn't take fits between three and five-thirty in the afternoon, that's good enough for me," said Barrow.

Everyone was relieved that Lazzeri, whose big, sad eyes belied his upbeat personality, hadn't suffered a single attack during a game or practice in '26. He'd been a shortstop in the minors but he moved to second to make room for Koenig who had a stronger arm. Tony was a steadying influence

Babe Ruth

on Gehrig and Koenig. Lazzeri was rewarded for a fine '26 season with a contract for $8,000 plus Pullman expenses for him and his wife Maye to travel from San Francisco to Florida in April and from New York back to San Francisco in October.

o o o

Miller Huggins had finally tired of second baseman Aaron Ward. He was solid defensively but his average fell to .246 in '25. The shortstop Pee-Wee Wanninger did even worse, just .236. It was time for a change so the Yankees bought easy-going Mark Koenig, a switch hitter, for $35,000.

Coincidentally, he was from San Francisco like his new double play partner, though they came from opposite sides of town. His father was an engraver and his mother ran a curtain cleaning business. She made thirty-five cents a set and paid Mark ten cents a week to deliver them. He made his runs on a coaster with his dog Buster tagging along.

Koenig started his career in Moose Jaw, Saskatchewan and had interesting stories to tell of moonlit nights with amorous Indian maidens. His favorite had been Sleeping Bear and he told his teammates that underneath her buffalo sleeping blanket she always was bare - and warm. "The tribe should have called her Hot Under the Covers," Mark chuckled to Lazzeri one day.

Mark was the most eligible bachelor on the team. He had blonde hair, ocean blue eyes and thick, sensuous lips. He was an inch taller and ten pounds heavier than Lazzeri. Whenever he got a new shipment of bats he would meticulously polish each one with a hambone. Then he would seep it in cottonseed oil, a trick he'd learned from an aging veteran in the American Association. Koenig made a lot of errors, in fact he'd led the league, but he had good range and a strong throwing arm.

The Yankees had Koenig leading off for the first two months of the '26 season with Combs batting second. In the middle of June, Huggins flipped them. Of his five home runs the one Mark remembered most fondly was on August 7 in Detroit. Lil Stoner was pitching and his curve was extra wicked that day. He bent two hooks over the corner and Koenig, though he later could not recall why, turned and winked at Lou Gehrig, who was in the on-deck circle. Stoner threw a fastball down the middle and Mark hit it into the right field stands. Ty Cobb watched as it sailed over his head. Then he waved his arms up and down to get Stoner's attention and then held his nose.

"What a swell teammate Cobb must be," thought Mark as he rounded the bases.

o   o   o

Koenig was making a thousand less than Lazzeri and he got no Pullman fare. His World Series performance hadn't helped his salary demands. Not that any player was in a position to make demands of Ruppert or any other owner. As the Yankees' leadoff batter he'd struck out seven times, sometimes in crucial situations, hit into three double plays and made three errors, one late in the deciding seventh game. Huggins was sticking with him anyway - at least for now.

The alternative was to put Ray Morehart, a good-looking twenty-six year-old from Texas, at second and move Lazzeri to short. Morehart, who held a degree in languages from Austin College, had batted .318 in seventy-three games with the White Sox in '26, though he'd racked up a lot of those percentage points in one double header when he rapped nine hits. He'd hit well enough that the White Sox had often used him as a pinch hitter. Morehart had made fifteen errors in '26, less than a third of what Koenig made, but Mark went after any ground ball hit between the foul lines and didn't care if he got an error. That impressed Miller Huggins. He'd done the same thing when he played the infield.

Huggins had been forced to earn respect his whole life. Always under size, he'd worked out with weights and pulleys as a teenager to build up his arms and legs. Playing for the St. Paul Saints in the American Association he earned the nickname "Little Mister Everywhere" because he tried to get to every ball hit within fifty feet of him. His play made it into the local newspapers and he broke in with Cincinnati in '04.

In 1910 Miller was traded to the Cardinals and he led the National League in walks three times. He became a sure-handed and slick fielder and he was a terrific bunter. Recognized as the smartest and most observant player on the squad, he was named manager in 1913 and he took the team from the basement all the way up to third place.

Babe Ruth

Over the vehement protests of his partner Tillinghast L'Hommedieu Huston, Jake Ruppert hired Huggins to take over the sixth place Yankees in 1918. Huggins, who was a bachelor, packed up his sister Myrtle and the two of them got a small apartment together in New York.

The team he took over was described by the New York press as a bunch of prima donnas. They referred to Huggins as a little girl. They'd gone through seven managers in twelve years and their indifferent play was driving fans away in droves.

"If the crowds get any smaller, we'll have to put fractions on the turnstiles," one club official moaned.

The players did their best to ignore Huggins. He'd hoped to rely on their professionalism but eventually he was forced to crack the whip. Bullet Joe Bush who'd won twenty-six games in his first year in New York called Miller stupid for ordering him to intentionally walk a hitter. Huggins shipped Bush off to St. Louis. That sent a clear message to the rest.

"He sent Bush to the *Browns!*" Herb Pennock told Waite Hoyt when he heard. "We'd better toe the line, he's liable to send us back to the cellar dwellers in Boston."

In spite of the contempt with which he was treated Huggins lifted the Yankees to fourth in his first year in New York and then, after two third place finishes, he brought Yankee fans their first pennant in 1921. It helped that the year before he'd suggested to Yankee general manager Ed Barrow that he should try to get Babe Ruth from the Red Sox. Ruth had posted pretty good numbers in his first two years in New York. He averaged forty doubles, twelve triples, fifty-five home runs, a .377 batting average, and a .522 on base percentage.

On a road trip in Huggins' first year with the club, Ruth, who'd been allowed to do pretty much as he pleased in Boston, grabbed his new manager by his ankles and dangled him over the tracks off the back of a speeding train. "If Huggins is a baseball manager, I can swim the English Channel," roared Ruth in the middle of a crowded bar a month later. "And I ain't much of a fuckin' swimmer."

There were times when Huggins was ready to give up. After another day of abuse he'd go home and tell his sister, "It's just too frustrating, Myrtle.

Life's too short for all this rotten stuff and the rowdy players I have to put up with. I think I'll chuck the whole thing." Myrtle told him to stick it out. "Things are bound to get better, Miller. You're a fighter, you never give up." He didn't.

Ruth's insubordination was largely to blame for his manager's wrinkled forehead and the deep creases around his eyes at a comparatively young age. Huggins called Ruth the most destructive force in baseball - and he didn't just mean the force of his home runs. When Barrow congratulated him on his first World Series championship in '23 Hug said, "I would not go through those last four years again for all the money in the world. My teeth rotted, I couldn't eat, and I sure as hell never slept."

During Ruth's second year in New York Huggins was on edge for weeks and his stomach was bothering him something awful. Mark Roth, the travelling secretary, was worried about him. The Babe was out carousing every night. "Ruth's going to be the death of you," Roth told Miller. "You ought to get rid of the bum. Watch, he'll show up late again today."

The Babe strolled in just before game time, three hours after he was supposed to. He tipped his flat cap, spit tobacco juice on the floor, scratched his groin, and changed into his uniform. The game went into extra innings and Mark Roth was stewing because they were going to miss their coach to St. Louis. Ruth saw that he was getting worried and went over to him and said, "Don't worry, I'll put an end to it." He grabbed his bat and hit one over the roof.

At the train station Ruth walked past them. Roth nudged Huggins and asked him if he was going to say anything. Huggins just said "Hi, ya, Babe." Roth stared wide-eyed at Huggins. Miller shrugged his shoulders and said, "What are ya gonna do with the big stiff?"

Things had turned around when Huggins finally stood up to Ruth, suspending him indefinitely and fining him the unheard sum of five thousand dollars at the start of the '25 season when he showed up late for a game. The Babe went crying to Jake Ruppert and the owner backed his manager over his star performer and biggest draw. Ruth finally got the message and realized he'd have to shape up. After a seventh place finish that year the Yankees and their most valuable player realized that Huggins

Babe Ruth

was the boss and they did what he said. All except Waite Hoyt.

Now Huggins and Ruth were getting along better than anyone could remember. Not just civil to one another but actually friendly nowadays, each man showing respect for the other's contributions to the team's success. Now, when Huggins talked Ruth listened.

Hug appreciated that Ruth was in shape now and taking his responsibilities seriously. "I admire a man who can win out over tough opponents; but I admire a man who can win out over *himself* even more," Huggins told James Harrison. "He's still no saint off the field, Jim, but here at the park, I couldn't be happier with him. He's turned into a real role model for the young kids and that's good cuz they all worship the big lug."

o o o

The Yankees' forte was their outfield. Centerfielder Earle Combs was in his fourth year in New York. After he batted .380 with 144 RBI for Louisville in the American Association in '23 the Yankees acquired him at a steep cost - five players and $50,000. He tried strengthening his below average arm with exercises and he made a point of getting rid of the ball quickly. Combs was one of the fastest men in baseball, an absolute necessity if you played the cavernous center field in Yankee Stadium. A timer from Churchill Downs clocked him in spikes at ten seconds flat for the hundred yards while he played for Louisville.

Combs had fashioned himself into the most effective leadoff hitter in the game. Huggins told him it was his job to get on base for Gehrig, Ruth, and Meusel and he did it splendidly, drawing a lot of walks in addition to his many hits. As a left-handed batter he got an extra couple of steps coming out of the box, which allowed him to beat out infield hits. He didn't try to pull the ball, he used the entire field, and when he lined one into the gap it quite often resulted in a three-bagger. The Kentucky Colonel led the AL in triples three times.

"Hark to the tombs, here comes Combs," was the warning that reporters attributed to enemy pitchers when Earle loomed in the on-deck circle.

Ruth called him Iron Ass because he could sit in a hotel lobby for an eternity without blinking an eye or twitching a muscle. Combs was one of a small group of Yankees who didn't head to the speakeasies after dinner.

He and Gehrig, Herb Pennock, Wilcy Moore, and Ben Paschal were labelled "the movie set" because they so often opted to take in a moving picture show in one of the newly air-cooled theaters.

"If you had nine Combses on your ball club, you could sleep like a baby," Huggins was fond of saying.

Earle was hoping for an improvement on his $9,000 salary, even though his average had slipped from .342 to .299 in '26. He'd gotten a kick out of a reporter's jibe about how much money some of the players were asking for. He'd written, "Once they've bought a new jalopy and have a brass spittoon in every room what more do they need?" Earle looked thin and pale when he arrived in Florida with the Yankee veterans. He'd just had his tonsils out. He signed for $10,500.

Six-foot three Bob Meusel was the only Yankee taller than Ruth. His older brother, a star in the National League, was called Irish, even though they were German. Bob hit .328 as a rookie when he joined the Yankee outfield in 1920, the same year the Babe arrived. He'd been prone to strikeouts at first but he'd learned to be patient and wait for his pitch. Meusel led the league with 33 homers and 134 RBIs in '25, so pitchers had to think twice about pitching around Ruth to get to him, especially if there was already another Yankee or two on base. Meusel had a rifle for an arm and he was deadly accurate to any base, his throws always arriving on the fly.

Fans often interpreted Languid Bob's effortless manner and long, loping strides as loafing, but no one appreciated Meusel's contribution to the team's success more than Miller Huggins. Unfortunately, dropping a routine fly ball that cost the Yankees a crucial game in the '26 Series had not endeared Meusel to the fans. His favourite expression was a scowl and his favourite utterance a grunt, but Meusel enjoyed nights on the town with the Babe or a drink or three of his expensive booze and a game of cards in Ruth's suite.

The third outfielder of course was the Bambino. He played right or left field, depending on which had the least sun, in order to guard against damage to his precious batting eyes and also because he'd once lost a ball in the sun while playing at the Polo Grounds.

Babe Ruth

Meusel always took the sun field. Ruth played in right whenever the Yankees played in Washington or Cleveland or at home. Meusel donned sunglasses when the Yankees played in Boston, Detroit, St. Louis, Philadelphia or Chicago. He wasn't happy about it, but what could he say?

The man who had the misfortune to be the Yankees' fourth outfielder was soft-spoken, sometimes brooding Ben Paschal. From a distance he looked a lot like Lazzeri. He had the same sunken eyes and sheepdog expression, though his face was longer and thinner.

Paschal was born in Alabama and had distinguished himself by tearing up the Sally League in '22 with two hundred hits including twenty-two triples and twenty-six homers that lead the Charlotte Hornets to the championship. He played in the low minors until August of '24 when Ed Barrow noticed that he'd batted .341 for the Atlanta Crackers of the Southern League and bought his contract.

Paschal and Combs had competed for the third outfield position at the start of the '25 season and Combs won out on the basis of his far superior fielding and speed. But when the Babe suffered "the bellyache heard around the world" Ben took his place, hit six home runs in May, and batted .360. On most teams he'd be a regular.

Stern-faced, left-handed Cedric Durst, the fifth outfielder, was from Texas. When the St. Louis Browns invited him to their training camp in '22 he made a big splash. He hit five homers in eighty-five at bats in '22, but his average was a dismal .212. When he hit .348 with the St. Paul Saints in '24 he earned a call up to the big leagues. But when his average sank to .237 the Browns traded him to New York along with pitcher Joe 'Pecos' Giard for Sad Sam Jones. Durst was good defensively but he wasn't going to be stealing anyone's job until he proved he could hit major league pitching. As the fifth outfielder, he got even less playing time than Paschal, usually just in exhibition games.

Pat Collins and Johnny Grabowski would share the catching duties. The Yankees hadn't had a regular behind the plate since Wally Schang turned thirty-five in '24 and lost fifty points off his batting average. Blue-eyed Pat Collins spent his first five years in the majors with the lowly St. Louis Browns. He had a sore arm. His cure was bowling as often as he could. He bowled so often he decided to open his own alley back home in Kansas City.

Ed Barrow had sent second baseman Aaron Ward to the White Sox for Johnny Grabowski during the winter to make room for Mark Koenig. Grabowski had batted over .300 in '23 and '24 for Double-A Minneapolis. His teammates called Grabowski Nig because of his dark complexion. The other teams called him Polack.

Twenty-nine-year-old Benny Bengough, who'd thrown stones into Niagara Falls when he was growing up, weighed only a hundred and forty-five pounds. He'd sat on the bench in Buffalo until his mother berated the manager for not playing her darling enough. Given the chance, he demonstrated a strong arm and fine defensive skills.

Miller Huggins liked Benny's aggressive leadership during his first training camp in '23. He made sure to say his name right. Most people, including the sports writers, pronounced it Bengow and Ruppert called him Benkopf. The correct pronunciation was Bengoff. Hoyt and Pennock wanted him behind the plate whenever they pitched.

Bengough had taken over from Schang in '25 on the same day that Gehrig replaced Pipp at first. Huggins wished he could be his regular catcher, but Benny had a bad arm. He'd been batting .381 in '26 when he was hit on his throwing arm by a slider from George "the Bull" Uhle.

Doctors did nothing to ease the pain in Benny's wing and he finally resorted to quacks and eccentrics. One of them painted him from the waist up with a terrible-smelling sticky solution that eased the inflammation - but only for a couple of days. Another quack sat him down in a kind of electric chair. When a powerful current pulsed through him Benny leaped out of the chair and tripped over the wires. Now he had a sprained ankle to go with his sore arm.

Benny was fun to have around. Completely bald though just 29, he'd take off his cap, shake his head, and run his fingers across his scalp as if he was taming a head full of luxurious locks.

Ruth thought he was a riot and invited him along on some of his romps. Benny loved jazz. His drink of choice was gin, bathtub or bootlegged, he didn't much care which. He and the Babe drank lots of beer together too.

Babe Ruth

"You really study for the priesthood?" the Babe asked him when they went to a downtown speak together.

"Ya, it was my mom's idea. I studied for it but I didn't much like it. The only booze they got's that ceremonial wine."

"I guess you know *I'm* a Catholic," said Ruth.

"What kind?" asked Benny.

"I'm what they call a roaming Catholic."

"Good one, Jidge. You know I just heard that a guy who was in the seminary with me's starting a home to save wayward girls."

"Ya? Well ask him ta save me a couple."

5.

FROLICKING IN FLORIDA

"She is not afraid of a man, a gun, or the devil himself."

Ruth boarded the Seaboard Airline sleeper train for St. Petersburg on Saturday, March 5. He wanted to get in a few rounds of golf before camp opened. He quite often played thirty-six holes in a day and sometimes as many as seventy-two. The Yankees had trained in New Orleans prior to 1925 - with disastrous results. Drinks and dames were the order of the day there. The most common activities in St. Petersburg, if they could be termed as such, were horseshoes, checkers, and dozing on park benches.

o o o

Bob Meusel, Waite Hoyt, and Bob Shawkey met the Babe at the Renaissance Vinoy club in downtown St. Petersburg. They were all scratch golfers like Ruth. The Babe took the game seriously. He took all his penalty strokes and always putted out, no gimmes for him.

"This is the first time Jidge has beaten everybody down here," said Shawkey as they drove a rented Packard out to the course. A convoy of noisy trucks carrying materials to build new roads rumbled by them.

"Whad'ya say, Gob?" asked Hoyt.

"I said this is the first time Jidge has beaten everybody down here to training camp."

"Ya, usually the only thing he's first for is the dining car," chuckled Hoyt.

As usual, Silent Bob Meusel said nothing, just like the way he ignored the fans when they cheered one of his bullet throws to home or a long hit. He just stared out the window at the barren landscape. An enormous turtle lay sunning itself by the side of the road.

Babe Ruth

"I hear he's lost fifty pounds," said Shawkey.

"Probably from chasing dames around Hollywood," said Hoyt.

"From what I hear about those actresses," said Bob, "some of them *like* bein' caught."

When he was younger, Sailor "Bob the Gob" Shawkey had been a fireman on the Pennsylvania Railway, mined for gold, worked on a logging crew, and driven race cars. He'd also done a stretch in the navy during the World War. He was the only Yankee with a tattoo, a large anchor on his forearm.

When he was twenty-three he'd married Marie Lakjer, a shapely thirty-one-year-old divorcee whose nickname was "Tiger Lady" because she often wore a massive robe of tiger skins and a matching hat. The fact that she had shot Herbert Clapp, her wealthy first husband, in the head may have contributed to her divorce. She was charged with aggravated assault and battery with intent to kill.

"She is not afraid of a man, a gun, or the devil himself," Clapp had told the wide-eyed jury.

Marie claimed self-defence and rather surprisingly the charges were dropped. Friends warned Shawkey not to marry her. Teammate Amos Strunk, who reluctantly agreed to serve as his best man, knew his friend liked fast cars and fast women but he told Bob that Marie might just be the death of him.

Shawkey was one of the players Connie Mack had jettisoned after the 1914 Series. The Yankees had picked him up for the waiver price of $2,500. He won twenty-four games in 1916 and ten straight in '19. He had some trouble that year with one hitter though, a Boston pitcher named George Ruth. Young Ruth hit three home runs off Shawkey including a grand slam in June, a game-winning two-run blast in July, and a game-tying shot in September that broke Ned Williamson's record. It sailed out of the Polo Grounds and was said to be the longest ball hit in the park's history. No one was more relieved than Shawkey when the Yankees bought Ruth that winter.

Bob had a mental book on all the hitters and their tendencies and a simple philosophy. "Pitching is first and last a study of the batter and a never-ending effort to give him something he doesn't want." Shawkey, who always wore a flaming red flannel undershirt under his short-sleeved tunic, won eight and lost seven in '26. He'd lost some of the hop on his fastball and wasn't being counted on for much.

o o o

There was a big crowd on hand to watch the Babe play. He wore a yellow knitted cardigan, brown plus-four knickerbockers, and brown and yellow-striped knee-high socks. The spectators gasped as his first drive rocketed off the tee. They'd never seen anyone including the club pro hit a golf ball so hard or so far. When he'd played a round with the great Walter Hagen he outdrove him a few times.

When Ruth swung his brassie the spectators could hear the whooshing sound it made. They applauded when his ball landed 345 yards away, right near the green. Ruth chipped on with his spoon and the ball landed three feet from the flag. He swore when he missed the putt. On the second hole he teed off with his mashie. He sliced and still had a hundred and fifty yards to go for his second shot.

"Gimme the niblick," he told the pimple-dotted caddy that the course had assigned him. Another kid who'd hoped to be sent out with Ruth because he was such a big tipper told him the Babe was fun to caddy for but the bag would be heavy because of all the bottles of beer and the bags of ice.

"You can hit a niblick a hundred and fifty yards?" asked the boy.

"Sure can, keed."

He hit it *over* the green and had to chip on with his spoon again. He hammered his putt ten feet past the hole and snarled at his putter in disgust.

After he teed off on the third hole Ruth bellowed "Fuckin' photographers!" loud enough that golfers three holes away turned to look. "Right in the middle of my backswing again!"

Meusel charged toward the photographers brandishing a 3-iron. "Get the hell outta here and leave the Babe alone, you picture-snapping bastards," he yelled. The photographers knew about Meusel's ornery disposition. They ran into the woods. The Babe took a tidy 36 to the clubhouse after

Babe Ruth

nine holes but shot 48 on the back. He blamed it on the photographers.

o o o

Waite Hoyt and Urban Shocker had breakfast together the next morning on the train ride to St. Petersburg. They'd had a lavish midnight lunch the night before. In spite of the hour, the dining car's menu featured porterhouse steaks, mutton chops, broiled salt mackerel, and veal cutlets. For breakfast they had wheat cakes with syrup, sausages, and scrambled eggs.

Shocker had thick eyebrows and a perpetual smirk. He'd been a catcher in Windsor, Ontario in 1913 when he stopped a fastball with the tip of the third finger on his throwing hand. When the broken finger finally healed it had a hook in the last joint.

"It isn't pretty to look at but it's been very useful to me," Shocker told reporters. "I tried pitching and found I could throw a slow ball that breaks straight down."

He'd started his career in New York but Miller Huggins thought he was a trouble-maker and he traded Shocker to St. Louis. Hug came to regret it. Urban racked up four straight twenty win seasons with the sad-sack Browns. Frank Ellerbe, their third baseman, said Shocker was the best fielding pitcher he ever saw. "If somebody tried to bunt on him he'd fly off the mound and pounce on the ball like a hungry cat."

Shocker, whose nickname was "Rubber Belly", become a Yankee nemesis. No one except the outlawed and disgraced Eddie Cicotte pitched tougher to Ruth. Shocker was one of the seven 'grandfathered' pitchers still allowed to throw wet ones after baseball banned all upcoming hurlers from throwing spit balls in the winter of 1920. Tragically it hadn't prevented Carl Mays putting an end to Ray Chapman's life on an overcast afternoon with a soiled fastball to the brain a few months later.

Shocker was the Browns' ace but he was also a thorn in his manager's side, often showing up late or just plain staying home if it wasn't his turn to pitch. He wasn't always in peak condition either. They traded him back to New York in '24 for Joe Bush and two pitching prospects. Miller Huggins never revealed to Lou Gehrig that if the Browns had insisted the young slugger be part of the deal he would have included him.

Urban was thirty-seven and he seemed to be aging fast. He didn't say much anymore. While his teammates bantered and ogled girls during breakfast he read a magazine. Sometimes a bunch of the players would head up to a place called the Blossom Heath Inn in Larchmont where Benny Bengough often sat in with the big bands on saxophone. Shocker never went.

No one, not even Huggins, knew that Urban had a degenerative valve in his heart. It was killing him. The other players noticed that he sat up all night on the sleeper cars. If he lied down he'd start to cough and even choke.

"Where's Gehrig?" asked Shocker. "I haven't seen him for a while. Did he get off to phone his mommy?"

"No, he's up in the observation car."

"Watching the scenery?"

"No, they have writing tables up there with stationery," said Hoyt.

"And he's writing a letter to Ma Gehrig?"

"Good guess. He's probably asking her to come down cuz he misses already."

Just then a man coming down the aisle bumped into the slim young waiter who'd been holding a coffee urn. Some of the hot coffee spilled onto Shocker's arm?

"What the hell!" yelled Shocker. "You stupid idiot!"

"Urban, settle down," said Hoyt. "It wasn't the kid's fault. That guy bumped into him."

"I'm so sorry," said the waiter as he patted Shocker's arm with a towel.

"Ah, forget about it," said Shocker, waving him away and dabbing water on the stain.

"You're in a lousy mood," said Hoyt. "You've been down in the dumps ever since we left New York."

"You know what? I had more wins from Twenty to Twenty-Five than any pitcher in baseball and I did it with the fuckin' Browns. And what happened? I got a rotten salary cut. With all the money Ruppert's got. And

Babe Ruth

then we miss out on two grand cuz we lose the fuckin' Series. Why d'ya think I'm in a lousy mood?" He didn't mention that he might be dying.

o o o

Waite Hoyt was nicknamed "Schoolboy" when he made it to the big leagues at seventeen after throwing three no-hitters in high school. He was broad-shouldered and handsome, with an aquiline nose and deep-set brown eyes. He'd given up no earned runs to the Giants in three complete games in the '21 Series. That tied Christy Mathewson's record from 1905, the Series in which Mathewson was to have been matched against the injured A's ace Rube Waddell, who might well have thrown three shutouts himself.

After having an off year in '25 Waite had done much better in '26 and he went in to Ruppert's office for his contract renewal with high hopes for a raise. Ruppert pointed to a picture of his brewery's 22-story headquarters. "The best location in Manhattan," the beer baron boasted. Then he pointed to a photo of his apartment building across from Central Park. "My fifteen room apartment is on upper Fifth Avenue," he told Hoyt.

Finally he pointed proudly to a picture of Eagle's Nest. "Thirty-three rooms, eight bathrooms, and fifteen servants," crowed Ruppert.

"Real nice, Mister Ruppert. I was hoping for a two thousand dollar raise, on account of how much better I did last year," said Hoyt.

Ruppert turned beet red and jumped out of his chair. "Two thousand dollars! What do you think I am? A millionaire!"

o o o

Hoyt went to see Miller Huggins the day after he checked into the Princess Martha, the Yankees' hotel.

"Hug, I know we haven't exactly seen eye to eye these last few years."

"You could say that," said Huggins. "You've been a bit of a hot head."

"I should never have taken a swing at you like I did in Twenty-Two ... and I know that throwing that ball into the stands when you came to take me out last year was dumb."

"Cost you two hundred. Enough to make a man think."

& THE 1927 YANKEES HAVE THE BEST SUMMER EVER

"I went for a walk by myself last night - down to the pier."

"What? Nobody around to drink with? On this club? I remember back when we held our camp in New Orleans and a reporter said the Yankees were training on Scotch."

"Lemme finish, Hug. During the off season I came to realize that I've been nothing but an egotistical, self-centered, pompous ass. And now I know that I've ignored pretty much every word of advice you or anybody else has given me. Last night, when I was out alone on that pier I felt the hand of God reach down and touch me. I felt him telling me it's time to make peace with myself and let go of my inner demons."

"You know, Waite, after you did so great in Twenty-One I thought you were on your way to being one of the best pitchers in the game. I told lots of people that. But then you let your temper and pig-headedness get in the way of your talent. How many times were you up 0 and two on a hitter and just would not waste a pitch to see if he'd chase a bad one? You had to show you could blow your fastball past him and you got burned every time. You just wouldn't listen to common sense. Some of us have been around a while and know a thing or two."

"Well from now on I'm going to change my ways and do what you say is best. I'm not gonna be a knucklehead anymore. You'll see."

"In that case I've got some news for you. You're my pitcher on Opening Day."

"Thanks, Hug. You won't regret it. I'm gonna have my best season yet."

Hoyt hadn't been able to find any of the veterans at the hotel his first night in town because they'd gone to the dog races. After signing at least a hundred autographs, the Babe blew two hundred dollars on the first three races betting on what he said were "sure things".

"I thought you were supposed ta bet on the pooch that pisses right before the race," he told Dutch Ruether as he ripped up another losing ticket.

"You are, Jidge. Your luck's bound ta change soon."

It did.

The next morning, as the players donned their uniforms, Ruth burst into the clubhouse carrying a grip. Everyone gathered round as he opened it

Babe Ruth

and spilled its contents - several stacks of ten and twenty dollar bills - onto the trainer's table.

"I had a good night at the dog track while you bums went to the pictures. There's eight thousand bucks here. We don't get paid 'til the season starts and I know some a yas are sending half your meal money home to the missus. Take what ya need. You can pay me back later."

"Imagine that!" a twenty-year-old from Tennessee who was hoping for a spot in the infield told a nineteen-year-old who threw hard but usually over the catcher's head. "I only took twenty. I probably won't make the team."

He didn't, but when he got back his old job at the Piggly Wiggly in Tennessee he made sure to send a twenty dollar check to the Babe care of Yankee Stadium along with a note explaining who he was. He was pretty sure the Babe wouldn't remember him. Ruth chuckled and tore up the check.

o o o

That afternoon some of the Yankees headed to Ruppert Beach which was located near their owner's orange groves along Pass-a-Grille Key. The Babe mugged for photographs with a group of beautiful dancers. A couple of them climbed up on his shoulders to show off their legs. He pinched a couple of well-shaped bottoms. There were giggles but no complaints.

"What show are the dancers from?" Waite Hoyt asked Herb Pennock, the Yankees' most cerebral player.

"They're from the cast of No, No, Nanette," said Pennock. "They're here for a holiday."

"Isn't that the show Harry Frazee sold the Babe to finance?" asked Hoyt.

"One of them," said Herb. "He's always looking for money to stage one new show or another. The Babe sale wasn't enough so he had to keep selling Ruppert more players."

Most observers considered southpaw Pennock, whom reporters had dubbed the Squire of Kennet Square, to be the ace of the New York staff. "If you cut that bird's head open the weakness of every batter in the league would fall out," said Miller Huggins.

Herb had an effortless, rag-arm style. Benny Bengough claimed you could catch him sitting in a rocking chair. Detroit's Bob "Fats" Fothergill, who had improved upon his .353 average in '25 by batting .367 in '26, said no left-hander could get him out. The next day Pennock fitted him with an 0-4 collar.

Pennock had an oval face atop a long neck, a thin, serious line for a mouth, and a squint-eyed expression that made him less attractive than he could have been. He bore a strong resemblance to Ty Cobb but he was a whole lot more pleasant. Of course, *everyone* was more pleasant than Cobb. Herb was relaxed and humble and his quirky sense of humor kept Ruth and Gehrig loose.

At the age of fifteen Pennock, whose parents were Quakers, was a weak-hitting first baseman playing for Cedarcroft Boarding School in Pennsylvania. His frail arm curved every throw he made which was why he played first base. A new manager decided that Herb's throws might just baffle hitters and when the regular pitcher failed to show for a game he sent Pennock to the mound. He struck out nineteen batters.

Word of his exploits spread across the state and reached Connie Mack, who called him up to the A's in 1912. He pitched four innings in relief in his debut and allowed just one hit. His second appearance the following Saturday was against Detroit but the Tigers didn't play. The entire team sat out the game in protest over Ty Cobb having been suspended for going into the stands to fight a heckler. It turned out the man had lost all but two of his fingers in a printing press accident. Pennock had no trouble with the replacement players, who lost 24-2 in their sole major league appearances.

In '14 Pennock's record was 11-4. Pitching coach Chief Bender had taught him how to throw a screwball, a pitch Bender had learned from Rube Waddell. Like Waddell, Bender called it a fadeaway. When Connie Mack dismantled his wonderful team after they embarrassed themselves in the '14 Series Pennock struggled and Mack traded him to Boston. Mack often referred to it as his biggest mistake.

In 1919 Pennock was 16-8, but when he slid to 10-17 in '22 Harry Frazee decided to sell him to his friend Jake Ruppert for fifty thousand dollars.

Babe Ruth

Herb and his wife Esther were returning from a tour of the Orient. They danced a jig on the San Francisco pier when they got the news. Pennock was the eleventh and last player Frazee sold to the Yankees. The others included Carl Mays, Bullet Joe Bush, Waite Hoyt, Babe Ruth, Joe Dugan, and George Pipgras.

Coming off a twenty-three win season in '26, Pennock was determined to get a raise out of Colonel Ruppert. "If I don't, I'll quit the game and breed foxes," he told reporters during the winter. "I haven't had a ball in my hand since last year and I don't really care if I pitch another game." Ruppert berated his ace hurler in the newspapers for demanding more money than any other pitcher including Walter Johnson was getting. "He wants a thirty-three percent raise. Has the price of Grade A milk, shoes, and neckties gone up that much?" he asked reporters facetiously.

After being told by Jake Ruppert that he was going to be placed on the ineligible list Pennock let Miller Huggins know that he was ready to talk. Huggins told Ruppert. Barrow reminded the Colonel that Pennock had, after all was said and done, led the team in wins in '26. The beer baron relented and gave the southpaw a huge raise - $3,000 - which boosted him to a whopping $18,000.

The beguiling dancers wore the new bathing costumes that consisted of a tight-fitting top with thin shoulder straps and a pair of shorts that showed off their long legs. They were having an awful time trying to walk in the sand in their high-heels though.

"I'm having trouble getting used to seeing women's legs," said Pennock. "I can't say as I'm minding the struggle, however."

"I'll bet Jidge'll have some of those legs wrapped around him tonight," said Hoyt.

"Ya," said Herb, "and he won't be struggling to get out."

Dressed in a pin-striped suit and a black derby that looked quite out of place on the beach, the portly fifty-five-year-old mayor of St. Petersburg shuffled his way through the sand to talk to the Bambino.

"Glad to have you in town again, Babe," he said. "Those are pretty nice looking gals. Dancers are they?"

"So they tell me. They're enough ta make a fellow think about goin' to them musicals."

The mayor chuckled. "Listen, Babe, the manager of a troupe of entertainers that are here in St. Petes this week has invited me and my wife, several clergymen, and some members of the Chamber of Commerce and their wives to a picnic he's organized for tonight. Since you're our city's most notable celebrity, he's asked me to invite you to join us."

"Gee, I dunno, your mayorship. A bunch a politicians and clergymen? Not really my cup of tea if you know what I mean. I hope ya understand. Besides, I gotta be up at 5:30 if I wanna play golf before practice."

"I understand, Babe. To tell you the truth I was going to tell the man I wasn't interested in going myself."

Ruth squinted into the sun, which had come out from behind a cloud. "What changed your mind?"

The mayor looked around to see if anyone was close enough to hear him. "He told me that his troupe includes a dozen lovely chorus girls."

"Why didn't you say that in the first place?" boomed the Babe. "I'll be there with bells on. I can beat the jokers I'm playin' tomorrow morning even if I'm still half asleep."

o o o

At nine o'clock that night a convoy of small boats carried the handsomely-dressed invitees across a narrow channel to a palm-fringed island. The full moon reflected off the water and the backs of dolphins who merrily provided an escort.

Near the shore a lavish assortment of goat cheese, sweet and spicy chicken, brioche rolls, pasta salad with asparagus and lemon, and an assortment of fruit cobblers and pies occupied wooden tables. Fried chicken and pork simmered in charcoal cookers. Drinks were served in tall icy glasses.

The Babe was the main attraction. Everyone wanted to shake his hand and he did his best to juggle his plate and his drink so he could accommodate them. He managed not to spill anything and then excused himself. A launch had pulled up to shore carrying the chorus girls. They were beautiful.

The girls headed straight for the punch bowl. Their manager looked around to see if anyone was watching and then poured a whole bottle of gin into it. Before long the girls were giggling up a storm. They spotted the Babe and crowded around him.

"Harry *said* you'd be here," a young blonde with an egg-shaped face squeaked.

"You sure are tall," said a tiny girl with copper hair and pale blue eyes.

A voluptuous brunette with vamp eyes who was squeezed into a tight skirt came over to Ruth, her hips swaying as she walked. She placed a hand on the Babe's arm. "You're as brown as a berry, Babe," she purred. "Are you getting lots of exercise down here?"

"I'm playin' a lotta golf."

"Are you? How many strokes do you usually take?"

To the shock of the town fathers and especially their wives an hour into the festivities Ruth took the hand of the voluptuous brunette and led her away through a line of palm trees and into the dunes. Twenty minutes later they returned. The Babe was grinning from ear to ear. The dancer tried her best to put her clothes and hair in order.

"Well I never!" exclaimed the mayor's wife.

The troupe manager elbowed the man next to him and said, "I'll bet she never!"

o o o

Huggins and his coaches stood beside a group of reporters and watched infield practice the next afternoon. The diamond at Crescent Lake Park looked terrific. Al Lang, a real estate developer anxious to attract chilled northerners to St. Petes, had lured the Yankees and the Boston Braves to the park and he'd spared no expense in providing them with top-notch training facilities. When Hug complained of the glare off the sandy infield Lang imported clay from Georgia to redo it.

Phil Schenck, the Yankee stadium groundskeeper, had come down to work on the outfield, supervising the laying of the sod - Bermuda grass and Italian rye. It was a thick, luxuriant bed of grass. Crescent Lake was just beyond right field and at a dollar and a quarter apiece Ed Barrow hoped not too many baseballs would be hit into it. To the left of the lake on the other side of the centerfield fence stood the West Coast Inn, which had rooms going for as high as four dollars a night.

"Have you changed your ways, Babe?" Dutch Ruether asked as they changed in the large locker room. "You're looking pretty fit."

"Up with the sun and to bed with the chickens," Babe told him.

"Don't you mean to bed with the *chicks*?"

o o o

A few minutes later the Babe stepped up to the plate for his turn in the cage. He took his swings with a towel shoved up into his armpit.

Gehrig leaned against the screen watching. "What's dat towel for, Jidge?"

"It's to keep my right arm close to my body, keed. You oughta try it, your arm was flappin' a lot last year."

Lou was always thankful to Ruth for giving him pointers. Once he'd been hit in the face when a ground ball took a bad hop and the Babe had told him to put a cold steak on it when he got home to keep down the swelling. Lou was too cheap to buy a steak. He used a piece of liver instead.

The Babe drove the first pitch over the fence between the lake and the hotel. He laughed as the bat boy climbed onto his bicycle to go get it.

"I kissed that one," he yelled to Gehrig.

Lazzeri stepped into the cage for his turn.

"Do you think the sophomore jinx is going to bite him this year?" James Harrison asked Richards Vidmer as they stood together near the on-deck circle.

"He'll be hard-pressed to match eighteen homers and a hundred and seventeen RBIs," said Vidmer.

"The kid can sure run. Hell, he's nearly as fast as Combs," said Harrison. He looked down at his *Sporting News*. "Fourteen triples and sixteen steals last season. And it's no wonder he hit so many balls out, look at the shoulders on him."

"He's built more like a *fullback* than an infielder."

"Too bad he's got that condition. A lot of clubs backed away when they found out."

"That's why Barrow got him for sixty-five thousand," said Vidmer. "I wonder how bad it'll affect him."

"I don't know, Richards, not at all last year. But I hear he had an attack on the train ride down here."

"He did. Koenig went back to his berth after breakfast to get something and Lazzeri was in convulsions on the floor, white foam seeping through his lips. Koenig stuffed his wallet into Tony's mouth and ran for Doc Woods. Not that there's much anyone can do for them while they're having a fit. I guess he was fine after a few minutes."

Spirited Charley O'Leary, who'd been with the Yankees six years, stood beside Miller Huggins watching the hitters take their turns. He was Hugs' first base coach, principal assistant, and closest friend.

"You staying with Myrtle?" O'Leary asked. He knew Huggins and his sister, a domestic science teacher, shared an apartment a short subway ride from Yankee Stadium.

"I am. We've got a little place on the beach. She likes it down here."

"I thought about bringin' me wife along," said Charley, who still hadn't lost his Irish accent.

"You did?"

"Ya. But not fer long."

After batting practice Art Fletcher hit infield. Charley sat in the dugout to get out of the hot sun and carefully studied the three second-year infielders. He knew he didn't need to worry about Dugan.

Tall, green-eyed Joe Dugan was turning thirty. He'd gone straight from Holy Cross to the Philadelphia Athletics in 1917. The A's were struggling. Disgusted with his star players after their half-hearted performance against the Phillies in the '14 Series Connie Mack had sent them all away. For the next few years the inept Mackmen played to disgruntled cranks who hissed and booed whenever Joe made an error.

Sensitive and temperamental, Joe left the team and Mack had to go after him and persuade him to come back. After a couple of disappointing years with the bat Joe's hitting picked up and he believed he was entitled to a raise. Mack disagreed. Joe took off again.

By the time he'd left the A's for the thirty-fifth time sportswriters had labelled him "Jumpin' Joe" and fans had taken to yelling "I want to go home!" whenever he took the field. Dugan struggled playing second base and shortstop, where he committed forty errors in '19. When Mack moved him to third he was terrific. He batted .322 in '20 but he still wasn't happy playing in front of the judgemental Philadelphia crowds. Joe finally escaped the City of Brotherly Love in '22. He'd told friends he'd be playing for the Yankees but Ed Barrow engineered a three-way trade that landed Joe in Boston. When Barrow moved to New York he quickly nabbed Joe for the juggernaut he was assembling, primarily with stars who'd played for him when he'd managed the Red Sox.

Dugan had a fine season in 1924. His third hit of the day on September 26 in Philadelphia, his former house of horrors, was a single to right field. Wally Pipp followed with a single to center that Al Simmons bobbled. Joe saw what had happened, raced to third and beat Simmons' throw with a Cobb-like hook slide minus the razor-like spikes. When he got to his feet he found he couldn't put any weight on his left leg. He had to be helped to the dugout and was through for the season. He had cartilage sown onto his knee during the winter but the trick knee would pain him the rest of his career.

Dugan had a strong arm and an even better glove, rated the best in the league by most. He handled bunts like a vacuum cleaner and had a consistent if not powerful bat even though he was a bit slow on the bases. He met with Jake Ruppert in February and asked for an increase from the $12,000 he'd been making for the past two seasons. He hadn't hit .300 either of those years, but he'd been close.

"How can you have the nerve to ask for a raise?" asked Ruppert. "Do you not know how much it costs to run a ball club and a stadium? I must pay for the players to take the train twice a week and to eat three times a day and to sleep in fine hotels. And there are the baseballs, and the uniforms, and the trainers, and the medical expenses."

"Listen, Mister Ruppert, you don't have to be embarrassed about it," Joe told him. "Do you need to borrow some money?"

Dugan hadn't meant it as a joke but Ruppert, who in spite of Prohibition's ban on his major money-making product had an estimated net worth of seventy million dollars, never forgave him.

o o o

Charley O'Leary had played a lot of shortstop and turned lots of double plays with Germany Schaefer in Detroit when he was young. He didn't bother to mention that he'd averaged fifty-five errors a year. The two infielders used to get a ride to the park in their friend Crazy Hank's motor car. He had a small factory on Mack Avenue where groups of two or three men assembled motor cars. Hank had invited Schaefer and O'Leary to get in on the ground floor as investors but they'd declined. "No thanks, you're crazy, Hank," Charley told him. Hank's real name was Henry Ford.

Charley had lots of stories about Ty Cobb, like the day the Georgia Peach had arrived for training camp in '07. The Negro groundskeeper'd had the temerity to put out his hand. How dare a black man pretend to be Cobb's equal! Instead of shaking it, Cobb punched the man in the mouth. The groundskeeper ran away and Cobb chased after him. When the man's wife tried to stop Cobb he put his hands around her neck and started choking her.

"Straddle the bag when yer takin' them throws, me son," Charley yelled at Lazzeri. "And let the ball come ta you, don't ya be reachin' for it. The same thing with the runner. Let him slide inta yer glove."

Art Fletcher was Huggins' other assistant. He was in his first year with the Yankees. Fletch had taken Fred Merkle's place as third base coach. Hug knew him from his National League days and he was delighted to get him. Art had been only a decent shortstop and an average hitter, but he was a real battler.

He'd fought enemy players, umpires, even fans and he got fined and he got suspended. Fletch was a world class bench jockey. He could ride enemy pitchers and berate umpires with the best of them. No one had appreciated his skills more than his manager, fiery John McGraw, who made Fletch the Giants' captain. He'd taken his lantern jaw and big mouth with him when he'd gone to manage the Phillies in '23. In his four years at the helm he'd done no better than sixth place and he'd been ready for a change when Huggins called him.

After the infielders headed to the clubhouse the Babe did one of his favourite drills. He handed Fletcher the towel he'd used to control his swing earlier and jogged out to right field.

"Lay it in the batter's box," he yelled to Fletcher.

Fletch looked puzzled.

"Right there," said Doc Woods, pointing to the box where left-handed batters stood. Art shrugged his shoulders and laid the towel down on the dirt.

O'Leary stood with a fungo bat along the third base line and hit fly balls to Ruth in deep right field. Pat Collins stood behind the plate. Fletch retreated to the dugout steps.

"Watch this," Miller Huggins told him.

o   o   o

"Holy shit!" muttered Fletch five minutes later.

The Babe had caught upwards of fifteen fly balls and after each one he'd fired the ball in to Collins. On a rope. Almost every one had either hit Collins' glove on the fly or bounced on the towel.

"Well, what do you think?" asked Huggins.

"Ya know, Miller, I never realized until now what a great player the Babe is. The man deserves to be rated among the best fielders ever. He covers a wide range of territory, he's sure death on fly balls and line drives, he plays ground balls as well as an infielder, and his throws are absolutely amazing. I've seen a lot of accurate throwing by outfielders over the years, mostly in the National League of course, but I never saw a man who had even a slight edge on the Babe in pegging runners out."

"Shame all everybody talks about is his power," said Huggins. "The man's one of the smartest players I ever coached and he's a terrific base runner."

o   o   o

Babe Ruth

The Babe took Richards Vidmer, James Harrison, and Waite Hoyt to play a round at the Renaissance Vinoy club that afternoon. Ruth and Vidmer each shot a three over par 75 and Hoyt shot 77. Waite added up Harrison's score.

"What did I end up with?" Harrison asked him.

"Just a second, Jim, I'm a ball player not an accountant. There are a lot of big numbers here. Lemme see, ten, eight, seven, twelve. You shot a hundred and sixty-eight."

Ruth handed his caddy a twenty dollar bill.

"What should I give *my* caddy, Babe?" Harrison asked.

Ruth laughed. "Your clubs!"

6.

LET THE GAMES BEGIN

"How long did it take for him to get the hint you wanted him to kiss you?"

On Sunday, May 13th, Koenig, Gehrig, and a team of rookies travelled to Auburndale to play the International League's Baltimore Orioles. Only five hundred people turned up. The town had heard the Babe wouldn't be playing. Gehrig was still not considered one of the veterans so he didn't get the day off. Not that he would have wanted it. He was always the first one on the field and the last one off it.

When the Yankees took their infield practice Art Fletcher ended it the usual way. He hit a ground ball to Mike Gazella who was playing third. Gazella had been up for a look in '23 before being sent to work on his hitting in Minneapolis and then Atlanta. Ed Barrow had put him on the roster in '26. He knew Joe Dugan needed the odd day off to rest his legs. Mike had batted just .232 in two hundred at bats and had little hope of cracking the starting lineup this year. Gazella fielded it and threw to Gehrig at first. Fletcher hit him another and he threw home to Johnny Grabowski and headed to the dugout.

Then Fletch hit a ground ball to speedy rookie Julie Wera, originally Werra, who was playing shortstop. The Babe had nicknamed him Flop Ears. Wera was hoping to hang on with the club as a spare infielder and late innings pinch runner. Julie badly needed the money he made in the off season as a butcher at a meat-packing plant back home. He had the distinction of having the lowest salary on the club, just $2,400. Wera fielded it, threw to first, then fielded another one, threw to home and ran off the field. Ray Morehart, who wanted a shot at shortstop if Koenig faltered, was at second. He repeated the ritual of first and then home.

Babe Ruth

That left Gehrig. Fletcher hit him a grounder which he fielded cleanly and fired home. Grabowski came up the line a little and slammed the ball back to Lou. He came in and one-handed it, wheeled, and whipped it back to Grabowski. They kept it up until they were throwing bullets to each other at close range. Gehrig broke into a wide grin and lumbered to the dugout.

Morehart and Cedric Durst had four hits each that afternoon. Walter Beall, who didn't expect to stick with the Yankees, and George Pipgras, who desperately hoped he would, held the Orioles to five hits and the Yankee scrubs won 11-2. This was likely to be the last chance Pipgras would have at making the club, he was twenty-seven now. He'd failed to stick in '23 and again in '24, starting a grand total of three games. His career had been delayed after he'd lied about his age and gone off to fight in France in 1917.

Huggins hoped Pipgras could take up the slack for Shawkey. He had great stuff but lousy control. In his forty-eight innings in the majors he'd walked thirty-three batters. Shawkey was mentoring the man who hoped to take his place. He taught Pipgras control, changed his pitching motion to add some hop to his fastball, and added a new wrinkle to his curve as well. George sure hoped it would pay off. He knew Mattie'd be heart-broken to leave New York and give up the friendships she was forging.

o o o

Back home in New York the Yankee wives cleaned the apartment, made sure the bills were paid, and then got together to shop. Ruth Combs and Mattie Pipgras met up with Mary Lieb, Fred's wife. Mattie had dark brown eyes and lovely ash blonde hair and was almost as tall as her husband. She always wore low heel oxfords. Red-haired Mary Lieb was a little overweight, like her hubby. Today she had on a bright gingham floral dress. Ruth Combs was pretty, but rather matronly looking. Her hair was always piled up in a beehive. She wore a simple cotton dress. Ruth thought she was a little too big in the hips but it didn't seem to bother Earle.

"What did you do yesterday, Ruth?" asked Mary.

"I stayed in. Earle Junior was home from school with the grippe. He insisted on going back today."

"What did you do, Mattie?" Mary asked.

"My sister and I went to a palm reader."

"Where *is* your sister?" asked Ruth. "I thought she was joining us."

"She and her beau entered a dance marathon on Coney Island."

"Well, spill the beans, what did the palm reader say?" asked Mary.

"She said that I'd have two children and my sister would meet a handsome man from Europe who was related to royalty."

"Anything about coming into money?" asked Mary.

"She said my husband would be getting a check for five thousand dollars sometime soon."

Mary whistled. "She's one heck of a palm reader."

"Why do you say that?" asked Mattie.

"That sounds like the winner's share for the World Series."

"Oh my, I hadn't thought. That could be it," said Ruth.

"What did the players get when they won in Twenty-Three?" asked Mary. "I'm sure Fred would know but I have no idea."

"Six thousand, one hundred and forty-three dollars and twelve cents," said Mattie. "It was the happiest day of our marriage. George was a rookie and his salary was only twelve hundred dollars. We could hardly believe it. He'd only won one game that year and he didn't pitch at all in the Series. It kind of felt like we'd robbed a bank."

"Did you offer to give the money back?" teased Mary.

"Hell no. And it's lucky we didn't go out and blow it on a new car and a radio and a clothes washing machine like we were going to. We ended up in Atlanta and St. Paul for two years before the team called George back up."

"What did you do yesterday, Mary?" asked Ruth.

"I went to lunch with a couple of the other reporters' wives and then I spent the afternoon reading Picture-Play and Motion Picture Classic. Well, looking at the pictures mostly."

Babe Ruth

"Some of those Hollywood mansions are unbelievable," said Ruth.

"Is it true the Babe went to Chaplin's house and to Pickfair as well?" asked Mattie.

"Apparently," said Ruth. "But Earle says he mostly raves about women he screwed - his name for it, not Earle's of course."

"Do you think he really met Clara Bow, the It Girl?" asked Mattie. "That's what he told some of the guys."

"I don't know," said Mary. "Fred wouldn't tell me even if he'd heard. Picture-Play says Bow's had affairs with Gilbert Roland the Latin lover, Victor Fleming the director, and some new actor called Gary Cooper. They had his picture. I know I'd be tempted. He's dreamy."

"I heard they sent Bow to a doctor about her promiscuity and she seduced him too," said Mattie.

"It's not just ball players that are easy to seduce I guess," said Ruth. "I'm luckier than most of the wives but I imagine it's tough even for Earle to say no with girls throwing themselves at the boys. At least he doesn't go to speakeasies like a lot of them. I know because he telephones from the hotels most nights."

"George doesn't do that. We can't afford it," said Mattie.

"He'll be able to if the fortune teller was right," said Mary.

They all laughed.

"Where did you and George meet?" Mary asked Mattie.

"We were high school sweethearts."

"When did it get serious?"

"None of this is going to end up in Fred's column, is it?"

"Of course not. None of the newspaper men write anything about the players' personal lives, you know that. Not even the Babe's and he's as public about his behaviour as anyone. So tell us. When did it get serious?"

"Well, he and his friends used to come in for sodas at the drug store where I worked. I thought he liked me and I did my level best to make him jealous by talking about other boys I'd gone out with or found amusing, even though I didn't care a hoot for them. I guess it worked because he took me to an amusement park and then a movie."

"You still haven't told us when it got serious," said Ruth.

"He started taking me for drives in his flivver. They were just romantic drives in the moonlight at first. George was really shy. He was too nervous to kiss me. Then I started moving closer and closer to him on the seat."

"How long did it take for him to get the hint that you wanted him to kiss you?" asked Mary.

"Heck, it must have taken eight or nine drives," said Mattie. "By then I was almost sitting in his lap. I'd bat my eyelashes and scrunch my arms in at my sides to make my breasts swell," she giggled. "He finally started taking me to secluded spots. You know, the kind where couples paw each other in struggle buggies."

The other wives laughed at the apropos term.

"I could tell he'd already looked for them. The first few times he just kissed me normally. Then he'd lift my chin up a little. Then George ran his fingers through my hair and then he ever so gently touched the back of my neck. Then he brushed the top of my spine with his fingertips. I don't know whether he knew he was driving me wild or not but I finally got all warm between my legs."

"I'm getting that way myself," said Mary. "Don't stop!"

"I finally had to help him out and moved his hands onto my breasts. He gulped and I noticed a big bulge in the front of his trousers. The next time he took me driving I wore a petting shirt."

"With the armpits cut out? You hussy!" teased Mary.

"And that's when I found out that his minor league manager had been right."

"What do you mean?" asked Ruth.

"He started out playing the infield and the manager said he had a great pair of hands."

Mary and Ruth laughed so hard they nearly fell down.

o o o

Babe Ruth

At Waterfront Park in St. Petersburg on March 15th, in a game against the Boston Braves, Cedric Durst belted a grand slam in the fifth. Hoyt, Ruether, and Moore pitched three innings each in a 6-5 win. Art Fletcher warmed up for the regular season by getting thrown out in the sixth.

The next morning St. Petersburg's sunny skies blackened and a torrential downpour drenched the town. Huggins had the team work out in the Princess Martha's huge lobby. After a few minutes of calisthenics the players got their gloves and played catch.

"The ceiling's real high. Throw me some pop ups," Lazzeri told Mark Koenig.

Koenig obliged. When one of his tosses passed right through the lobby's chandelier, somehow managing to avoid hundreds of glass crystal prisms Huggins told them to keep them down.

"That was close," said Mark. "Coulda cost ya half your salary."

As the players waited for the skies to clear Carl Sandburg, the poet and biographer from Illinois who was working for the *Chicago Daily News*, came in to interview Ruth.

"What advice would you give to kids, Babe?" Sandburg asked.

"Cut out smoking and drinking, eat the right foods, and get to bed early," Ruth told him with a straight face.

Several of the Yankees nearly choked.

"What books should boys read?" Sandburg asked next.

The Babe, who thought he was being a pretty good sport since Sandburg hadn't offered him any money for the interview, snarled, "They don't ask me that question, Mister Sandfield, they ask me how ta play ball."

Sandburg persisted. "Millions of ball fans in this country believe that the Bible and Ulysses by James Joyce are the two greatest books ever written. Some of them would like to know what parts of those books are favorites of yours."

Now the Babe was getting steamed. "A ball player don't have time to sit around and read. And it isn't good for his eyes. A player lasts only as long as his legs and his eyes hold out and there ain't much he can do about his

& THE 1927 YANKEES HAVE THE BEST SUMMER EVER

legs. He can't take any chances with his eyes."

"Is there one character in history you are especially interested in? Lincoln? Washington? Napoleon?"

"I never met any of 'em," said Ruth, getting up and stalking away.

Three days later Bob Meusel hit a home run into the left field seats and the Yanks nipped the Cincinnati Reds 2-1. When Ruth batted in the third inning the Cincinnati catcher, Val Picinich, questioned the umpire's eyesight.

"That was low and outside, ump," Picinich grunted.

The Babe went to the ump's defense.

"Low and outside, ya busher? If it had been a strike, don't you suppose I woulda knocked it into the palmettos?"

o o o

The next morning Ruth went to the Duval County courthouse to see the Sheriff, W.H. Dowling.

"Thanks for gettin' me outta that speeding ticket, Sheriff," said the Babe. "Mighty nice a ya."

"We don't want you leaving here with bad memories, Babe," said Dowling. "I think the county can spare the six dollars."

"Who's the doll?" Ruth asked, pointing to a pretty blonde who was being led into the courtroom in handcuffs by a pair of deputies.

"That's Billie Jackson."

"What did she do?"

"She's accused of shooting her husband."

"Think she did it? She looks awful sweet."

"She claims it was self-defence."

"Hey, Billie," called Ruth.

She and the deputies stopped and looked over to see who was calling her. They were startled to see that the booming bass voice belonged to Babe Ruth.

"Hello, Babe," said Jackson. "You come to watch my trial like everybody else?"

"No, I came to visit the Sheriff. You got a good lawyer?"

"I hope so. I'll find out soon enough. If not, I'll get to be famous like you. First gal in Florida to get the electric chair."

"You wanna come watch us play if you get off?" asked Ruth.

"I'd love to, Babe," she gushed. "Being out *anywhere* after these jail cells'll be a relief."

Just before the Yankees headed north for the season Herb Pennock, who read the papers wherever he went, told Ruth that Jackson had been found guilty but was spared execution.

"Good. It woulda been a shame ta fry a doll like that," the Babe told Pennock.

o o o

That afternoon the Yankees blasted the Boston Braves 16-7 at Al Lang Field. Neither Bob Shawkey nor Myles Thomas was effective, but Wilcy Moore showed promise, giving up only an unearned run in four innings of work.

Moore was a blue-eyed, broad-shouldered, good-natured dirt farmer from Hollis, Oklahoma who couldn't pitch without a wad of chewing tobacco in his cheek. Ed Barrow spent his spare time reading the *Sporting News* where he came across a pitcher who was racking up win after win for the Greenville Spinners. He bought a mail-order subscription to the *Greenville Gazette* and followed Moore's progress.

Barrow found it a little odd that no one, not even the most diligent scouts, seemed to know who Moore was. No one seemed to know how old he was either, twenty-eight, perhaps twenty-nine, maybe even thirty. His receding hairline made him look more like thirty-five. Bob Gilks, the scout Barrow sent to check him out, said, "Hell, he looks like he's *forty*."

The only thing everyone *could* agree on was that Moore had a baffling sinker and exceptional control. When the Sally League wrapped up play in September his record stood at 30-4. Barrow went to Huggins and told him about Moore. "I don't know why no one's noticed the man all this time but I sent him a contract anyway. With a record like that he must have *something*."

Huggins was sceptical at first, but Moore won him over. He later told reporters, "Moore's built for hard work. He has a low fastball that's a wonder and as soon as he masters control he should win some games for us."

"Why hadn't anyone heard about you?" Richards Vidmer asked Moore when he arrived.

"I was toilin' away in Armore and Okmulgee before headin' to Greenville. From the Injun leagues ta the Sally League."

"And now the big league. What changed for you last year, Wilcy?"

"Funny story. I got hit by a line drive a couple a years ago. Dang thing fractured my wrist. When I tried to pitch overhand it hurt like the dickens so I had to start throwin' sidearm. The ball'd sink at the last second and it was real hard to hit."

A small, dimple-cheeked boy sat a few rows up in the stands with his father as Moore sent one Brave after another to the bench muttering to himself. The boy had eyes for only one player though. He was still a huge fan of Babe Ruth in spite of the things he'd heard about him. He watched his hero's every move - at the plate, in the field, and even in the dugout.

"See how he gets ready for a fly ball," the boy told his father. "He swings his arms, then he pounds his glove, then he crouches and puts his hands on his knees. And when a ball's hit he seems to be moving in the direction it's gonna go before it even leaves the bat."

The Babe struck out his first time up, greatly disappointing the lad. Ruth next came to bat in the fourth against a big twenty-year-old hurler who was hoping to catch on with Boston.

"Come on, Babe, hit us a homer, will ya," yelled the boy.

Ruth covered his eyes and squinted through the sun at the lad.

He smiled. "Sure kid, I'll sock ya a couple," he bellowed.

After two wide ones the Braves' rookie came in with a strike. Seconds later it landed with a splash in Crescent Lake. It was Ruth's first home run since he'd won the game for the Los Angeles Angels in *Babe Comes Home*.

When the Babe came up in the seventh the boy yelled, "You said you'd hit two, Babe. That's what you said." Ruth chuckled as he dug in at the plate.

Babe Ruth

The rookie'd tried to sneak a curve past the Babe the last time. This time he tried to zing a fastball by him. Ruth's eyes lit up and he swung with everything he had. Heads turned and mouths gaped as the ball climbed higher and higher and finally disappeared over the palm trees beyond the center field fence.

An elderly couple sat on the porch of the second floor of the West Coast Inn.

"Can you believe the prices here, Agnes?" said the old man. "Two dollars for a steak!"

Agnes waved a fan in front of her face. "I told you …"

Something whizzed through the air. Thud!

The baseball landed on the sidewalk right below them. It bounced high in the air and smacked into the wall beside Agnes.

"Jumping Jehoshaphat!" yelled her husband. "Are you all right, dear?"

"We need to find a new hotel," declared Agnus. "The prices are sky high and now things are *falling* from it."

Up in the press box, John Kieran began typing his story for the *Times* on his Remington Portable typewriter. As always, he said out loud what he was composing, so he'd know how it would come across to his readers. "It had been feared that the lights of Hollywood had affected the King of Clout's vision, giving him an ailment known as klieg eyes. Apparently the Babe's eyes are just fine."

"I want that one measured," Ruth told Eddie Bennett as he headed to the shower.

"Sure Babe," said Eddie. I'll get one of those city surveyors that are working up the street to do it."

Eddie came back half an hour later while Ruth was getting into his street clothes.

"Well, how far did I hit that son of a bitch?" asked the Babe.

"The surveyors asked people at the hotel and one of them pointed to the skid mark in the sidewalk. The ball travelled six hundred and twelve feet and then bounced another thirty feet before hitting the second story wall above the porch."

"I think I'll go find a couple a gals and tell them about what I can do with my bat," said Ruth.

"And get them to measure it?" asked Urban Shocker.

"Ya, or maybe test the grip."

Worrywart Huggins knew he'd sleep well for a change. His team had rapped sixteen hits, including a homer and double from Meusel and a Gehrig triple. Hug was happy to see the big guy hitting them again as well. "Feel good to finally get a couple?" he asked Ruth as he tied his necktie.

"Ya know what, Hug? I love hittin' 'em anytime, regular season, World Series, exhibition, doesn't matter. The crack of the bat, the sight of the ball soarin' out into the sky. I tell ya, they're as big a thrill for me as they are for the fans."

○ ○ ○

After five straight wins the Yankees were feeling a bit cocky, even though these were just exhibition games. That ended when the Braves hammered them 18-0 on the 24th. It was a wild one. The Yankee bench was all over umpire Frank Wilson from the start. Richards Vidmer had dubbed Wilson the "ousting arbiter of the National League". When he went over to their dugout, nine players came out to berate him. He threw all of them out of the game. They chuckled and trudged to the clubhouse. When Wilson went to challenge players on the Braves' bench, the ejected Yankees snuck back into the dugout one at a time and gradually re-entered the game. Nineteen players were ejected. Everyone agreed it had to be a Grapefruit League record.

A Curtiss Candy Company plane flew over the field throughout the game dropping Baby Ruth candy bars. They'd been called Candy Cakes and they hadn't sold very well until they were given their new name.

"The pricks use my name and don't gimme a red cent!" Ruth swore as the plane made its fourth pass. "I tried to sue the bastards and they claimed they'd named it after President Cleveland's daughter. They musta paid off the judge. Marshall Hunt told me Ruth Cleveland's been dead for twenty years!"

○ ○ ○

When the Yankees played the Cincinnati Reds at Crescent Lake, the Babe went hitless in four trips to the plate and lost a fly ball in the sun. Earle

Babe Ruth

Combs ran after it as it scooted toward the lake shore. As he reached for it he heard a splash. Out of the corner of his eye he saw something move.

A man-sized alligator slithered his way, its bulging eyes fixed on him. Combs shrieked. He forgot about the baseball and ran for his life. He jumped over a five foot high embankment and sprinted all the way into the Yankee clubhouse as his teammates laughed themselves silly.

"Why didn't you come up with that ball?" Dugan teased Earle as he opened his locker after the game. "It's a dollar and a quarter to replace it. Barrow's gonna be some pissed."

o o o

Throughout the game Art Fletcher watched carefully to see how well in sync Lazzeri and Koenig were. Lazzeri made a nice play on a shot up the middle but a minute later Koenig misplayed a ball hit right to him. James Harrison approached Miller Huggins after the game ended. "What are you gonna do about shortstop, Hug?"

"I don't know what you're talking about," snapped Huggins.

"Koenig's made seven errors in the exhibition games and he's batting o forty-six," said Harrison. "He's a nice kid, but are you sure you shouldn't go with Morehart at second and move Lazzeri to short? Morehart's leading the team with a three sixty average and he's handled fifty-two chances without a single error."

Huggins ignored him. Harrison tried again. "What about it, Hug?"

The manager puffed on his short-stemmed pipe and then stared daggers at Harrison. "His fielding will be fine. And as for him not hitting, maybe he believes, as many players do, that there are only so many hits in each bat and he's saving them for the season. Koenig's my shortstop," he grunted. He walked away, muttering to himself about know-it-all reporters.

When he got to his office after the practice he called Koenig in. Mark had heard the buzz and he knew how well Morehart was playing.

"I'll understand if you want to go with Ray," said Koenig.

"Stop right there. Don't say another word. It's me that's runnin' this club, not the goddamn sportswriters. I don't give a fig how well you've done down here. Just be ready when we get to New York."

& THE 1927 YANKEES HAVE THE BEST SUMMER EVER

Mark's face brightened. "Thanks, Hug, I will be. I won't let you down."

"I know you won't."

o   o   o

The Yankees finished Spring Training with a series of exhibitions with the championship-winning Cardinals labelled "the Little World Series" in eight different towns on their way back north. The Cards walloped the Yankees 13-2 on the 27th. No one had much confidence in their pitching staff after that, especially considering the 18-0 drubbing from the Braves three days before. The Babe didn't care to dwell on it. He spent the afternoon riding a sea-sled around Lake Worth to cool off.

o   o   o

Huggins called a meeting in the clubhouse after the team's last workout before heading north. The players sat in front of their lockers, the familiar smells of liniment and sweaty socks competing in the air. Eddie Bennett collected wet towels and threw them into a hamper.

"Pipe down, boys," said the tiny manager, "I need to tell you about the rules for this year."

Several players groaned.

"What's it gonna be this time, Hug?" asked Shawkey. "A two blonde a night limit for the Babe and a brunette each for the rest of us?"

"Like he'd stick to two a night," chortled Hoyt.

Huggins ignored them and continued. "Pinochle and bridge are okay in the clubhouse but this year there's gonna be a fifty cent limit on card games."

"Fifty cents!" said Ruether indignantly. "My *grannie* plays for more than that. How we supposed to take Jidge for half his paycheck?"

"Jidge can afford it, the rest of you lot can't," said Huggins. "Four bits it'll be or nothing. There's to be no shaving at the ballpark, no smoking while you're in uniform, no stayin' out past midnight - you check in at 10 a.m. whenever we play - and there's to be no golf on game days."

"Better to walk a golf course than run around after dames, isn't it?" bellowed Ruth.

Babe Ruth

"You play a round every night, don't ya Babe?" asked Joe Dugan.

Huggins had one more thing to say. "This isn't a rule, boys, it's just a piece of advice. Whether your pay check's big or small, think twice about buying stocks like every other Tom, Dick, and Harry is right now, especially on margin. That's a fool's game. Times are swell right now but the bubble's bound to burst sooner or later."

o o o

"Here you are boys," said Mark Roth as he handed out one hundred dollars in crisp ten dollar bills to each player for meal money on the trip north when they were boarding the train. "No more signing checks in the hotel dining room."

Their first stop was in Jacksonville on April Fools' Day. So many people showed up they crowded the outfield fences and both foul lines and some brave souls perched atop the bleachers' roof. The Babe's blast into the overflow crowd in right was the margin of victory in a 3-2 win.

The next day they played in Savannah, Georgia where the Cardinals hammered the Yanks 20-10. Ruth hit a single, a double, and, to the delight of the crowd, many of whom were youngsters who'd skipped school, a home run. Hundreds of kids swarmed the Babe when the game ended and he barely made it off the field.

"Doesn't that ever bother you?" Joe Dugan asked the Babe as he peeled off his sweaty undershirt.

"Nope," he beamed. "I wish they were all mine."

o o o

Even though it was pouring rain when the Yankees' train stopped for coal and water in Etowah, Tennessee at midnight the whole town was there to see them. They lined the platform ten deep. The Babe took a break from his bridge game and stepped out into the downpour to say a few words to them. When he stepped back inside the Pullman he shook himself like a big sheepdog, spraying half a dozen groggy teammates.

In Montgomery, Alabama there wasn't enough room for all the players in the locker room. Miller Huggins still needed to make some cuts to the roster before Opening Day. Gehrig and Pennock sat on top of the dugout with a couple of rookies who likely wouldn't be around much longer. Only a wire screen separated them from some drunk and vocal fans.

"You guys'd be bottom feeders if you didn't have Ruth!" one bellowed.

"I've seen better arms on a clock," shouted another.

"I've seen better swings on a porch," shouted a third.

"We're so close to those hooligans they can hurl epithets at us," cracked Pennock.

Lou looked at Herb quizzically and then said, "Don't worry Hoib, dey can't hit us with anything. Da screen'll protect us." Pennock just shook his head.

Down on the field Ruth drove in two runs with a pair of doubles. After his second, in the ninth, Gehrig came up with a chance to end things.

"Knock me home and get this thing over with, keed," the Babe yelled at him from second.

Lou stepped into the batter's box. He dug in, a picture of concentration. His body rocked back and forth in a smooth rolling movement. His knees were bent a little, his legs parallel and committed to an open stance so he could see the pitcher release the ball. He waggled the bat around in a semicircle, his eyes trained on the pitcher's movements. Lou got a pitch he liked and blasted it to right center. Ruth scored easily and the Yankees downed the Cards 4-2.

o o o

In Atlanta the next day the Yankee bats were booming. They pummelled four different Cardinal pitchers for a 15-8 win. Ruth banged a pair of doubles and nailed two Cardinals at home with throws that bounced into Pat Collins' waiting mitt. The re-creation of the previous fall's World Series now stood at three wins apiece. In Chattanooga Joe Dugan hit a grand slam in the fourth to tie things up. In the tenth Combs singled and so did the Babe. Earle scored on Gehrig's sacrifice fly to end it, 10-3 New York.

o o o

The Babe was bored as they travelled to their next stop. It was still two hours until dinner time and no one wanted to play bridge. He asked a woman passenger if she had a hairpin he could borrow.

"I beg your pardon. A hairpin?" she asked him.

Babe Ruth

"That's Babe Ruth!" her husband whispered. "Find him a hairpin for God's sakes."

She rummaged through her bag. "Here you go, Mister Ruth," she said, handing him one.

"Why on earth do you suppose he has need of a hairpin, Ralph?" she asked her husband.

"With the Babe you never know," he answered, staring after him.

Ruth took the hairpin to the drinking fountain outside of the men's smoking room and proceeded to punch holes in all of the paper cups in the dispenser. Then he giggled like an eight-year-old as passengers struggled to control the mysterious leak as they attempted to drink from the cups.

o o o

In Knoxville another huge crowd called in sick or played hooky to see the Yankees play. They barely made it to their hotel rooms; the lobby was packed to the rafters with gawkers. The state legislature adjourned discussion of an important railway bill for the afternoon to attend. St. Louis won the last game of the eight-game, thousand-mile tour 10-3 and the series ended with each team having won four.

Knowing the club's total payroll for 1927, with some allowance for bonuses, came to $250,000, Ed Barrow telegraphed Jake Ruppert that night to inform him of the take from the Spring exhibitions.

> *Yankees share of gate receipts three hundred thousand dollars STOP Sufficient to cover all training camp and travel expenses and pay all team salaries for the year END*

7.

Now They Count

"I put the jinx on them, Pop."

The Yankees finally got down to business on April 12. A light wind stirred the flags and bunting as the mercury inched its way up to 59 degrees. Subways and buses arrived at the Stadium crammed to the gills and taxis arrived by the hundred. The fact that Jake Ruppert had decided to reduce the price of bleacher seats from seventy-five to fifty cents was an incentive for many of the subway users. Red-coated ushers scurried to seat the majority of the boosters, or fans as most writers were now calling them because so many were fanatics who couldn't bear to see their heroes lose. Some would have to stand behind the last row of seats. They didn't mind, the gatekeepers had told them that twenty-five thousand people had been turned away. Still, 73,206 was the most ever to attend a ball game.

In the Philadelphia clubhouse Connie Mack, who'd made the cover of *Time* magazine for signing Ty Cobb, went over the Yankee hitters with his pitching staff. Mack wore a black suit, a high starched collar, a yellow knit tie, and a straw boater.

"It's going to be difficult for us or any other team to keep Combs off the bases," Mack began. "He drives balls to the gaps, knows how to draw a walk, and can drag bunt his way on base. Koenig's a different story. He has none of those skills. We simply *cannot* let him get on. As for Ruth, the last time I checked we are not allowed to station a man in the fortieth row of the bleachers. So, any pitcher that puts a ball in the strike zone will find his next pay check is light. Gehrig is a line-drive hitter. Pitch him on the outside corner and he'll hit a lot of balls to the wall but not over it. You have to pitch to him because Meusel and Lazzeri are next and both of them can put balls in the seats. You can relax when you get to Dugan and the catcher and pitcher's spots. Don't throw anything hard to them - if they get a single here and there, it's no concern. Save it for their big guns."

A few minutes later, on the diamond, photographers snapped pictures of Ty Cobb in his new uniform with the grey elephant on the tunic instead of the Gothic *D* he'd worn on his chest for twenty years with Detroit.

A cub photographer noticed that Ruth had finished playing long catch with Benny Bengough and saw an opportunity to get one of his pictures on the front page for a change. He approached Cobb and motioned toward the Babe. "Could I get a picture of the two of you shaking hands?" The experienced photographers looked at the kid like he'd just asked Attila the Hun to make brownies for tonight's PTA meeting.

"You expect me to mug with the gorilla that's ruining baseball?" snarled Cobb.

"D'ya hear the news, Cobb?" Ruth shot back. "The war's over. The South lost."

"Fuck you, Ruth," Cobb snapped over his shoulder as he headed to the Philadelphia dugout.

In the stands above vendors shrilly advertised their wares. "Frankfurters, peanuts, Cracker Jacks," yelled one.

"Ginger ale, sarsaparilla, charged mineral water," bellowed another.

"Got any cold beer?" a rotund man asked him.

"This may be the only place in New Yawk you can't get one," the boy answered.

o o o

As they waited for the game to start, the regular patrons chatted about the change in the Yankees' home uniforms. They now had YANKEES across the chest of their wool jerseys instead of NEW YORK. But navy blue vertical pinstripes accentuated the uniform as they had since 1915, five years before Ruth had joined the Yanks. Their long-time announcer, short, stout, animated Jack Lentz, who wore a derby as always, informed the crowd of the proceedings through a megaphone. He called out the lineup that would remain virtually the same throughout the season.

The Seventh Regiment Band, looking like the Duke of Wellington's guards, marched briskly onto the field. They were outfitted in shakoes, long grey coats, and white trousers with white belts. A beefy man led them. John Phillip Sousa's tiny spectacles and huge brown beard were familiar sights on Opening Day. His band played the *National Anthem* and things got under way.

Jimmy Walker, the dashing and handsome 45-year-old mayor of New York, wore a dark grey top hat, a black, pinch-waisted, one-button suit, the slenderest of cravats, a silk shirt from his collection of hundreds, a swallowtail coat, and pearl gray spats polished to a gleam. Walker seemed more cut out for entertainment than politics. He'd dabbled in song-writing when he was young and had a hit called *There's Music in the Ruffle of her Skirt*. Jimmy never missed a prizefight or a Broadway premiere and he spent many an afternoon at the Stadium or the track.

'Beau James' as many voters called him had always enjoyed the company of feather-clad showgirls. He was now said to be spending a lot of his spare time frolicking with 23-year-old actress and former Ziegfeld Follies dancer Betty Compton in a penthouse suite at the Ritz-Carlton paid for by his Tammany Hall friends. They were making a fortune in graft from the building of the subway system thanks to Jimmy. The voters didn't care; Walker was keeping to his promise to hold fares to a nickel in spite of construction costs that were skyrocketing for some strange reason.

Walker's wife conveniently spent a lot of time in Europe. Jimmy went there a lot too, once to meet Benito Mussolini. He'd racked up 143 days in vacation in his first two years in office and had just returned from a $10,000 trip paid for by an agent for the city's bus lines. When a little-known Congressman named Fiorello LaGuardia tried to take him to task for raising his salary from $25,000 to $40,000, Walker responded, "That's cheap! Think what I'd cost if I worked full-time."

When Jimmy wasn't on vacation he conducted business to the sound of popping Black Velvet champagne corks in his private booth at the 21 Club. *Time* reported that the mayor was rarely seen at City Hall, especially before noon. He'd been ninety minutes late for his own swearing-in ceremony and there'd been a further delay when a smudge of red lipstick was discovered on his collar. Jake Ruppert had hosted a party for the new mayor in his Fifth Avenue apartment the night before.

Babe Ruth

The mayor threw out the first ball to the Yankees' primary bat boy and good luck charm, hunched-back Eddie Bennett, at 3:25. A few months after he was born in the Flatbush section of Brooklyn Eddie had fallen from his crib. His parents had been too poor to afford the operation the infant had needed and his shoulder had never healed properly. But Eddie seemed to have mystical powers that compensated for his disfigurement.

In 1919, in the stands at the Polo Grounds where the Yankees played their home games, Eddie focused on a visiting player, Happy Felsh of the Chicago White Sox, who was anything *but* happy. In fact he was a nervous wreck, riddled with anxieties and self-doubt. For some reason, Eddie's gaze soothed Happy's inner demons and he told Ed Cicotte about the hunchback kid. On Cicotte's recommendation the Chicago manager, Kid Gleason, hired Eddie as the team batboy. The White Sox fought off a late season charge by the Cleveland Indians and won the pennant. That some of the White Sox mysteriously dropped easy fly balls, purposely swung at pitches over their heads, and subsequently lost the '19 World Series was no fault of Eddie's.

He was disgusted when the stories of the players' conspiracy hit the newspapers. Eddie quit his job and went home to Brooklyn, where he was hired on by the Robins, a second division club for three years. With Eddie putting a Flatbush hex on the rest of the National League, the Robins went on an astounding tear and finished seven games ahead of the heavily-favoured New York Giants.

After beating the American League pennant-winning Indians twice in Brooklyn, the now proud Robins packed up to head to Cleveland. Eddie wouldn't be making the trip. Charles Ebbets, the Brooklyn owner, had decided he couldn't afford to send Bennett to Cleveland. Stunned and on the verge of tears, Eddie appealed to the players to try to change Ebbets' mind. They told him to get lost and headed to the train station. Eddie's psychic powers went with them to Cleveland.

Aided by the first grand slam home run in Series history and the only unassisted triple play, the Indians won the next four straight to win the Series. Eddie's father read the news of the Robins' defeat and told his son the score of the final game.

"I put the jinx on them, Pop," said Eddie.

Waite Hoyt had seen Bennett at a basketball game working as the mascot for the Brooklyn Visitations in the winter of '21. Between halves Bennett entertained the crowd with his free-throw shooting skills. After the game Eddie managed to convince Hoyt that if the Yankees hired him they would win their first pennant. Hoyt talked to Huggins who talked to Barrow who talked to the superstitious Ruppert and the deal was done. Of course the Yankees did win the pennant that year, and the next, and the next. The '23 flag made Eddie a perfect five-for-five.

After catching the mayor's surprisingly accurate first pitch Eddie returned to the dugout and got bicarbonate of soda for the Babe, who thanked him and rubbed his hump for luck.

"Make sure nobody but you and the wee fella touch my bats," Ruth enjoined him.

"Don't worry, Babe, nobody'll get near 'em."

o   o   o

Graham McNamee, a 38-year-old former concert baritone, had been given so few opportunities to sing on stage that he'd reluctantly tried his hand at sales. It hadn't gone well. While earning a much-needed $3 a day doing jury duty in a Manhattan courthouse he went for a walk during the lunch break. He passed the AT & T building at 195 Broadway that housed WEAF, a new radio station, and on a whim decided to go in.

McNamee was given a job opening and closing piano lids for performers, answering the telephone, and escorting young ladies home after their programs. One night the regular announcer who was supposed to do commercials and public service announcements during station breaks didn't show up.

"McNamee!" yelled the station manager. "Read over this script for tonight's broadcast."

"Why?" asked McNamee.

"Because you're doing Finley's job tonight." He pointed to the microphone. "Good luck."

Babe Ruth

"I'll do my best, Mister Abrams."

The station manager went into the sound booth. "Let's hope he isn't too awful," Abrams muttered to himself as he lit up a cigarette and put on his earphones.

"The time is eight o'clock and you are listening to the WEAF Evening Report. I'm Graham McNamee. Settle back in your easy chair and enjoy this evening's programming," wafted like smooth honey into Abrams' earphones.

"Holy shit!" he yelled to the empty booth. "This guy's voice is amazing. Why the hell haven't we had him on air all this time?"

After listening to him speak in deep, mellifluous tones for the rest of the show the manager promoted McNamee to full-time announcer and reporter. He covered political conventions and then sporting events, starting with the first coast-to-coast broadcast of the Rose Bowl game and he did so well that after a few months he was given his own afternoon show. McNamee became a welcome and familiar presence in people's living rooms. His voice was so perfectly pitched that recordings of its cadence were used to train aspiring announcers.

"You did a great job at that boxing match the other night," Abrams told McNamee one afternoon in early April.

"Thank you, Mister Abrams."

"I felt like I was at the damn fight myself."

"That is exactly the effect I was striving for."

"So you're covering the Yankees' home opener on the twelfth."

"The home opener of what?" McNamee asked.

"Their regular season."

"Oh, I see. I'll do my best, Mister Abrams. But I have to warn you, I don't know much about baseball."

"I can tell," said Abrams. "Don't worry. I've hired Will McGeehan, the baseball editor of the Tribune, as your co-announcer. Just describe what you see. He'll fill in the rest."

McNamee sat in an open box seat holding a large microphone connected by telephone lines that fed his account of the action back to the radio station. The game was transmitted over a hook-up to stations that extended from New England to Washington. He described the signs around the park, the hats ladies in the stands were wearing, the planes that flew over the park pulling advertisements, the chill in the air, and the birds that landed in the outfield. Listeners had no trouble imagining they were sitting beside McNamee in Yankee Stadium.

"A fifteen foot deep copper façade adorns the front of the roof that covers much of the stadium's third deck," crooned McNamee. "It lends the occasion an air of dignity, even elegance."

McGeehan set down his coffee, stared at McNamee, and muttered, "What the *hell* is he jabbering about?"

McNamee carried on. "The stadium has eight toilet rooms for men and an equal number for ladies, which I am told is quite unusual for a baseball park. All of the wooden seats, which go for between fifty cents and a dollar and ten cents, are painted blue. The place in which the Yankee pitchers warm up, which is called a bullpen for no apparent reason, looks out onto left-center field. The dark green Yankee dugout is on the third base side of the playing field."

He paused to take a quick sip of water. "The umpire, Billy Evans, is behind the plate now, putting on a mask and adjusting his chest protector. He wears an olive-drab whipcord outfit. I understand that the officials had worn blue serge suits prior to this season. The home side is in white, their guests are clad in grey. The diamond and grounds look beautiful. The rich dark brown chocolate infield contrasts sharply with the lush green outfield."

A newspaper reporter sitting next to McNamee commented that there were two games that day, the one being played on the field and the one McNamee was describing.

"Leading off the festivities and moving into the batting box is Earle Combs, who is six feet tall and weighs one hundred eighty-five pounds," intoned McNamee.

Babe Ruth

"It's pronounced Coooms," McGeehan whispered.

"My abject apologies ladies and gentlemen, Earle's surname is pronounced Coooms, not combs like we use to straighten our hair. And the loud crack you just heard was the sound of Coooms' bat making contact and driving the sphere toward the outfield perimeter. Coooms slides into second with a two-base knock."

He took another drink of water.

"Now stepping to the plate is Mark Ko e nig, from San Francisco, California," said McNamee.

McGeehan cringed. "It's pronounced Kaynig," he whispered.

"Once again I must beg your pardon dear listeners. I stand corrected on the pronunciation of Mister Kaynig's name as well. Rest assured I shall not make those mistakes again."

"I have no trouble pronouncing the next batter's name. Babe Ruth is coming out of the dugout. He's talking to a young boy in a Yankee uniform. His name is Ray Kelly. He's Ruth's personal batboy and has been since he was four years old. He's seven now. Mark Roth, the Yankees' travelling secretary, told me how the lad came to be the Babe's bat boy. It seems the Babe was walking to his apartment in Riverside Park one day and he saw Ray playing catch with his father. He thought the boy was pretty good and he was amazed when his father told him little Ray was only three. So Ruth told Miller Huggins he wanted him to be his batboy and Huggins went along with it. I asked Mister Roth if the other players objected to it and he told me, 'It's like Ruth playing left field when the sun would be in his eyes if he played in right. It's the Babe, what's anybody going to say.'"

"Which one are you gonna use?" little Ray asked the Bambino. "Black Betsy?"

"I sure am," said Ruth.

Ray got Black Betsy from the bat rack and handed it to his hero. Ruth's signature had been bone-rubbed into it. There were cleat prints on the barrel because he banged the bat against his shoes to clean his spikes and pin knots he had the manufacturer add because he thought they gave his hits more distance. It was ash, not hickory like the ones swung by Joe

Jackson, after whom Ruth had patterned his uppercut swing.

McNamee continued. "Kaynig swings at the first pitch and hits a shallow fly ball to Ty Cobb in right field."

McNamee put his hand over his microphone and whispered to McGeehan, "I don't know much about baseball, but I thought Ty Cobb played for Detroit."

McGeehan nodded. "I got this," he told McNamee, who slid the big microphone over.

"It's about time," McNamee muttered to himself.

"Cobb was shockingly released by the Tigers after allegations that he and Tris Speaker had conspired to fix the last game of the 1919 season. Judge Landis was presented with letters that seemed to prove the allegations to be true but the baseball czar uncharacteristically elected to sweep the whole thing under the carpet. Speaker has been released by Cleveland and will patrol centerfield for the Senators this year. The Yankees offered him fifty thousand dollars, but he turned them down when they told him they couldn't promise he'd play full time."

McNamee nodded to McGeehan and took over again. "It is now Babe Ruth's turn at the bat. As you can no doubt hear through the airwaves, he is taking a great round of applause, exuberant adulation from this New York crowd. As Harry Stevens, the inventor of the scorecard and the hot dog said, 'You can't tell the players without a scorecard' and it must be difficult indeed from the third deck to tell one player from another. But there is no mistaking the Babe. Stevens is also helping youngsters watch today's game."

McGeehan took off his fedora and scratched his head. He tried and failed to figure out what the hell McNamee was babbling about now.

"And how exactly is Stevens doing that?" he asked.

"He made straws available at ball parks so that kids can sip their sodas while they watch the game," explained McNamee.

"Thank you so much," said McGeehan sardonically. "I was not aware of that."

"Wait," said McNamee, "the umpire has called time. Mayor Jimmy

Babe Ruth

Walker is coming out onto the diamond."

Walker waved his top hat toward the stands and went to the plate, where he presented Ruth with a three-foot tall silver loving cup.

"This was donated by William Randolph Hearst, the newspaper baron," Walker told the Babe. "It's in recognition of your having been voted the most popular player in baseball."

"How come it ain't fulla booze, Jimmy?" asked Ruth.

"Didn't ya hear? It's against the law," Walker answered.

"Ya, I guess that's why you got three speakeasies on every corner," chuckled the Babe.

"Are you sure about that?"

"Ya, Jimmy, I've been in most of 'um. You taking care a the dolls at the Twenty-One Club?"

Walker winked at Ruth. "It's my sworn duty as mayor to attend to the citizens' needs."

Walker returned to his seat and Eddie Bennett took the cup to the dugout. McNamee cleared his throat and continued, "The Babe had doffed his cap to converse with the mayor. He's put it back on now. I'm told he has his caps especially made, they're broader than his teammates' caps and the tops are higher. He bats left-handed, with his right foot extended toward the plate. He spits on his hands and raps each shoe with his bat. Now he's waving his wand over the plate and he's so big it looks like a toothpick in his hands. The stadium is eerily quiet. All of the peanut vendors have taken time out from peddling their wares to watch Ruth's turn at the bat. The first pitch is low, too low according to the umpire - ball one. Another ball, outside and low - two balls to the Babe now. One out, a man on first, Earle Coooms. Babe takes a tremendous slice at the ball, throwing his entire weight onto his right leg and pivoting on it. He misses. Another pitch, again a little low, but over the pan. The home plate arbiter declares it strike two. And now the Sultan of Swat takes a mighty swing at an outside offering ... and misses. Strike three. A collective groan rises from the huge crowd."

o o o

After Philly ace Lefty Grove had pitched scoreless ball for three innings Miller Huggins told his starters, "Stop swinging and just try to meet the ball - short, snappy cuts." It worked.

Combs lined a double to left center in the fourth to drive in Dugan and Grabowski and Gehrig smashed one of Grove's fastballs into right field with two aboard to make it 4-0 New York.

The A's plated two in the top of the sixth. In the bottom of the inning Lazzeri doubled and Dugan singled him home, before getting picked off by a bullet from Cochrane when he took too big a lead off first. Grabowski singled and Hoyt moved him to second with a sacrifice. Combs hit a slow grounder to the shortstop Joe Boley, who was playing his first big league game. The ball went through Boley's legs.

"What the fuck was that, Polack?" Cobb yelled from right field. The ball rolled into left field and Hoyt jogged home.

"It's bad enough you call *me* that, Cobb," Al Simmons yelled from centerfield. "Don't start in on the kid."

On the Yankee bench Dutch Ruether turned to Herb Pennock. "I sure am glad the Colonel didn't go after Cobb. Can you imagine having to put up with that prick every day?"

o o o

Up in the press box James Harrison and Richards Vidmer drank lukewarm coffee and smoked. A short, homely man in his early twenties, his hair parted in the middle and slicked back with a lot of pomade, sat down beside them. They'd never seen him before.

"How the fuck are you two gents doing?" asked the man.

"Ah, fine, I guess," said Harrison. "I don't think I can recall seeing you at the Stadium before."

"I never cover sports. I'm on the entertainment beat."

"Which paper?" asked Vidmer.

"The New York Graphic. It's a fuckin' tabloid, but I'm hoping for something bigger. Name's Ed. Ed Sullivan."

Babe Ruth

"Good to have you aboard, Sullivan. I'm James Harrison. And this is Richards Vidmer. We travel with the Yankees."

Sullivan cut to the chase as he usually did. "I gotta be honest with ya, I don't know a fucking thing about baseball. But I do know that stories about the Yankees are really fuckin' popular. I've decided to write a piece about the Yankee wives."

"Interesting," said Vidmer. "I'm sure the players will be happy that their wives are going to be famous too."

"Are any of them here today?" asked Sullivan.

"There are a few of them right down there," said Harrison, pointing to box seats a few rows up from the Yankee dugout.

o o o

Dorothy Hoyt had ginger hair and hazel eyes. Her most distinguishing features were her button nose, swept bouffant hairstyle, and large bosoms. She and Marie Shawkey, in an expensive dress rather than her Tiger Lady getup because of the temperature, looked at a mousy-looking woman a few seats away. She wasn't sitting with the other wives. It was Dorothy Dugan, who went by Dot.

"Poor Dot," said Marie. "All she does is worry that Joe's cheating on her."

"Who's to say he isn't?" asked Dorothy. "After all, he hangs out with Ruth and there are loose women around him everywhere he goes."

The Babe watched them from the dugout steps, ogling Dorothy's cleavage.

"I'd give about a year's pay to take a peek down that blouse," he muttered to himself. Dorothy saw him staring. She pulled her sweater closed and gave him a withering look.

"Dot's problem is they got married before Joe was a big star," said Marie. "Now she thinks he just wants glamour girls."

"Did you hear what happened when they went for marriage counseling?" asked Dorothy.

"No. What?"

"The counselor asked Joe if he knew what Dot's favorite flower was,"

Dorothy explained. "He said, 'Sure I do. It's Robin Hood White Enriched.'"

"He didn't! Maybe I should lend Dot my gun in case she catches him with a floozy."

"And if she shoots one, Waite can take care of the body," said Dorothy.

Marie stared at Dorothy, mystified by what she had just said.

o o o

Waite Hoyt finished with an eight-hitter, which he thought was not too bad at all against the Athletics' powerful lineup. Miller Huggins met with reporters after the game. Ed Sullivan wasn't among them, he'd cornered Eddie Bennett to find out which wife was which. "Beating Grove is bound to give the entire team a lot of confidence," said Huggins, puffing away on his pipe. "I was pleased because it proves the fallacy that our club can be stopped by hard-throwing left-handers."

"I think he means disproves," Richards Vidmer whispered to James Harrison.

Hug continued, "Teams figure that if they can shut down Combs, Ruth, and Gehrig they have us beat. But we have some pretty husky right-handed batters too. They had better get over the idea that we're suckers for southpaws."

o o o

After hitting two theatres and three speakeasies that night, Ed Sullivan wrote his article. James Harrison couldn't wait to read it. He wondered if Sullivan would write that the wives were really fuckin' beautiful. He found it on page three of the *Graphic*. The boy at the newsstand had been quite surprised that Harrison would buy the rag. The piece began …

> *In the reserved seats of the grandstand to the rear of home plate at Yankee Stadium there is an interesting gathering when the Yankees are at home - the wives of the players watching their hubbies plying their trade. You can spot Mrs. Pennock, Mrs. Shawkey, Mrs. Ruether, Mrs. Lazzeri, Mrs. Shocker, and Mrs. Hoyt. They talk of this and that and are tactful enough to talk about other matters when one of the hubbies pulls a boner on the field. The players will tell you that the cost of dressing their wives is no small item. New York sets a high standard in fashion. Other cities are not as tough on the*

Babe Ruth

bankrolls of players with wives. They say that the wife of a New York player never thinks of coming to the park in the same outfit two days running.

The Yanks clobbered the A's 10-4 the next day. Koenig, again the number two hitter in Huggins' seemingly already set batting order, went 5-for-5, and Gehrig drove in three runs with a double and a triple. Dutch Ruether struggled against the hard-hitting A's but the Yankee defense sparkled. When Cy Perkins tried to steal in the fourth Mark Koenig hauled down Pat Collins' high throw and applied the tag. In the seventh Bob Meusel made a great throw from left to nail Ty Cobb at the plate.

"Slowin' down are ya, Cobb?" yelled Charley O'Leary. "Too bad, old man."

Cobb shot him a murderous look and Charley suddenly recalled that they'd never gotten along in Detroit and that Cobb toted a gun wherever he went.

Dutch Ruether, the Yankees' other southpaw, was in his eleventh year in the majors. He'd been 19-6 with a sparkling 1.82 E.R.A. in 1919 for the Cincinnati Reds and held Joe Jackson and the White Sox to just six hits in winning his only start in the '19 World Series. He was still proud of it, refusing to believe that some of Chicago players hadn't been trying as hard as they might have. "I thought I worked a tight game," he told sceptics.

Dutch won twenty-one for the Brooklyn Robins in '22 but he got into an argument with Charles Ebbets and was traded to the Senators. Ruether started well in Washington but when his E.R.A. ballooned to 4.84 in '26 the Senators put him on waivers. Six teams passed on him. They'd heard that Dutch was 'surly', which everyone knew really meant that he drank too much. Ed Barrow got him for next to nothing and the small investment had paid off.

Herb Pennock visited Dutch's locker as he was about to head to the shower after his lop-sided win.

"You lucky son-of-a-gun," said Pennock.

"What are you talking about, Herb?" asked Dutch.

"You give up fourteen hits and you win by six runs."

"So? Maybe they'll score that many for you when it's your turn."

& THE 1927 YANKEES HAVE THE BEST SUMMER EVER

o o o

The third game of the series had to be called due to darkness with the score tied 9-9 after ten innings and almost three hours of play. The fact that the Yankees had scored twenty-seven runs in three games against the team that was predicted to win the American League flag did not bode well for the rest of the circuit.

o o o

After batting practice before the fourth game on Good Friday the Babe looked for Benny Bengough. He always wanted Benny as his partner for long toss to bring him good luck.

"Where's that Googles guy?" yelled Ruth. Notorious for not remembering names, the Babe thought his name was Barney not Benny and the only Barney that came to mind was Barney Google, the comic strip character.

"Sorry, Jidge," said Bengough, panting as he ran out of the dugout. "Had to fix a busted strap on my mask."

"Not much use protectin' that ugly puss," said Ruth.

"We can't all be matinee idols like you and your pal Fairbanks, Jidge."

Bengough turned out to be lucky for Ruth once again.

o o o

Howard Ehmke, the six foot-three "Silver Creek Sapling", looked to be off to a promising start. He got Combs and Koenig to tap easy comebackers to him to begin the first inning and was glad to have the bases empty when Ruth came up. The Babe had pounded more home runs off Ehmke than anyone else in the league.

Ehmke threw a high one, then a strike, then another high one. Then he decided to try a curve on the outside corner to even up the count. The Bambino sent it on a high arc into the tenth row of seats for his first home run of the season. In the top of the second Ruth threw out Al Simmons at home, a perfect strike to Pat Collins from deep right.

The Yankees scored again in the second, third, and fourth but the A's rallied for three in the top of the seventh to shrink New York's lead to 4-3. The Yankees' two runs in the bottom of the inning gave them a 6-3 margin of victory.

Babe Ruth

"They only got me six," Pennock told Ruether.

"That's terrible," said Ruether. "You poor man. They only got you six runs. How's a fellow expected to win when they only score six?"

"Damn straight. Pretty tough getting wins pitching for these guys," moaned Pennock facetiously.

"The Babe took a while to hit his first. Had to come sooner or later though."

"Only ten rows up. Must still be feeling a bit punk."

"Hard to believe they had him pitching when we played with him in Boston," said Pennock. "Mind you he won twenty-two games two years in a row."

"They don't send twenty-two game winners out to the pasture very often," said Ruether.

"He's done okay playing every day though."

"Ya, not *too* bad. Seems to have worked out all right for him."

o o o

When the Yanks hosted the Red Sox the next day it was even worse. Urban Shocker had to win it with his playmates scoring only five times. He profited from some terrific defensive plays. Bob Meusel drove in three which was all that the Yankees needed for a 5-2 win.

Waite Hoyt had a little more breathing room the day after, Easter Sunday. There was a delay at the start of the game because one of the umpires had taken ill.

"Could you smell the smoke last night?" Herb Pennock asked Bob Shawkey as they sat in the dugout.

"From the big fire?" asked Shawkey.

"Ya, the Sherry-Netherland."

"Hell, ya, Herb. We could see the *flames* from our place. Morning papers said you could see 'em twenty miles away."

"It was going to be the tallest residential building ever erected," said Herb.

"It was the scaffolding that caught, wasn't it?" asked Bob.

"Apparently. There was a report on the radio this morning. Fifty-foot sections of it fell five hundred feet down to the streets and the flames from it set four other buildings on fire. So many thousands of people showed up to watch the blaze it took seven hundred cops to keep them back far enough to where they'd be safe."

"How far up did the hoses reach?" asked Bob.

"Only a few floors," said Herb. "It must have been pretty frustrating for the firemen, knowing they couldn't really do anything."

"The buildings are goin' higher and higher. What are they callin' 'em? Oh ya, skyscrapers. The same thing's liable to happen all over town. Somebody really shoulda seen this comin'."

"It was just lucky this time, what with it not being finished yet and nobody living there."

o o o

"Look at those two," Richards Vidmer said to James Harrison as they sat in the press box puffing away on Camel cigarettes.

Making their way down the aisle in the grandstand above first base were two interesting looking characters. A garish platinum blonde wearing a huge yellow Easter bonnet walked ahead of a short, florid man in a mauve suit. The blonde wore a necklace strung with large gold padlocks and a bracelet that held a gold police whistle.

"There's something you don't see every day. Who are they?" Harrison asked his co-writer.

"The guy is Tammany Young," said Vidmer.

"Who's he?"

"He's big in the theater scene. Rarely has anyone gotten so much mileage out of so little talent though. The most he's ever done is walk-ons in a few plays but he knows everybody who's anybody and he's the world's greatest gate crasher. Young's had box seats at World Series games and last year's Army-Notre Dame championship and at the last five opening nights at the Metropolitan Opera without ever buying a ticket. He's called the reverse Houdini because he can get into any kind of box."

Harrison laughed. "That's rich. Who's the dame?"

Babe Ruth

"Mary Louise Guinan. She goes by *Texas* Guinan."

"I've heard about her. She has a nightclub doesn't she?"

"She's had several. She came to the Big Apple from Waco, Texas. Started out as a chorus girl then performed on vaudeville. She made an oater called The Wildcat a few years ago and got dubbed the Queen of the West. Did all her own stunts. She opened a club here and hired forty scantily-clad teenage girls to dance beside the tables. She praises them up and down no matter how bad they are and says 'Let's give the little lady a big hand' as long as the men like the way they look. A lot of swells were there the night I went, George Gershwin, Gloria Swanson, and John Barrymore. Al Jolson got up and played the piano."

"Sounds like I should check it out," said Harrison. "How much are the drinks?"

"A lot more than we can afford," said Vidmer. "Twenty-five dollars for champagne or a fifth of Scotch and two bucks for a pitcher of water if you bring your own hooch. She greets all the customers with, 'Hello, sucker'. When government agents showed up she welcomed them the same way. They padlocked her place and now she's starring in a new play called The Padlocks of 1927. Apparently it's a riot."

When the game got underway Koenig was batting .600, with twelve hits in five games. It looked as though Huggins had been smart to go with him in spite of Morehart's great spring training. He'd made some terrific stabs at short and all of his throws to the still not sure-handed Gehrig were right on the money.

Columbia Lou celebrated Easter with two home runs. The second one was so well hit that Ruth who was on first just stood and watched it. Gehrig almost ran him over. Later, Lou very nearly took the ear off Phil Todt the Red Sox first baseman with a vicious line drive. Infielders had always played back for the Babe, now they did for Gehrig too. There was bravery, then there was insanity. The Yankees clobbered Boston 14-2.

○ ○ ○

"Are you happy now?" Ruether asked Pennock after the game the next day. "I didn't need a cushion at all." He'd just shut out Boston on a three-hitter and the Yankee record stood at 6-0. In the first inning the Babe

& THE 1927 YANKEES HAVE THE BEST SUMMER EVER

was on second when Meusel caromed a single off third baseman Topper Rigney's glove. When the ball rolled away from him, Ruth dashed home and scored with a beautiful slide over the corner of the plate.

In the last game of their opening home stand the Boston bats finally came to life. The Yankees finally showed themselves to be human and suffered their first loss. Bob Shawkey, who'd given up three runs in the third of an inning he'd lasted in his only other start, the 9-9 tie game, surrendered five runs in five innings. Boston won it 6-3.

Babe Ruth
& the 1927 YANKEES have the BEST SUMMER EVER

8.

Leaving the Big Apple

"You could be a pitcher, you got pretty nice curves."

The team hopped aboard the Quaker City Express and headed to Philadelphia. Their three Pullman cars were coupled to the back of the train. When Ruppert travelled with the club an additional car was added. The first car had private drawing rooms for Huggins, Mark Roth, and Doc Woods who often brought his pet poodle along.

Hug, who spent a lot of the time playing pinochle with his two coaches during the long train rides, loved road trips. He was able to indulge his favourite hobby of going to roller rinks and watching the skaters go round and round. He'd bought a rink when he was in Cincinnati and dreamt of owning a chain of them some day. The Babe saw there was a fourth drawing room in the car and he took it over so he could play his portable Victrola. No one minded.

The other two cars were for the players, who all slept in curtained lower berths according to seniority. None was forced to endure an upper berth.

"Puttin' a veteran player in an upper berth," Joe Dugan explained to Wilcy Moore, "would be like takin' a swell dame to a show and sittin' in the second balcony and then takin' her home in a trolley car."

Ray Morehart munched noisily on penny candy from a paper bag. Gehrig and Paschal played checkers and talked about the meal money.

"You can live pretty high on the hog for four bucks a day," said Paschal. "I did that for a while. Then I started sendin' some of it home for the little woman to stash away for the winter when we don't get paid."

"I save most of it to give to my mom," said Lou.

Babe Ruth

Ruth was in the smoking car contentedly puffing large perfectly-shaped rings into the air from his huge black cigar. Myles Thomas, a five-foot-nine college man from Pennsylvania, sat beside him. He was writing in some kind of small book.

"What's that you're writin' in, Duck Eye?" asked the Babe.

"I decided to keep a diary - in case this is my last year in the big leagues," Thomas answered.

"Wasn't last year your *first*?" asked Ruth.

"Ya, but you never know."

Shawkey and Ruether sat in facing seats playing gin rummy. Ray Morehart worked on a crossword puzzle. Hoyt startled the conductor when he walked along the aisle. Waite was reading a book on undertaking, a business his father-in-law was encouraging him to take up when he was done playing ball.

Joe Dugan looked over at Earle Combs, who was reading his Bible.

"Still reading the good book, are ya Earle?"

"I'm no saint, Joe, but when I die I want to walk with Jesus," said Combs.

"That's great, Earle," Joe chuckled. "As for me, I'd rather walk with the bases loaded."

o o o

Urban Shocker sat down beside Benny Bengough and reached into his bag. He took out a book of his own.

Bengough gave him an odd look. "I didn't know you went in much for books, Urban," said Benny. "What's that you're reading?"

Shocker turned the book around so Benny could read the title.

"*Pride and Prejudice,*" Benny read aloud. He whistled. "Geez, I'm impressed. I wouldn't have guessed …"

Shocker opened up the book. It did not contain pages of Jane Austen's wonderful prose. It contained a silver flask. Shocker took a sip and offered some to Benny.

Pennock, who was sitting between Koenig and Lazzeri, read the newspaper.

& THE 1927 YANKEES HAVE THE BEST SUMMER EVER

"Anything interesting in the sports pages, Herb?" asked Pipgras.

"Johnny Weissmuller set a new record in the hundred-metre free style, Henry Steinbrenner won the NCAA low-hurdles championship, and some comedy basketball team's starting up. They're calling themselves the Harlem Globetrotters. I guess they're all colored fellas."

"How did the A's do?" asked Lazzeri.

"They beat the Senators, three to one. Got all their runs off General Crowder."

"So what are they now?" asked Dutch.

"Three and four, three games behind us," said Pennock.

"So after this series we could be six ahead or we could be all tied up," said Pennock.

"We'd better not be tied," said Ruether. "Hug'd be a nervous wreck."

Things were quiet for the next few minutes. Pennock went back to reading his newspaper.

"Anything about the flooding out west in there, Herb?" asked Lazzeri.

"No, not today," said Pennock.

"Any *hot* news in there?" asked Koenig.

"Not that I've seen."

"Anything about a fire?" Tony asked.

"No."

Mark and Tony waved to the other players to watch and then put their hands over their mouths to hide their wide grins. Tony struck a match on his shoe and touched it to the edge of Herb's newspaper.

"Any train cars catch on fire, Herb?"

"What? No, there weren't any fires ..."

Everyone howled.

"Lazzeri!" yelled Pennock, trying madly to extinguish the flame in his newspaper.

Babe Ruth

"That spontaneous combustion's really something, ain't it fellas?" chuckled Tony.

"There's somethin' to put in that diary yer keepin', Duck Eye," bellowed the Babe.

o o o

In the first game in Philadelphia Lefty Grove gave up three runs, but Urban Shocker's spit balls weren't fooling anybody. The Yankees got on the scoreboard with one in the top of the fourth but in the bottom of the inning Mike Gazella, who was playing third, dropped a popup in foul territory off the bat of Al Simmons. Given new life, Simmons ripped the next pitch to center and legged out a triple. He scored on Sammy Hale's sacrifice fly to Ruth. Branom singled to right, Cochrane tripled to center, and Boley singled to left. The A's were getting their revenge for the season opening series. They led 4-1.

In the seventh Shocker gave up back-to-back singles and then walked Cobb. Huggins sent Wilcy Moore in to restore order. Simmons singled and scored on a groundout. That put the A's ahead 7-4 and they held on for their fourth win in their last five games. It looked like they might be on their way to a pennant after all.

o o o

At the start of batting practice the next day Ruth was waiting his turn with Waite Hoyt.

"Seems as though I can't get ahold of the doggone ball these days," said the Babe.

"Are you seeing them all right, Jidge?" Waite asked.

"They come in as big as balloons and then I bounce 'em into the ground or miss 'em by a mile. But I'll get going one of these days and when I do some poor pitcher is gonna suffer plenty."

"Your turn, Jidge," said Hoyt.

The Babe stepped in and put on a show. He entertained the reporters and groundskeepers by smacking six balls out of the park. The first one landed on the roof of a tannery, the next three bounced on the street, the last one took a chip out of a telegraph pole. Connie Mack, dressed in a suit as always, watched from the shade of the dugout.

"That's just great," Hoyt muttered to himself as the sixth ball left the premises. "He's sure to see lots of good pitches today after that exhibition."

The A's lineup got to Waite Hoyt early and often, scoring six times in the first four and a third innings. Their senior citizens, Cobb and Collins, had two hits each. Huggins decided to see if Wilcy Moore could do better than he had yesterday. 'Cy' shut down the mighty A's the rest of the way. They kept asking Brick Owens, the home plate umpire, to check if Moore was scuffing the ball or rubbing it with rosin or slippery elm.

After his bombastic display in batting practice the Babe was issued four free passes to first. But Connie Mack couldn't have his pitchers walk the next three men in the order as well. Meusel tripled in Combs and Gehrig in the first, Lazzeri tripled home Ruth and Meusel in the fifth, Gehrig's homer scored Koenig and the Babe in the sixth, and Lazzeri's four-bagger scored Gehrig and Meusel in the eighth. It ended 13-6 New York.

Lazzeri and Gehrig each ended up with five runs batted in. Gehrig, whose .459 average led the majors, already had nineteen RBIs. Meusel, who was batting .439, had fourteen RBIs and Lazzeri had thirteen. If the Babe ever started hitting the rest of the league would really need to look for shelter. He still had just eight safeties and one RBI on his lone home run of the year. His other seven hits were all singles. He was being referred to as the empty spot in an otherwise explosive lineup. It hurt.

"Look at those numbers," Ruth said to Dugan. "I'm the worst hitter on the whole fuckin' club. Why am I battin' ahead of you? Hell, I should be hittin' behind the catcher!"

There was plenty of speculation that Father Time and countless late nights had finally caught up with the Bambino.

○   ○   ○

The Yankees were rained out in Philadelphia on Friday the 22nd and the Babe was frustrated and bored. He decided to have Joe Dugan and Marshall Hunt up to his suite at the Ansonia. When they came in he was wearing his silk bathrobe and, as usual, smoking a big cigar.

Babe Ruth

"Always gotta have somethin' in his mouth," Dugan remarked. "A hot dog, a pipe, a pinch of snuff, somethin'." Ruth picked up the ornate white porcelain telephone.

"Three guesses who he's calling," said Hunt.

"He's got one in every town," said Dugan.

"Gus there?" asked the Babe.

"No? Well can *you* take my order? All right, I need a case of scotch and a case of rye - the good stuff - and beer. So what happened to Gus?" He waited for the answer.

"He's got amnesia? Well send me up a case a that too."

Dugan tried not to burst out laughing.

"Must think it's an after dinner liqueur," Hunt suggested.

"I suppose," said Dugan. "He can sure hold his booze though. One night last year we went to Belmont and he won a bunch of money so he took me to a speak. We got back to the hotel around four. The next day Hug looked at my eyes and took me out in the first."

"How'd the Babe do?"

"The bugger's eyes were as clear as a baby's. Played the whole game, made a great catch, stole a base, belted two home runs. The man's not human I tell ya. He fell out of a tree. I remember one game at Griffith Stadium a couple a years back, first game of a doubleheader. Jidge chased a fly ball into foul territory in the first game and ran headfirst into a cement wall. Knocked him unconscious."

"Who got to him first?" asked Hunt.

"Combs. When the Babe started to wake up Earle asked him who was the president before Coolidge and the Babe said. 'I don't know, and I didn't know *before* I got knocked out.'"

Hunt laughed. "Did he go to the hospital?"

"Hell no. He played the rest of the game, went three-for-three, and played the late game too."

o o o

Ruth and Gehrig hit back-to-back solo shots to stake Dutch Ruether to a 2-0 lead in the top of the first in the final game of the shortened series with Philadelphia. The Yankees added another run in the fourth but Eddie Collins scored once and Cobb scored twice to even things at 3-3 after eight.

The Yanks failed to go ahead in the top of the ninth. The second out in the bottom of the frame was a force out, Lazzeri to Koenig. Trying for a double play, Koenig, who'd made three terrific plays earlier, spoiled all that with a high throw to first. A more experienced first baseman would have jumped and caught the ball. Gehrig kept his foot on the bag and stuck up his glove. The ball skidded off the side of it. Joe Boley had gone from second to third on the grounder to Koenig. He saw the ball rolling toward the grandstand and dashed home to win it for the A's.

o o o

With Sunday baseball banned by Philadelphia's Quaker forefathers the Yankees headed to Washington for a single game.

"Let's get sloppy," Bob Meusel said to Joe Dugan as they got into their uniforms.

"We did that last night, Bob. Drinkin' after the game not enough for ya anymore? You're gonna start drinkin' while you're playin'?"

"No. He's pitchin'."

"What the hell are you … Oh, I get it. Ya, let's."

Meusel homered off Sloppy Thurston in the second. When Sloppy, whose nickname facetiously referred to the fact that he always wore immaculately cut suits, singled and scored on Sam Rice's triple to center in the bottom of the fifth it seemed to wake the Yanks up.

The Babe led off the sixth. When he left the on-deck circle and headed to the plate he looked back to the dugout and bellowed, "Time ta swing them bats, boys."

Thurston tried to sneak an inside fastball by Ruth. He lined it over the forty-foot wall in right. The ball landed on the other side of a garbage-strewn alley. Two mangy-looking cats pawed at it as it rolled by them.

Babe Ruth

Worried that Gehrig might do the same, Thurston walked him. Lou took a good-sized lead and Cochrane fired the ball behind him. Joe Judge caught it and fired to second base. Gehrig was out by a mile. Sloppy felt a little better. Meusel took several vicious practice swings and the infielders backed up two steps. Bob laid down a bunt and was safe at first. Thurston was so mad he walked Lazzeri and then Gazella too.

"Grab a bat, Cedric," Huggins told Durst, "you're batting for Collins."

"Finally," Durst muttered. It would be his first at bat of the season and first as a Yankee.

Sloppy's first pitch was high but outside. Durst laid off it. The second pitch was high and fast but not high and fast *enough*. Durst drilled it to right field for a bases-clearing triple.

"What's with these guys this year?" Harris said to the shortstop Buddy Myer. "Even their scrubs are tearing the cover off the fuckin' ball."

The Yankees won it 6-2.

o o o

The two teams climbed aboard the Congressional and headed to New York for a single game on Monday. Waite Hoyt was sailing along with a seemingly comfortable 4-1 lead in the top of the seventh when he mysteriously came unglued. Rice and Harris singled and Rice scored on Tris Speaker's long fly to Ruth in right. Huggins thought about bringing in Wilcy Moore.

Art Fletcher looked at his notebook. "The man's given up ten runs in the twelve innings he's pitched, Miller."

"Some of them were unearned, weren't they?" asked Charley O'Leary.

"At least three, I think," said Huggins. "I don't know. I'm just not sure I trust him all that much. At least not yet. I'm sticking with Hoyt."

Goose Goslin homered to left and the Yankee lead was gone.

Bucky Harris sent in Hod "Lizzie" Lisenbee, a twenty-nine-year-old rookie who'd pitched a grand total of two innings in the big leagues. It was his game to win or lose. When he jogged in from the bullpen the fans had no idea who he was. Neither did the Yankees.

& **THE 1927 YANKEES HAVE THE BEST SUMMER EVER**

It looked as though this was too close a game to risk sending in a rookie when Lazzeri singled up the middle. Gazella sacrificed him to second and the Yankees had the go ahead run in scoring position. Huggins sent Durst in to bat for Grabowski. He bounded one back to the mound and Huggins decided to let Hoyt bat for himself. He grounded out.

In the eighth the Babe came up with a chance to put New York back in the lead. Lisenbee struck him out. Gehrig doubled to left but Goose Goslin's perfect throw to Ossie Bluege persuaded Koenig to stay on third. Now it was Meusel's turn to be the hero. He hit a long fly to left. Goslin tracked it down near the wall for the third out. In the ninth Lazzeri struck out, Ray Morehart popped out, and Pat Collins flied out. Lisenbee had his first win.

o o o

The Bronx Bombers headed to Boston for a rare two-game series. Before the Friday game Ruth whistled while he boned his bats.

Mark Koenig whose locker was across from the Babe's looked puzzled. "What are you doing, Jidge?"

"If you rub your bats with a bottle like this they don't chip or splinter."

"Where did you learn that?"

"Beats me, keed. Ya know, hitting's a funny business," Ruth mused as he rubbed oil into his glove. "Some days they just can't get you out and the next day you can't hit the side of a barn with a bass fiddle."

"Which pitchers give you the most trouble?" asked Mark.

"All of 'em when I'm in a slump. I'm a sucker for everybody. If I'm hitting, I'll hit any of 'em. I don't suppose I'll ever break that Twenty-One record though."

"Why not?"

"To do that you've gotta start early and the pitchers have got to pitch to you. I don't start early and the pitchers haven't really pitched to me in four seasons. I get more bad balls to hit than any other six men - and a lot less good ones. I'd love to hit five hundred. I got three hundred and fifty-nine now. That leaves a hundred and forty-one to go." The requisite number was down to a hundred and forty an hour later.

Babe Ruth

○   ○   ○

It didn't seem possible but the Red Sox were playing even worse than they had in '26. They'd won just two of their first dozen games. It didn't help that five of their regulars were batting well below their weight.

Koenig, Gehrig, Meusel, and Collins each tripled home a run and the Babe walked, singled, doubled off the top of the left field wall and homered, propelling one of Slim Harris' best fast balls into the right field stands to crush the Red Sox 9-0. It was Ruether's second shutout of the young season. Dutch thought he might just have a couple of extra bourbon and branch waters to celebrate.

Pennock kidded Ruether in the shower. "They got you nine this time," he shouted over the sound of the water. "What are you doing, promising them easy broads after the game or just free booze?"

○   ○   ○

The Yankees led 2-0 heading into the bottom of the ninth on Saturday but Miller Huggins started worrying even earlier than usual when the first two Boston batters reached base. There wasn't too much noise from the crowd. Most of the fans had already left. It spoke volumes about Boston's struggles when Bill Carrigan sent Jack Rothrock in to bat for Bill Regan.

Rothrock had lifted his average to .179 with a four-game hitting streak. Regan outpointed him with a .185 average. Huggins groaned as Rothrock made it five straight with a double to right to tie the game.

With runners on second and third Huggins sent in Wilcy Moore with orders to walk the next batter and set up the double play. He did. Then, with the bases now jammed, he threw a sinker that sank right through Johnny Grabowski's shin guards. A rare win for the Red Sox.

○   ○   ○

The Yankees ended the first month of the season 9-5-1. They were tied with the A's and just a game ahead of the White Sox. With just four home runs so far Ruth was on a pace to hit twenty-five in '27 and he was batting just .267. In spite of the Babe's woes the starting lineup was batting an astounding .369. Gehrig, Koenig, Collins, and Meusel were a combined .419 for the month.

Nobody could claim the Bombers were a one-man attack anymore and, with Buster behind him in the order, Ruth was finally beginning to get some pitches to hit. That would make it a bit easier for him to earn his huge salary.

o o o

That night, to impress a couple of flappers at a speak, Ruth showed them his pay check.

"This is for *two weeks!*" gasped Gladys, a strawberry blonde in a white and silver sequin dress.

"Two and a *half* actually," Ruth corrected her.

The other girl, a mousy brunette whose name was Hilda, took the check and read aloud. "The American Base Ball League Club of New York, Inc. Manufacturer's Trust Company, Yorkville Bank Office. Pay to the order of George H. Ruth, seven thousand, six hundred and eighty-five dollars and twenty-three cents. Signed, Jacob Ruppert."

Gladys took a drag from her cigarette and exhaled the smoke slowly. "I make fifteen bucks a week, Hilda. How many weeks would I have to work to get a pay check for that much?"

Hilda thought for a minute. "A little over five hundred," she told her friend.

"Maybe I shoulda been a ball player," said Gladys.

"You could be a pitcher," said the Babe. "You got pretty nice curves."

"And you gotta pretty swell *bat*, George H Ruth," Gladys giggled. She grabbed the check from Hilda and tucked it into her brassiere. "Now I'm going to have to see your bat again."

"So long as you don't want me to sign it for you," said the Babe.

o o o

On May Day the Yanks took on the A's with first place on the line. Seventy-thousand squeezed into the Stadium for the Sunday afternoon tilt, the biggest crowd since the opener. Many of the spectators were from Philadelphia, where Sunday baseball was still deemed sinful.

Connie Mack started forty-four year-old Jack Quinn. He'd started out pitching for the Highlanders in 1909 and five years later won twenty-six

Babe Ruth

games for the Baltimore Terrapins of the Federal League during its brief existence. Herb Pennock started for Millers' men.

Koenig drew a walk in the first, after Combs had lined out. The Babe's sixth home run of the year was a thing of beauty. It flew almost on a line to the exit gap in the bleacher section. Cobb didn't even bother to turn around to see where it landed. He raised a disgusted eye skyward and spat out a stream of tobacco juice.

Cobb singled to lead off the third. Al Simmons, the cleanup hitter, followed, slashing a ball to right. The Babe raced in and scooped it up. Cobb tore around second and headed for third. Ruth fired the ball to Dugan. The throw was right on target, low enough for Joe to catch the ball and set his glove on the base line in front of the bag for Cobb to slide into.

But Cobb's foot didn't slide toward the bag. It slid right up Dugan's shin instead. Blood gushed from it and Joe yelped in pain.

Meusel had a clear view of the whole thing. He tore in and grabbed Cobb. "You lousy fucking cheater!"

"Get away from me," said Cobb. He saw that not one of his teammates was coming to back him up. Plenty of Yankees were on their way to the scene. Ruth arrived.

"You're not a Tiger anymore, but you still haven't changed your stripes, Cobb. Still slicin' people up. How long d'ya sharpen those fucking things this morning?"

"I never spike anybody on purpose, you big ape. He was blocking the bag. The base paths belong to me."

Before Ruth could answer, Cobb broke free of Meusel and went after the Babe.

Ruth swung hard, but as his fist was about to hit Cobb it was intercepted by the jaw of Miller Huggins, who'd run onto the diamond to intervene. He fell to the ground dazed.

"You miserable prick," Ruth said to Cobb. "Look what you made me do."

Cobb growled back. As he was about to try again to hit Ruth the umpire, Brick Owens, arrived. "Don't even think about it, Cobb," he warned. "You've already done enough."

& THE 1927 YANKEES HAVE THE BEST SUMMER EVER

o o o

When the Yankees took the field for the fourth inning the sky was overcast. Bob Meusel left his tinted glasses on the bench and jogged out to left field. Two A's reached on sharply-hit singles and Jack Quinn lofted a high fly to left. Meusel ran in under it and suddenly stopped as the sun peeked out from behind a cloud. Like a boxer trying to protect himself from a torrent of blows he covered his head with his arms. There were audible groans from the grandstands.

Quinn's fly dropped safely a few feet from Meusel. He still didn't know where it was. Combs had seen his teammate's dilemma. He raced over and picked up the ball, but by that time Quinn was jogging into second and the two runners had scored.

Ty Cobb led off again in the fifth. Pennock tugged at his cap, fingered the baseball and examined it as though it were a rare stone or object d'art, hitched his belt, tossed the rosin bag into the air a few times, rubbed up the ball, stared in at Cobb, and re-adjusted his cap.

"Throw the fucking ball, ya cocksucking slowpoke!" Cobb finally yelled at him.

Herb was happy. He'd rattled Cobb. Not that it took much to get the bastard angry.

Cobb grounded the ball to Gehrig and then tried to run him over. Lou stepped out of the way just in time and yelled, "You're not gettin' *me*, Cobb."

Gehrig hit his fifth in the sixth inning and Ruth regained the home run lead with a long poke in the eighth, to his delight over the head of Cobb once again. Pennock yielded a dozen hits to the Philadelphia powerhouse and there would have been even more if not for some great plays behind him. Considering how long he took to deliver the ball to the plate it was a wonder his fielders were still awake when a ball was hit their way. Tony "the Wop" Lazzeri handled four ground balls faultlessly to bring his streak to seventy-nine chances without an error. Slowpoke Pennock won, 7-3.

o o o

Babe Ruth

Christy Walsh met Ruth for breakfast the next day. Walsh was handsome, with deep-set eyes and jet black hair that he parted neatly on the left side. He always dressed well, a double-breasted suit, a starched collar, a Kelly green tie, and black and white wingtip shoes.

Though he'd graduated from law school, Walsh's first job was as a cartoonist. He got into the promotion business after getting Eddie Rickenbacker, the World War ace, to ghostwrite an account of the '19 Indianapolis 500. It made all the front pages and he and Rickenbacker split eight hundred and seventy-four dollars for a few hours' work.

He'd first impressed the Babe when he asked him how much he got paid each time he wrote an account of a home run he hit in a World Series game.

"Five dollars," Ruth told him.

"How would you like to get five *hundred* dollars?"

He'd earned the Babe a lot of money. Now he thought his famous client needed some advice. He set down his coffee cup and wiped his mouth. "Babe, do you realize you've spent almost five hundred thousand dollars on gambling and high living the last three years?" asked Christy. "You've owned nine different high-priced automobiles, you've spent a bundle on hotel suites, and I can only imagine what you've spent on women, cigars, and booze. To top it off you tip more than most people earn. Isn't it time you settled down just a little?"

The Babe set down his coffee. "Do ya really think I'm gonna find a sweet girl and live happily ever after listening to Amos 'n' Andy with her on the radio every night?"

o o o

The team boarded the Chesapeake Overnight and headed back to Washington for four games, the start of a four city, twenty-one day road trip. In the first one Ruth and Gehrig took a day off from pounding baseballs over the fence. Meusel, Lazzeri, and Dugan picked up the slack with three hits each and Waite Hoyt contributed two of his own, good enough for a 9-6 win. Hoyt went eight innings and Wilcy Moore took over in the ninth to earn what some people thought deserved to be called a save and maybe even recorded as such.

& THE 1927 YANKEES HAVE THE BEST SUMMER EVER

o o o

Gehrig knocked in a pair in the top of the seventh the next day off Washington's Firpo Marberry to give his side a 4-2 lead. Marberry, whose real name was Fred, much preferred Red to Firpo. His teammates called him Firpo because he bore an uncanny resemblance to Luis Firpo, the homely "Wild Bull of the Pampas" who had sent Jack Dempsey to the mat in their sensational bout in '23. George Pipgras got his first start for New York. He was great for six innings but he fell apart in the seventh. Five batters and two runs later he was on the bench. He knew he was running out of chances. If he got sent down a third year in a row it might just be the kiss of death.

Huggins sent Wilcy Moore to the rescue again. Cy earned some new respect from his manager when he shut Washington down and the Yankees scored another two in the eighth to give Moore his second win.

o o o

On Wednesday, May 4 the Yankees scored three runs in the first inning and Dutch Ruether, who had won all three of his starts thanks to huge run production from his teammates, was feeling pretty confident about running his record to 4-0. He faced seven batters and the Senators rocked him for six hits and six runs, all earned. Bob Shawkey and Myles Thomas held Washington off from there on, but the Yankees couldn't rebound against Sloppy Thurston. Herb Pennock resisted the temptation to tease Ruether after the pounding.

o o o

In the get-away day game on Thursday the Yankee bats weren't the story. It was their porous gloves. They matched their six hits with six errors, one by the infield, two by the outfield, and three by the battery. Hod Lisenbee painted the black all afternoon. No New Yorker reached second base after the first inning. Meusel struck out his first three times up, Pat Collins his last three. Hod chuckled his way to a 6-1 win, his third straight. For the series Ruth had four hits in sixteen trips. All singles. He'd had high hopes of hitting fifty home runs for the first time in five years and maybe even breaking his record. That didn't seem very likely now.

The Yankees had a rare day off on their way from Washington to Chicago for the start of their first western swing of the season. They played an

Babe Ruth

exhibition game in Fort Wayne, Indiana against the Lincoln Lifes, a team sponsored by the local insurance company. Ruth was one of the only regulars to play the whole game. The score was tied in the ninth and the last thing anybody wanted was extra innings. Cedric Durst grounded out and Benny Bengough popped out to short.

"That's two down," groaned Combs from the end of the bench.

"Let's hope Jidge can do something," said Koenig as Ruth grabbed a bat.

"We're gonna miss our train if this game doesn't end soon," said Huggins.

"Why didn't ya say so, Hug?" asked Ruth.

He called for quiet and then announced to the crowd that he was going to end the game. He hit the first pitch high over the right field fence and across Clinton Street. It was a happy train ride to Chicago on the Sunrise Special. Ma Gehrig had sent a big batch of fried chicken for her darling son to share with his playmates.

Koenig and Lazzeri sat together as usual, doing their best to gnaw every scrap of chicken off the bones.

"Say what you will about Ma Gehrig hanging on to her precious son and Lou being such a momma's boy," said Mark, "but, damn, the woman sure can cook."

"You can say that again," said Tony. "I wonder if she'll still be cooking for him when he's forty."

"Wouldn't surprise me in the least. Remember what I told you about trying to introduce him to some girls."

"Like my father always said, 'Si può portare un cavallo all'acqua ma non puoi farlo bere.'"

"Really? Is that what Papa Lazzeri says?"

"Ya, it means you can lead a horse to water but you can't make him swim," Tony explained.

"That would be Lou when it comes to the fairer sex," said Mark. "Course you gotta spend some jack if you wanna date a gal. Lou wouldn't be real keen to do that."

"So he just sat there the whole time?" asked Tony as he grabbed another chicken leg.

"Ya, Googles and I arranged for these three real pretty girls to meet us at a soda fountain. He showed up in a nice suit with his hair all combed and we introduced him to the girls. We told him he could go after whichever one he wanted. He hardly even looked at them. One of 'em was this sexy brunette who took a real shine to Lou. So we moved her over so she was sitting right beside him. She asked him what he did with the Yankees. He said, 'I play first base'. She asked him if he liked music and he said 'A little'. Then she asked him what he liked to read and he said 'Comics.'"

"Talked the poor girl's ear off did he?" Tony chuckled. "Such a charmer."

"You suppose he's nervous about what a girl's gonna think if she ever sees him naked?" asked Mark.

"Could be."

"I mean he's got those blue eyes and big shoulders and a normal-sized pecker, but between those two tree trunks he's got for legs the poor thing looks like a straw."

o o o

At a staggering cost of seventy million dollars, Chicago's Union Station had been completely rebuilt. After several delays caused by the Great War, it had finally reopened in the spring of '25. It was being hailed as a stupendous achievement in railroad facility design. Its ornate Beaux-Arts waiting area, dubbed the Great Hall, had a vaulted skylight, statuary and connecting lobbies, grand staircases, and enormous balconies. A wide concourse led out to and along the river. The Babe took one of the staircases down to the specially-designed taxi shelter built to protect travelers from the elements and hopped into a yellow cab.

"Hi, ya, Babe, good to see you," said the balding driver. He reeked of garlic. "Hey, that big Gehrig kid's really poundin' the shit outta the ball, ain't he? You may have a tough time winning the home run crown with him around."

"We'll see about that," grunted Ruth.

"Where'll it be? You headin' to a speak?"

Babe Ruth

"Not tonight. I'm goin' to the House of All Nations on Dearborn Ave. I'm in the mood for a little ... female companionship."

o o o

"It's been a while, Babe," said the muscle-bound bouncer who tended the front door. "Go on in. It's kinda quiet, even for a Thursday night."

"Maybe everybody's decided to behave themselves," Ruth suggested.

"Or they spent all their dough on hooch and they ain't got any left for hoochy coochy," chuckled the bouncer.

The Babe entered through the walnut-paneled drawing room with brocaded draperies and damask upholstered divans. Paintings of Lady Godiva, Cleopatra, Marie Antoinette, and Catherine the Great hung on the richly-papered walls and a stringed orchestra played softly in the salon. The club's food was prepared by a cordon bleu chef and in this high end bordello there was no wriggling of skinny, gaunt-faced girls in teddies, gingham baby rompers, or see-through shifts displaying their wares.

The House of All Nations girls were chosen for their beauty, good health, and freedom from drug addiction. Their speech and manners were ladylike and they all mastered in sexual artistry. A mahogany staircase led to the Copper Room, the Turkish Room, where the customer reclined on hassocks and silver bolsters, and the Chinese, Egyptian, and Japanese Rooms, which were heady with the fragrance of incense. Each of the parlors had a gold spittoon and a fountain that sprayed perfume mist.

After eating a huge roast beef dinner and sipping a dark amber cognac the Babe headed upstairs. He decided to start with the Japanese Room. A geisha girl awaited him. She had blossoms in her hair, powder white skin, bright red lips, and large red dots on her cheeks.

She set down her fan and served Ruth sake and then ran her fingers through his hair. Then she felt his biceps and ran her hand along his thigh. "You very big man. You give Maiko much pleasure tonight, yes?" The Babe tried his best.

He visited the Turkish room next. The girl inside was Greek. She had long, jet black hair, and perfect white teeth. She was a belly dancer and she was good at it. She wore a turquoise, nearly see-through costume. She had small breasts but beautifully shaped hips and smooth thighs. When they were done Ruth took a break. He smoked a cigar and downed a glass of smooth bourbon.

He didn't know what to expect in the Copper Room. When he went in he was abruptly ordered to "Sit down!" by a schoolteacher. She wore glasses and had her hair tied in a bun, but she was beautiful. She had on a high neck silk blouse and a tight-fitting skirt that had a slit that ran all the way up to her thighs. She held a ruler in her hand and she ran her fingers slowly up and down it.

"I don't care what she costs," the Babe thought to himself.

The teacher took the pin out of her hair and long brown curls cascaded out. She slowly unbuttoned her blouse and ordered Ruth to do several things to her, each one sexier than the last, including spanking of course.

"Naughty boy, bad boy," she told him.

He was bad three more times before he left.

Babe Ruth
& the 1927 YANKEES have
the BEST SUMMER EVER

9.

HANGIN' OUT WITH AL

"What's so unusual about an aquarium in the living room?"

The Yankees would be out of town for a while. Esther Pennock invited Dorothy and Tony Lazzeri's wife Maye over for coffee at the Grand Concourse apartment in the Bronx that Herb had rented for forty dollars a month. Esther, Herb's wife of twelve years, was tall with curly, dark brown hair and delicate features and she was as smart as a whip. Dorothy wore an ankle-length grey skirt and a long-sleeved white cotton blouse that was inevitably snug in the chest.

In the next room Herb and Esther's pig-tailed, freckle-faced, seven-year-old daughter Jane was taking care of her little brother Joe, a cute and precocious two-year-old. She was helping him assemble the new train set his daddy had bought him. Herb had paid a lot for it and Esther thought he'd really gotten it for himself. She didn't mind, Herb had just bought her a new vacuum sweeper. And, when she'd dragged him to see *The Sheik* a few months ago he'd sat through the whole picture without rolling his eyes at Valentino even once.

Dorothy asked Esther if Herb had bought her a refrigerator yet.

"Yes and I love it. It keeps everything so cold, even on the hottest days. I felt bad having to tell the ice man we wouldn't need him anymore though. He was such a dear fellow. He knew we were wrapping newspaper around the ice so it wouldn't melt as fast but he never said a thing."

"I felt bad when we got rid of our ice box too," said Maye. Her auburn hair was pinned up in a sleek French twist and she wore a grey chiffon dress. "Then I found out our ice man was doing a lot better for himself now delivering stuff people put ice into."

Dorothy snickered. She looked at the windows. "I love your new curtains."

"Thanks, Dorothy. I made them myself, on my new Singer sewing machine."

"I wonder how much longer women will be making their own curtains?" asked Maye. "You look at the way the young girls are dressing and you wouldn't think they ever intend on settling down with one man and making a home for him."

"I'll tell you one thing," said Esther. "Some of them are positively *obsessed* with showing off their legs."

"And their bobbed hair looks so ridiculous," snorted Maye. She took off her $1.95 Lido hat and pushed her fingers through her own sandy waves. "Did you know that Macy's won't hire girls with bobbed hair?"

"Good for them," said Dorothy. "And the hussies smoke in front of men and get them to light their cigarettes and talk about how many men they've kissed. Really! Why don't they just hold up signs that say I'm easy?"

"Where did you and Waite meet?" asked Esther.

"At a costume ball," said Dorothy. "I was there as Marie Antoinette and I was feeling miserable because no one had cut in on me and any of my partners the whole night."

"You poor thing!" teased Esther. "I'm surprised though. With the low-cut bodices the women of her day wore you should have been the belle of the ball with *your* big bosoms. As Marie Antoinette you must have had enough décolletage for the whole French court."

Dorothy ignored her and went on. "Then Waite arrived dressed as Robin Hood. He was so tall and he looked so athletic in his green tights, he was enough to turn any girl's head. As soon as he saw me he cut in on the man I was dancing with. He told me I was probably a lot prettier than the real Marie Antoinette and we danced the rest of the night."

Dorothy got a faraway look in her eye and then realized that she'd stopped talking. She felt the tips of her ears begin to warm. Then she blushed and pretended to cough. "What about you and Herb, Esther? Where did you two meet?"

"We went to high school together. Well, not *together*. Herb was a senior and I was a junior. My parents knew what a clever boy he was. They asked him to tutor me in mathematics."

"And did he tutor you in anything else?" snickered Maye.

"A gentleman never tells, nor should a lady," Esther answered coyly. "But I will say that things got a lot more interesting when he taught me about ratios by taking my measurements."

"Your parents were *right*," said Maye.

"What do you mean?"

"He was very clever."

"Esther," said Maye. "You know how Herb works so slowly when he's pitching. Does he do *everything* that slow?"

"Never you mind," said Esther. "What about you and Tony, Maye?"

"We lived a few blocks apart in the Cow Hollow district of San Francisco," Maye explained. "One day I was riding the bus and a man told me I had a great shape. He stared right down my shirt and then he went to grab my behind."

"The rotten swine!" Dorothy exclaimed.

"Tony was standing nearby and before the creep reached my bottom Tony dropped him to the floor with one punch. He dragged the louse the whole length of the bus and threw him down in front of the door."

"And when the bus reached the next stop?" asked Esther.

"Tony tossed him to the curb like the morning trash."

"A bit rough, mais très galant," said Esther.

"You know there's only one problem with our husbands not fooling around on us when they're on these long road trips," said Dorothy.

"I know just what you're going to say," said Esther. "They're absolutely ravenous when they get home."

"That's for sure," said Maye. "The last time Tony got home from four weeks on the road we went at it like rabbits and I could hardly walk for a week."

Babe Ruth

Esther giggled. "Oh, but what a *terrible* hostess I'm being. What would you girls like to drink?"

"Coffee, I suppose, it's a bit early for gin," said Dorothy.

"Speaking of gin, you'll never guess what Mrs. Stevens, the woman next door, has in her living room," said Esther.

"What?" asked Maye.

"An aquarium," said Esther.

"What's so unusual about an aquarium in the living room?" asked Maye.

"It's filled with gin," said Esther.

"It's not!" said Maye. "You're making that up."

"It is so. When you ask for a drink she just ladles out a cup and hands it to you. Her husband makes it in the bathtub. It's pretty dreadful, but if you add enough tonic water it's not too bad."

"More and more people are adding things to their liquor these days," said Esther. "Ginger ale, soda water, tonic, branch water, Coca-Cola."

"Can you blame them?" asked Maye. "Some of the stuff the bootleggers try to pass off as alcohol would peel the paint off a battleship."

Esther continued. "Mrs. Stevens throws a mean party and she always sends out clever invitations. Bring your corkscrew. Wear a bib in case you spill something. Arrive thirsty, or bring a whistle to wet. Her speciality's giggle juice. It's gin mixed with orange and sugar. And there's always homemade whiskey cut with Coca-Cola for the men. She walks around saying things are divine, or mad, or the cat's pyjamas, and asking people if they're embalmed yet."

"Well I say we grab some ladles and head over to Mrs. Stevens' place," said Esther.

o o o

Almost forty thousand rooters swarmed into Comiskey Park to see the Yankees and Chisox on Saturday. One of the dignitaries on hand was Cardinal Joseph O'Donnell. Ruth was the first player to greet him. He knelt and kissed the ring on the cardinal's right hand. Benny Bengough and Tony Lazzeri followed suit.

The surprising White Sox were only a game behind New York. They sent their ace Ted Lyons to the hill and Miller Huggins countered with undefeated Herb Pennock.

Thousands of heads turned toward the box seats above the White Sox dugout just as play was getting under way. A large man in an apple green suit, spats, and a Panama hat was leading a boy to seats in the third row.

"Who's everybody lookin' at?" drawled Wilcy Moore.

"It's Capone," answered Dutch Ruether. "His son's a big Yankee fan."

"I thought Capone was a lot older. He doesn't look much older than thirty-five, maybe forty tops," said Pat Collins.

"He's only twenty-eight," Ruether told them.

"Only twenty-eight? Done pretty good for hisself," said Moore.

"Look at all the big wigs goin' over to greet him," said Dutch. "Capone's almost as popular as the Babe. That guy shaking his hand's the mayor, Big Bill Thompson. He's as crooked as a dog's hind leg. When they ask him if he's wet or dry he says he's as wet as the Atlantic Ocean."

"Did you hear about Capone's car?" asked Collins.

"His custom-built V-8 Cadillac?" asked Ruether.

"Ya, the thing's steel-plated with bullet-proof windows. It's got a hidden machine gun compartment and the back window drops down so you can shoot out of it," Collins explained. "The thing's got a police siren and an exhaust system that can spray out a smoke screen. It set Al back twenty grand but he raked in around sixty million last year so I guess he can afford it."

"How'd he get those nasty scars on his cheek?"

"Doherty the reporter knows Capone pretty well," said Dutch. "He told me Al was a bouncer in a Coney Island dance hall when he was seventeen or eighteen and he told some dame she had a nice ass. The girl's brother didn't like it and a big brawl broke out. The brother slashed Capone three times with a broken beer bottle."

"I hear he's real self-conscious about them, tries to hide them with talcum powder," said Collins. "Nobody ever dares to call him Scarface like the press does."

"What do his friends call him?" asked Moore.

"King Alphonse or Big Fella, or Snorky," answered Ruether.

"Snorky?" asked Dutch.

"It's slang for classy, elegant. The guy's quite a dresser, always looks real sharp."

"I can see his ring from here it's so damn big," said Moore.

"Eleven carat blue diamond. It matches his cufflinks and tie pin," said Ruether. "He and Machine Gun Kelly love golf. They play for five hundred bucks a hole. His business card reads Al Brown, Second-hand furniture dealer."

"Good money in used furniture," offered Collins.

"Hey! Get your heads in the game," Miller Huggins yelled at them.

"Sorry Hug," said Ruether.

"Ya, sorry Skip," said Moore as he sauntered out to his home away from home in the bullpen.

o o o

The game was still close in the eighth. Ted Lyons had held Hug's men to just two runs. Herb Pennock hadn't allowed Chicago any. In the ninth Gehrig blew things wide open and started the big crowd heading for the exits when he wacked a grand slam into the pavilion. Pennock wound up with a five-hit, 8-0 shutout.

The Babe bought the evening edition of the *Chicago Tribune* from a newsstand as he and Shawkey and Meusel walked to the Pullman Building. Ruth had finally forgiven the *Trib* for not going to bat for him when he was fined and suspended for barn-storming in '21.

He'd just received a check for $2,500 from Christy Walsh for an endorsement. He couldn't remember ever saying anything good or bad about the Murphy-Rich Company's soap. He usually went with Ruether, Pipgras, and Gehrig to a German restaurant on Wells Street between Madison and Washington that had terrific Wiener schnitzel and Koenigsherger klops. But this time he decided to use some of his windfall to treat Shawkey and Meusel to a meal at The Tip Top on the top floor of the Pullman Building.

The Tip Top had several rooms that diners could choose from, the Colonial Room, the Nursery, the Flemish room, Charles Dickens' Corner, and the French Room. But the Babe liked the Whist Room. Its walls were decorated with gigantic playing cards and it was lit by lanterns with symbols of hearts, spades, clubs, and diamonds. After a careful examination of the menu he ordered.

"Stuffed artichokes, Lobster Cardinal, quail stuffed with firejack cheese, Columbia River salmon with mayonnaise, pickled lamb tongues, and a double helping of breaded veal cutlets," he told the deferential young waiter before tucking his linen napkin into his shirtfront.

What to do after dinner in Chicago was more of a challenge than it used to be. Rector's, Voegelsangs, Stillson's, and Mangler's were all closed up now, victims of the Eighteenth Amendment. Ruth had bought the newspaper to find a show to go see. Not a moving picture show, some live entertainment.

Beneath ads for lovely printed chiffon frocks and Coty's toilet water he found notices of several productions. Shawkey and Meusel poured whiskey from their flasks into their coffee cups and listened as between puffs on his cigar the Babe read out the choices.

"We got Ralph Chapman and his orchestra at the Hotel La Salle's Roof Garden, Sophie Tucker in Gay Paree, a show for the whole family at the Majestic – fuck that – Walter McNally, the Irish baritone at the New Orpheus, and ... wait. This is more like it, a mammoth production of jazzy tunes and funny skits at the Rialto."

"You interested in the jazzy tunes or the funny skits, Jidge?" asked Shawkey as he eyed a society gal at a nearby table.

"Neither," answered Ruth. "They've also got a burlesque show with gorgeous girls from Joyland."

"That's more our style. What time's it start?"

o o o

The Babe had their cab driver stop at a cigar store on their way to the Rialto, and then at a dilapidated house on a dimly-lit street. A stocky man with a beefy neck who was already in his pyjamas came to the door and led

Babe Ruth

Ruth around the back to his garage. A minute later the Babe came out with two paper bags full of bottles.

"Fill up your flasks, boys," he instructed when he got back into the taxi.

They weren't sure the show merited the 'mammoth' descriptor but the music was good and the skits were hilarious. What impressed them the most were the babes from Joyland.

"Wherever Joyland is the men must be real fuckin' happy," whispered Shawkey.

Ruth took a shine to two long-legged beauties in the chorus. They winked at him throughout the last dance number and came over to introduce themselves when they were done.

"I'm Beatrice," said the taller girl, a brunette with a beauty mark beside her nose. She indicated her friend, a willowy blonde with chocolate brown eyes, "And this is Fanny. We're from Peoria."

"Not Joyland?" asked Shawkey.

Fanny looked puzzled. "What? Oh, I get it. That's funny. Ya, we're from Joyland."

o o o

An hour later Ruth dropped Shawkey and Meusel off at the hotel and headed back out on the town with the chorus girls. When the Babe got back to the hotel at about 4:30 a.m. there was no one in the lobby. A lone clerk stood at the front desk. He looked up and grinned when he saw it was the Babe coming in at his usual time.

Ruth strode to the elevator whistling a tune from the show at the Rialto. A young boy in grey livery with thin red piping and brass buttons sat on a stool inside earnestly chewing a fingernail. He pulled his finger out of his mouth and jumped up when he saw who it was that needed a ride. He smiled as he noticed a trace of lipstick on the Babe's thick neck.

"Hello, Mister Ruth. Good to see you again. You appear to be in a fine mood. Did you have a good evening?"

"Just fine, sonny. Good food, smooth whiskey, and sexy women. Now I've gotta get some shut-eye. If I'm not at the park by ten Hug'll wet his knickers."

The boy closed the gate and pulled the lever. The elevator grunted, jerked, and began its climb up. They both watched the large dial as the arrow crawled from left to right, one to ten. When the floor of the elevator car was even with the tenth floor carpet the young operator opened the gate and the Babe stepped off.

"What's the biggest tip you ever got, keed?" he asked, pulling his billfold out of his pocket.

"A hundred dollars," said the boy.

"A hundred dollars! Really? That's a helluva tip! Well, here's two hundred."

The boy stared at the two one hundred dollar bills.

"Thanks, Babe! I mean, Mister Ruth."

"Glad to." The Babe started walking down the hall toward his room but stopped and turned back toward the boy. "Say, who's the fool that gave you a hundred bucks?"

"You did. Last night."

○ ○ ○

Joe Dugan and the inseparable Tony Lazzeri and Mark Koenig went out to eat after the blowout. Tony was a symphony in grey, from his snappy fedora to his grey-top shoes. Mark was a riot in a light brown hat, a salmon-colored suit, a tan shirt, a salmon tie with blue spots, and light brown shoes.

They walked past the Wrigley Building and then the Drake Hotel, outside of which two well-dressed but apparently quite available women eyed them up and down. They tipped their hats and carried on to the Green Mill Cocktail Lounge on Broadway Street. They'd heard that it was the hottest speak in town. It sat between a funeral home and a suspicious-looking dry cleaners.

A clutch of flappers crowded around the entrance, apparently hoping someone would invite them in. They clearly didn't know the password. Dugan knocked crisply on the door three times. A slit opened and an eye gruffly demanded, "Who is it?"

Joe had learned the password from the hotel concierge. "Wobbly knees," he said.

Babe Ruth

The slit disappeared and the door opened.

Inside, young men in tuxedos sipped amber drinks at the mahogany bar and unsavoury older ones in pin-striped suits and crumpled fedoras sat in plush green booths puffing on cigars. The thick cloud of smoke was pierced by beams from the stage and the sparkles of the sequined dresses of skinny, bob-haired flappers pretty enough to adorn the covers of fashion magazines.

They were variations on a theme - cigarettes dangling between pouty red lips, peacock feathers shooting out of silver headdresses, strand upon strand of multi-colored pearls, and boas wrapped around inviting bare shoulders. Their lithe bodies swiveled and swirled with abandon as a group of black musicians played *Doin' the Racoon* and the flappers madly danced the Charleston. Two particularly captivating ones stood at the bar. One ordered a Buck Fizz and the other asked for a dirty martini.

While they waited for their drinks to arrive Joe, Mark, and Tony talked in hushed tones about Chicago's gang warfare and about the way Hymie Weiss and Paddy Murray and three other man had been killed the day after the World Series ended in a hail of machine-gun fire in front of a cathedral.

"Pushed poor old Pete Alexander and his heroics against us right off the front pages," said Dugan.

"Which was lucky for me," said Lazzeri.

"It was the same spot that other North Side boss got gunned down," said Joe. "Not too hard to figure who was responsible."

"Speaking of which, I hear this is Capone's favourite hangout," said Koenig.

"I wonder if he'll come to another game," said Dugan. "Everybody makes such a big fuss over him. The poor guy can hardly watch for people wantin' to shake his hand or introduce their wife and kids to him."

A beautiful blonde cigarette girl in a short red and black dress and a matching pillbox cap came to the table.

"Cigars, cigarettes, cigarillos, or anything else your heart desires?" she asked coyly, looking straight into Mark's blue eyes.

"Sorry, honey, our boss doesn't like us to smoke," said Mark.

"You can't sin *at all?*" she teased.

"Maybe the occasional glass of joy juice is all," said Dugan.

She winked at Koenig. "Well, if you think of anything just whistle."

Mark looked her up and down, "I'll bet you get whistled at a lot."

"I get off at two, I live just up the street," she whispered in his ear.

"What was that all about?" asked Tony.

"Friendly gal. I might have a date later," said Mark.

The girl blew Mark an air kiss as she disappeared into the back to replenish her tray.

o   o   o

When a gaunt waiter with slicked back hair brought their drinks Dugan asked him if Capone had been in lately.

"He was here last night. Had two dames with him, real firm peaches. That's his booth over there," he said, pointing to one that had a RESERVED card on it. "I hadda be careful not to spill their drinks I was so busy gawking at 'em."

"Not a real smart move to spill drinks on Capone and his friends," said Joe.

"Al was telling the girls you guys were in town and he might go see yas. The broads didn't seem too interested."

o   o   o

A few minutes later the club manager came over to the three Yankees' table. He was about forty and had a bulbous nose and bags under his sunken eyes. His voice was low and scratchy.

"I heard you boys was askin' about Capone," he said.

"We didn't mean anything," said Lazzeri.

"We were just wondering if he'd been in. We heard he likes this place," Dugan explained.

"Al's a big baseball fan. I guess you knew that," said the manager. "His buddy Jack McGurn's one a da owners a this joint."

Babe Ruth

"Capone, I mean Al, was at our game today," said Dugan. "With his kid."

"You boys wanna meet him?"

"Jack McGurn?" asked Tony.

"No. Al. Do yas wanna meet him?"

"Sure, when's he comin' in?" asked Joe.

"Lemme call him," said the manager. "I'll be right back."

The three players stared at each other.

"He's gonna call Capone?" asked Dugan.

"That's what the man said."

o o o

Five minutes later the manager came back to their table.

"I talked to Al. I told him you guys were here. He doesn't feel like going out tonight."

"Oh well, that's ..." Lazzeri started to say.

"He wants you to come over to his place."

"Pa, Pa, Pardon?" Mark stammered.

"Al's sendin' a car for yas. Be here in ten minutes."

"Oh. That'll be great," said Joe, thinking that you don't turn down an invitation from Al Capone.

o o o

Sure enough, ten minutes later a limousine pulled up in front of the Green Mill. The players climbed in. A man who wore a pin-striped suit that barely concealed his bulging muscles sat beside the driver in the front seat. The limo took them to the Lexington Hotel at the corner of Michigan Avenue and 22nd Street. The body builder led the players through the huge lobby filled with leather chairs.

Several men were reading newspapers and smoking cigars. Other men in shirtsleeves were drinking and having a tournament on an artificial putting green. One of them sank a long putt. "That'll be twenty each, suckers," he crowed.

The Yankees had stayed in some pretty nice hotels but the three marvelled at the ornate architecture. Their burly guide led them to the elevator and grunted to the operator, "They're goin' ta George Phillips' room, fifth floor."

When they got off the elevator another burly man patted them down. "They're clean," he told the other henchman. "Go ahead, Al's waitin' for yas."

Capone sat behind a huge mahogany desk. He had a flat nose, a bull neck, and a receding hairline. The players noted his monogrammed shirt and diamond cufflinks.

On a table behind him sat two bowls of fresh yellow roses. Between them was a Tommy gun. A log burned in the huge fireplace. On either side of it were portraits of George Washington, Abraham Lincoln, Mayor "Big Bill" Thompson, and two movie stars, Fatty Arbuckle and "the Vamp", Theda Bara. Enormous bay windows offered a spectacular view of downtown and the lake beyond. Along one wall lay piles of padlocked canvas bags.

"You can bet that's cash," whispered Lazzeri.

"Good ta see yas, gents," said Capone. "You guys are off to a helluva start. Better not think about beatin' my White Sox though. Might not be healthy for yas."

As he laughed at his joke Tony tried hard not to stare at Capone's scars.

"Not as good a year as you from what I hear, Al," said Dugan.

"Ya. Not that *fuckin'* good," Capone roared. "Nobody's havin' as good a year as me. And I didn't even finish grade school."

"What happened, Al?" asked Joe. "You have to go to work?"

"Nah. Nuthin' like that. I got kicked out for sluggin' my teacher, but she hit me first."

"So business is good?" asked Tony, anxious to change the subject.

"I come a long way since I was swillin' drinks at the Four Deuces or out front with my collar turned up whisperin' ta guys, 'Hey, we got some nice-looking girls inside.' But now I got the whole fuckin' police force on my payroll."

Babe Ruth

"D'you hear what a Treasury Department captain in New York did last week, Al?" asked Lazzeri.

"No. What?"

"He had all his agents line up. He told them to stick out their arms. Then he said, 'Every one of you sons of bitches with a diamond ring is fired.'"

Capone laughed. "Good for him. But I'll bet the jerk's got an angle of his own. When it comes down to cases, nobody's legitimate. It's a funny thing, boys, when I go to a whole lotta trouble and expense to provide for the needs of my clients they call it bootlegging. But when the swells serve the booze I get 'em on shiny trays in their fancy houses on Lakeshore Avenue, it's called hospitality. And now I hear the Supreme Court's sayin' bootleggers gotta pay income tax. It'll be a cold day in hell when I do that. And as for the gamblin' houses they complain about, I never saw anybody point a gun at a guy and tell him to go in. Hey, you fellas wanna hear somethin' funny? My mother called me the other night and said she had some news about my brother James. He's moved to some Godforsaken place in Nebraska and changed his name to … well, I better not tell you that. Anyway, you'll never guess what he's doin' there."

"Is he a priest?" Tony asked.

Capone chuckled. "No. Worse. He's a fuckin' fed. Can ya imagine that? Bustin' up stills in Pigshit, Nebraska when he could be makin' a good livin' here runnin' one a my casinos."

A swarthy-looking man with a large lump under his jacket came in and interrupted their conversation.

"Scuse me, boss, but you said I should let you know as soon as I took care of that business matter we discussed."

"Pardon me for a second, boys," Capone said to the players.

"No problem, Al," said Tony.

"So what's the news?" Capone asked his henchman.

"I'm happy to report that the individual that we discussed, your former business associate, has been taken for a ride and will not trouble you further."

"I'm happy ta hear it," said Capone. "Why don't you pick out one of the expensive whores for yourself tonight? You earned it."

"Thanks, boss," said the hood. "Anything else?"

"Ya there is. Ya know those people who bin puttin' up a fuss about a whorehouse openin' up on their street?"

"Ya, boss."

"Tell 'em I'll get 'em a new roof or a new furnace, or even pay their mortgage. And, of course, I'm in the furniture business so they can have some a that too," he chuckled.

"Sure thing, boss."

"All right, gents, where were we?" asked Capone.

"Is it true you have a shooting gallery here in the hotel, Al?" asked Koenig.

"We sure do. Gotta keep in practice for hunting season," he said with a wink.

"And tunnels and secret passages and stairways?" asked Lazzeri.

"You just never know when uninvited guests might show up that you really don't wanna see just then," Capone explained.

"Did you really say you can get more with a kind word and a gun than you can with a kind word?" asked Mark.

"Nah. Wish I had though. Pretty fuckin' clever. And true most a the time. You boys want somethin' to drink? I usually drink Templeton's myself but I got some great whiskey that fell off a boat from Canada the other night." He got up and went to the huge bar in the corner of the room. He was right. It was good stuff.

"Swell guy," Lazzeri said as their cab pulled away from the Lexington an hour later.

"If you're on his good side," said Mark.

"That's exactly where I'm planning to stay," declared Tony. "I don't want to end up six feet under, wrapped in a Chicago pine overcoat."

Babe Ruth
& the 1927 YANKEES have
the BEST SUMMER EVER

10.

IN THE HOUSE OF THE GOOD SHEPHERD

"Pitchin' to you guys is like juggling a case of nitro glycerine."

On Sunday the Yankees scored runs in every other inning and Waite Hoyt coasted to a nine-hit, 9-0 shutout in front of fifty-two thousand. Bob Meusel did most of the damage, scoring three runs and knocking in three others. The game took two hours and six minutes, which made Fred, the stats man Lieb, happy. He'd just written a piece for the *Telegram* about how some games were lasting as much as two and a half hours.

o o o

Red Faber held New York to one run over ten innings in the wrap up game on Monday the 9th. In the bottom of the frame catcher Harry McCurdy singled and, when Faber attempted to sacrifice him into scoring position, Wilcy Moore adeptly fielded the bunt and threw to where he thought first base was. Except it wasn't. Later Tony Lazzeri made his first error in twenty-three games and Chicago salvaged the final match of the series 2-1.

o o o

After the game the Yankees took the Wabash Blue Bird to St. Louis. As the train rolled over the tracks that night and the wheels clicked away beneath him Urban Shocker, who as usual couldn't sleep, tiptoed between the berths. He weaved a little, having drunk a fifth of Old Kentucky he'd hidden in his grip.

The car was dark save for the corridor lights at each end. He passed berth 5 and recognized the hissing noises Benny Bengough made because he always slept on his back. He passed lower *11* and heard the familiar guttural sounds the Babe made. As usual the occupant of lower 3 made no sound. Gehrig was probably dreaming of washing dishes with his mom.

Babe Ruth

"That Lazzeri, what a joker," Shocker chuckled when he passed berth *16* and saw that KISS had been printed on Herb Pennock's forehead and he had M and E on his cheeks.

o o o

Babe Ruth borrowed Charley O'Leary's stats book before the opening game at Sportsman's Park. He suspected the gap between him and Gehrig was sizable, but he was startled by just how huge it had grown. He had six home runs, eleven runs batted in, and a respectable - but hardly impressive - .314 batting average. Young Gehrig had seven home runs and thirty-five RBIs and *his* average was .404.

Combs walked and Koenig reached on an error to lead off the first inning. Milt Gaston, the Browns' starter, decided he couldn't afford to load the bases with Gehrig following the Babe and gave Ruth a pitch to hit. He dispatched it to the right field bleachers. That lifted his spirits a little.

George Pipgras couldn't hold the lead and when they trailed 7-5 after eight it looked as though the Yankees would lose to the lowly Browns. But in the top of the ninth Gehrig, with two out, two men on, and one run in, stroked a single that plated two runs and Hug's men took an 8-7 lead. The home team loaded the bases in the bottom of the ninth but with one out Wally "Spooks" Gerber bounced one to short, which Koenig shovelled to Lazzeri. He swept his foot across the bag and threw to Gehrig for a walk-off double play.

o o o

"Why don't you choke up on the bat and hit to left field more often?" one of the St. Louis writers asked Ruth after the game. "You could hit a ton of doubles. You'd probably bat .400 every year."

"I ain't doin' that!" the Babe retorted. "The fans'd rather see me hit one homer to right than three doubles to left. Hell, if I went for singles I could have a lifetime average around .600, but they don't pay out on singles. There's more jack in it for me in this home run racket. They pay me all that dough for them four-base knocks and I keep swingin' for the fences."

"Which park's the easiest for you?" asked another reporter.

Ruth paused. Then he belched so loud water fell from the shower spouts. Eddie Bennett hurried to get him some bicarbonate of soda.

"This park's a good one. So's Navin Field in Detroit, and League Park in Cleveland is too. Comiskey's even better since they extended the grandstand and I like Shibe. They're all good except the Stadium. Boy, how I used to sock 'em at the Polo Grounds. I cried when they took me outta that place."

"I just talked to Dan Howley, the Brown's skipper," the first reporter told Ruth. "He said you fellows hit too hard."

"That so?"

"Ya, Babe, he says the league oughta penalize you one strike every time you come to the plate - to give everybody else a chance. And the fellow you guys beat today, Milt Gaston…"

"He pitched a few games for us in '24," said Ruth. "Poor fella had a rough time out there today. I kinda felt bad hittin' that one off him."

"Well, he said he'd rather pitch a doubleheader against anybody else than one game against you guys. He's says a fellow doesn't get a minute of rest, that pitchin' to you guys is like juggling a case of nitro glycerine."

The Babe pulled off his jersey, undershirt, pants, white socks, blue wool stirrups, and sliding pads and headed to the showers. He thought back to when Howley had been one of the Red Sox coaches in '18. Harry Frazee had assigned Howley to room with the Babe and told Ed Barrow, then the Boston manager, he should keep an eye on the wild young phenom.

Barrow knew that the 24-year-old kid from the Baltimore orphanage was staying out late. One night he decided to find out just how late. He sat in the lobby and read two newspapers, then the *Baseball News*, the *Racing Form*, and six chapters of a novel. He finally went to bed at four. No sign of Ruth.

Barrow had no intention of spending another night in the hotel lobby. He gave the porter five dollars to wake him up when Ruth came in the next night. At 6 a.m. there was a knock on his door.

"Mister Ruth just got in, sir," whispered the porter.

Barrow put on his dressing gown and slippers. When he reached Ruth's door he saw light shining through the transom. When he knocked, the light went out. He knocked again and Howley came to the door. When Barrow

Babe Ruth

went in he saw Ruth lying in bed smoking a pipe. Howley went and hid in the bathroom.

"Why are you smoking a pipe?" asked Barrow.

"It helps me sleep," answered Ruth.

Barrow whipped back the covers and saw that Ruth was fully clothed. He was even wearing his shoes and socks.

"I want to see both of you at the park at ten sharp," he said loud enough that Howley could hear him from the bathroom.

When the Babe got to the park Barrow told him not to bother putting on his uniform. He was suspended.

That night on the train out of town the Babe told Barrow about his childhood and that he was living it up now because he'd been deprived of so many things at St. Mary's. "I just want to play ball, Ed. You know I give it everything I got whenever I'm on the field."

"I'll tell you what, George, when you come in at night slip a note under my door saying what time you got back to the hotel."

Ruth did as he was asked and Barrow chose to trust that he was always telling the truth. He never checked up on him again. Ruth played great and Barrow got some sleep.

Bill Carrigan, the Red Sox manager before Barrow took over, had never bothered to check on what time the Babe got back to the hotel. When a reporter questioned Carrigan about Ruth's conduct he said, "How can I complain about all the late nights when there are all those home runs in the afternoons?"

o o o

In the first inning the next day the Babe hit a ball 450 feet into the centerfield seats with Koenig aboard. Only 1,500 were on hand to see it. Herb Pennock, who told Dutch Ruether he was pretty sure he'd pitched in front of bigger crowds in high school, pitched his usual slow and methodical game, saving his arm and pitching to spots. He had the Browns hitting them on the ground the whole afternoon. Koenig gobbled up nine and Lazzeri fielded twelve others flawlessly. The Yankees won 4-2.

o o o

"Sad Sam" Jones, who was in his first season with the Browns, was the scheduled starter for the third game of the series. He had trouble getting into the park. A policeman stopped his roadster as he tried to drive into the parking lot. Jones rolled down his window. "I'm Sam Jones, officer."

"Sam who?" the policeman asked.

"Sam Jones, I'm a St. Louis pitcher."

"The Browns don't have any pitchers," cracked the cop.

Jones did better than most of the St. Louis hurlers had. He struck out Combs, Koenig, and Ruth to start the game but the Bronx Bombers scored two in the fourth and two in the fifth for a 4-3 win.

In the Friday the 13th game the Yankees prevailed again. Waite Hoyt gave up ten hits but only a lone run in a 3-1 win. Ruth raced and caught up to a line drive and made a spectacular bare-handed catch in the fifth, but he twisted an ankle in the ninth going after a shallow fly. He decided it was time for some healing.

"We're gonna be rained out again tomorrow. Mark my words," Dutch Ruether told Bob Meusel after the Saturday game had been called off.

"I imagine so. What are we gonna to do on a Saturday night in St. Louis?"

"Do you guys wanna come with me?" asked Benny Bengough.

"You heading to some jazz joints?" asked Dutch.

"I sure am. St. Louis is getting bigger in the jazz world than New Orleans. There's a load of places to hear great music."

"Do they serve booze?" asked Meusel.

"Should any guy who says he doesn't like flappers be locked up in Bellevue?" Benny asked sarcastically. "Of course they serve booze, they just don't call it that."

They had no intention of going to any place in the north end. Herb Pennock had read that Egan's Rats and the Hogan Gang had chalked up twenty-three murders in North St. Louis in the last two years. First they went to Tony Scarpelli's Plantation Club, which was modeled after the Cotton Club. While all of the entertainers were Negroes only white customers were admitted. The sign out front advertised *Friendliness and Merriment from dusk 'til dawn. 11, 1 and 3 a.m. floor shows.*

Then they went to Katy Red's club in East St. Louis where they heard the Chocolate Dandies. Their guitarist was Steady Roll Johnson. His brother Lonnie Johnson played guitar and sang *Cat You Been Messin' Around* and *Hot and Bothered.* They liked the music but the booze tasted awful, even when they added ginger ale. They headed to a place on Biddle Street, which Benny said was known as Deep Morgan. Charlie Creath played trumpet and Roosevelt Sykes pounded away on the piano. Mary Johnson sang *Delmar Blues.*

After their second beer Dutch elbowed Bob. "Benny's happier than a pig in mud."

"I'll bet he wishes he was up there with 'em," said Meusel.

Benny overheard. "You got that right. I'd give my eye teeth to play with them."

o o o

A little past midnight they headed down to the wharves on the Mississippi where the riverboats tied up and their bands played on the top decks. Fate Marable's band, the Jazz-a-Maniacs, had Barrelhouse Buck McFarland on piano, Pops Foster on string bass, and Baby Dodds on drums.

"The music here's pretty racy stuff," said Dutch after Little Alice Moore sang *Blue, Black, and Evil.*

"The later it gets the raunchier the songs'll be," Benny explained. "A lot of these performers sang or played in brothels before they had hit records and could play in decent joints."

Speckled Red Perryman, who was an albino, sang *Wilkins Street Romp* and Down on the Levee. He belted out,

> *I wants all yous women to fall in line*
> *And shake your shimmy like Ize shakin' mine*
> *You shake your shimmy and you shake it fast*
> *If you can't shake your shimmy, then shake your ass.*

Joe King Oliver's band came on next and their singer, Dixie Nolan, sang My Back to the Wall and Good Grindin' and then I Must Get Mine in Front.

"I'm gonna have to go to confession tomorrow after listening to this stuff," said Benny.

o o o

"The House of the Good Shepherd," the Babe told the cab driver after he'd showered, dressed, and waded through a throng of admirers after the game.

"You said you were in need of some healing. Are we goin' to church, Jidge?" asked Marshall Hunt. He'd decided to tag along with the Babe and he seriously doubted they were headed to a place of worship.

"Not exactly. Good for the body. Maybe not the soul."

Hunt had a feeling he knew what that might involve. "There liable to be any dames at this house of healing, George?"

"There just might be," Ruth told him. "Best steaks in the world, that's for sure."

"Oh. It's a restaurant then."

"Not exactly."

o o o

"The 32-ounce prime rib, rare," Ruth told the dark-skinned waiter. "With garlic and mushrooms, and potatoes on the side."

"And I'll …" Hunt started.

"And four pork chops smothered in onion gravy, with black-eyed peas on the side for an appetizer," Ruth added.

After dinner Hunt went to the ornately decorated sitting room and smoked one cigarette, then another, then several more. The Babe went upstairs to avail himself of the establishment's after dinner delicacies.

The first girl looked to be about eighteen. She had dark brown hair, watery blue eyes, and beautiful legs. She was dressed in a French maid outfit.

"Je m'appelle Angelique," she told Ruth as she pretended to dust the furniture in the elaborately furnished bedroom.

Babe Ruth

"Damn, you're really French," said the Babe as he took off his jacket and loosened his collar. "I love this place."

"I am from New Orleans. My ancestors were Acadian," she explained. "They were expelled from their homes by the English and many of them settled in Louisiana."

"Is that why they call their food cayjun?" asked Ruth.

"C'est vrai. I mean, it is true. You are very clever."

"Horny as a hoot owl is what I am. Now stop your dusting, girl. I got something here you can polish."

The second girl was a lithesome green-eyed cowgirl. She wore a ten-gallon hat, a red brassiere with fringe along the bottom, a black leather skirt, and high-heeled boots. She tossed a lasso around the Babe's shoulders, pulled him onto the bed, whooped "Yippie Yi Yo Kayah", and rode him hard for half an hour.

The third girl was little Bo Peep. Her butter-colored curls were held in place with a baby blue ribbon. She wore a frilly light blue and white skirt with white stockings. She had large red dots on her cheeks and she held a shepherd's staff. She smacked the Babe's ass with it and then stretched a rubber over his throbbing member.

The fourth girl had to be at least twenty-five. She had coal-black hair and was dressed as a pirate. She wore a tricorner hat, tall boots, leather arm bands, and a black leather corset that was laced tightly enough that it pushed her large breasts together and out the top. She brandished a sword and ordered the Babe to get down on his knees.

"Are you gonna shiver me timber?" asked the Babe.

"I'll do more than shiver it," she told him.

"The last one was on the house," Ruth grinned when he told Hunt he was finally ready to leave.

"Is four the most for you, Babe?" asked Hunt.

Ruth laughed. "Are you kiddin' me? Hell, I've been known to work my way through a whole stable of hookers and some of the brothels have a dozen girls."

"Gehrig ever been with a women?" Hunt asked as they stepped into a cab.

"Nah, I offered to get him laid a couple a times but he just turned red and said he wasn't interested. He'd probably faint if a dame touched him."

o o o

To avoid the crowds at Union Station the team met the Wabash they were taking to Detroit at the Brandon Avenue station in the suburbs. It was more of a crossing than a station. They were waiting there, sitting on their trunks when a delivery truck pulled up.

"Hey, keed, just in time," said Ruth as the driver got out and started unloading bags and boxes. Some were packed with ice. Clouds of steam wafted from a clothes basket.

The man smiled as the Babe handed him three twenty dollar bills.

"The usual, just like you ordered, Babe. Three gallons of home brew, five boxes of beer on ice, and thirty-five racks of baby back ribs."

When the Yankees got to Detroit Ruth cashed a pay check at the front desk of the Book Cadillac and booked four adjoining rooms. The players couldn't believe the place had thirteen elevators and their rooms had gold-leafed ceilings.

o o o

The weather was raw and miserable for the time of year and only four thousand die-hards showed up for the Monday game. Lu Blue, the Tigers' first baseman and leadoff hitter, did his job, reaching base four times, three of them on bases on balls. He and Jack Warner, who batted second, each scored a run. No other Tiger did. In the fourth Gehrig singled and Lazzeri hit a grounder to second. Charlie Gehringer scooped up the ball and tossed it to five-foot three, 138-pound Rabbit Jack Taverner, who was covering the bag. Knowing it was his job to break up the double play, Lou barrelled into Taverner. He went ass over tea kettle up into the air.

There were only two umpires working the game but the experienced Bill Dinneen was in perfect position to make the call. Gehrig had gone outside the baseline in order to collide with Taverner.

"Interference," Dinneen hollered, "the runner is out."

Gehrig dusted himself off and headed for the dugout.

Babe Ruth

After Taverner landed it took him a while to get his wind back. When he did, he let Lou know just how he felt about him.

"You're a fuckin' cheater, ya cocksucking Kraut!" he yelled as Gehrig walked away. Lou turned around and started toward Taverner but Lu Blue persuaded him to leave things as they were.

"He's just pissed cuz you knocked him over, Lou, he don't mean nuthin' by it."

Gehrig hesitated, shrugged his shoulders, and headed off.

Gehringer went over to see if Taverner was all right.

"I thought a goddamn truck had hit me!" Taverner told him.

Bob Meusel tested the arm of the Tigers' rookie catcher Mervin Shea by stealing second and then third after singling in the seventh. Then he caught pitcher Ken Holloway napping and stole home too. His feat made all the papers that afternoon. He may just have been in a hurry to get back to the comparative warmth of the dugout. Gehrig ended up with three hits including a homer in the eighth and Hug's crew beat the Tigers 6-2 in the nasty conditions. Gehrig was one of the only players to pass on Ruth's invitation to a party in his suite that night. He stayed in his room and wrote a letter to Ma Gehrig.

o   o   o

A group of girls came in just after nine o'clock. They were fond of ball players and they knew that Babe Ruth threw great parties. They looked the players up and down and whispered to one another. Most looked to be between eighteen and twenty-two, but some were older. Almost all of them were rail thin and each had short, bobbed hair, some peroxided, some hennaed. Though some were blondes and others were brunettes or redheads they all looked remarkably alike. Their eyebrows were plucked, their eyes were penciled with kohl, their eyelids beaded, their cheeks piquantly rouged, and their lips thickly glossed. Most had feather headbands, long strings of pearls around their necks, black stockings and high-heeled pumps. They wore long-waisted, fringed-beaded dresses that stopped at the knee and showed off their gorgeous legs.

"Get an eyeful a that one!" Dugan said to Ruether. He tilted his head in the direction of a girl with black-lined doe eyes, false lashes, and a thick fringe of bangs above rosy cheeks. She was wearing a sleeveless and nearly transparent dress that didn't even reach her knees.

They overheard a girl go up to her and say, "Abby, what were you thinking wearing a dress like that?"

Abby said, "This dress just happens to be the latest thing on the streets of Paris."

The other girl said, "Don't you mean the latest thing on the street *walkers* of Paris?"

The man working the phonograph turned up the volume. He'd been sure to bring along all the appropriate hit songs, *Everybody's Doin' It, I Want to be Bad, Makin' Whoopee, Let's Sow Some Wild Oats, Good Little, Bad Little You, No Wonder She's a Blushin'*, and of course *Let's Misbehave*.

Most of the younger girls ignored the food and headed straight for the magnums of champagne. The older-looking ones stuck to gin. Normally they'd have asked for lemon juice to go with it, but they knew the Babe always got the good stuff.

"Help yourselves. Plenty more where that came from," Ruth told them. "And these boys have worked up quite an appetite waitin' for ya."

Some of the women smoked cigarettes which the players still found an odd thing for women to do.

"Ladies don't smoke," Paschal whispered to Dugan.

"Seein' as the Babe invited these dames, I'm guessing they probably ain't ladies."

The younger girls kept their powder tins, pencils, brushes, rouge pots, and lipstick tubes in their vanity cases. The older ones carried makeup and contraceptives in theirs.

A brunette with long eyelashes hiked up her skirt and pulled a flask from her lavender garter. She carefully filled it with the expensive gin the Babe was serving.

"As I live and breathe, a girl's gotta be careful," she told a bleached blonde flapper beside her. "Them lousy Feds have dogs that sniff for flasks. Ya don't want some schnauzer stickin' his snout up yer skirt."

"How d'you burn your finger?"

"On my curling iron."

"Now Rachel has *her* hair shingled too," said the blonde.

"Every gal has. Are your stockings silk or rayon?"

"Silk of course." She looked at a raven-haired girl who was standing in front of a mirror adding another line of kohl along her eye lines. "Poor Daphne has an awful time flattening her big breasts."

"Are you sure she's really trying?"

"Maybe not. She won't wear a corset, but we all know men won't dance with a girl if she's wearing one."

"What's she doin' now?" asked the blonde.

"Beats me," said the brunette.

Daphne crossed the room and sidled up to Joe Dugan. She slid a cigarette out of a copper case and looked straight into his eyes.

"Be a doll and torch me, will ya?" she asked seductively.

"Sh … Sh … Sure," Joe answered, shoving the crab-cake hors d'oeuvre he'd been munching on into his pocket and fumbling for his matches.

"You wanna get a breath a fresh air together later?" she asked Joe. She inhaled deeply, well aware of the effect that would have on her chest and most likely on the ball player too.

Joe looked into Daphne's kohl-lined eyes and then down at her breasts. "Ya, that'd be swell."

"Or, swell*ing*," cooed Daphne, "if ya get my drift."

Most of the players drank beer, the hard drinkers drank whiskey. The Babe had lots of both. Some of the women held their liquor well, others not so much. One, who said her name was Susy, caught her high heels on the edge of the carpet and fell backwards onto the hardwood floor. It was so well-polished that when she landed on her rump she slid a couple of feet. When she came to a stop, apparently unhurt, Dugan bent over her, put one hand over his other palms down, thrust them wide apart, and yelled, "Safe!"

& THE 1927 YANKEES HAVE THE BEST SUMMER EVER

o o o

Around eleven o'clock Ruth climbed onto a table and yelled at the top of his lungs, "Listen girls, we're happy ta see ya enjoying the food and the booze, but this ain't no college pettin' party and we ain't no glee club. Any of yas that don't want to screw can clear out now."

A few girls snickered at their host's bluntness but almost none of them left.

o o o

As the Tigers took their infield practice the next day Gehrig stood in front of the Yankee dugout watching Taverner.

"He's looking at me like he's gonna bore a hole right through me," Taverner told Gehringer.

Taverner stayed out on the diamond as long as he could, hoping Gehrig would stop staring at him. Finally he had to come in and he hurried for the Detroit dugout. Gehrig marched toward him. Taverner looked around for somewhere to hide.

Lou stuck out his hand. Taverner gulped.

"I shouldn'ta done it, Rabbit. It wasn't right," said Lou.

Taverner was startled. "F.. F.. Forget all those names I called ya, Lou. I didn't mean 'em."

"I know that, Jack. Have a good game."

"What was that all about?" Gehringer asked Taverner when he got back to the dugout.

"Big lug came up and shook my hand like he was greetin' the president," said Taverner. "Whad'ya think a that?"

Fats Fothergill whaled a long smash to deep center to open the fifth, but Combs dashed back, stuck his glove up beyond his right shoulder and the Kentucky greyhound made one of his most dizzying catches of the season. Ruth slammed his ninth over the scoreboard in left center to lead off the eighth, one of fifteen Yankee hits in a 9-2 mauling of the Bengals. Dugan had none. His average slid to .157. Five weeks into the season "Jumping Joe" had just three RBIs and no home runs. If he hadn't been so slick at third base Mike Gazella would have had his job long ago.

Babe Ruth

○ ○ ○

On Wednesday, May 18th the Yankees boarded the Cleveland Mercury for a four-game series with the Tribe. When they arrived they checked into their rooms at the Hollenden House, the city's largest and most glamorous hotel. It was the first in the world to have electric lights in each room and several presidents had stayed there. The lobby featured paneled walls, redwood and mahogany fittings, and crystal chandeliers. It had a theater and a barbershop where business tycoons, entertainers, and politicians got shaved.

"The Colonel sure is puttin' us up in swell places," Ruether told Pennock on their way in. "Only problem is when you get back to your apartment you think you're living in a fuckin' hovel."

○ ○ ○

Garland Buckeye, a southpaw from Minnesota, got the start in the first game in Cleveland. He'd been 6-9 in '26 but he'd given up just over three runs a game and was getting lots of work in '27.

After the ump yelled, "Play," Buckeye struck out Combs and got Koenig to ground out to third. Knowing better than to give him anything near the plate he walked Ruth semi-intentionally. He planned to pitch Gehrig outside. Word had gotten around. Let the big kid hit a long one to left center. Better than giving him something inside he could jerk out of the park.

Gehrig drove Buckeye's first pitch to right center, the deepest part of the outfield.

"Go, Lou, go!" shouted Art Fletcher.

His arms flailing, Lou churned his thick legs like a locomotive's pistons all the way around the bases for an inside-the-park home run. The Babe helped out the ump by declaring Lou safe.

"Didn't I tell you that you can get around just fine on the lefties?" Huggins told him when Lou reached the dugout.

Apart from Gehrig's ninth homer, Buckeye pitched well in the opener, much better than Urban Shocker who allowed three runs in the first two innings. Huggins signalled for Wilcy Moore. He scratched his head, picked

& THE 1927 YANKEES HAVE THE BEST SUMMER EVER

up his glove, hitched his trousers, bit off a chew of black plug, and headed to the mound. He was lights out for the next seven innings.

The affair stood knotted at three in the top of the ninth when Dugan and Collins singled to put runners on the corners. The Indians were happy to see that Moore was due up.

"You gonna leave him in?" Charley O'Leary asked Huggins.

"The man can't hit, but he can bunt with the best of them," Hug answered.

With the skill of a master Wilcy laid down a beauty and then lumbered after it. He blocked the first baseman's view and Dugan crossed the plate with the winning run.

o o o

That night most of the Yankees went to the Show Boat room at the Hollenden House. They never went to the hotel's other night clubs. The Parisien and the Vogue Room were for stiffs. The stage of the Show Boat room was designed to look like the front of a large steam boat. It was mostly couples and, though the band was terrific, few of the players knew how to dance nor cared much to learn. They attracted a few stares.

"I'm pretty sure that's Jumpin' Joe Dugan," a man with a handlebar mustache told his wife, who clearly had no idea who Jumpin' Joe Dugan was and turned away to talk to the other woman at the table. Joe chuckled and poured some more whiskey from his flask into his mug.

A waiter came to the table with something in a fancy glass dish. "Someone ordered this and then had to leave. Would anyone care for a shrimp cocktail?"

Gehrig, who was sitting closest to the waiter, politely said, "No thanks, I don't drink."

Everyone burst out laughing.

"It's not booze, ya big dope," said Ben Paschal. "It's just shrimps."

Oh well, then. Sure," said Lou, taking the dish from the waiter and digging in.

"I thought German guys were usually smart," said Ben.

Babe Ruth

"Smarter than Polacks maybe," said Joe. "Oh, speakin' a which, I heard a doozy the other day. Three Polish guys go up to the Pearly Gates at the same time. Saint Peter says he doesn't see anything bad on their records but he needs to give them a test, a religion test. So he asks the first Polack what Easter's all about. The guy says that's the time when kids put on foolish costumes and go trick or treating."

Ben chuckled and took another swallow of his bourbon and branch water.

Joe took another drink himself and then continued, "Saint Peter says no, that's not it, that's not even close and asks the second one the same thing. The guy says at Easter a roly-poly guy in a red suit comes down the chimney and leaves presents for the kids. No, that's not it either says Saint Peter. Third guy. What's Easter? The third guy says, Well the Romans put Jesus on a cross and they crucified him. That's more like it says Saint Peter. Keep going. The guy continues. And his body was placed inside a cave on a Friday. *That's* it, says Saint Peter. Are you other guys listening? Sorry. Go ahead and finish. And the guy says and then three days later Jesus came out of the cave and saw his shadow and they had six more weeks of winter."

Paschal howled. Lou said, "I don't get it."

o o o

There was a break without any music and then the band returned. The trumpet player, who was clearly the group's leader, asked everyone to be quiet and then introduced a girl singer named Jane Cooper.

"That's more like it!" said Johnny Grabowski.

"It sure is, Nig," said Dugan. "She's a real dish."

The girl had a sweet voice but it was her looks that impressed the ball players. She wore a short flame dress with multi-colored chains of beads. She had high cheekbones, long eyelashes, and a beautiful smile. She swayed her hips to the music as she sang.

"I like this band a lot better now," said Paschal.

"You gonna ask anybody to dance?" Benny asked Koenig.

"I don't think so, Benny, I'm holding out for Jane Cooper."

o o o

On May 20, as Gehrig was in the lobby buying penny postcards to send home, his teammates sat in the leather chairs speculating as to whether Benny had scored with the girl singer. Back east, Charles Lindbergh climbed into *The Spirit of St. Louis* to begin his attempt to fly across the Atlantic. The Yanks were up against their nemesis George Uhle that afternoon. He'd beaten them six times in seven tries in '26.

In the first, with Combs on base, he fanned Gehrig on three curve balls. With two on in the fifth Lou struck out again, this time looking for curves and getting nothing but fast ones.

Lucky Lindy did better than the Yanks. They managed just seven singles and lost 2-1 to snap their winning streak at seven. That night at Yankee Stadium 50,000 boxing fans stood for a moment of silent prayer. Lindbergh was somewhere over the ocean and it would be hours before anyone knew his fate.

Babe Ruth
& the 1927 YANKEES have the BEST SUMMER EVER

11.

Scott and Zelda

"My hips are absolutely wild tonight. You don't mind, do you?"

The Yankees were all over Dutch Levsen in the first inning on Saturday. Combs singled to left, Ruth singled to right and Gehrig doubled, scoring Combs and sending the Babe to third. Durst's single scored Ruth and Dugan's scored Gehrig. But Cleveland's ace, Willis Hudlin, came in and cooled off the Yankees' hot bats. They plated one more run in the fourth and that was it.

Dutch Ruether had a tough go of it. Cleveland left fielder Charlie Jamieson hit a ball back to the mound in the first that looked like a routine grounder until it hit a pebble and ricocheted up and hit Dutch right in the mouth. Ruether yelped but threw Jamieson out with the blood-stained ball. Two innings later Lew Fonseca drilled a line drive right off Ruether's shoulder.

The game was interrupted in the bottom of the seventh when news arrived by telegraph that Charles Lindbergh had landed in Paris. The band struck up the *Star-Spangled Banner* and the Cleveland fans bared their heads and sang proudly. Then they called for their team to rally and got their wish.

The Tribe scored one in the third on a rare error by Joe Dugan, two in the sixth, and one in the eighth to tie things at 4-4. Miller Huggins took on the third base coaching chores and exhorted his charges as they headed into extra innings. His efforts were to no avail.

In the twelfth the Indians loaded the bases and then celebrated a second straight win over the Yankees when Moore uncharacteristically walked in the winning run.

Babe Ruth

LINDBERGH DOES IT! TO PARIS IN 33 HOURS; FLIES 1,000 MILES THROUGH SLEET AND SNOW; CHEERING FRENCH MOB CARRIES HIM FROM THE FIELD.

Every word in each news column on the first five pages of the was devoted to the one event, Lindbergh's nonstop flight across the Atlantic.

The series finale at Dunn Field was played on Sunday in front of the Tribe's biggest crowd of the season. In the sixth inning Ruth hit a fly ball so high the right fielder, Homer Summa, had time to eat a sandwich and wash it down with a soda. He watched helplessly as the ball fell into the stands behind him. The Yankees rebounded with a 7-2 win, Urban Shocker's fourth.

o o o

On their way home to New York the Yankees played a single game in Washington on Monday the 23rd to wrap up the road trip. Ruth blasted his tenth homer in the first, a solo shot off Sloppy Thurston into the centerfield seats 441 feet away. Gehrig followed with his tenth, but that was it.

Sloppy tired in the eighth and, as he so often did, Bucky Harris called for Firpo Marberry. Red threw nothing but fastballs and slammed the door on the Yanks. The Senators tallied one in the third to make it close. In the seventh Goose Goslin hit a Myles Thomas fastball to shallow right. The ball got by Ruth and rolled to the fence as Goslin sped around to third base. Joe Judge lofted a long fly to left and Goslin tagged and jogged home with the tying run. Muddy Ruel grounded one past Koenig for a single, then Topper Rigney, the Senators' shortstop, hit a grounder right at Koenig.

"Double play ball, inning over," Huggins said contentedly to no one in particular.

Koenig fumbled the ball. Hug cringed as both runners were safe. Thomas was so flustered he walked the next two batters. Washington won it 3-2.

o o o

The players walked the four blocks to the train station talking about how much money they should invest in the still soaring stock market. They hopped on the Congressional and headed to New York. It rained on Tuesday and their game was postponed.

"Let's go look for a new car," Waite Hoyt said to Dorothy when he heard there would be no game and he'd actually have a day off. They were both tired. After the long road trip they had caught up for lost time until the wee hours on Monday night.

"Are you sure, Waite?" asked Dorothy. "I know you got a raise but it wasn't that much."

"What do you mean? A thousand bucks is a pretty nice raise. Besides, we don't have to pay for the car all at once. Haven't you seen the signs in front of the dealerships? All of them except the Ford ones say the same thing. 'Why wait?'"

"Isn't that pretty risky?"

"A little. But the team's looking pretty good. I lost my last game but I've got five wins already. I might just win twenty. Then Ruppert will have to give me the thousand dollar bonus he promised."

"All right then," said Dorothy. She went to the closet and picked out a hat to wear, a taffeta applique. Waite grabbed his fedora and an umbrella and they headed out on a tour of nearby dealerships in their 1922 Nash Coupe.

"What kind of automobile are you thinking of buying, dear?" asked Dorothy as they waited at a red light.

"Not a Model T, that's for sure. You hate black for one thing. General Motors has different colors and new models every year. The new ones have safety glass, hydraulic brakes, shock absorbers, and chromium plating."

"Are they expensive?"

"The Chevrolet's seven hundred dollars. The Pontiac Coupe is a bit more expensive and it looks like a police car. The Chrysler Imperial looks like a gangster's car. I don't want another Nash, but we could get a McFarlan, or a Studebaker, or a Peerless 6-72. That's a nice car. Or we could get a

Hudson Essex Super Six. They're not expensive and the new model they started making last year has an all-steel enclosed body."

"It sounds as though you've done some research," said Dorothy.

"I've been talking to the fellas about it. We all want better cars than we can afford. Say, we could get what the Babe's thinking of buying."

"What's that?"

"A Pierce Arrow."

"How much are they?"

"The one he's considering is only eight thousand dollars."

Dorothy gasped. "Don't even dare think about it!"

They ended up buying a navy blue Chevrolet for thirty-six twenty dollar payments. It had a large trunk, which was important to Waite. The gas gauge was on the tank at the rear. Waite ran out more times than he could count.

o o o

That night Ruether, Dugan, and Bengough headed to Harlem.

"Did you ask Hoyt and Shawkey if they want to come along and bring their wives?" Dutch asked Joe. "I know they wouldn't go without them."

"I did," said Dugan. "Seems Waite's wife Dorothy read this article about jazz in the *Ladies Home Journal*. It warns women that the new jazz craze is a threat to young people. It said jazz is a base form of dancing that stirs up one's lower nature or some such nonsense."

"Who says we have to dance?" asked Benny.

"Just hearing it's bad apparently," said Joe. "Its primitive rhythms and the moaning saxophones are sensuous and capable of hypnotizing people."

"Gee! We'd better close our eyes and cover our ears then, boys," said Dutch. "Where are we goin' anyway?"

"It's getting pretty hard to pick a spot," said Joe Dugan. "I hear we're up to thirty thousand speakeasies in New York."

"Let's eat at Connie's Inn and then go to Chumley's," suggested Benny, leafing through the Entertainment section of the *Daily News*. "Then we

& THE 1927 YANKEES HAVE THE BEST SUMMER EVER

can hit The Stork Club or the Cotton Club for a nightcap. Fred and Adele Astaire are at the Trocadero. Duke Ellington, Bojangles Robinson and Ethel Waters are at the Cotton Club. Fats Waller and Fletcher Henderson are at Connie's Inn and Louis Armstrong's at the Stork Club."

o o o

"Googles, what's the password?" Dugan asked Bengough when they reached Connie's Inn.

"Iced tea, Joe," Bengough told him. "At Chumley's it's buttermilk."

After they'd ordered their dinners and drinks, the pudgy waiter whispered, "We serve the booze in tea cups, like most joints. If there's a raid you go out the Bedford Street doors. The police always come in through the Pamela Court entrance to give everybody a chance to get out. The owner pays 'em well."

At the Stork Club they heard Louis Armstrong and his band perform *Ol' Man River, Hotter Than That,* and his big hit, *Savoy Blues.*

"The piano player's cute," said Joe.

"That's Armstrong's wife," said Benny.

"We better get going if we wanna make another stop," said Dutch.

Bojangles was dancing up a storm as they were seated at the Cotton Club. After he finished, a lot of other people got up to dance.

"I've never seen so many pretty colored girls in my life," said Dutch. "And those bare midriffs? I didn't know such things were allowed. Even in New York."

Bare legs were flying everywhere. "What's that dance called?" asked Dugan.

"The Black Bottom," answered Benny. "Mostly people do the Turkey Trot or the Bunny Hop. Or the Charleston of course."

"What's *she* doing?" asked Joe, pointing to a flapper swinging her arms and rotating her perfectly-shaped hips provocatively on top of a table. She was in her early twenties and she was absolutely stunning. Her nose, cheek bones, and rosebud lips were perfectly formed and her wavy golden hair shone in the club's lights.

Babe Ruth

"It's called the shimmy," said Bengough. "You know who she is?"

"No, but I'd sure like to," said Dugan.

"Zelda Fitzgerald, Scott Fitzgerald's wife," answered Benny.

"Who's Scott Fitzgerald?" asked Dutch.

"An author," answered Benny. "He's got a new book everybody's talking about called The Great Gatsby. It's about some swell who throws big parties. Zelda's the wildest flapper there is. She swims in a beige bathing costume that makes her look naked and she's almost always drunk. She's been known to strip at cocktail parties or toss her knickers at someone in the middle of a dinner party."

"What's the husband like? The writer?" asked Dutch.

"Fitzgerald's no Caspar Milquetoast," said Benny. "He lights his cigarettes with five dollar bills and throws brandy glasses out of windows. Last week he took his clothes off in the middle of a Broadway play."

"She's a real sexpot," said Joe. "When she gets down from there I'm gonna ask her to dance."

He was delighted when, after grabbing a cigarette out of a man's mouth and guzzling a class of champagne that someone had abandoned, Zelda accepted his invitation.

She danced close. Very close. "My hips are absolutely *wild* tonight. You don't mind, do you?" she yelled into his ear.

"Isn't your husband here?" Joe asked, trying his best to conceal his erection.

"Of course, but he's a good sport and he knows I can't be bothered resisting things I want. I'm afraid I'm just not good for anything but useless, pleasure-giving pursuits. Don't you think life is all about having fun and doing whatever you want?"

"I suppose …" Joe began.

"And right now, what I want is another drink," announced Zelda.

"Sure, come on over to our table," said Joe.

"You're handsome. You know what?"

"What?" asked Joe.

"Lips that touch liquor … can always touch mine."

Zelda sat on Joe's lap while he signalled for a waiter to bring another round. "And a drink for the lady, as well."

"An orange blossom," she instructed the waiter. "And don't dare be stingy with the gin." She looked down at her chest and played with her string of pearls. "Don't you just hate the way we're supposed to flatten our breasts? I'd much rather men were able to see them. Then they'd know if they'd like to touch them."

"Your husband really doesn't mind it when you pay attention to other fellas?" Joe asked Zelda. "If *I* were your husband, I'd be awful jealous."

"He was a bit shocked when he heard I'd gone into another man's washroom at a weekend get-together and asked him to give me a bath," she said. Joe could feel his erection coming back. "But I've told Scott that sleeping with other men doesn't affect my feelings for him. Fidelity is so puritanical after all. Don't you think?"

The drinks arrived and so did Scott Fitzgerald. He was a tall man with an intelligent, friendly face and wavy brown hair.

"Speaking of your husband, Mrs. Fitzgerald," said Benny, "here he is."

Fitzgerald grabbed an empty chair from another table and sat down. Zelda moved over onto his lap and gave him a peck on the cheek. "I'm Scott Fitzgerald. It appears as though you've met my enchanting bride. Quite a woman, isn't she? Always the life of the party. Say, haven't I seen your pictures in the paper?"

Zelda downed her orange blossom in one gulp. "I believe they are ball players, dear. And mushcular ones too, espeshially Joe here," she slurred.

"We play for the Yankees," said Dutch. "Usually it's the Babe that gets his picture taken."

"You play with Babe Ruth!" shouted Zelda. Several people looked over, though many of the men hadn't taken their eyes off her since she'd leapt up on the table. "How exciting! I hear he's slept with a thousand women."

Babe Ruth

"We wouldn't know anything about that," said Dutch, "just that he's a great guy and a helluva ball player."

"Didn't he go to Hollywood and make a pa… pa… picture last year?" she hiccupped.

"Ya, his mug's on the big screen now," said Dutch.

"Did he meet Lilian Gish and Clara Bow?"

"I don't know. He said he met Chaplin and Fairbanks. I think he may have said something about going for a drive with Clara Bow too," said Benny.

"Douglas Fairbanks! Oh, he is so handsome," gushed Zelda. "I would love him to sweep me away and …"

"All right, Zelda, I think we get the idea," said Fitzgerald,

"You're one to talk. When you were drinking with Hemingway in Europe last year the two of you were positively crude."

Fitzgerald helped his wife up on her feet with some difficulty. "Why don't we get you some fresh air? You're squiffy. *Again.*"

"But I was just …"

"Good seeing you, fellas, good luck the rest of the season."

"Damn, but she is one hot number," Joe exhaled.

"We could tell you liked her a lot," said Dutch, indicating Joe's crotch.

Dugan blushed. "That writer fella has his hands full with that one."

"I expect a lotta guys have had their hands full with that one," chuckled Benny.

12.

None of that Gets Into the Papers

"It beats the tar outta shovelin' pig manure back home."

In the first game of the Friday doubleheader with the Senators, Huggins sent Herb Pennock to the hill and had to trudge there in the third to get him. His ace leftie had already surrendered nine hits and seven runs. Hod Lisenbee, who'd already beaten the Yankees twice, gave up one run in the first and then coasted to a four-hit, 7-2 win. The New Yorkers had now dropped four of their last five and the White Sox had caught up to them. Hug wasn't sleeping much.

Bump Hadley went for a sweep of the twin bill. Combs, Koenig, and Ruth scored in the third, Gehrig homered in the seventh and that was all the Yankees needed. Hoyt did the Capitol Hill squad in with a tidy three-hit, 5-0 shutout. He jumped in his new Chevrolet after the game anxious to celebrate another win with Dorothy. He ran out of gas two blocks from the Stadium.

o o o

In the first game of the Saturday, May 28 doubleheader, Meusel hit a two-run homer and Ruth hit a single, a triple, and his twelfth home run of the year to raise his average to .333 and power the Yanks to an 8-2 win.

With the late game being the fourth in two days it was no surprise when both managers had to use their relievers as starters. Moore and Marberry each had their best pitches working and the score stood at 1-1 after seven. Ossie Bluege lined out to Koenig to start the eighth. Marberry singled and Earl McNeely did too, sending Firpo to second. Bucky Harris hit a grounder to Koenig and charged for first base with fire in his eyes. Mark's throw reached Gehrig in time, but it was a little up the line and Lou had to step off the bag to get it. When he did, Harris stomped hard on his big left

Babe Ruth

foot. His spikes went right through the top of Lou's shoe.

Gehrig yelped in pain and fell forward onto his face. The ball dribbled out his glove. Cy called out, "Lou, you all right?" He raced over and picked up the ball but it was too late. Firpo Marberry raced across the plate with the go-ahead run. Gehrig stayed in the game in spite of the pain and a blood-soaked sock but he grounded into a double play his next time up. The Senators won 3-2 on Harris' dirty play. Gehrig said nothing but that he'd be fine to play the next day.

Huggins closed the door to his office after it was over. He didn't feel much like shooting the breeze with Fletch and Charley. The White Sox were right on the Yankees' tail and the dreaded A's weren't far behind them.

o o o

The Red Sox, who were wallowing in last place, came to town for one game on Sunday.

"Christ, Cy, we better get back on track," said Hoyt as he and Moore jogged in the outfield before the game. "We've dropped five out of eight since that winning streak."

"Seems like a long time ago already," said Wilcy. "We'd better beat these guys or Hug'll be as nervous as a pig at a bacon factory."

Art Fletcher was hitting groundballs to the infielders. The Babe joined them. He'd borrowed Ray Morehart's right-handed glove and was showing off how adeptly he could field with it.

Pennock and Gehrig watched from the dugout. Even though Lou's foot appeared to be all right, Huggins had Mike Gazella practising at first in case Lou ever got seriously hurt - though he never seemed to miss an inning, much less an entire game. Herb could see how impressed Gehrig was with Ruth's ease with the wrong-handed glove.

"They couldn't afford to buy left-handed gloves at St. Mary's, so Jidge got pretty good fielding with either hand," Herb explained.

"I'm not dat good usin' just da one hand," said Lou.

"I'd give my *right arm* to be ambidextrous," quipped Herb.

"What?" asked Lou.

& THE 1927 YANKEES HAVE THE BEST SUMMER EVER

"Never mind," Herb told him.

o o o

Forty thousand New Yorkers watched uncomfortably on Sunday, the 29th of June as the Beantown crew scored two runs off Dutch Ruether in the first, another in the second, and yet another in the third. Myles Thomas came in and gave up another two and it was 6-0 Boston.

For the sad-sack Red Sox it was too good to be true. The Yankees scored two in their half of the third and added four the next inning. They didn't stop there. Koenig and Meusel had three hits each, Benny Bengough stroked four singles to raise his average to .314, and Ruth hit his thirteenth, into the left field stands for a change, to power the Yanks' 15-7 comeback win.

Miller's Maulers headed to the train station after the game.

"How come Jidge calls red caps stinkweeds?" Koenig asked Lazzeri as they boarded the Quaker City Express.

"No idea," said Tony. "I get why he calls Collins Horse Nose, but Stinkweeds … I got no clue."

"We better watch our asses this week," said Mark. "If the A's win four or all five of the games they'll climb right over top of us."

The Yanks and A's would play double headers on Monday and Tuesday and then a single game on Wednesday. Their train pulled into Philadelphia just after 1 a.m. Most of the weary players went straight to the Aldine. Ruth, Shocker, and Meusel lit out to Rose Hick's place on Broad Street.

o o o

"We've bin here four hours, Jidge, can we call it a night?" asked Shocker as the grandfather clock in the parlor chimed five o'clock. Meusel was doing his best to keep his head from falling into his drink.

Ruth sat in a big leather chair. He'd been upstairs five times. A brassy brunette sat on one knee and a tiny redhead on the other. They poured champagne over the Babe's head and pretended to shampoo his hair.

"Is this a great life or what?" bellowed Ruth.

He went upstairs again and the three finally got back to the Aldine at 6 a.m. Shocker threw up twice the next morning and spent the afternoon

Babe Ruth

sawing logs in the bullpen. Meusel played, but he looked like he was sleep-walking. Ruth whistled as he got into his uniform and then played both games of the doubleheader. He threw out two runners and had a single and a double in the first game and a single and a homer in the second.

He sought out Shocker and Meusel in the clubhouse after the game. "You boys have trouble sleepin' last night?" the Babe asked when he found them propped up against opposite walls of the shower in hopes the cold water would bring them back them to life.

"Fuck off, Jidge," growled Shocker.

Meusel said nothing. He just closed his eyes and groaned.

○ ○ ○

In the first game on Monday the Yanks led 4-1 after two but the A's scored three off starter George Pipgras, three off Bob Shawkey, two off Joe Giard, and one off Walter Beall in what would be his only appearance of the season. The A's proved why they had been picked to capture the American League flag in '27, winning 9-8.

"We get to Grove for fifteen hits and eight runs and we lose it?" Huggins moaned to Art Fletcher.

"Pipgras is just no match for them, Miller," said Fletch. "We knew that comin' in. Let's just hope Pennock does better this afternoon."

○ ○ ○

The forty thousand fans who'd watched the morning game were politely ushered out of Shibe Park and another forty thousand streamed in for the afternoon one. It almost ended up being played in the dark.

The Yankees scored twice in the third inning but the A's got one back in the fourth and they reached Pennock for another three in the sixth to take a 4-2 lead. In the top of the seventh Pennock walked, Combs singled to left, Ruth walked, and Gehrig ripped a single up the middle to score Pennock and Combs and send the Babe to third. Meusel's sacrifice fly sent Ruth home and New York led 5-4.

The lead lasted all of ten minutes. Jimmie Foxx and Eddie Collins singled and Foxx lumbered across the plate with the tying run when Bill Lamar plunked a dying quail in front of Ruth.

& **THE 1927 YANKEES HAVE THE BEST SUMMER EVER**

"At least we didn't use Moore in the opener," Huggins told Fletcher. "Go get him."

Wilcy and Rube Walberg matched one another, each putting up zeroes for the next hour.

"It's startin' to get dark, Jidge," Mark Koenig told the Babe as he left the on-deck circle in the top of the eleventh inning.

"Ya, keed, and I'm getting mighty fuckin' hungry. We been here since nine this morning."

"Maybe you could put an end to it."

He nodded and did just that. The Babe hit a moon shot into the bleachers in left center. Moore shut out the A's for the fourth straight inning, and the Yanks avenged their morning loss.

"Doesn't it ever bother you that you can't crack the starting rotation?" Richards Vidmer asked Moore after the game.

"No, it don't. Not one bit. I ain't one a the high price startin' pitchers 'round here. I'm just a day labourer. Ain't none a my nevermind how Hug wants ta use me. Truth be told, I'm lovin' it." He stuck a chew of tobacco into his cheek and grinned. "It beats the tar outta shovelin' pig manure back home."

o o o

Pierre du Pont's wife Alice had called Herb Pennock over to her box seat before the game and invited him to the Du Ponts' Delaware home for a garden party.

"Feel free to bring some of your teammates," she told Herb. "Perhaps Mister Ruth would like to come."

Pennock knew that her garden parties were the highlight of the summer social season in Philadelphia and he also knew that it was really the Babe she wanted most. He invited Ruth as well as Bob Meusel and Earle Combs, two players he was fairly sure wouldn't embarrass him.

Herb told Earle what the Babe had said when he asked him to come with them. "Jidge asked me to tell him the names of the hostess and the hoster."

Babe Ruth

The du Ponts had come a long way since their forebears had started making gunpowder on the shores of the Brandywine River. Pennock remembered seeing Pierre du Pont's face on the cover of *Time* last winter and he recalled reading about how he'd bailed out General Motors. The du Ponts' home was a thousand acre, 32-room estate called Longwood. The house was a large stone edifice with a Corinthian portico and fluted pilasters between its windows and a series of terraces bordered by balustrades.

After passing through an arched Moorish gateway they were met by a woman in her late fifties who introduced herself as Pierre du Pont's sister, Louisa. She led them through the house, pointing out paraphernalia as they went.

"Daddy got that tribal mask during a trip along the Amazon," she explained. "The piano is from an opera house in Paris. Those tusks are from an elephant in Kenya. The tapestry is from a castle in Bavaria."

"Your father was quite a collector," said Herb.

"My father? Oh, I'm sorry, I meant Pierre."

"But you called him Daddy?"

"Pierre is my younger brother, Mister Pennock."

"Then why do you call him Daddy?"

"Because when our father died Pierre took over the family and the entire business."

"Was he in his twenties or thirties when your father died?" asked Combs.

"He was fourteen. But he was already a financial wizard. He built the gunpowder company into a multi-million dollar corporation and thanks to him our family owns more than a third of General Motors," she said with visible pride.

"I heard Pierre made fifty million bucks last year," Pennock whispered to Combs.

"That's almost as much as Capone!" exclaimed Earle.

The players gawked at the glistening chandeliers, the imported Italian furniture, and the gigantic potted palms drenched in the sunlight that streamed through the tall windows.

"Nice joint," muttered Ruth.

They passed groups of people in a huge parlour. Some were playing mah-jong, some were rehearsing a skit they were apparently performing later, and others were deep in conversation with a spiritualist.

Louisa led the players out a doorway to the backyard, a vast, manicured, rolling lawn that stretched toward the horizon. There were enormous greenhouses, groves of exotic trees transplanted from various parts of the world, two small lakes surrounded by swans and flamingos, and a spectacular fountain.

"There are six hundred jets in nine separate displays shooting water from the six pools," Pierre's sister explained. "Daddy, I mean Pierre, likes fountains. He installed a forty-foot tall jet fountain at the end of the central allée. It can be turned on with a switch."

She pointed to a large open-air theater. "And beneath the theater's stage there are secret fountains. Pierre gets no greater delight than soaking unsuspecting guests in the middle of a performance."

Underneath a magnificent terrace on which a twenty-piece orchestra played show tunes was a marble swimming pool with a slide and, of course, a fountain. Well-scrubbed, smartly outfitted guests meandered between sculptured shrubs and Greek statues. Young men in sheer linen shirts and white trousers mixed with girls in billowing coral, apple-green, and lavender dresses, some playing croquet, others throwing lawn darts.

"Suppose they have any horse shoes? I could make some dough betting these swells," said Meusel.

"Quiet!" whispered Pennock. "Have some couth."

"They didn't have any couth stores where I grew up," said Meusel.

Pennock hoped he was making a joke, but he wasn't all that sure.

A waiter in a crisp white jacket offered glasses of pink champagne on a silver tray. Mrs. du Pont told the guests she was terribly sorry, but one of the servants had inadvertently spilled an entire bottle of vodka into the punch.

Babe Ruth

The Babe, who wore a natty brown suit that verged on a plum shade and a beige silk shirt, demonstrated his home run swing with a celery stick and let ladies feel his biceps. Pennock was delighted when he kept his pinkie in the air while drinking something from a tea cup and said how charmed he was with everyone and everything. He was being a real gentleman. So far.

Pierre du Pont invited Ruth into his library, where he explained that the company had begun with gunpowder but was now making paints, heavy chemicals, dyestuffs, polymers, and plastic.

Ruth pulled a flat round tin container of Copenhagen from his vest pocket and shoved some into his cavernous nostrils. "You lost me at heavy chemicals," he said. "I never heard of those other things."

"How would you like some Bushmills, Babe?"

"I'm not exactly sure what that is, but I got a feeling my old man never served it in his bar," said Ruth.

"It's one of the oldest and finest Irish whiskeys that ever crossed the Atlantic."

"I suppose a sip or two would serve."

Though du Pont wasn't much of a drinker, he poured them each two fingers of whiskey from a crystal decanter. Guessing the question the Babe was about to ask, du Pont said, "Fifty dollars a bottle."

Outside, Earle, Herb, and Bob mingled as best they could. All that the guests wanted to talk about were Charles Lindbergh, the scandalous Fitzgeralds, and the stock market.

"Lindbergh was given the key to another city yesterday," said a man with tiny spectacles perched on his nose. "I believe that's ten now. People positively can not get enough of the man."

"He's so modest, and polite, and wholesome," said a woman in an embellished vest dress and mauve toque hat. "I wish our daughter was attracted to men like that. I'm surprised she hasn't hooked up with those ball players Alice invited."

"I was in New York for the weekend," said a woman with a glossy pout and heavy lidded eyes. "The two of them were absolutely zozzled at the

Plaza Saturday night. Fitzgerald knocked over a huge potted plant in the middle of the lobby and she jumped into the fountain."

Two well-dressed men passed by on their way to the punch bowl. "The Standard and Poor's industrial stock index was at forty-four point four in Twenty," said the taller one, who wore an Ivory linen suit and a beige Trilby. "This month it hit a hundred and four point four."

"Their industrial rail stocks index has shot from a hundred and fifty-six in Twenty-One to three hundred and fifty-six," said the other man who had on a custom wool suit in spite of the temperature. "I tell you what, Charles, I'm not waiting any longer. I'm going all in."

o o o

After several glasses of Bushmills the Babe was literally in fine spirits. Soon after he rejoined the others on the lawn a curvaceous brunette in a tight-fitting outfit offered them canapés. Ruth's eyes lit up. As he was about to make a comment that would likely not be appreciated in mixed company - especially of this pedigree - they heard screams coming from the open-air theater. The group they'd seen rehearsing earlier in the parlour was on stage. They were laughing hysterically. The audience was absolutely drenched. In the wings, wearing a huge grin, was Pierre du Pont.

"That Du Pont's a real joker. He's got mighty good whiskey though," boomed the Babe. "D'you see the caboose on that dame?"

"Pretty gal," said Earle.

"*Pretty?* Are you kidding me, Iron Ass? She's a *fuckin' doll!*" asserted Ruth even louder this time.

After knocking back a couple of glasses of punch the Babe started chasing the girl all around the garden.

"We gotta get the big ape outta here," said Meusel.

"Jidge," called Pennock. "We have to leave. We've got a double header tomorrow."

"I want a piece a that broad," Ruth announced.

"I'll see if I can get the girl's phone number for you when I go to thank the du Ponts for inviting us," Pennock promised the Babe. "Get him into a cab," he whispered to Meusel and Combs.

Babe Ruth

○ ○ ○

In the early game the next day Gehrig doubled, tripled, and homered, but couldn't manage a single.

"Tough luck, Lou," drawled Wilcy Moore after the game. "I'll have ta give ya some tips on hittin' little ones."

The Yankees breezed to a 10-3 win; Hoyt's seventh against just two losses.

Howard Ehmke started for the A's in the second game. After he'd been pounded for eight runs Connie Mack sent in Eddie Rommel, who'd won twenty-seven games as a starter in '22 but was being used more and more in relief. Rommel did much better than Ehmke. He only gave up seven runs.

Among the Yankees' twenty-four hits Combs had five, Lazzeri had four, and Koenig, Ruth, and Urban Shocker had three. Shocker was batting .391, three points behind Meusel. Even Pat Collins got in on the fun, lifting one over the double-decked grandstand in left.

"Where'd that come from, Horse Nose?" Ruth asked Collins after he'd finished his rare home run trot.

"I've gotta have *something* to brag to the flappers about, Jidge."

Gehrig had just a pair of singles and his batting average dropped to .413. The Babe hit a ball just fair over the right field fence. He wasn't hitting very many homers this season, but he could still hit them a long way. This one soared over a two-story house across the street and ended up on a front lawn.

A woman came out her front door and noticed it lying there. "Jimmy!" she yelled inside. "How many times have I told you not to leave your things on the lawn?"

Whad'ya mean, ma?" came a young voice from inside.

"There's a baseball on the front lawn."

A nine-year-old boy ran out the door. "We don't use a real baseball when we play stickball, Ma. They're way too expensive."

He picked up the ball and read the lettering.

& **THE 1927 YANKEES HAVE THE BEST SUMMER EVER**

OFFICIAL
AMERICAN LEAGUE BASEBALL
PAT'D RE 17200

He rubbed his chin and looked at Shibe Park between the houses across the street. "The Yankees are playing the A's today," he said to himself. He grabbed his bicycle, which he *had* left on the lawn, and tore off to tell his friends that he was pretty sure Babe Ruth had just hit a ball into his front yard.

The Babe drove in five in the 18-5 nail-biter. What a difference a day made. On Monday the A's had come close to sweeping a doubleheader and putting a scare into the Yanks and today the window breakers had absolutely humiliated them. Thirty seven hits and twenty-eight runs in the double header, a record.

The Yankees finished May with twice as many wins as losses, a 28-14 record. They had a six game lead on the A's, the team that was supposed to win it all and still hoped to overtake the New York juggernaut.

o o o

In the fifth and last game in Philadelphia on June 1st, Myles Thomas got a rare start. The slew of double headers had worn out the other starters. Koenig hit a solo home run in the first and Dugan singled home Ben Paschal in the ninth. Thomas came through with a surprise six-hit, 2-1 win.

After the game, reporters went to visit Thomas at his locker. He told them how thrilled he was to have kept Cobb off the bases the whole afternoon but he didn't say much else that was interesting. John Kieran got bored and began watching other players.

Gehrig had just come out of the shower. Kieran marvelled at his finely-honed physique. When he opened his locker Kieran looked inside. Lou's street clothes were neatly folded and piled as though by a valet and his shoes were perfectly aligned beside each other on the bottom. On the shelf sat a pile of Gehrig's comic books and beside them were a hair brush and a bottle of inexpensive cologne. Lou took out his shoes and set his shower slippers neatly in their place. He took out his hair brush and after using it, set it back exactly where it had been.

Babe Ruth

Ruth came out of the shower room. He took off his towel and whipped Tony Lazzeri's ass with it. His large member swayed in front of him as he walked to his locker. He loved to show it off.

"Hey, keed," he boomed to Kieran when he saw him looking at him, "guess you don't see one this big very often." Kieran blushed.

The Babe opened his locker. It was an absolute mess. Letters and telegrams spilled all over the floor.

"I'll get those for you, Babe," said Doc Woods.

"Thanks, Doc. Ya mind signing a couple dozen balls for me? I'm going to see some kids at St. Jude's before I head to dinner."

"Sure, Babe, no problem. Hey, remember that time I found a check for six thousand dollars you'd forgotten you had in your locker."

"Ya, I lost most of it on a lead-footed nag that night," said Ruth.

o o o

Ruth's street clothes lay in a heap on the bottom of his locker. On the shelf were bottles of cologne, cans of snuff, and girlie magazines. Above the chalk letters RUTH that were printed across the top of the locker was a huge green gourd. He never told anyone what it was doing there, they just assumed it was for good luck.

o o o

The Yankees headed home to play Detroit on Thursday. They might just as well have left their bats on the train. Luckily, Dutch Ruether, who had not been sharp of late, pitched even better than Thomas had the day before. Lil Stoner limited the Yankees to eight singles but Dutch held the Tigers to two and won 2-0. It took him all of ninety minutes.

The Yanks managed ten hits the next day, but with the exception of Gehrig's solo home run in the second inning, they were all singles. Herb Pennock was sailing along with a one run lead when the Tigers' two best hitters came to bat in the seventh. Harry Heilmann grounded one to Koenig which he booted for an error. Then Charlie Gehringer ripped a single between first and second.

Rabbit Jack Taverner stepped into the batter's box. He had one home run to show for his last one thousand plate appearances. Pennock hoped for a double play groundball but knew Taverner would be tough to double up. As it turned out, Taverner was tough to keep in the ball park. He deposited the ball in the left field bleachers. It would be a long while before the grin left his face. Gehrig's thirteenth made less of an impression on the scoreboard. The Tigers won it 3-1.

o o o

After a rainout on Saturday Wilcy Moore started the Sunday game and somebody bailed *him* out for a change. Cy surrendered a run in the seventh as the Tigers knotted things at three a piece but Myles Thomas, who'd pitched so well on Wednesday, went in and shut Detroit down. The Yanks scored two in the eighth and won 5-3.

o o o

The White Sox had finished fifth in '26. The Yankees and A's each had plenty of big name players. Chicago had none. Now the Pale Hose were in the middle of a hot streak that would see the no-names win twelve of fourteen. They had a lot of people checking the nightly box scores and scratching their heads.

Everyone knew Ted Lyons was a first-rate pitcher but Red Faber, who'd won fifteen in '26, was considered over the hill now at thirty-eight. He wasn't. Ted Blakenship and Tommy Thomas were doing fine too. Harry McCurdy and Bibb Falk were hitting better than ever and newcomers Alex Metzler, Bud Clancy, and Wild Bill Hunnefield were all batting well over .300. Third baseman Willie Kamm hadn't hit a single homer in '26 but he was hitting some now.

The A's had started slowly and had never really gotten going. Some thought it was because they had to put up with Cobb every day. The White Sox had bolted out of the gate, stumbled, and then recovered quite nicely with seven and five-game winning streaks and now they'd just won *another* seven in a row. Their record stood at 31-17 and they trailed the Yanks by just a game when they came to New York for four games starting June 7.

Ray 'Cracker' Schalk, who'd taken the managerial reins from Eddie Collins at the end of the '26 season, sent Tommy Thomas out against the Yankees. He'd won thirty-two games for Jack Dunn's Baltimore Orioles in '24 and then held out for a raise the next year. Unwilling to pay him more, Dunn sold Thomas to the White Sox for $15,000 and he won fifteen games in '26 and led the league in opponents' batting average with .244. Now he had ten wins against just two losses. Schalk was using him even more than Lyons.

Thomas got through the Yankee lineup without difficulty the first time around in the first game. But, as so often happened, the second time through the Yankee sluggers had seen what was working for the starter and, more importantly, what was not and they knew what to expect. In the fourth inning Ruth and Gehrig lined back-to-back homers.

As usual the Babe's was a towering fly that dropped deep into the right field bleachers and Lou's was a wicked liner into the front rows. Fans stood up and admired the height and length of Ruth's towering homers and hoped to catch them. They dove out of the way of Gehrig's.

Waite Hoyt had his good stuff and was breezing along in the seventh. He threw a third strike past Aaron Ward, whose place Mark Koenig had taken over.

"Dat's the old fight," yelled Gehrig.

Then Hoyt struck out Tommy Thomas.

"Way ta go," yelled Lou.

Hoyt shot him a dirty look. Gehrig missed it. Waite threw a fastball by Alex Metzler and then got him to chase a curve for strike two.

"Stick it to him," yelled Lou.

Hoyt signalled Red Ormsby, the home plate umpire, that he wanted time called.

"Time!" yelled Ormsby, taking off his mask and waving his arms.

Hoyt waved Gehrig over. Pat Collins thought about joining them on the mound but decided against it. He was pretty sure what Waite had to say.

"What's up?" Lou asked, looking puzzled. "What'sa matta?"

"Is this a high school game we're playing out here, Lou?" Hoyt growled.

"No. Why?"

"Because you sound like a fucking cheerleader over there."

"I do?"

"Ya. And I don't need a damn cheerleader. I know what I have to do and I can supply my own inspiration. You're bugging the shit out of me with all your Go team, Go bullshit."

"Sorry, Waite I guess I get a little carried away."

"Well cut it out!"

"All right. Can I go now?"

"Yes. And play farther off the bag."

"Right. I got it. Farther off the bag and keep my mouth shut."

Waite had a hard time not cracking up. "Yes."

Hoyt, with less encouragement the rest of the way, limited the White Sox to a lone run to boost his record to 8-2 with a sparkling 2.19 E.R.A. Now the Yankees led by two.

"What's your hurry, Waite?" Herb Pennock asked him after the game. "I've never seen anybody shower and dress so fast. Afraid if you get home late you'll get hot tongue and cold shoulder for dinner?"

"No. It's not that. I … I … I can't tell you."

"What do you mean you can't tell me? You got a dame on the side Dorothy doesn't know about?"

"No. It's nothing like that."

"Well what is it then? I won't tell anybody. Promise."

Waite looked around the room. No one was in earshot. "You know how my father-in-law's a mortician and I'm studying to be one too?"

"Ya, he's got a funeral parlor in New Jersey, doesn't he?"

"Yes, and, well, sometimes he gets me to pick up corpses from morgues in Manhattan and take them out there."

"All right. What's that got to do …"

Hoyt looked around again, nervously.

"You don't!" gasped Pennock.

Babe Ruth

"Keep your voice down. Yes, I have one in the trunk of my new Chevy. I didn't have time to drive it all the way out to the funeral parlor before the game."

"Holly Moses! Now I get why you're in such a hurry."

"Don't breathe a word of this," whispered Hoyt.

"I won't. But, Waite …"

Hoyt grabbed his hat. "What?" he asked impatiently.

"I don't think you really have to hurry."

"Why?"

"The corpse isn't likely to leave without you."

13.

A June Swoon for the Yanks?

"Ya, and I hit marshmallows for a living."

The next morning the Babe left the Ansonia early. As he stepped out onto 73rd Street he was bombarded by now familiar sensations: the smell of gasoline and garbage and warm pretzels hawked from pushcarts; the clanging of trolley cars, shouts for taxi cabs, shrieks of traffic cops' whistles, and the incessant jackhammers. Skyscrapers were springing up all over New York and you got used to the incumbent racket. Missing now though were the once familiar grunts and curses of drivers struggling to crank start their autos.

Ruth thought about how his life had changed so often and so much, from the squalor of the alleys of Baltimore, to the cloistered routines of St. Mary's, to the excitement of Boston where a kid with a few dollars in his pocket could buy whatever he wanted, and finally to the seemingly endless possibilities of New York.

Who would ever have thought his life would take the turns it had? He'd figured he had it pretty good when he was making thirty-five hundred a year to pitch for the Red Sox. Now, with Jake Ruppert's big checks and Christy Walsh's schemes and vaudeville and the picture shows, he was making far more than he would ever have dreamed.

Best of all, by far - beyond the silk shirts and the dollar cigars and the expensive cars and the good whiskey and the eager to please dames - was the way kids' faces lit up when they saw him, especially when he paid them even the least bit of attention, even if that wasn't happening anywhere near as often as it had before he hit rock bottom in '25.

The Babe passed a street vendor with a pushcart. He was selling sausages on a bun. Ruth stared hungrily, his mouth watering.

Babe Ruth

"Hey, Babe, your usual?" the man asked. "Two footlongs with lotsa garlic and onions."

"Sorry," Ruth told him. "They ain't on my new diet."

The Babe stopped at a newsstand. Lindbergh's now all too familiar face was on the cover of *Time*. Lefty Grove's was on the *Sporting News*. Some men stood reading newspapers. On the back pages the Babe saw Gehrig grinning inanely on a *Wheaties* box, Ty Cobb drinking a *Coca-Cola*, Walter Hagen enjoying a *White Owl* cigar, and Gehrig holding up a bar of *Murphy-Rich Company* soap.

On either side of the newsstand were billboards with Bill Tilden smoking a *Lucky Strike* beside a tennis court and Red Grange running for a touchdown with *"Pinch-hit Chewing Tobacco"* over the goalposts.

The newsstand owner noticed Ruth standing there. "Hey, Babe," he called out. He saw what he was looking at and said, "It used to be *your* face plastered all over the place."

Ruth stopped to pet the head of a cocker spaniel puppy and startled its owner. He ducked in to his favorite barber shop to get a shave. As he entered he took off his brown derby and, as always, threw it in a perfect line onto one of the hooks on the hat rack twenty feet away.

The barber was sharpening a razor on his leather strop. "You wanna haircut witta your shava today, Meester Ruth?"

"The works, Tony," bellowed the Babe.

The barber's name was really Lorenzo, but to Ruth all barbers were Tonys.

"I cutta da hairs offa you ears anda you neck too den, Meester Ruth," said Lorenzo as he threw a cover over the Babe. "Isa good?"

"Ya, gimme back my movie star looks."

As the scissors whirred like a hornet around Ruth's ears a handsome young man in a well-cut suit was on his way out the door. He stopped to check himself out in the mirror and then walked back to the barber and handed him a five dollar bill.

"Thanks, Meester Raft," said the barber.

The man gingerly placed his black fedora on his new haircut and left.

"Who was that?" asked Ruth.

"Hesa one a Owney Madden's drivers. Comes in alla da time."

Lorenzo stopped snipping and went to the window. A group of boys was pointing and staring in at the Babe. He pulled down the shades and returned to work.

"He's a reala smooth operator. Namesa George Raft. Hees always checking heemself out inna da mirror. Heesa good tipper though."

"And he drives for Owney Madden? The gangster?"

"Ya, but Madden passes heemself off as a respectable nightaclub owner. When he got outta Singa Sing for bumping offa Patsy Doyle he botta the Cotton Club and then Madden and a couple a hees cronies muscled their way ina to da Storka Club."

"No wonder it's so easy to get a drink there. The hat check girls are out of this world and some of the dancers got great gams, but those places are too fuckin' loud for me. What's Raft deliver for Madden?"

"Milk."

"Ya, I'll bet, and I hit marshmallows for a living."

Lorenzo laughed. "Thatsa a gooda joke, Meester Ruth. Can I tella you one?"

"Sure, Tony, I love havin' jokes for those long train rides we're always takin'."

"Well thisa one is *about* a train ride."

"Perfect. Fire away."

"Okay. Luigi gets back froma hees honeymoon in Florida with hees new bride Virginia and he stops by his barbershop to say hello to his friends. Giovanni da barber says 'Hey Luigi, how wasa da treep?' Luigi says, 'Everyting wasa perfect except for da train ride down.' 'Whata you mean, Luigi?' asks Giovanni. 'Well, we boarda da train at Granda Central Station. My beautiful Virginia she pack a beeg basket a food. She broughta da vino, some nice cigars for me, and we open upa da lunch basket. The conductor comes by, waga hees finger at us and say, no eat indisa car. Musta use a dining car. So me and Virginia we go to da dining car, eat a beeg lunch and open da bottle of vino. Conductor walka by again, waga hees finger and say, No drink indisa car! Musta use da club car. So, we go to da club car. We drink da vino and I lighta my beeg cigar. The conductor waga hees finger again and say, No smoke indisa car. Musta go to smokin car. We go to da smokin car and I smoke a my beeg cigar. Then my beautiful Virginia and I, we go to a sleeper car and go to bed. We just about to go boombada boombada and the conductor, he walka through da hallway shouting at a top of hees a voice Nofolka Virginia! Nofolka Virginia! Nexta time, I'm gonna take da bus.'"

The Babe laughed so hard Lorenzo was afraid he was going to choke. When he finally recovered he said, "I can't wait to tell the dago that one."

o o o

The skies were clear for the Wednesday, June 8 game with the White Sox. Huggins had been relieved to win the important first game of the series, but he was far from relaxed. Not that he ever really was. As usual, the Babe eyed the stands for pretty women after his turn in the batting cage.

"Wow! What a knockout!" he muttered.

She was sitting with an attractive man in his early thirties. They were in Florenz Ziegfeld's box. Ruth guessed they were entertainers. She was a sultry beauty in her mid-twenties, with lustrous, wavy black hair, piercing brown eyes, and puffy, red lips. Ruth wondered what kind of a body she had. He went to the edge of the grandstand and called up to Ziegfeld.

"Howdy, neighbor. Who d'ya bring this time?"

Ziegfeld looked confused for a second and then realized the Babe was referring to the couple sitting behind him. "Hello, Babe. My guests today are John Boles, who starred in my big hit Rio Rita last winter, and Claire Hodgson, who's in a play at the National Theatre. She's really a model more than an actress."

"I can see why," said Ruth. Boles wrinkled his brow, which made his face at least a little less handsome.

"It's a pleasure to meet you," said Claire with a soft Georgian accent.

The Babe nearly melted. Then he noticed that Huggins was glaring at him. "Well, I got to get back to work. Good ta see ya, Flo. I hope you enjoy the game, Miss Hodgson. You too, Mister … ah, I gotta go." He tipped his cap to Claire and went to get his glove.

○ ○ ○

The game was a slugfest. Dutch Ruether, Wilcy Moore, and Chicago's Red Faber all got roughed up. Lazzeri hit a long fly into the right field seats in the second and hit one to the centerfield wall in the sixth that he legged out for an inside-the-park homer. But the White Sox held a 7-5 lead and seemed to put the game out of reach when they added two more in the top of the eighth.

When they added another pair in the top of the ninth to make it 11-6 many of the not so faithful Yankee faithful headed for the exits. As they filed out and made their way to the 161st Street subway station the five o'clock whistle sounded at a nearby factory.

"I guess those people haven't been to a game before," a man in the front row of the right field grandstand said to his son. "It seems like whenever the Yanks are losing, that factory whistle wakes them up."

"I bet they pull this one out too," the boy told his father. Like more and more young fans he'd taken to bringing his baseball glove to games in case the Babe hit one his way.

After Combs led off with a single to start the bottom of the ninth, Cecil Durst, who was in for the injured Bob Meusel, rapped his second hit of the day. He'd smashed one to the fence earlier for a triple.

"Seems like anybody Huggins puts in this year plays better than he ever has," said the father as Lazzeri stepped to the plate.

"Poosh 'Em Up, Tony! You can do eet," yelled a man with a black handlebar moustache.

"Think Tony'll hit another one, pa?" the kid asked his dad.

"You never know with this bunch, son. They've all been tearing the cover off the …"

"Pa! It's coming this way. Right to us!" yelled the boy as he leaned out over the railing extending his glove out in front of him.

"Careful, son," warned his dad, grabbing the back of his son's jacket.

Babe Ruth

Thud. The ball landed squarely in the boy's glove. He beamed with pride and held his prize high in the air for everyone to see.

"Nicea catch, keed," said the man with the handlebar moustache.

The Yankees plated two more for a total of five runs in the inning. Their "five o'clock lightning", as the reporters would start describing their late innings surges, had put them back in the game. Ray Schalk finally put an end to Faber's misery and sent in Sarge Connolly, who held the Yankees off the score sheet in the tenth.

"Ma Gehrig's got supper waitin'," yelled Lou as he ran off the diamond after catching a popup to end the top of the eleventh.

"I hear ya," said Cedric Durst as he grabbed a bat.

"You gonna get on again?" asked Lazzeri.

"Why not?" shrugged Durst.

Cedric ripped Connolly's first pitch into left field for a single. Then Lazzeri smashed one right at Bill Hunnefield, the Chicago shortstop. Durst was off with the pitch and looked to be an easy out at second. He would have been if Hunnefield had made the play, but the ball caromed off his glove into center. Durst rounded second and slid safely into third ahead of Alex Metzler's throw.

Ray Morehart was in for Koenig and he had two hits already. He sent Connolly's second pitch into shallow center field and Metzler charged in for it. He hadn't been playing very deep. He made the easy catch and came up throwing.

"Go!" yelled Art Fletcher.

Durst took off for home. He and the ball arrived at the same time. Durst was lucky, Buck Crouse, the White Sox backstop, was light for a catcher, just over a hundred and fifty pounds. Durst smashed full tilt into him.

As the home plate umpire waited for the dust to settle the baseball rolled out of Crouse's mitt.

"Safe! That's the ball game!" yelled Owens.

"Cedric, you are coming home with me for the best chicken dinner you've had in your life," Gehrig told the grinning sub as he wiped the dirt from his pinstripes.

Ruth patted Durst on the back. "Swell job, keed."

"Thanks, Jidge," beamed Cedric.

The Babe headed over to see Ziegfeld. He saw that Claire and the man she was with had already headed up the steps. "Where's that doll from? I love her accent."

"She's from Atlanta."

"She's *gorgeous*. You gotta give me her address, Flo."

Ziegfeld thought for a minute. "I'll tell you what, Babe. I will give you her address if you'll tell everyone that you can't wait to see my next production. It's called Show Boat."

o o o

The next morning the Babe took Meusel and Shawkey to a drug store. They knew he wasn't shopping for bandages or liniment or Ivory soap. They were careful that no one saw them go in.

"This place sells medicinal whiskies," Ruth explained. "Good for what ails ya."

"I hear Old Grand-Dad Bourbon is now the Medicinal Spirits Company," said Shawkey. "And last week a train pulled into Boston with seven thousand gallons of Old Forrester from Louisville for sale to the drug stores."

The pharmacist, a pale, splotchy man with thick glasses, took the three players to the back of the store.

"Pretty nice watch you got there," said the Babe.

"Oh, thank you."

"I guess the medicinal whiskey business has been good to you."

The pharmacist blushed and coughed lightly. "There does seem to be a rather great demand," he admitted.

"Folks gotta be careful," grinned Shawkey. "Ya don't wanna let a fever get the best of you."

As usual Meusel said nothing. He was surveying the shelves, his eyes wide in disbelief.

Babe Ruth

"Let's see," said Ruth, reading the labels. "Paul Jones Rye, Red Star Gin, White Star Brandy, Broad Ripple bourbon, and what's this?"

"Old Pirate Rum," the pharmacist told him.

"Those are pretty well-known medicines where I come from," said Shawkey.

"I bin' gettin' the stuff from my dentist, but he ain't got nuthin' like this," said Meusel.

"My grocer's got some pretty good bourbon," said Shawkey. "Course it's labelled apple juice. Cy Moore gets stuff sent from home. They make up a hash of roots and herbs. Stuff'd grow hair on a cue ball."

"He oughta give some to Googles," said Ruth.

"You gotta add lemon, sugar, and water, else it'll knock you on your ass," Shawkey continued.

"Dugan's wife takes cough syrup that's about eighty proof," said Ruth. "And her sister takes a tonic from Kentucky for the vapours that's even stronger." He turned to the druggist. "I'll take a case of the Broad Ripple bourbon and three cases of the Paul Jones Rye."

"Oh, I'm terribly sorry, but I can only sell customers one bottle at a time," said the druggist. "And you need a prescription."

Meusel and Shawkey smiled at one other. They knew exactly what was coming.

"I have a *couple* of prescriptions," said the Babe, pulling a wad of bills from his pocket and tearing off two hundreds. "From Benjamin Franklin."

The pharmacist looked around to see if anyone was watching and took the bills. "Doctor Franklin. Very well then. I'll have the ... medicines delivered to your hotel."

o o o

Ted Blankenship had his best stuff in the third game of the White Sox series that afternoon. He'd yielded only a pair of singles and had a shutout and a 3-0 lead when the Yanks came to bat in the sixth. In the dugout the White Sox held their breath waiting for the New Yorkers to strike again. They did, an inning earlier than the day before.

& THE 1927 YANKEES HAVE THE BEST SUMMER EVER

Combs led off by grounding out. Morehart singled to left and Ruth singled to right, but Blankenship struck out Gehrig. When Blankenship saw that the next batter was Cedric Durst he relaxed a little. Normally he would have been facing the dangerous Bob Meusel.

Morehart took his lead at third. The Babe spit a stream of sunflower seeds and edged off first.

"Lazzeri's next," Blankenship thought to himself. "I gotta strike out Durst or make him hit the ball."

Durst chose a pitch he liked and ripped it into the gap in left field. As Bibb Falk, nickname Jockey, raced to get it, Morehart jogged home and Durst chased the Babe around the bases. Ruth crossed home standing up and picked up Durst's bat. Durst arrived at home a second after Falk's throw.

"Yer out!" yelled the ump.

"Nice try, keed," the Babe told Durst.

Ray Schalk sent lanky Bert Cole in to take over from Blankenship. Bob Meusel stood on the dugout steps and yelled. "Who ya gonna throw at today, Cole?"

Some of the younger Yankees were stunned. They'd never heard Meusel speak, certainly nothing above a grunt.

"He generally doesn't use that many words in an entire day," Combs told Durst. "G'morning's about all you normally get out of him."

"What was that all about?" asked Cedric.

"Meusel started a bench-clearing brawl a couple of years ago when Cole threw a fastball that just missed his head. It was a real donnybrook. They both got suspended for ten games and fined a hundred bucks."

Cole glared in at Meusel. "Too bad you ain't playing, dickhead," he yelled at him.

"If I was I'd be sure to line one right down your damn throat!" shouted generally Silent Bob.

The Yankees did more damage in the seventh. With two men on, Ray Morehart slashed one between third baseman Willie Kamm and the bag.

Babe Ruth

The ball bounded to the left field stands and bounced off them right past the charging Bibb Falk. By the time he retrieved the ball Pennock and Combs had scored. Morehart crossed the plate behind them with the first and only home run of his career.

Falk's follies weren't over. The Babe hit a ball to the left field corner. Falk sprinted toward it, reached it, and dropped it. Ruth raced all the way around to third and slid in, just safe.

Cole didn't pay much attention to him as the Babe stood on the bag catching his breath. He thought to himself that he should spend some more time at Art McGovern's gym. Cole started into his slow, rocking windup and Ruth took off.

"Jidge!" yelled Art Fletcher. "What are you …"

Cole had been around long enough to know that Ruth had deceptive speed. He'd stolen home nine times and was trying to make it an even ten. As the Babe arrived at the plate Buck Crouse reached up to pull down Cole's high pitch. Ruth hit the ground and deftly executed the hook slide Brother Matthias had taught him. Crouse's tag was late.

"Safe!" yelled the umpire.

Inspired by Ruth's daring theft the Yankees scored five more runs in the inning and won 8-3.

"Where did you learn to slide like that, Babe?" Marshall Hunt asked Ruth after the game. "You hook the bag as well as Cobb."

"From Brother Matthias, back at St. Mary's," the Babe told him.

"Did you read about what happened to him last week?" asked Hunt.

"No, what?"

"Sorry, Babe, I thought you already knew. He nearly got himself killed. He stalled the big Cadillac you bought him on the railway tracks just outside of Baltimore. He got out in plenty of time but the car was demolished by a freight train."

"Good Lord must have been keepin' an eye on him. I guess I'll have to buy him another Cadillac though. Lucky they give me a deal 'cuz I say nice things about them," said the Babe over his shoulder as he headed to the showers.

& THE 1927 YANKEES HAVE THE BEST SUMMER EVER

The "frolicking, rollicking, walloping Yankees lit up the White Sox," wrote Richards Vidmer in the *Times*. Their lead was up to four games.

○ ○ ○

Ted Lyons, who boasted a 10-2 record, wore the Yankees to a frazzle in the Friday finale. When Ruth came to bat in the eighth, with no hits to his credit like most of his teammates, Lyons went into his windup, swinging his arms back and forth and back and forth and back and forth again.

"If you're gonna jump, jump, for Christ sakes," yelled the Babe. "Otherwise throw the fuckin' ball." He stepped out of the box.

"What do you think you're doing?" snarled Brick Owens. "You can't step outta the box once you're in there! Throw it," he yelled to Lyons. "If it's anywhere near the plate it'll be a strike."

Ruth stepped back in and struck out.

The White Sox won 4-2, but they'd missed their chance to pass the Yankees.

The Babe had looked hopefully for Florenz Ziegfeld the last two days, but he hadn't been in his box for either of the games since the sultry southern beauty had been his guest. Ruth had been thinking about her a lot. When he got to the clubhouse after the disappointing loss Eddie Bennett handed him a piece of paper.

"What's this?"

"Beats me. A messenger gave it to me. He said it was for you."

The Babe unfolded it. Inside was an address. Underneath it were the words, "This is Claire Hodgson's address. Best of luck, Babe, you may need it. Don't forget to tell people about *Showboat*, Flo Ziegfeld."

Ruth slapped plenty of his expensive cologne on his puss after his shower. Once he'd dressed he headed to the address Ziegfeld had given him. His exits from the Stadium were quicker these days with so few kids waiting outside for him now. After the first game of the Chicago series the Babe had been thrilled to finally see a big group of kids outside the gates when he came out. They'd just stood and stared at him and he couldn't figure out what was going on.

Babe Ruth

Then Gehrig came out and the kids mobbed him. But he didn't pick up the kids, or hug them, or sign their penny scorecards or scraps of paper like Ruth always did no matter how much of a hurry he was in, or who was waiting for him. Gehrig just looked embarrassed and hurried away after mumbling something about having to do something for his mom.

Worse, when the Babe got out of his car near the address he was looking for a group of boys was playing stickball in the street. He heard the big kid holding the stick declare, "I want to be Lou Gehrig."

"*I* should get to be Gehrig, said another boy. "You always got to be Babe Ruth whenever you wanted."

When the Babe reached Claire's brownstone she was coming out the front door wearing a chemise dress and a brown cloche hat. He figured she was only five foot two, but she seemed taller. She was in five-inch heels. Claire ran down the steps and was obviously quite surprised to see him. He had a huge bouquet of red roses in his arms he'd bought on his way.

"Hello, Claire," said the Babe. "I've been thinking about you."

"I was just on my way out," she told him. "Ty Cobb's in town. My father handles all his investments in Atlanta. He was born there and he spends his winters in Atlanta. He says Detroit might as well be Siberia after November. He called on me a couple of times after I got divorced. He's invited me to have dinner with him tonight."

It could hardly have been worse news. Ty Cobb of all people. Knowing that she was seeing a handsome actor too didn't help. He told himself he should have expected this, given her amazing looks. Deflated, he simply held out the flowers. "I brought these for you."

"They're lovely. You can leave them with my sister."

A taxi pulled up at the curb.

"There's my cab now. Sorry, but I really do have to go. I'm running late."

"Ty *fucking* Cobb," Ruth muttered to himself as the taxi drove off. He thought about stuffing the flowers into a garbage bin and going to find another woman to spend the evening with. Or maybe two or three. He doubted they'd lift his crushed spirits much. No. He wasn't even in the mood for frisky flappers.

He took the flowers up to Claire's apartment. A woman that Ruth assumed was Claire's sister answered the door. There was a little girl with her. "This is Claire's daughter Julia," she told the Babe. The wide-eyed girl was only six or seven, but she already had some of her mother's good looks.

"Aren't you a little sweetheart?"

"You're Babe Ruth?" Julia gasped.

"I used to be," shrugged Ruth. "I think I'm losin' what little charm I had."

Julia look confused.

The Babe realized he still had the flowers in his arms. "These are for your mother."

"They are! The actor fellow has never brought her flowers, just some stale chocolates."

Ruth chuckled. He liked this little girl. "Well, that's somethin' in my favour at least. Maybe I have a chance with your mom after all."

"I sure hope so," said Julia.

The Babe shook her little hand, winked at her, and said he hoped he'd see her again. He said good-bye to Claire's sister, who was busy trying to fit all the roses into a vase. Then he went home, drank some of his expensive whiskey and thought about ringing Ty Cobb's scrawny neck.

o o o

The Indians came to town for four games, the first on Saturday, June 11. The Babe backed away from a pitch in the middle of batting practice.

"Whatsa matter, Jidge?" asked Lazzeri, who was waiting for his turn.

"I feel a homer coming. I wanna save it for the game," Ruth explained.

The Babe walked his first time up. His next time at bat, in the third inning, he belted one off Garland Buckeye almost to the scoreboard above the seats in right field. It landed six rows beyond the 465-feet sign. In the fifth he blasted one to the top of the bleachers and almost out of the park.

The Indians' catcher Luke Sewell turned to Billy Evans, the home plate umpire and said, "Nobody could hit a ball like that without havin' a slug of lead in the end of his bat."

Babe Ruth

Evans motioned to Eddie Bennett to let him look at it.

Bennett handed it to Evans and he examined the end and the handle. Then he sniffed it. He handed it back to Eddie. "It's real heavy, but there's no lead in it so far as I can tell."

"I *still* think there's got to be somethin' fishy about it," Sewell told Evans.

In the seventh Lazzeri hit one that carried beyond the cinder track into the bull pen and rolled under a bench. The Indians scored three in the ninth to make it somewhat interesting, but only for a moment. The fireman, as the reporters were beginning to call Wilcy Moore, doused the Indians' smoke signals. The final was 6-4 New York.

A frustrated Lou Gehrig went hitless and saw his average drop below .400. He stomped out of the locker room after getting dressed and went to take his dog to the park for a run.

Richards Vidmer got back to the hotel late that night after visiting friends in Queens. As he passed the front desk the clerk said there were several messages for him and handed him a pile of notes. They all said the same thing, "Come up to room 436." Vidmer knew who was in room 436. It was the Babe. His suite at the Ansonia was being painted as was Vidmer's house.

Ruth answered the door within seconds of Vidmer's knock. He was wearing a robe and a pair of Moroccan slippers and puffing on one of his dollar cigars.

"Where the hell have you been?" the Babe demanded.

"At a friend's place, in …"

"Never mind. Get in here."

"It's almost midnight, Babe. I'm bushed."

Ruth ignored him and went to the bar. He poured Vidmer a drink of Paul Jones Rye.

"What's this all about?" the reporter asked.

"What did we do last night?"

Vidmer thought for a second. "We killed a couple of bottles of your rye."

& THE 1927 YANKEES HAVE THE BEST SUMMER EVER

"And what did I do at the park today?"

"You powdered a pair of homers, nearly five hundred feet each."

"So why d'ya think you're here?" asked the Babe.

"You don't want to break the spell."

"That's right. Drink up."

In front of 45,000 fans, many still in their Sunday best, the Babe hit his twenty-first, half way up the right field bleachers. He waved to Vidmer and nodded as he rounded the bases. He wasn't grinning like he often did on his home run trots though. The ball had landed among signs that read "WE LOVE LOU" and "GEHRIG'S the GREATEST".

o o o

Cleveland seemed to be the one team that could give the Yankees a run for their money. The Indians rocked Waite Hoyt for six runs in an inning and a third. George Pipgras took over and, though he smacked a two-run homer, he gave up another two runs, just enough for an 8-7 Cleveland victory. Pipgras seemed to be sealing his own fate.

The Tribe scored six in the finale on Monday but the home team tallied fourteen. Ben Paschal was still in for the ailing Meusel. He homered twice, doubled off the left field screen, and lined a triple over the head of six-foot three Baby Doll Jacobson in center. Ben's four hits on the day raised the super sub's average to .333. He might easily have had four home runs.

"It really tells you something when that guy can't crack the lineup," James Harrison told Richards Vidmer.

Babe Ruth
& the 1927 YANKEES have
the BEST SUMMER EVER

14.

Lighting it up, but no Lucky Lindy

"I held back as long as I could, but it had to come."

The snowstorm of ticker tape and paper - 1,800 tons of it according to the supervisor of the crews that took four days to clean it up - was so dense above the parade that the open car carrying Charles Lindbergh had to be bailed out every ten minutes. Four million delirious New Yorkers packed the sidewalks along his route.

No game was scheduled for Thursday so Fred Lieb took the opportunity to postulate about the effects of aviation on baseball in the *New York Post*. He wondered if it would bring the Pacific Coast within reach of the big leagues. He thought it within the realm of possibility that within a few years the San Francisco Seals might touch down somewhere near Coogan's Bluff and head to the Polo Grounds to play the Giants and the Los Angeles Angels might fold their wings near the Concourse Plaza and prepare for a series with the Yankees. Aviation might just bring the west coast cities as close to the eastern hubs as St. Louis was now.

Three days later a million admirers clogged downtown Brooklyn to catch a glimpse of America's new idol. Lindbergh attended a ceremony at Roosevelt Field where his historic flight had begun and was scheduled to arrive at Yankee Stadium in time to throw out the first pitch of game one of a three-game set with the Browns. Five hundred white-gloved policemen stood at attention ready to form a flying wedge through which Lindbergh would pass. The start time of 3:30 came and went and there was no sign of him. The game was delayed for twenty-five minutes. Still no Lucky Lindy.

"I feel a homer coming," the Babe told Joe Dugan as they waited in the dugout.

Babe Ruth

"How d'ya know?"

"My left ear twitched. It's a sure sign."

"Lindbergh's not coming to see you hit home runs. He's coming to see me pitch," said Waite Hoyt. "I think I'll ask him for an autographed airplane."

"I left a couple of passes for him at the gate," said Dugan.

"How are your silver foxes doing, Herb?" Lazzeri asked Pennock.

"Just fine, Tony," he answered, looking up into the clouds as if Lucky Lindy was going to arrive in the Spirit of St. Louis instead of in the middle of a motorcade.

"And your chrysanthemums?" asked Tony.

"They're fine too. Good of you to inquire."

"You reading any good …"

Herb suddenly jumped to his feet and grabbed at the shoe on his left foot. Someone had stuck a burning match into the back of it.

"Lazzeri. You are a despicable cur!" Pennock yelled.

"You're a despicable cur," Mark told Tony. "Whatever *that* is."

After another twenty minutes had passed the umpire had waited for the adored aviator as long as he was prepared to. "That's enough," he yelled. "Play."

In the bottom of the first, St. Louis starter Tom Zachary committed the cardinal sin of throwing Ruth a strike. It wasn't exactly the pitch the King of Clout had been looking for and he held off for a split second. Then he swung hard and sent the ball high up into the bleachers in left-centerfield. There was applause, but nothing close to the tumult that usually followed a Ruthian blow. All eyes turned immediately back to the gate through which Lindbergh was supposed to enter.

"I held back as long as I could, but it had to come," Ruth said later. "When you get one of those things in your system, it's bound to come out."

Gehrig followed with his fifteenth. It was also all but ignored, a mere smattering of polite applause. Everyone's gaze returned to the gate.

Lindbergh had missed both of the blasts. Later on Lou hit a ball that dropped among a group of St. Louis fielders.

New York Times writer James Dawson lampooned the Browns' struggles in his article that night.

> With the bases filled, Mister Lou Gehrig hit a high fly to center. The Browns held a district convention around the spot where the ball descended. They chatted about this and that and someone told a funny story and then there was a discussion of the Russian situation. Inevitably an argument arose as to which player should catch the ball and it was a wonder one of them wasn't hit on the head. The sphere dropped onto the beautiful Stadium greensward and two smirking Yankees crossed the plate.

At 5:30, with the motorcade still stuck in traffic, Lindbergh's handlers decided to abandon all thought of getting to the game. They took him instead to collect the $25,000 check Raymond Orteig had promised the first pilot to fly across the Atlantic. Few people knew that Prohibition was ruining Orteig's lucrative hotel business and Orteig could barely afford to cover it.

After the Yankees walked off with an 8-1 win the reporters went to talk to the Babe.

"Here I was saving that homer for Lindbergh and he doesn't even show up," Ruth told the throng of newsmen who'd hoped to write about the meeting of America's two greatest heroes. "I guess he figures this is a twilight league."

"Though you got off to a very slow start this year, you've starting hitting balls out, Babe," said a reporter. "Do you suppose you still have a chance to hit fifty again?"

"If I did it might just shove Lindbergh off the front page for a day."

The reporters scribbled that one down. "You might need that many to beat Gehrig," one said.

∘ ∘ ∘

In the second game, under murky leaden skies and in front of a small gathering of eight thousand, the Yankees managed only eight singles off Lefty Stewart. The down and out Browns got just four off Urban Shocker,

Babe Ruth

though Earle Combs had to flag down a few long drives and make a shoe-string catch of Bing Miller's shot to center in the seventh.

With his buddy Koenig resting a sore arm, Tony Lazzeri played shortstop and chased George Sisler's high foul pop to the grandstand before plucking it from the lap of a paying customer. Joe Dugan electrified the small crowd in the ninth when he back-handed a line drive. The brilliant fielding made a 3-2 lead hold up.

o o o

The Babe slapped on another large dose of cologne after the game. He put on one of his best suits, and a brand new shirt and collar, and drove to Claire's. On the way he stopped at Macy's and another flower shop.

Julia opened the door when Ruth arrived. Claire was behind her.

"Mommy! The Babe's here to see you!" squealed Julia.

"Hi, sweetie pie. This is for you." He handed her the beautiful doll he'd bought, the most expensive Macy's sold.

Julia's eyes lit up. "Thank you, Babe, she looks just like a real princess!" She gave him and her new doll each a big hug.

"And these are for you, Claire," said Ruth, handing her the roses. "I was hoping you'd go see a picture with me."

"Well, I'm not sure if I ..." she started.

"C'mon, Mommy! Can't you see he's crazy about you?"

"Smart girl you've got there," said Ruth.

"Will there be a lot of people there?" asked Claire.

"I sure hope so," said the Babe. "It's my movie."

o o o

In the closer on Saturday St. Louis second baseman Ski Melillo committed his fourteenth error of the young season after Combs had singled up the middle. It put two men on for Gehrig who belted one of Elam Vangilder's slow curves into the seats. Lou tripled his next time up and hit his seventeenth homer his last trip to the plate. Gehrig's five RBIs won it for Myles Thomas. The final was 8-4. Moore shut out the Browns the last three innings. The Babe bowed out after eight with a sprained knee.

& THE 1927 YANKEES HAVE THE BEST SUMMER EVER

"Shit. If Ruth don't get ya, Gehrig does," Ski Melillo told Guy Sturdy, the Browns' first basemen whenever George Sisler took a rest, as they trudged off the field,

"That's not necessarily true," said Sturdy. "Sometimes it's Meusel, or Lazzeri."

"And what about their pitching?" asked Bing Miller. "Jesus Christ, we got four guys battin' well over .300 and they're makin' us look like little leaguers. Anybody Huggins sends out there pitches like Christy fucking Mathewson."

"Not bad, Duck Eye," Ruth told Thomas as they headed to the shower after the game. "That new bride a yours gettin' ya all revved up?"

"I got Cy to thank for it, Jidge, not all the lovin'. The cowboy shuts 'em down every time. You pitch a few decent innings and when you get in trouble in comes Wilcy with his fire hose."

o o o

The Yankees headed to Boston to play five games in three days. It was clear before the series even got underway that the Red Sox pitching staff was not made of the same stuff it had been back in the teens when Bill Carrigan could trot out the likes of Smoky Joe Wood, Sad Sam Jones, Herb Pennock, Carl Mays, Ernie Shore, Dutch Leonard, and Babe Ruth.

Now Ted Wingfield went all the way in the first game of the Tuesday double header even though he was 1-5 with an E.R.A. close to five. He got rocked for thirteen hits. Pennock tired in the seventh and gave up three runs but held on to win 7-3 without help from Wilcy.

In the stands sat Billy Kennedy and his father. Billy had wavy brown hair and wore a striped shirt and blue dungarees. His dad was tall and thin, with a slightly receding hairline. They'd come down from Manchester, New Hampshire so Billy could see his hero, Babe Ruth.

It was almost a year since Billy had been struck by a car while playing ball on the street in front of his house. He was hurt so badly that four operations were needed just to keep him alive.

"He's so weak," Billy's mother told her husband.

"What can we do, Mary?"

Babe Ruth

"I don't know, Jim, what is there that would cheer him up? We've tried giving him toys and games. Nothing interests him. He just lies in his bed staring out the window."

"I can't think of …" Jim noticed that his son was gazing out the window at the ball diamond. "Wait. Wait a minute. I know what we can do."

"What? What can we do?"

"Who's his hero?"

"Babe Ruth, even I know that. But I don't see how …"

That night Billy's father wrote a letter to "Babe Ruth, Yankee Stadium, New York" in which he enclosed a check and asked for an autographed baseball "from Babe to Billy."

o o o

In the afternoon tilt Gehrig slammed a three-run homer, his eighteenth. This time it was Waite Hoyt who benefited from more support than he needed. He won 7-3 as well, a five-hitter. Billy was crestfallen when the Babe didn't hit a home run in either game. Jim Kennedy went down to the railing above the Yankee dugout. Eddie Bennett was cleaning up the bench.

"Can I have a word?" Kennedy asked him.

"Sure, what can I do for you?"

Jim explained what had happened to his son. "Is there any chance you could get the Babe to say hello to Billy? It'd mean the world to him."

"I'll see," said Bennett. "He may already be in the shower."

The Babe was standing at his locker looking around the room and smoking a pipe. "Nice pitchin', Walter," he yelled to Waite Hoyt.

"Thanks, Jidge," Hoyt called back.

"Hey, Babe, you got a minute?" Eddie asked Ruth.

"Sure, keed. What's up?"

Eddie explained about Billy and his accident.

"Ya, Doc read me his letter. I signed a ball for the kid."

"That's right. And you told him to come see you play when we came to Boston."

"I did?"

"Apparently."

"So?"

"So he's here today. His father just talked to me."

"Where is he?"

"Up top."

Ruth set down his pipe, buttoned up his shirt and went back up to the dugout.

"Is this Billy?" he asked Jim Kennedy.

Billy's eyes lit up at the sight of his hero.

"Yes, Babe. This is my son Billy. He's your biggest fan. He's had a rough time of it these past few months. It sure meant a lot for him to see you play today."

"I wasn't much good. A lousy double and two singles. Knee's still buggin' me."

"You played great, Babe," said Billy.

"You two comin' back tomorrow? We're playin' two again. Maybe I can make it up to ya and hit one."

"We were going to head back to Manchester tonight."

"Please, dad! Please! Couldn't we stay over?"

"We can't really afford …"

"Never you mind about that," said the Babe. "Go ta the Buckminster. Tell 'em to charge your dinner and room to me."

"Are you sure, Babe?" asked Jim Kennedy.

"Absolutely. I'll see ya back here tomorrow. I'll leave passes for yas at the gate."

As he turned and headed back down to the clubhouse Billy and his dad stood staring at him.

"Can you believe what just happened?" Jim asked his son.

"Wait'll I start back to school and tell everybody we talked to Babe Ruth."

They hadn't heard what the Babe had said to himself on his way back to

Babe Ruth

the clubhouse. "At least there's one kid that still loves me."

In the first game the next day Wilcy Moore bailed Myles Thomas out again. He'd already allowed the punchless Red Sox four runs when Huggins went to get him with one out in the fourth. Moore shut out Boston the rest of the way.

The Babe blasted one to right center in the fifth. It exited Fenway and landed on an office building across the street. He contributed to a four-run seventh with another shot. This one flew through an opening in the right field bleachers before bouncing into a garage.

"I thought your knee was bothering you," Dugan said to Ruth.

"It was. Couldn't you see I wasn't able ta dig in like I normally do?"

"Ya, Jidge. You were really struggling. Tell that to whoever picked up your first homer across the street."

"I told a sick kid I'd hit one for him. Guess he'll be happy I got two."

o o o

That was an understatement. Billy would never forget the stay at the fancy hotel, the talk with the Babe, his deep voice, meaty paws, big brown eyes, broad smile, the smell of his sweat, his grass and tobacco-stained uniform, his speed and grace pursuing and catching a liner headed for the gap, the oooh of the crowd as he pegged out a runner with a strike to third base, and the thunderous roar from the grandstands when he hit two long homers just for him and then trotted around the bases head down with a big grin on his moon-shaped face.

o o o

In the second game, the fourth in two days, the Yanks managed just three scratch hits off Charlie "Red" Ruffing. He'd been struggling and thinking he'd probably be doing a whole lot better with another club, any other club. He had no idea that Miller Huggins thought Ruffing would be a perfect choice to take the place of one of his aging hurlers.

Wilcy Moore took over for Urban Shocker and shut out the Red Sox in the ninth to hold on to a 3-2 lead produced by three walks and a Boston error in the first and a Ray Morehart double in the fifth. The winner, Urban Shocker, was 8-4 now. Not bad for a thirty-seven-year-old.

& THE 1927 YANKEES HAVE THE BEST SUMMER EVER

∘ ∘ ∘

The Yankees had their bags packed for the trip back to New York but had to play the Red Sox one more time before heading out. Dutch Ruether got his sixth win in seven decisions. He got three hits as well.

"Way ta show me up, Lou," Ruether chided Gehrig after the game, an 11-4 romp. "I get three hits and knock in two and you steal my thunder. What a show off. Three homers and five ribbies."

"I was seein' da ball pretty good, Dutch," said Lou.

"Apparently."

"I'm Paul Gallico, from the *New York Daily News*, Dutch," said a young reporter wearing a fedora that looked like someone had sat on it. "How you feeling? I'm guessing it was pretty hot out there today."

"I just weighed myself. I sweated off twelve pounds. Always good to beat your old team though."

"Whatever you were throwing worked pretty well. From my angle I couldn't really see. A lot of benders?"

"I haven't thrown a curve in three seasons," said Ruether. "I just mix 'em up is all, fast ones and slow ones, inside and out. It's great that Hug doesn't call every pitch. He relies on a fellow's experience to know what to throw without bein' told. I wish he'd give me more work though. Today was the first I've pitched in more than two weeks. I hope it doesn't have anything to do with…" He stopped himself short.

"Anything to do with what?" asked Gallico.

"Nothin', never mind." He wasn't allowed to tell anyone that Barrow had promised him a $2,500 bonus if he won fifteen games.

∘ ∘ ∘

The White Sox had absolutely fallen apart. Beginning with their series in New York they'd lost thirteen out of seventeen. The Chicago fans were glum. Their team had been breathing down the Yankees' necks and now they trailed New York by nine. Ray Schalk wasn't sure if his first year at the helm might not be his last.

Babe Ruth

The Yanks had a glittering 44-17 record, a nine-game winning streak, and a ten-game lead over Philadelphia as the A's came to town for six games. If they could win five or six Connie Mack's club could lop off a good chunk of that gap. They got off to a good start.

In the first game of the Saturday double bill the powerful A's pounded Herb Pennock for fourteen hits. For a change Huggins opted not to bring in Wilcy Moore even when the Philadelphians scored four times in the top of the ninth. If he'd gone in and prevented even one of those runs from crossing the plate it might have been enough.

Lefty Grove had given up five runs after eight and Connie Mack elected to bring in Joe Pate, his corpulent knuckleballer, for the ninth. He'd broken in a year ago at the age of thirty-five and had gone 9-0, all in relief, proof that the A's could mount big comebacks too. The Texan got two men out but allowed two base hits and a walk. Gehrig came to the plate with the bases loaded and the Yankees down by a run.

"Come on Buster," shouted Koenig from third base.

"You got him this time, Lou," yelled Art Fletcher.

Mickey Cochrane went out to the mound. "Ya think Sacco and Vincetti are gonna get the chair?" he asked Pate.

"Wouldn't surprise me if they did," Joe drawled.

"Everybody says they're innocent," said Mickey.

"They both got real good alibis. All depends on the judge I reckon," mused Pate. He nonchalantly spit out a stream of tobacco juice.

"I hear their wives pleaded with the governor for two hours to spare their husbands and he turned them both down." Cochrane looked in at Gehrig. "Think he's nervous enough now?"

"I reckon so."

Pate's first pitch was a fast ball. Half way to the plate it looked as though it would come across belt high. The overanxious Gehrig swung hard but by the time the four-seamer reached the strike zone it was neck high. Lou missed it. Pate came back with a knuckleball. Gehrig let it go by.

"Strike two," called Pants Rowland.

& **THE 1927 YANKEES HAVE THE BEST SUMMER EVER**

Gehrig glowered at him but said nothing.

The next pitch was another fastball. Lou calculated that it was another four-seamer. He wasn't going to chase this one. He let it go by too.

"Strike three," called Rowland, "that's game."

Gehrig dropped his bat, glared at the umpure, turned on his heel, and stormed off to the dugout. The Yanks lost it, 7-6. The A's pulled a game closer.

Later that afternoon Frank Graham wrote:

> *Lou Gehrig is not another Babe Ruth because there will never be another Ruth. No one else has ever hit a baseball as far as the Bambino does when he truly leans on it, and doubtless no one else ever will. Nor has anyone ever had quite the color of the Babe, except perhaps for Rube Waddell.*

In the second game Rube Walberg, who'd been named after Waddell, yielded only a pair of runs in seven innings. This time Joe Pate came on in the eighth. Six men up, six men down. The Yankees couldn't do a thing with his wobblers and lost 4-2. Their lead was down to eight. Huggins dug into his desk drawer for his nerve pills when he got back to his office.

As he swallowed one and then another Gehrig stopped on his way to the showers and asked the other members of the movie set, "You fellas want to take in a picture show tonight? Might take our minds off the A's."

"Good idea, Lou. I could use an hour or two in one a them theaters where they blow in ice-cooled air with electric fans," said Wilcy Moore. "They're worth the price of admission even if the picture show's worse than an angry squirrel in yer britches."

"I wouldn't mind joining you guys," said Pennock. "Esther's taking care of her mother."

"Great. What's playing?" asked Ben Paschal.

Pennock went and got a newspaper from the bench in front of his locker. "The Roxy's playing the new Buster Keaton picture called The General."

"I hear that's hilarious," said Ben.

"Dey gawt a swell awchestra dere," said Lou.

Babe Ruth

"In between the pictures you can play that new bingo game they've got," said Herb. "It's called Screeno."

"They got drinking fountains?" asked Lou.

"Young Gehrig don't want to pay a nickel for a soda," kidded Wilcy.

"That's our Lou," said Pennock. "What about two cents for one of those new Eskimo Pies? Could you afford that?"

"Leave the kid alone," said Ben. "What else is playing?"

Herb turned back to the paper. "There's a Laurel and Hardy picture, one with Harold Lloyd, another one with Mary Pickford, and a horror picture with Lon Chaney."

"Which one'll it be, gents?" asked Ben.

"Whichever one's playin' in the coolest theater," said Cy.

They ended up picking *The Unknown*. It was playing at the 5,900 seat Roxy Theatre on West 50th Street between 6th and 7th Avenues just off Times Square. It had a soaring, Spanish-inspired auditorium. The main lobby was a columned rotunda that featured the world's largest oval rug. Music swelled from an enormous pipe organ on the mezzanine.

"I read somewhere that it cost twelve million to build this place," said Pennock as he swiveled his head to take in the wonders. "It's got a dry-cleaner, a hairdresser, and an infirmary. They've even got a gym and a library for the staff."

"No wonder it cost so much," said Paschal.

Pennock read aloud from the poster for *The Unknown*. "A criminal on the run hides in a circus and seeks to possess the daughter of the ringmaster at any cost. Starring Lon Chaney and introducing Joan Crawford."

Moore looked at the picture of Crawford.

"She is one *fine* lookin' filly," said Cy. "I'd sure like ta saddle her up and ride off into the sunset."

The movie didn't start right away. There was a cartoon first. It starred a mouse and his girlfriend and it was called Steamboat Willie. The players didn't like it much. The mouse was followed by newsreels. Of course there was footage of Charles Lindbergh's triumphant tour of America.

"People just can't get enough of the guy," whispered Herb. "I hear waiters are selling the food he leaves on his plate at diners."

Then came pictures of the devastation from an earthquake in Palestine that had killed two hundred people.

"I hope the picture starts soon," said Moore, "I wanna get a load a that Crawford gal."

"It shouldn't be much longer," said Pennock. "Here comes the sports news, that's usually the last thing before the picture."

The sports started with grainy film of Henri Cochet beating Jean Borota in the Wimbledon finals after eliminating Bill Tilden in the semis. Then they showed Bobby Jones defending his British Open title at St. Andrews.

"What? No baseball news?" asked Lou.

"Wait, here comes something," said Pennock.

The image of a large man in a camel-hair coat appeared on the huge screen. He was entering a hospital for sick children.

"Oh, no, it's not …"

"It is," said Pennock.

The man turned and waved. It was Babe Ruth. Next came footage of him sitting on the edge of a little boy's bed handing him a baseball.

"Our beloved and once adored right fielder," continued Pennock.

"We gotta see the big goof here too?" groaned Paschal.

Finally there was a newsreel of the Babe running the bases after a home run.

"Hey, Jidge don't run like that," said Moore. "He runs just like everybody else."

"Why's he look like he's taking tiny steps, all pigeon-toed like that?" asked Paschal.

"It's because of the speed of the film," explained Pennock. "That's what makes him look like he's running that way."

"Quiet, fellas," said Cy. "Here comes Joan Crawford at last."

○ ○ ○

Babe Ruth

Fritz French, whose nickname was Piggy, had not been happy that he was getting a lot less playing time due to Ty Cobb's arrival. But with all the double headers the A's were playing, Connie Mack decided to give Cobb's aging legs a rest the next day. Piggy got a chance to play and he took full advantage, rapping three hits, scoring twice, and leading the way in a 4-2 Philly win in the first game of the Sunday double header. Combs was the only Yankee who did anything at the plate. He had a double and a single, but the big guys behind him didn't drive him in this time. Gehrig struck out three times and bounced out weakly to second in four trips.

"Nice work, Heinie," Cobb called out from the dugout after Lou's last time up. "You were great today, ya Deutch dick."

"Shut up, ya Confederate fag," Art Fletcher yelled at Cobb.

"Maybe the movie hurt your battin' eye last night," Ruth suggested when Gehrig flung his bat at the dugout wall.

The Babe hadn't played. He'd finally decided to give his bad knee a day off. He was painfully aware that when you reached thirty things didn't heal as fast as they once had. He envied Gehrig's youth. Ruth had read Arthur Mann's piece in the *New York Evening World* in which he said that "Gehrig is in perfect health and since he takes care of himself and eats well he should guard first base for the Yankees for another ten years."

Gehrig's lousy day at the plate had come at a bad time. The A`s had gained yet another game on the Yanks.

But in the afternoon contest the Yanks scored five in the first and coasted to a 7-3 win, a complete game five-hitter for Wilcy Moore, who was pressed into service as a result of all the double headers. Gehrig was delighted to hit his twenty-second off a Joe Pate knuckler in the seventh.

o o o

Dutch Ruether ran his record to 7-1 at the Stadium on Monday, a 6-2 win over Howard Ehmke. Durst was a disappointing 1-5 filling in for the Babe in the number three slot but Tony Lazzeri hit his ninth homer of the year and Earle Combs hit his first.

In the series finale on Tuesday Gehrig hit his twenty-third into the sun worshippers in right field. Lou singled in a run in the ninth after Al Simmons had robbed him of a sure triple with a fantastic full-speed backhand catch. Fans from Johnny Grabowski's hometown of Schenectady presented him with $1,500 in dollars, quarters, and nickels to show their appreciation. Unfortunately Nig wasn't in the lineup.

Urban Shocker had a five-hit, 9-0 lead after eight. Then the roof caved in. Simmons, Cochrane, Dykes, Cobb, Foxx, and Billy Lamar reached base. In went Moore to save things. Two batters, two more hits. Out came Moore. In went Pennock. One batter, one more run, the A's eighth. Then a base on balls.

Huggins threw his cap on the ground and called for Myles Thomas. It was a lot of pressure to put on a second-year pitcher. Especially since the batter due up was Al Simmons. After him would be Mickey Cochrane.

"When he reached the mound Hug said, "It would be really great if you could get someone out, Myles."

"I'll try, Skip."

Two batters, two outs. A 9-8 win for New York. Huggins breathed a huge sigh of relief. He hadn't wanted the A's drawing any closer than they already had. They had won the first three games of the series. But they'd lost the last three and they left town demoralized and once again ten back.

Babe Ruth
& the 1927 YANKEES have
the BEST SUMMER EVER

15.

Murderers' Row

"I hope you lose the next twenty and then run into a whole slew of injuries."

With the score tied 2-2 in the fifth inning against Boston on Wednesday, June 29, Gehrig hit his twenty-fourth. The pitch was a slow curve. Gehrig didn't seem to put much of a swing into it but the ball sailed high and far into the seats in right. He got a huge ovation from the crowd.

Ruth sat on a crate resting against the right field seats. After grounding out he'd seen no point in going to the dugout. He had a clear view of Gehrig's poke. "The kid's sure gonna be hard to beat," he muttered to himself.

"God damn that son of a bitch is strong," Ruether said to Koenig on the bench. "Looked like he was hittin' a fungo and the thing went half way up the grandstand."

Pipgras finally got his first win and it was a beauty, an 8-2 three-hitter. For good measure he hit a single and a triple to raise his average to .313. Ruth went 4-for-5 to raise his to .354, the highest it had been since April 15. His only out, a line drive up the first base line, tore the glove of first baseman Phil Todt apart when he tried to backhand the bullet behind the bag. He picked the ball up, threw it to the pitcher for the out and then checked to see if he still had all his fingers.

"The beast near took my ear off in April and now he rips my new glove in half," muttered Todt.

o o o

On Thursday, in their last game of the month, the Yankees scored five runs in the first two innings, including Gehrig's twenty-fifth round-tripper. Myles Thomas was stung for six runs in the third and Huggins had to send

Babe Ruth

in Wilcy Moore, his one-man fire department. The Yankees scored one in the third, three in the fourth, one in the fifth on the Babe's 425-foot homer to right - and three in the sixth. "Take that!" their bats seemed to say. The Red Sox got nothing off Moore. New York 13, Boston 6.

With a 49-20 record the Yankees stood ten and a half games ahead of their nearest challengers, the Senators and White Sox, and now twelve up on the A's. A lot of people were starting to ignore the pennant race and focus on the long ball competition between Ruth and Gehrig, the Home Run Derby as some scribes were starting to call it. James Harrison wanted to know if there was any animosity between them.

"Lou's a great kid," Ruth said of Gehrig. "If anybody's gonna break my records I hope it's him."

"Dere'll never be another guy like da Babe," was all Gehrig said.

o o o

Before the first game of July rookie Danny 'Deacon' McFayden, the Boston starter, was warming up along the sidelines as Koenig and Lazzeri chatted on the bench after taking batting practice.

"Ever see a guy wear glasses to pitch?" Mark asked Tony.

"Can't say as I have. Looks pretty funny, don't it?"

"Herb says he's blind as a bat without 'em."

"Well, let's just be happy he's got 'em on then, else we might be getting a fast one up side the head."

McFayden had no trouble seeing the plate and the Yankees had no trouble seeing his pitches. Combs led off the first with a home run to left and a few minutes later, after Ruth lined a single through the box, Gehrig hit his twenty-sixth to right to give New York a 4-0 lead.

McFayden helped his own cause in the third, spearheading a three-run rally that brought Boston within a run. But Ruth singled home Combs and Gehrig doubled home the Babe in the fourth. Herb Pennock had to leave the game with a sore arm with one out in the fifth but Shawkey came in and shut out the Red Sox the rest of the way and the Yankees cruised to

& THE 1927 YANKEES HAVE THE BEST SUMMER EVER

a 7-3 victory.

"I guess dey call him da terrier," Gehrig told Koenig before the Saturday game got under way.

"Who?"

"Their pitcher," said Gehrig.

"Why? What's his name? Hugs never said."

"His name's Russell. Jack Russell."

"Jack Russell," Koenig repeated. "Oh. Like the dog. I get it. Good one, Lou. They teach you stuff like that at Columbia?"

"Dey didn't teach me much at all. Christ, I flunked German and I tawk da fuckin' language."

"A lot better than English," Koenig chuckled.

"Wha d'ya say?"

"Nothing, Lou, nothing. Never mind. Hug say what the terrier throws?"

"Mostly hooks, pretty good ones."

Bill Regan tripled in two in the third off Ruether, but Dutch got help from Morehart and Lazzeri who made two nifty double plays to get him out of jams. Tony enjoyed playing short, his original position, when Morehart was in for Koenig.

Russell's curves gave the Yankees fits. They mostly swung at air. Meusel singled home Gehrig and Collins singled in Dugan in the fifth. An inning later Combs singled home Lazzeri. That was it, just enough for a 3-2 win over the cellar-dwelling Red Sox. The loss was Boston's fifty-third in sixty-four games.

o o o

On July the third in Washington thirty thousand Senators fans showed up hoping to see their club win their tenth in a row. Though they lacked the Yankees' power, five of their starters were batting better than .300.

"We sweep 'em and we'll be five back," Bucky Harris told his team as they changed into their home white uniforms. "Let's keep things rolling."

Babe Ruth

Ruth dampened their enthusiasm in the very first inning with a solo home run into a concrete sun parlour beyond the centerfield fence. Judged to have flown 450 feet, it was the longest one ever hit at Griffith Field. But Goose Goslin hit a much shorter two-run four bagger minutes later to put the Senators ahead.

The Yankees retook the lead with two in the top of the third, but the Senators tied it in the bottom of the frame. Urban Shocker had to leave the game when he twisted his ankle. In the fifth, Tris Speaker singled to left off Shocker's replacement, Myles Thomas. Goslin drew a walk and Joe Judge hit one down the first base line.

"Peanuts, five cents," a vendor who was standing on the field yelled up into the right field stands. The ball hit him in the leg.

The umpires huddled to decide whether to penalize the home team for interference. The gate in centerfield opened and a booster who was rip roaring drunk staggered through it. To the amusement of everyone but the umpires he plunked himself down on the outfield grass and took something out of his coat pocket. He unwrapped a sandwich and took a big bite out of it. The umpires waved him off the field. He smiled and waved back at them with a pickle.

"Hey, ya mule-headed bum, get off the field," Ruth yelled at him.

The sot pawed at the grass with his hooves and yelled "Hee haw! Hee haw!"

Ruth belly laughed as two burly policemen appeared and led the souse away to a loud chorus of cheers. The next batter, Ossie Bluege, ripped a two-run single and the Senators won it 6-5. The sot hadn't missed much.

o o o

The two teams hopped aboard the Congressional after the game and headed to New York. Miller Huggins and Bucky Harris met for supper in the dining car. Harris wore a serious expression. He set his boater down on the seat beside him and picked up his menu. Then he set it down again. He looked at Huggins and said, "You know what, Miller, I hope you lose the next twenty and then run into a whole slew of injuries." Harris handed the waiter a five dollar bill and whispered, "Slip me a double bourbon with a beer chaser."

"And for you, sir?" the waiter asked Huggins.

"Milk."

Joe Dugan and Tony Lazzeri sat across from the managers. A waiter with a dish-laden tray held high over his head hurried passed them.

"Does Jidge always carry around hundreds?" Tony asked Joe.

"A lotta the time. Sometime he does it to get free drinks cuz most bars can't change a hundred so they just let him drink for free."

"He sure goes through a lot of money."

"Funny thing," said Joe. "I asked the Babe for money when we were in Cleveland in May. He was standing in the lobby of the Hollenden House and I says to him, 'Jidge, your pal's empty.' So he pulls a bill out of his pocket and hands it to me. I thought it was a fifty until I went to pay the restaurant tab that night. The waiter asks me if I thought I was a wise guy. I say, what do you mean? He says a restaurant this size can't cash this. It was a *five hundred* dollar bill. They had to get the owner outta bed to make change. A few days later I give the Babe five one hundred dollar bills and he asks me what it's for. I tell him and he says 'Great, I thought I'd blown it. Thanks, keed.'"

"That's the Babe for you," said Tony.

"But sometimes he needs to *borrow* money cuz he goes through it so fast," Dugan continued. "Last spring he needed money to pay his income tax."

"A while back he told Frank Costello he was short of cash," said Lazzeri.

"The mob boss?" asked Dugan.

"Ya, that Frank Costello," said Lazzeri. "Costello set up a golf match with Jidge for five thousand bucks knowing he'd lose so he wouldn't have to lend him the money. I guess he figured Jidge would forget to pay him back and he didn't want to have to send his hoods to collect it."

o o o

An estimated 75,000, the largest crowd ever to see a baseball game, turned up for the Yankees' Fourth of July doubleheader against Washington. Thousands more were turned away. Fans stood five deep behind the back row, others stood in the runways or sat in the aisles. They knew the Senators had a chance to close to within a few if they could beat the Yankees in New York like they just had in Washington.

George Pipgras gave up nine hits, eight of them singles, and limited the Senators to one run. He breathed a sigh of relief when it was over. Sloppy Thurston, the Washington starter didn't fare so well. The Yankees battered him for ten hits and eight runs in four innings.

Desperate to stop the barrage, Bucky Harris called for Walter Johnson. The Big Train hadn't pitched in almost a month. He'd been throwing on the sidelines during batting practice in spring training when his best friend Joe Judge lined a ball off his right ankle. His teammates, especially Judge, were mortified but it turned out that Johnson was fine. He put some ice on it and was as right as rain.

"My arm feels good, I'm in fine shape, and I don't see why I shouldn't have a successful season," the 39-year-old told reporters after the workout.

Four days later Johnson stood near the boxes just beyond third base chatting with some admirers. All of a sudden he crumpled to the ground. Judge had hit another line drive at him. This one hit him in the left ankle. Al Schact and Nick Altrock, who never took anything seriously, hurried over to Johnson. He was rolling on his back holding the ankle and groaning. They broke into a chorus of *London Bridge is Falling Down*. Altrock, imitating a fight referee, sent Schact to a neutral corner and began counting Johnson out. By the time he got to ten it was clear that Johnson was badly hurt. Teammates helped him off the field and the trainer put ice on the ankle, which was bright purple, but the swelling wouldn't go down.

Two days later, after trying vainly to run on it, he finally submitted to an x-ray. It revealed a 45-degree fracture of the fibula. He couldn't walk at all for a month and was delighted when the doctor put his ankle in a light cast that enabled him to go back to his farm to inspect his prize-winning White Leghorns, Rhode Island Reds, Budd Rock chickens, and Bourbon Red turkeys.

When he finally rejoined the Senators' staff Johnson wanted to pitch right away, against the Yankees. Harris elected to boost his confidence by holding him back for weaker competition. Two weeks later he delighted everyone by hurling a three-hitter at the lowly Red Sox.

"D'ya notice he threw nuthin' but curves, Skip?" catcher Muddy Ruel asked Bucky Harris after the game.

"I sure did, Muddy, curves and control were all he had."

"Not a single strikeout."

He'd been roughed up for five runs in five innings in his next start but things looked hopeful when he got Lazzeri to swing at a sweeping curve on the outside corner for strike three. He tried the same thing with Dugan and Joe ripped it into left field for a double. Then Johnson threw a fastball to Pat Collins and he sent it into the left field seats.

Two innings later Lou Gehrig deposited another Johnson fastball into the right field seats. It was almost too painful to watch. The aging warrior didn't have to face the Bronx Bombers every day but he wouldn't do much better against everybody else. Johnson was done at the end of the year. The Senators lost 12-1.

Though it seemed impossible, in the second game of the double header the Yankees treated the Washington pitchers even worse. It looked a lot like an afternoon at the driving range. The hosts loaded the bases on General Crowder in the first inning and Gehrig hit a grand slam. The crowd rose en masse and shrieked in delight, shaking the huge stadium to its rafters. Many of the fans covered their ears, never having heard so loud a racket.

The Yanks bashed emergency reliever Firpo Marberry around for another ten runs and finished off with six more off Bobby Burke for a 21-1 victory. Morehart, Ruth, Gehrig, Lazzeri, and Grabowski each scored three times. Lou and Tony both drove in five. The Babe hit a triple that flew forty feet over Tris Speaker's head and bounced on the cedar track beside the flagpole 475 feet from the plate. In the seventh, Julie Wera hit the only home run of his career, considerably less distance than Ruth's drive.

Richards Vidmer set down his pencil. "I just did some math," he told James Harrison. "What do you think the Yankees batted in the two games today?"

Babe Ruth

"I don't know. It must have been way over .300," guessed Harrison.

"Try .468."

"That's unbelievable. I've never even heard of a mauling like that one."

"And if Wilcy Moore, who couldn't hit water if he fell out of a boat, hadn't gone 0-4 in the second game they'd have batted .493."

Over in the Senators' locker room their pitchers hung their heads and licked their wounds.

"The Yankees can pound anything or anybody and would on the slightest provocation," drawled Sloppy Thurston. "They have treated me very shabbily."

"I'm sure there are worse things in this world than facing the Yankee batters," moaned Firpo Marberry, "but I wish you could tell me what they are."

"I used to think I was a pitcher," said Bobby Burke, "but the Yankees have knocked that notion clear out of my head."

o o o

Reporters resurrected the term "Murderers' Row" to describe the Yankee powerhouse. It was a reference to the second floor of New York's City Prison - which everyone called the Tombs - the floor on which rapists and murderers awaited execution. The nickname had originally been applied to the 1918 squad in Miller Huggins' first year as manager. It referred to Frank Gilhooley, Del Pratt, Wally Pipp, Frank "Home Run" Baker, Ping Bodie, and Roger Peckinpaugh. It was a sign of the dead ball era that the six sluggers had combined for a whopping fourteen home runs that year. Now Ruth sometimes hit that many in one month.

Dan Daniel and Fred Lieb, the *Telegram* reporters, went to dinner after the twin bill.

"That was really something today," said Lieb.

"Murderers' Row nothing, they ought to call them the bomb squad," said Daniel.

"The poor Senators thought they were gonna put some pressure on them and instead they got beaten to a pulp."

& THE 1927 YANKEES HAVE THE BEST SUMMER EVER

As a bushy-haired waiter handed them menus Lieb asked Daniel if he thought Gehrig was going to stay ahead of the Bambino in the home run derby.

Daniel thought for a moment. "Gehrig has everything in his favour. Power, youth, perfect physical condition, and splendid co-ordination. If he could only learn to pull the ball more like Ruth does he'd be further ahead of the Babe than he is."

"If it ends up being close, it's going to be real interesting to see which one has the most people cheering for him," said Lieb.

As they ate, a reporter from the *Washington Evening Standard* was writing a piece about a new phenomenon. Almost all of the owners of major league teams had decided that, if the new NBC and CBS radio stations that were springing up all over the country decided to broadcast regular season games, it would kill their attendance. But dwellers in the apartments that fringed Wrigley Field had learned the trick of watching the Cubs play through their front windows while they listened to the game on their radios. They claimed they knew more about what was going on than the fans inside the park.

The team's management had been horrified by the development at first but soon discovered that many of the freeloaders had developed a keen interest in the club and a lot of people who'd never been to a game started buying tickets to see the players they heard described on their radios in person.

o   o   o

In the final game of the series the Senators scored five runs off Herb Pennock and Joe Giard in a wild first inning. Bucky Harris decided to throw Bump Hadley to the wolves and he gave up two runs in a third of an inning. Then Harris sent in Garland Braxton from Snow Camp, North Carolina. He swallowed his chewing tobacco in the midst of giving up four runs in five innings.

The game was all tied up in the seventh when Harris sent in Hod Lisenbee, the one man the Yankees hadn't beaten all year. He threw a fastball to Tony Lazzeri and it wound up in the right field seats. A 7-6 Yankee win. The demoralized Senators staggered to twelve and a half back.

Babe Ruth

∘ ∘ ∘

The Yankees rode the Advance Empire State Express train to Buffalo and beat a local team 18-1 even though they lent them several players. Then they boarded the Maple Leaf Liner for a game in Toronto. Most of them thought to bring along racks of ribs to barbecue in Ruth's private car and Dutch Ruether pitched in with a case of beer. As the train steamed toward the Canadian border friendships strengthened, gnawed ribs flew out the windows to the surprise of grazing deer, and slurring off-key voices belted out *The Beer Barrel Polka*.

"Here's good news for the wets," said Herb Pennock as he read the *Toronto Mail and Empire*. "The government of Ontario has just passed the Act to Regulate and Control the Sale of Liquor in Ontario, which repeals the Ontario Temperance Act." Cheers erupted from all corners of the Pullman.

After an uneventful exhibition game on Centre Island, Ruth, Meusel, Dugan, Shawkey, and Ruether eagerly took the ferry back to Toronto and went up and down Yonge Street, stopping at every reopened bar. Each one was holding a boisterous celebration of the end of prohibition in the province and the Yankees joined in.

"Christ almighty! King Street, Queen Street, Princess Avenue, Parliament Street, the Royal York Hotel? It's like you're in jolly old fuckin' England up here," said Ruether after many here legal whiskeys.

Dugan ignored him. "Ya know what? I'd forgotten that women don't go to saloons."

"That's right. We've gotten used to seeing them in the speaks," said Bob. "They never went to bars when they were legal in the States either."

"The speakeasies have got music and dancing, the saloons never did," said Joe. "And dames can get gin and wine and mixed drinks in the speaks. It was all beer and shots of whiskey in the bars before Prohibition."

"The Canadian gals we've seen sure are pretty," said Bob. "I don't imagine the Tiger Lady has any spies up *here*."

"You wouldn't want her want to know that you'd even looked at a woman," said Joe. "She still keeps a loaded pistol in her underwear drawer, doesn't she?"

"Yup. But she's got some pretty sexy outfits in it too."

At their last stop, a tavern that looked as though it belonged on a narrow street in Dublin, a huge man with an ugly scar on his face charged up to the Babe. Everyone tensed. They were pretty sure Ruth hadn't slept with anyone's wife or girlfriend in Toronto though.

"I remember seeing you play here in Fourteen, just before I headed off to France to fight the Hun," the man rasped at the Babe. "I got them and their damn mustard gas to thank for this voice of mine. You were playing for the Providence Greys back then, weren't you?"

"That's right. I hit my first homer as a professional on Centre Island," said Ruth, glad to be recognized north of the border.

"You pitched a whale of a game. Shut our side down on three hits as I recall. Let me buy you gents a pint."

"That'd be swell, but we've got a train to catch," said Ruether.

Ruth bought a few cases of Canadian whisky and paid some teenagers to help carry them to the train station. They hadn't seen American bills before and they found it strange that they were all green and not one of them had a picture of the king on it.

○ ○ ○

The Yankees, some badly hung over, were back on American soil for a Friday double header at Navin Field in Detroit on the 8th. Ruether, whose eyes looked awful, lasted an inning and a third in the early game. Myles Thomas came in and did well at first but then gave up a pair of runs in the fifth and another two in the sixth.

Gehrig smacked a triple and two singles to raise his average to .405. The Babe had the worst game he could remember and wore an 0-5 collar to the between games snack table. In disgust, he passed on the food and drank a half gallon of water from the drinking fountain instead.

"I was such a bum I don't deserve a goddamn breadstick," he growled.

Myles Thomas, who'd started the year so well, felt no better. He'd given up eleven hits in his five innings of work and, worse, he'd let Huggins

Babe Ruth

down again. The Tigers won 11-8.

Jake Ruppert always insisted that his team look sharp and, alone among major league clubs, they were issued with three sets of home and away uniforms. They put on a fresh set of grey flannels for the second game.

Every Tiger in the lineup got at least one hit in the afternoon contest. After his fine performance July the 4th Pipgras lasted just two and third and Huggins had to send in Moore. He did no better, yielding five runs in five innings. Then Pennock took over and gave up another.

But, as the experts had predicted in April, the Tigers had the bats, but precious little pitching. Ray Morehart singled home Combs in the first inning. In the second Lazzeri, Dugan, and Collins singled. Combs doubled and with two on and two out the Babe smashed a ball to deep center. Heinie Manush raced back and finally picked it up as it rolled to the fence at the 440-foot sign. He heaved it in to Charlie Gehringer who relayed it to Johnny Bassler, the Tiger catcher.

Another perfect hook slide. Bassler's tag was late. Ruth had an inside-the-park home run. The long drive and the hell-bent for leather base-running were the margin of victory in a 10-8 Yankee win, Moore's tenth. With his frequent relief appearances and the numerous Yankee late-inning comebacks Wilcy now had more wins than almost all of the league's starters.

o o o

A crowd of 33,000 poured into Navin Field for the early Saturday game. The Tigers scored seven runs off Pipgras and Moore but the home team's pitchers got bombed yet again. The Yanks scored three runs in the first, seventh, eighth, and ninth innings. They notched four in the fourth and two in the sixth. Only in the third and fifth were they shut out.

The Babe had two singles, a double, and two home runs, his twenty-eighth and twenty-ninth. He ended the game 5-for-6 with seven RBIs and now boasted a .373 average. The scoreboard read 19-7 New York when the whipped Tigers trudged off the field.

Because the Yanks had spent so much time smacking baseballs in the early game the afternoon match started late. Shocker did miserably and his replacement Joe Giard was worse. The Tigers scored three runs in the second, third, and fourth, and then four more in the fifth for good measure. Giard's E.R.A. mushroomed to an embarrassing 10.13 in the 14-4 drubbing.

o o o

In a single game on Sunday, July 11 Herb Pennock gave up six runs in his six innings on the mound. Earl Whitehill took the hill for Detroit. He'd told the Tigers' owner that if Cobb was kept on as manager in '27 he would quit the team. Whitehill was Detroit's most reliable starter, but he'd lasted only an inning and a third against the Yanks two days ago.

Whitehill had his good stuff today and he limited the Yanks to three runs. The Babe failed to get the ball out of the infield in five tries and struck out twice. The Tigers scored four in the fourth and won 6-3.

In the get-away game on Monday afternoon Ruth went hitless again but the Yanks scored five runs in the sixth as part of an 8-5 win. Waite Hoyt yielded five runs in six and a third but got a lot more run support than Pennock had. Gehrig doubled to start a five-run rally in the fifth and hit his twenty-ninth homer of the season in the seventh.

The injury bug had finally bitten the Yankees. Among the starters, Ruether, Pennock, Hoyt, and Shocker all had troubles of one sort or another. That left Moore, Pipgras, and Thomas to pick up the slack. Koenig was hurt and Huggins put Ray Morehart in at second and moved Lazzeri to short. Morehart had a bit of speed but not much power. Gehrig had a bad ankle but he soldiered on. People were starting to notice that he refused to miss a game or even an inning.

o o o

When they got off the train at the still under construction Union Terminal depot in Cleveland the Yankees looked up at the 700-foot skyscraper that was rising above downtown and would soon be the world's tallest building.

"Come on, dago, time ta use some a your Eyetaliano," Ruth said to Lazzeri as they hopped into a cab.

"Where are you two going?" Dugan called out to them.

"Mayfield Road," Ruth shouted as he ducked into the taxi. "You wanna come with us?"

Babe Ruth

"Pretty rough part a town, Jidge," said Joe.

"The wop'll make sure we're okay," said the Babe.

"Count me in then," said Dugan, hurrying to reach the cab before it pulled away.

"What's the guy's name," Ruth asked Lazzeri as the taxi driver threw the yellow cab into gear.

"Moe Dalitz. He's the head of Little Italy's Mayfield Road mob."

"He got good stuff?" asked the Babe.

"The best you can get these days," said Tony. "Brings it across the lake from Canada at night on launches."

"Hey Mack, how many cases a hooch ya think we can we fit in the trunk?" Ruth asked the driver.

"Six," the cabbie answered knowingly.

"That should hold me for a couple a weeks," boomed the Babe. "I still got a few cases from Toronto."

"If ya pace yourself," said Dugan.

When they arrived at their destination, which wasn't much more than a garage, they saw several trucks out front. *Kowalski's: Purveyors of Fine Furniture since 1898* was printed across their side panels. Lazzeri led the way to the back entrance.

Two large men stood on either side of a door that said "Absolutely no admittance!"

They immediately recognized the Babe and led the three Yankees inside.

"Sei signore Dalitz?" Lazzeri asked a large man sitting at a desk covered with empty coffee cups and whisky glasses.

"Sono io," answered the man.

"Saluti, signore, abbiamo sentito che hai buon whisky," said Tony.

"Ho i migliori whisky," said Dalitz.

"We need six cases," said Ruth.

"Vogliamo sei casi," Lazzeri translated.

Dalitz shook his head at Tony. "Is okay. I speak pretty good English."

"How much?" asked the Babe.

"A hundred a case," Dalitz told him.

"Sounds about right. If it's good stuff. I keep hearin' about hooch that's laced with all kindsa nasty shit."

"Not this whisky, Mister Bambino. Itsa from Canada. You gonna like it just fine."

"All right then." The Babe took a wad of bills out of his pocket. He tore off six one hundred dollar bills and gave them to Dalitz.

Dalitz looked at them. He stuffed two in his pocket and slid the others into a drawer. "Get dese boys the good stuff," he told a man who was stacking cases against a wall.

"We're back in town in a month," Ruth told Dalitz. "If this hooch is as good as you claim I'll be back with *two or three* cabs."

Lazzeri shook hands with Dalitz and headed out the door with the others.

Joe Shaute from Pickville, Pennsylvania was the Indians' starter in the first of a four-game series in Cleveland. He went the whole way and suffered a 7-0 drubbing, allowing fourteen hits. Koenig celebrated his return to the lineup after a two and a half week absence with a pair. After failing to hit in fourteen consecutive tries, Black Betsy came to life in the ninth. Ruth smacked a ball over the high right field fence. It bounced off the roof of a passing taxi cab on Lexington Avenue. The cabbie decided not to get the roof fixed. He enjoyed telling his fares how it got dented.

"That feel good?" Charley O'Leary asked the Babe as he passed his third base coaching box.

"Sure did," answered Ruth.

"You may not catch Biscuit Pants, but nobody hits 'em like you do, Jidge."

The Babe grinned.

In the seventh he backed up against the wall, reached up, and knocked down a ball on its way out of the playing area. In the ninth, when the last batter of the game dribbled one to the mound, Urban Shocker preserved his shutout with an easy scoop and then twisted his ankle turning to throw to first. He had to be carried off the field. Ruth went to his locker and gave him a bottle of 'medicine' to ease the pain.

o o o

On Wednesday the Yankees pushed the Indians twenty-four games behind them with a 5-3 win. Koenig had three hits and the Babe went four-for-four to raise his average back among the league leaders.

"Geez, you couldn't buy a hit but ever since that jazz guy gave you that saxophone you bin squawking on, you've bin hittin' up a storm," said Joe Dugan as he passed Ruth's locker on his way to the showers. "What's the guy's name, Googles?" he asked Bengough, knowing the Babe wouldn't remember. "He came up from New Orleans. I think he did *Rhapsody in Blue*."

"Paul Whiteman," answered Benny.

"Ya, that's the guy. But you got to teach Jidge how to play that fuckin' thing, Googles. He's driving us all nuts."

"I've been trying, believe me," shrugged Benny.

"I can't stop playin' the thing no matter how bad I sound." said Ruth.

"Why not, Jidge?" asked Lazzeri.

"Cuz I'll stop hittin' again, ya dumb wop."

Up in the press box Richards Vidmer turned to James Harrison and asked, "What's up with Gehrig?"

"What do you mean?" asked Harrison.

"Only one homer and not a single three-bagger in seven games. That's pretty strange."

"He needs pickled eels," said Harrison matter-of-factly.

"Did you say pickled eels?" asked Vidmer.

"That's what I said."

Vidmer thought for a minute. "Well he isn't likely to get any in Cleveland."

"The Babe told him about a place in St. Louis, a delicatessen two blocks from the hotel. Gehrig says he's going there as soon as we get to town."

& THE 1927 YANKEES HAVE THE BEST SUMMER EVER

○ ○ ○

Thursday's game was a scorcher. The mercury hovered near a hundred. The Indians got two unearned runs in the first when Ray Morehart dropped a pop fly and Lazzeri followed with an uncharacteristic bad throw. Huggins knew the heat was getting to him and took him out. Meusel dropped a ball near the fence two innings later. The sweat-soaked Yanks lost 4-1.

In the series closer on Friday, the fifteenth, the Indians reached Waite Hoyt for five runs in four innings and Myles Thomas for three in his two innings of work. The Tribe led 9-2 but then George Uhle fell apart. The Yankees pushed across three runs to get back in the game and when Garland Buckeye took over they lit him up, scoring four more to win it in the ninth.

"That's two in a row with three hits for Meusel," Vidmer told Harrison after the last out.

"What's he hitting now?" asked Harrison.

"He's up to .379, his highest mark of the season," said Vidmer.

"How many guys are ahead of him?"

Vidmer shuffled through some papers. "Let's see, the Tigers have Gehringer at .350, Heilmann at .349, and Bob Fothergill at .360. Speaker's hitting .347 and Goslin's at .364 for the Senators. The A's have Dykes at .363, Wheat at .348, Chuckles Cobb at .355, and Simmons at .401. Ruth's at .365, Gehrig's down to .390. So Meusel's third best now."

"Think he might actually crack a smile about it?"

"I doubt it."

Babe Ruth
& the 1927 YANKEES have
the BEST SUMMER EVER

16.

SWEATIN' IN ST. LOUIS

"I had a piece a cabbage in my hat, not a block of ice."

The first game in St. Louis was played in front of only nine thousand.

"Pretty small crowd for a Saturday," Meusel yelled to Combs as they played long toss.

"With this heat and humidity it's a wonder *anybody's* here," Combs shouted back.

"Hug says this is their biggest crowd of the year," said Dugan, who started throwing with Lazzeri.

"Well it's one of the *smallest* ones we've played in front of," said Tony.

"If it weren't for the Babe versus Lou thing I'll bet there wouldn't be as many here as there are," said Joe. "I'd be sittin' at home in front of a fan drinkin' a cold beer if I were them."

A thick mass of humidity blanketed the field and Sad Sam Jones smothered Ruth all afternoon. As part of a nothing-for-five day the Babe grounded into two double plays and fouled out to the catcher. There were runners on base every time he came up. Gehrig still didn't manage a triple or home run, but he did knock in three with a single and a double. The Yankees came out on top 5-2. Pennock, who allowed just six hits, got his tenth win.

"Thanks for fannin' me with the towel when I come off the field, Eddie, but could ya get me a cabbage tomorrow?" Ruth told Eddie Bennett after the game. "I musta sweat off fifteen pounds out there."

"Sure thing, Babe," said Bennett. "I'll make sure the ice box is plugged in too."

"Wait!" yelled Ruth.

"What is it, Babe?" asked Eddie. "What's wrong?"

"Nothing. I could have sworn I just felt a breeze. Musta bin my imagination."

"Hey, Jidge, whad'ya say dat deli was cawled?" Gehrig asked Ruth.

"I got no idea, Buster. I just know it's two blocks the other side of the hotel, on the corner across from the telegraph office, next door to a haberdashery. I got fifteen real nice silk shirts there. Not that *you'd* shell out five bucks for one."

o o o

As the Yankees were dressing for the Sunday game Lazzeri went over to Gehrig's locker.

"Did you get your precious eels, Lou?"

"Ya, Tony, dey was good too. I bought a bunch and gave 'em to da chef at da hotel ta cook up for me again tonight."

"Hey. You're startin' to think like the Babe. That's somethin' *he'd* do. Now we'll see if they put any zip back in those big arms of yours."

A few feet away Ruth tore a piece of cabbage off the head Bennett had put in the ice box for him. He placed it inside his cap.

"Least I'll be a bit cooler today," the Babe told Urban Shocker who was going to start. "I had ta drink about twenty beers after yesterday's game. McGovern says I shouldn't get dehydrated."

"I wish I could take a cold one out to the mound," said Shocker.

"Whenever I pitched here in the heat I tried to get everybody to swing at the first pitch. I didn't wanna be out there any longer than I had to."

"That's exactly what I'm gonna do, let 'em hit the ball. Only ones ya gotta worry about are Sisler and Ken Williams."

"Ya, don't give Williams anything too juicy. The fucker'll hit it a ways," said Ruth as he gently put on his cap before heading out to the sun-baked field.

The Yankees trailed 3-2 after five but rallied for a pair in the top of the sixth to go out in front. Shocker wilted in the heat and gave up two runs in the seventh.

& THE 1927 YANKEES HAVE THE BEST SUMMER EVER

"Might it not just be time fer Mister Moore?" Charley O'Leary asked Huggins.

"He hasn't pitched for a couple of days and being from Texas he can handle the heat better than most," said Art Fletcher.

"Hell, I'd be putting him in if he was from Alaska," said Huggins.

In the eighth Gehrig sent one of Milt Gaston's fastballs deep into the centerfield seats and Bob Meusel hit one just a few rows shorter. That was all Wilcy needed. He shut St. Louis down cold, in spite of the heat and gave his team a 5-4 win.

"Where you sleepin' tonight?" Shawkey asked Ruether as they were getting into their street clothes, minus a necktie with Huggins' blessings.

"I'd like to sleep in that cold shower I just got out of, but I guess I'll sleep in the park like I did last night," said Dutch. "The last time we were in St. Louis I soaked the bedsheets in cold water and wrapped myself up in them. I got some sleep but my fuckin' joints ached for a week."

"Too bad they don't have air-cooled hotels here like the air-cooled movie theaters in New York," said Bob.

"They sure need 'em. Where are you gonna sleep?"

"It wasn't too bad on the roof last night. There were a few of us up there. Jidge got room service to send us up crabs on ice and a bunch of cold beer."

"Well, that cinches it. Gehrig and Morehart can sleep in the park, I'm goin' up to the penthouse with you swells for some Ruth service."

o o o

It was George Pipgras who had to swelter on the mound in the Monday, July 18th game. He let the Browns get the odd hit but allowed them only one run, in the fourth. The score was tied at ones at the end of six, but the Yankees piled on a half dozen runs in the seventh and two more in the eighth. Gehrig hit one into the centerfield seats.

"I told ya he just needed pickled eels," Harrison told Vidmer, who was using a rolled up newspaper as a fan. "That's number thirty-one. He's *well* ahead of Ruth now. And in this heat Gehrig's definitely got the advantage."

Babe Ruth

The Yankees were up ten to one until the ninth when Bing Miller singled home Wally Gerber. George Sisler followed with a three-run homer. Then came Ken Williams, who'd hit more home runs than the Babe in '22. Williams hadn't hit one in a couple of weeks. He was due. The muscular slugger tapped his bat on the far side of the plate and dug in.

With the count two-and-two Williams took a vicious swing at a curve that got a bit too much of the plate and drove it to left. Meusel took off after it. Two feet from the fence, running at full tilt, he reached up and snagged it for the third out. Huggins wondered where that effort and determination had been in the '26 Series. Maybe, like everyone else, Silent Bob just wanted to get to the showers.

"Thanks for givin' us a scare, George," said Dugan on the way to the dugout.

"Thanks for keepin' us out there in the heat," growled the Babe as he ran by Pipgras. "I had a piece a cabbage in my hat, not a godammed block of ice."

In the last game in St. Louis, Ruether had his way with the Browns. He shut them out for six innings then flagged from the heat and allowed one in the seventh. Fresh from a day of rest, Wilcy Moore came in, got out of the inning, and blanked St. Louis in the eighth and ninth. The visitors, anxious to wrap things up and be on their way to cooler climes, scored five runs on Lefty Stewart.

"We're just far enough from downtown that you can't smell the stockyards or hear the traffic of the Loop," said the hotel manager when the Yankees reached Chicago and checked into the swanky Cooper-Carlton at 53rd and Hyde Park Boulevard on the shore of Lake Michigan. The Babe liked that it was far from the newspaper offices. Photographers weren't around to snap his picture whenever he went out. The H-shaped red brick hotel rose ten stories above the adjacent park.

"I want my usual room with big windows, on the lake side so I can watch the sailboats," said Ruth.

"As if he ever stays in long enough to look out the windows," Lazzeri whispered to Koenig.

"Actually - now that you mention it - Jidge doesn't seem to be going out at night any more," said Mark.

"Haven't you heard," said Dugan. "The Babe's got a big crush on some model from Atlanta."

"Really? He usually has a crush on whatever woman's nearby," said Tony.

"Meusel's roomin' with me, like last year," the Babe told the manager.

"Would you like the same arrangement for the bath, Mister Ruth?" asked the manager.

"Ya, stock it with beer and plenty of ice," said the Babe, handing the man a twenty.

Meusel watched as the Babe unpacked his trunk a few minutes later.

"Didn't you buy a bunch of silk shirts in St. Louis?" asked Meusel.

"Fifteen a them."

"So where are they?"

"I left 'em for the maid."

"You left them for the maid! You said they cost five bucks each."

"She said they were really beautiful and I thought she'd like 'em for her husband."

"Ya, Jidge, I imagine she will."

Ruth and Meusel shared a cab to the park with Dutch Ruether. On their way into the stadium they passed Billy Evans and George Hildebrand.

"You guys are sure working a lot of our games this season, Billy," said Ruether. "Like the big crowds, do ya?"

"No, Dutch. We was here for the Sox and Senators' series."

"I heard the Senators wiped the floor with 'em," said Ruth.

"Four straight," said Hildebrand. "Put 'em eighteen behind you lot."

"Ya, but now Washington's only eleven back of us," said Dutch.

"You must be shakin' in your boots," chided Evans.

"Ya. That's what we're doin', shakin' in our boots," said Ruth. "Say, those

Babe Ruth

specs you ordered come in yet?"

"That's a real knee-slapper, Babe, haven't heard that one in a while. Have a nice game."

o o o

Along the outfield walls of Comiskey were signs advertising Eight O'Clock coffee, fur coats for $100 at Miller & Company, and RCA Radiola 66 cedar panel electronic radios for $129, just $10 down.

Koenig and Lazzeri threw a ball back and forth along the sidelines after taking batting practice.

Distracted by thoughts of the beautiful cigarette girl, Koenig threw the ball wide of Lazzeri.

"Look out, Earle!" he yelled too late.

The ball hit Combs square in the right temple. It make an awful sound. He fell to the ground like a stone. Koenig rushed over to him.

"I'm real sorry, Earle. You all right?"

Combs lay on the ground. His eyes were closed and he wasn't moving.

"Holly shit! You killed Earle!" said Lazzeri.

Mark and Tony carried their stricken centerfielder into the dugout.

"What happened to him?" Huggins demanded.

"I hit him with a throw," Mark admitted sheepishly.

"Well get him into the clubhouse and get him some ice," ordered Huggins.

Luckily the doctor who treated the White Sox was in the stands. He'd seen Combs lying on the ground and had hurried to the Yankee clubhouse.

"He is not badly hurt but he could use some whiskey," said the doctor after looking at Combs up close.

"He doesn't touch the stuff," said the Babe, who'd come in to see what all the fuss was about.

"Well he needs some now," said the doctor. "Somebody run to the drug store."

"I'll go," said Eddie Bennett.

⚓ THE 1927 YANKEES HAVE THE BEST SUMMER EVER

Ruth went to his locker and grabbed a bill out of his trousers.

Ten minutes later the doctor forced a bit of whiskey into Comb's mouth. His eyes popped open and he sat straight up.

"What the heck was that?" he yelled.

"It's what's kept me in the big leagues all these years," chuckled Ruth.

Huggins gave him a dirty look. Combs sat up.

"How are you feeling, Earle?" asked his manager.

"I'll be fine in a minute."

"Are you going to be able to play?"

"Of course."

"Because Paschal can …"

"I'll be fine, Skip. Don't worry."

Paschal had already grabbed his glove in anticipation of a rare start. It was exactly a month since he'd been in the lineup. He slumped back down in frustration.

Sarge Connally, a twenty-eight-year-old from Texas, started for Chicago. It was his first year as a starter and hooks were his speciality. For seven innings he had the Yankees swinging at nothing, a seeing-eye double by Gehrig their only hit.

"Maybe it's you that needs the specs," Billy Evans told Ruth when he came up in the sixth.

Harry McCurdy, the Chicago catcher, singled in a run in the fourth and that was it. Until five o'clock rolled around.

"Time to get to work and earn those big pay checks you fellows cash," Miller Huggins announced before the start of the eighth inning.

Lazzeri had seen enough of Connally's curves now to know where they crossed the plate. He knocked one to the fence for a triple, but Mike Gazella, who was often filling in for Dugan at third in the late innings, popped out.

"Grab a bat, Ben," Huggins told Ben Paschal, "you're hittin' for Grabowski."

Babe Ruth

"You got it, Hug," said Paschal, happily jumping off the bench.

Paschal laced a double to left on the second pitch and nodded to Huggins when he got to second base standing up. Lazzeri scored. Tie game.

Combs, who was 0-3 and still rubbing the large bump on his head, drew a walk. Connally couldn't afford to be too careful with Koenig. Not with Ruth and Gehrig following him. He threw a fastball over the plate. It wasn't fast enough. Koenig lined it over the second baseman's head for a single. Paschal scored.

Ruth followed and smacked a pitch to right center. "See, the eyes are just fine," he yelled at Evans as he took off. Combs scored. Koenig scored. It ended 4-1, making Hoyt the proud owner of a 12-4 record.

o o o

Huggins decided to give Combs a couple of days off. Ben Paschal was thrilled to take his place. Cedric Durst would play left field. He'd gone almost as long as Paschal without a start. Durst came out of the gate swinging. Batting leadoff he doubled and scored in the first and was robbed of another hit when first baseman Bud Clancy hauled down his line drive in the fifth. The four men that followed him in the order, Koenig, Ruth, Gehrig, and Meusel each had two hits, but hitting wasn't the problem. Herb Pennock, who was 10-4, gave up three earned runs, a Koenig error scored two more, and Myles Thomas allowed another pair in a 7-5 Yankee loss.

Thirty-five thousand came to see if the White Sox could make it two in a row over the front-runners on Saturday. Gehrig drove home a pair with his thirty-third double but Koenig, anxious to atone for his error the day before, provided most of the offence with two hits, two runs, and three RBIs. Urban Shocker held the White Sox to two runs over seven innings at which time five o'clock lightning struck again in the form of four Yankee runs. Wilcy Moore allowed nothing in the seventh, eighth, and ninth for a 5-2 win.

"Ten games now without a homer," moaned Ruth, who'd had a line drive single and two walks, after the game. "I'm sure as hell not gonna catch Gehrig or break my record now."

o o o

& THE 1927 YANKEES HAVE THE BEST SUMMER EVER

Fifty thousand rooters squeezed into Comiskey for Sunday's game. In the first inning the Babe hit a Tommy Thomas curve to the furthest reaches of the outfield grass, 450 feet from home plate, and wound up with his fifth triple of the year.

In the third Ruth *really* powdered one, into one of the last rows of seats in right field.

"Jidge really got ahold of that one," Meusel told Gehrig as he replaced him in the on-deck circle.

"Shouldn't that count as two runs?" Ruth chuckled to Billy Evans as he crossed the plate.

"Probably," said Evans.

His next time up the Bambino just missed catching one on the sweet spot. He popped it high over first base. Bud Clancy camped out under it.

"Oive heard about mile-high pop ups and da like," he muttered to himself, "but Lord tunderin', dat ting's gotta be even higher'n at."

Clancy finally caught it, but he was almost knocked over.

"That should probably be two *outs*," deadpanned Evans.

"Ya, probably," agreed the Babe.

George Pipgras gave up just three hits and two runs over eight innings, his best performance of the season and his fifth straight win. Moore pitched a no-run ninth and the Yankees left town with a 3-2 win and a healthy twenty-game lead on the White Sox. Huggins celebrated by going to one of his favourite roller skating rinks.

Babe Ruth & the 1927 YANKEES have the BEST SUMMER EVER

17.

OFF TO MA GEHRIG'S FOR KASEPATZLE AND SAUERKRAUT

"Did anybody ever drop by to borrow a cup of bullets?"

When Pipgras got home Mattie met him at the door with a big hug and then a passionate kiss.

George sputtered, "I'm sorry I didn't call, hun. I didn't think I should spend …"

"Five wins in a row, Mister Pipgras? I don't care *how* much money we have in the bank. We're going out to celebrate. And when we get home, I'm putting on my petting shirt."

"In that case, I'm taking you to a place with really fast service," said George.

"We can have our dessert in bed," said Mattie.

o o o

After seventeen days on the road the Babe was anxious to spend some time with Claire. The next morning, a rare off day, he took her and Julia to the New York Zoological Park, which most people now called the Bronx Zoo. Julia loved the snow leopard kittens and thought the rhinos and giraffes and silverback gorillas were fascinating. They took a boat ride on the Bronx River to cool off and to get a break from the curious on-lookers that were following them around. People weren't used to seeing Babe Ruth with a woman in the daytime.

"Has Mommy said she'll go see your movie yet?" Julia asked the Babe while he was getting her an ice cream cone.

"Not yet, sweetie. But I got my fingers crossed."

Babe Ruth

Julia crossed her own fingers. "I do too, Babe."

o o o

That night Combs, Gehrig, Moore, and Paschal went to the Longacre Theatre where *Babe Comes Home* was starting a six-week run. They'd tried to talk Ruth into going with them.

"Come on, Jidge. Ya *gotta* come," said Gehrig.

"Ya, Lou might even buy you a candy bar and some popcorn," said Paschal.

"I'm hopin' Claire's gonna go see it with me," the Babe told them.

"How are we supposed to make fun of you if you aren't there?" asked Combs.

o o o

When the Babe got to the Stadium the next day the movie set told him they'd enjoyed his picture.

"The ending was a bit predictable," said Paschal.

"And some of the actors that were supposed to be your teammates looked like they'd never been anywhere near a ball diamond," said Combs.

"But you were pretty good in it, Jidge," offered Gehrig. "You looked like a real actor."

"Hell, I know I'm no Doug Fairbanks. Long as you enjoyed the popcorn," shrugged Ruth.

"Oh, we did, Babe. The *popcorn* was great," said Paschal.

o o o

Desperate to beat the Yankees after eleven straight losses, the Browns sent their ace Milt Gaston out to face them in the first game of their double header the next day. The Yankees led 5-0 after three and 8-1 after six. In the first inning Ruth hit one over the exit next to Row 50 in the right field bleachers. In the sixth he hit another one not quite as far up.

"There's no need for their five o'clock lightning today," Richards Vidmer told James Harrison as they watched Gaston throw his warm up pitches before the bottom of the seventh.

"They could leave the man with a *shred* of dignity," said Harrison.

After several more loud cracks of the bat the score was 15-1.

"You said they didn't need the five o'clock lightning today," said Harrison.

"I guess they can't help themselves," said Vidmer.

Every starter had a hit except Mike Gazella, whose average dropped twenty points to .314 with an 0-for-5. Ruether gave up just six hits and boosted his record to 11-2. Winning fifteen and getting his secret bonus was looking like a sure thing.

In the late game the Browns did a little better at the plate, managing eight hits off Hoyt. Gehrig hit his thirty-second homer in the third with one on to give the home side a 3-2 lead, which they held as of the middle of the seventh. Then it started yet again. A half inning, three St. Louis errors, thirteen batters, and seven hits later the Yanks led by nine. The final was 12-3. The total score for the double header was New York 27, St. Louis 4.

"Ruth enjoyed a rather productive day, wouldn't you say?" asked Harrison after the carnage had ended. "Bumped his average twelve points to .376. Not a bad day at the office."

"Yes, but should the Yankees be allowed to play him and Gehrig against St. Louis?" asked Vidmer facetiously.

"It's not like they couldn't win without them," said Harrison.

"Hell, I think their B squad could handle the Browns," said Richards.

"Their B squad? Oh, like they have for spring training games."

"Exactly. Wait a minute." Vidmer started scribbling. He erased a couple of names, thought some more, and wrote in new ones. A moment later he turned the paper around so Harrison could read it. "Look at this. That's as weak as I can make them."

Harrison read aloud. "Leading off, Durst in center field. Second, playing second base, Morehart. Third, in right, Paschal. Hitting cleanup, playing left field, Meusel. Batting fifth, at first, Koenig. Hitting sixth, playing third, Gazella. At short, batting seventh, Wera. Catching and hitting eighth, Bengough. And pitching and batting ninth, Giard." He paused to consider the lineup. "Not weak enough. They'd probably still win."

o o o

Babe Ruth

On Wednesday at the Stadium, Bing Miller tripled in the second and Ski Melillo singled him in to give St. Louis a 1-0 lead. No one imagined that the Browns were expecting it to hold up. The Yankees tied it in the third but Win Ballou pitched carefully and it was still 1-1 in the bottom of the sixth. He was a little *too* careful with the Babe, who took him to a full count and then tossed his bat aside and trotted to first after Ballou threw one several inches wide of the plate.

"It's up to you, Biscuit Pants," Ruth called to Gehrig.

Ballou's first pitch to Lou was a chest-high fastball. He swung hard and the ball shot into the upper reaches of the right field bleachers. The Babe waited at home and shook Lou's hand. They headed to the dugout together and Meusel stepped to the plate.

Lazzeri came out to the on-deck circle. As Ruth and Gehrig passed him Tony said, "I'm gonna show you two a *real* home run."

"Are you now?" asked Lou.

"I tell ya what, ya dumb wop," boomed Ruth. "You hit one farther than that and I'll buy you the biggest plate of spaghetti in town."

Meusel tried to hit one himself but Ballou threw him a two-seam fastball that sank to the bottom of the strike zone and Meusel grounded out to second. Tony belted Ballou's third pitch into the extreme corner of the left field stand, his longest of the year and a rival of many of Ruth and Gehrig's blasts.

"I like mine with mushrooms," he yelled in to Ruth.

"You got 'em," Ruth yelled back.

It ended 4-1, Pennock's eleventh win against just four losses. All of the Yankee starters were having career years.

o   o   o

In the first inning of the last game of the series on Thursday it looked as though the Browns were finally going to beat the Yankees. Urban Shocker was in trouble from almost the very first pitch. Frank O'Rourke doubled to right and Herschel Bennett hit a fly to left that Meusel lost in the sun. George Sisler drove one to left which Meusel finally tracked down in the corner.

But by the time he'd fired the ball in, both runners had scored. Ken Williams grounded out to second but Bing Miller singled to right, scoring Sisler. Huggins told Wilcy Moore to get ready but Shocker earned a reprieve when Ski Melillo grounded to Lazzeri and he flipped the ball to Koenig who fired it to first for a double play.

"All right, let's hold 'em for once," George Sisler yelled to his teammates as they took the field for the bottom of the first.

Sisler shook his head in frustration as a caravan of Yankees ran past him on their way to second and beyond. Combs scored. Koenig scored. Ruth scored. Gehrig scored. Meusel scored and it was 5-3 New York.

The Yankees led 7-3 when the Babe came up in the eighth. With Combs on base he drilled one among the customers in Ruthville, as fans and writers had taken to calling the right field bleachers in '21. They hadn't much since '25. The overmatched Browns scored a futile run in the ninth to make it 9-4, their fifteenth straight loss to the Yankees.

After the game Lou took the other players with German backgrounds home for some of his mom's cooking. Benny Bengough and Mark Koenig, who shared an apartment not far from the Gehrig's place, went in Lou's '24 Flint that he'd bought from a neighbor who couldn't keep up the payments. Dutch Ruether, George Pipgras, and Bob Meusel went in Ruth's brand new 100-horsepower, six-cylinder Pierce Arrow. They were able to stretch their long legs; it was one of the few five-passenger cars on the road.

"Du siehst wunderschön wie immer, Mama Gehrig," bellowed the Babe as he walked into the apartment. She blushed. He gave her a big hug and thought that her huge bosoms might just tempt him if she were thirty years younger and a hundred pounds lighter. "Sind Sie sicher, dass Sie genügend Nahrung für alle von uns haben?"

"You still speak German pretty good, Babe," said Lou, taking Ruth's hat and putting it on the shelf in the front closet. He went around and got all the other players' hats and told them to sit down.

"That's mostly what I heard in Pigtown when I was a kid," said Ruth. "A course *a lot* a what I heard around my old man's saloon I can't repeat in front of your mom."

Babe Ruth

"What are you serving, Ma Gehrig?" asked Ruether.

"I haff bratwurst, kasepatzle, sauerkraut, sauerbraten, and pickled eels," she told him.

"What? No dessert?" teased the Babe.

"Of course, George, there's apfelstrudel," Ma Gehrig told him.

o o o

The food was delicious. The players had to keep from snickering at the way Lou doted on his mother. He helped carry the huge servings of food and cleared away the plates. After dinner he told his mother he'd do the dishes later and finally relaxed. He got his pipe and lit it up.

"Öffne das fenster," Ma Gehrig told him.

"Es tut mir leid, Mama," Lou said sheepishly. He got up and opened the window.

"Das war köstlich," said the Babe.

"Yes, delicious," said Benny.

She took off her checkered apron and smiled.

"Is it true you used to do Owney Madden's laundry, Ma Gehrig?" asked Mark.

"Yes, but he vas not often at home ven I vas dere," she said. "Just his vife. She vas a nice voman."

"Did anybody ever drop by to borrow a cup of bullets?" chuckled Benny.

"Vat?"

"Nothing. I was just making a joke."

"We better get on our way," said the Babe. "Thanks for the great meal, Ma Gehrig. I always love comin' here."

"Thanks for inviting us," said Meusel, who hadn't said much as usual.

"Yes, thanks, Mrs. Gehrig," said Pipgras.

"Vielen Dank," said Ruether.

"You boys must come back again soon. I used to think baseball was for bummers, but now I luff to haff Lou's playmates here."

The players grinned. Lou gave them their hats.

"This is quite a son you have here," said Ruether, putting his arms around Lou's big shoulders.

"He's a goot boy, my Louie."

"I guess you're looking forward to him finding a wife and giving you grandchildren," said Dutch.

Ma Gehrig frowned. "He is still just a boy," she said. "And he's the only big egg I have in my basket. He's the only one of four that lived so I vant heem to haf da very best."

The Babe elbowed Ruether hard in the stomach on their way to the car, almost knocking him to the curb.

"Owww! What the hell?"

"Ya shouldn't have said anything to Ma about Lou findin' a girl," Ruth told Dutch.

"Why? Cuz no one would be good enough for her darling boy?"

"It's not just that. You think she's gonna let her baby take up with another woman and stop paying all his attention to her?"

"I guess not."

o o o

On Friday Cleveland's rookie manager Jack McAllister ordered his starter Willis Hudin to pitch extra carefully to Ruth and Gehrig and take his chances with Meusel. It worked. Four times Meusel came up with men on base and failed to drive them in. The only times Hudin gave Ruth anything near the plate was when the bases were empty and he smacked two doubles.

Combs ripped four straight singles and was robbed of an extra base hit by centerfielder Fred Eichrodt his last time up. Eichrodt had been playing fairly shallow for Combs, unlike his location when the Babe was batting, which was close to 400 feet from home. He felt like his position should be listed as center bleachers. Thanks to Meusel's rough day at the plate Combs scored only once. The Indians won it 6-4 to put a halt to New York's six-game winning streak.

o o o

Babe Ruth

George Uhle was the Cleveland starter for the first game of a twin bill on Saturday. He'd won twenty-seven games in '26. Now, at the end of July, he'd won only five. The Yankees scored a run in the first and Uhle looked shaky.

Joe Sewell scored in the top of the second. Then his brother Luke scored. Then Fred Eichrodt scored. Hug left Ruether in anyway. It was a smart move. That was all the Indians got. The Yankees knocked Uhle out of the box in their half of the second. McAllister sent in six foot-four, 300-pound rookie Jumbo Brown.

Jumbo gave up a run in the third and in the fifth Ruth singled and Gehrig hit his thirty-fourth into the right field seats. The young giant was still on the mound when Gehrig hit his thirty-fifth in the eighth. It bounced over the fence into the left field stands.

Two of the umpires talked at the end of the inning.

"Ya think they're ever gonna change that rule, Bill?" Red Ormsby asked Bill Dinneen.

"I dunno. You'd think they'd a changed it by now. Heck, we've been suggesting it for years."

"It should be a double, just like if there were fans on the field when there's an overflow crowd and somebody hits a ball into them," said Ormsby.

"Any a Ruth's bounce into the seats this year?" asked Dinneen.

"Nope. They've all been on the fly," said Ormsby, "and a few have flown right outta the neighborhood."

On the fly or bounced over, Lou was still in the lead. The Indians failed to score in the ninth and the Yankees beat them 7-3. Now Ruether was 12-2.

"I shoulda gotten more than eleven thousand," he muttered to himself as he stripped off his sweaty uniform.

o o o

In the second game of the Saturday double header Joe Shaute was the Cleveland starter. He had fond memories of his major league debut when he came into a game in the eighth inning with a one-run lead, two outs, and the bases loaded. The next batter, Shaute's first, was George Herman Ruth

& THE 1927 YANKEES HAVE THE BEST SUMMER EVER

and Joe struck him out in four pitches.

In the sixth the Yankees got to work and scored a pair on a homer by Meusel and an RBI single by Hoyt. Waite gave up six hits, all singles, half of them by Shaute. Ruth helped preserve Hoyt's third shutout with a perfect strike to home to nail Chick Autry at the plate. Hoyt was 14-4. He was rewarding Huggins' faith in him and then some.

o o o

Ruth picked up Claire after the game. After three beseeching phone calls - as well as a bit more encouragement from her daughter - she'd finally agreed to go to see the Babe's movie. She wore a red cloche hat that matched her lipstick, a black dress from Chanel, a Gabardine cape, and as usual, five-inch heels. They went to dinner first, during which Claire explained that she would have agreed to step out with the Babe sooner but needed to terminate things with John Boles. Then they headed to the movie. *Babe Comes Home* was playing at a little theater in the Bronx. Ruth pulled his hat down over his face on the way in so no one would recognize him.

As always, there were newsreels before the picture, shots of protesters in Vienna angry about the acquittal of three accused murderers, the premiers of Japan and Germany signing a trade agreement in Tokyo, and the Prince of Wales arriving in Quebec for a tour of Canada.

Last came the sports news. "Ty Cobb, now playing for the Philadelphia Base Ball Cub, registered his four thousandth hit on June eighteen," announced the narrator. "Fittingly, he did so in Detroit, where he accumulated most of that total."

"Are you still seeing Cobb?" Ruth asked Claire.

"No. We just had dinner that time. I told him I was seeing someone. Then it was John Boles and now it's you." The Babe smiled at that news.

"You know, I've never really courted a girl before," he said. "Am I doing all right at it?"

"You're doing just fine."

"Has anyone ever told you that you have very kissable lips?"

"Is that your way of asking if I'd like you to kiss me?"

"How did you know?" asked the Babe.

"A woman can tell. And yes I would."

The Babe kissed her once and then again.

Claire said, "I hope we do a lot more of that."

They sat back and held hands through the whole movie. Ruth loved the picture. There was no applause when the lights came up as he'd hoped, but there had been a few laughs.

"The Babe better stick to smackin' baseballs," a man said to his wife as they left. "That picture'll soon be playing exclusively to ushers."

18.

An Enchanted Day Off and A Rough Afternoon for Pants

"See, daddy, the moon really is made of cheese!"

The first day of August at the Stadium was damp and gloomy. It looked as though the game would be a washout like Sunday's had been. Lazzeri and Bengough had taken advantage of the rare Sunday morning off to go to church together. Combs went too, a Presbyterian church though, not a Catholic one. As usual, Tony had prayed that he wouldn't have a seizure during a game.

The rain held off and Dick Nallin yelled "Play!" at three o'clock.

Jake Miller, the Cleveland starter, struck out Combs and got Koenig to pop up meekly to short.

"Are we really gonna play this thing?" Ruth asked Nallin as he stepped to the plate. "For the love of Pete, I can't see what Miller's throwing."

"Get up there, you big stiff," Nallin told him. "You can't see what he's throwing on a clear day."

"Look who's talking about not being able to see," the Babe muttered.

"Watch it, Ruth, I've thrown men out for less than that."

Miller and Herb Pennock posted zeroes for three innings. Koenig smacked a crisp single to start off the fourth. Ruth looked down the third base line for the signal from Art Fletcher, who'd just looked into the dugout for a sign from Huggins. The indicator that inning was a pull of the right ear and the sign after it had been a swipe across the chest. Fletcher repeated it for the Babe.

Babe Ruth

"I guess Hug doesn't figure we're gonna get much offa Miller today the way he's throwin'," Ruth thought to himself.

He took a couple of mighty practice swings, made a point of eyeing the right field bleachers, and laid down a nifty sacrifice bunt. Koenig moved to second. The technique was repeated a minute later when Gehrig laid down a bunt to move Koenig over to third.

"Nice job, Lou," Huggins told Gehrig when he returned to the dugout. Gehrig beamed, happy to have pleased the boss.

As it turned out, the sluggers' perfectly executed sacrifices weren't needed. Meusel lashed a double to the gap that would have scored Koenig from first. The score held at 1-0 New York until the sixth, when Ruth made a perfect throw to home and Bengough dropped the ball.

The Yanks trailed 2-1 when the skies opened in the seventh. In three minutes the diamond was a lake. The Cleveland dugout filled with water. After another ten minutes of steady downpour it overflowed and the floorboards began floating away. In hopes of encouraging Nallin to call the game the Indians took off their shoes and socks and ran through the rain, splashing and frolicking. Soaked to the skin, Nallin held the fort as long as he could. He finally had enough and called the game.

James Kahn mused in the *New York Graphic* that the Master Mauler was now the pursuer and the question was now not whether Gehrig would beat out Ruth but whether Ruth could catch Gehrig. He predicted unhappy days ahead for the Colossus of Clout. Those favoring the Babe said he'd been a pretty good king in the past and the Gehrig faction pointed out that a lot of good kings were losing their thrones and maybe it was time for Buster to take over the chair.

o o o

The Yankees had a rare day off. Attendance had been so high throughout the year that for once Ruppert and Barrow elected not to send them to some one-horse town to play an exhibition game. Waite Hoyt, Herb Pennock, and Bob Shawkey took their wives and kids to Steeplechase Park on Coney Island. They met outside the park under the enormous Funny Face that grinned frightfully through its forty-four teeth. The grotesque and diabolical jester hinted at a promise of the irresponsible hilarity visitors would experience inside. And they could experience it all by purchasing a combination ticket: twenty-five amazing attractions for twenty-five cents.

After the Dads paid, the families passed through the boardwalk entrance and climbed onto naphtha-powered launches. The French Voyage carried them briskly past a scale model of the Eiffel Tower. Then they hopped onto the Scenic Railway which took them by a replica of the Palace of Westminster's clock tower, the Big Ben.

"Let's go on the Thunderbolt, Gob," Waite told Shawkey, who had turned the other way to sneak a look at a cute blonde a few seats away.

"They built an even bigger, faster, and scarier one this spring," said Herb. "It's called the Cyclone. It's the biggest in the world."

"It's a riot," said a man sitting across from them who'd overheard. "But don't take your wives. I took mine and she screamed her head off the whole way."

"You're not leaving me behind," said Marie Shawkey.

"I'm going too," Esther Pennock told them.

"I guess I'll have to go too," said Dorothy. "I'll just close my eyes and chew on my hankie."

The younger children went for rides at the pony track, which featured three adorable, pure white Shetlands. The older kids went on the mechanical race course from which the park derived its name. The Steeplechase Horses was an undulating, curving metal track. It was a gravity-driven ride with six horses that coasted along six parallel 1100-foot long tracks. Tilyou, the man who'd built the park, had given his ride realistic touches. There were attendants dressed as jockeys, buglers to announce the start of the race, half and quarter-mile posts, and a finish wire at the end. Unlike actual horse races, where the lightest jockey was most likely to win, here the heaviest riders usually sped through the finish gate to victory.

The families went on the Earthquake Stairway, the Dew Drop, the Whichway, and the Razzle Dazzle, a great circle of laminated wood suspended by wires from a center pole. Seventy people teetered precariously on its frame while four muscular workers rocked it back and forth. A pretty teenage girl lost her balance. Her skirt flew up to her waist and she clutched onto her smiling escort as everyone caught a glimpse of her bloomers.

The Earthquake Stairway featured a flight of steps split in the middle. One half jerked abruptly upward while the other half jerked down. The Whichway was a swing that whirled its passengers eccentrically in all directions. The same girl was catapulted into her date's lap. He looked to be having a wonderful time. The Dew Drop had fair-goers climb to the top of a fifty foot high tower where they whirled feet first downward in a spiral until they were thrown outward onto a billowy platform.

The wives talked their reluctant husbands into taking them on the Barrel of Love, a slowly revolving, giant cylinder of polished wood about fifteen feet long through which, by careful diagonal movement, you could remain upright as you passed through. If you lost your footing you could end up in an intimate arm and leg tangle with complete strangers. The players looked for the pretty teenager. Her escort was pulling her out of the clutches of another boy who'd been admiring her. The Yankees were much too coordinated to lose their balance but their wives enjoyed that they hugged them close to keep them from falling into the morass.

On their way to the Monte Carlo Building the group passed a ticket booth. For scenic purposes, Tilyou had put his beautiful blonde sister Kathryn in the booth as a cashier. She didn't have much to do but smile since, like the Yankees, most people had bought combination tickets.

Shawkey nudged Hoyt. "Did ya get a look at the body on that blonde?"

"She's pretty hard to miss," said Waite. "But don't let the Tiger Lady catch you gawking."

"Ya, I'd better not. Might not be too good for my health. Which reminds me, I gotta go through Marie's underwear drawer again."

"Why would you do that?" asked Hoyt.

"I check every few weeks to see if she's still got a gun in there."

"Oh, ya, Joe told me about that. I thought he was pulling my leg."

"Nope. She does. It's scary to find her revolver in there, but it's fun to see what she might have on when she meets me at the door after the next road trip."

Inside the Monte Carlo Building was a 25-foot diameter Human Roulette Wheel where patrons could play King of the Mountain. Next to it was the Jumping Floor, a large room of warped mirrors where people could grin at their badly distorted reflections.

"Hey, your stomach's as big as the Babe's used to be," Hoyt told Shawkey.

"And your head's as big as Lou's ass," said Pennock.

Their next stop was a 125-foot diameter wheel with twelve cars that each held eighteen passengers. The group crowded into two of them. From the top they could see the whole park, from the concession stands spaced around the wheel all the way to the beach and beyond. The wheel was covered with hundreds of incandescent lights.

The kids hurried their parents to the Aerial Slide, the Bicycle Railroad, the Double Dip Chutes, and the Parachute Jump.

We saved the best for now," Pennock told everyone. "The Trip to the Moon."

The attraction was housed in a large round building. Sixty passengers boarded a winged spaceship and sat in steamer chairs on an open deck. They could watch the ship's flight to the moon through portholes in the walls and the floor. Scenes painted on movable canvas screens gave the riders the illusion of liftoff from the fairground, a flight over Niagara Falls, and then up into space away from the shrinking Earth. The children stared wide-eyed as the ship rocked and wind blew from hidden fans. Cables and rods linked to the motors made the ship's huge wings flap.

"This is amazing, Daddy," Jane Pennock told her father.

"It sure is, Sweet Pea."

En route to the moon the space travelers encountered a fierce electrical storm with thunder and lightning flashes. Eventually the ship approached the moon and swept over deep canyons and craters before making its landing. The disembarking passengers, now inside an extinct crater, were greeted by midget Selenites with spiked backs who led them down a long illuminated avenue filled with toadstools and fantastical trees and then over a drawbridge across a moat to the castle of the Man in the Moon. Comely moon maidens escorted the visitors into the Green Cheese Room where they offered them tasty pieces of cheese that they tore off the walls.

"See, Daddy, the moon really is made of cheese!" Jane Pennock told her father.

They spent an hour in the Pavilion of Fun, a gigantic indoor enclosure covered in steel and glass. There was a huge array of booths with games of chance. The proprietors didn't recognize the players and let them play the throwing games. They easily won the biggest prizes at each one.

The group finished off their day in an illusion cyclorama called Darkness and Dawn and a ride called the Giant See-Saw, which featured two small Ferris wheels on each end of a giant tether. The 235-foot long structure lifted passengers 170 feet into the sky. In the dusk they could see the streetlights and in the distance the Statue of Liberty, as well as the lights of hundreds of liners, barges, and freighters, most of which they knew were rum runners.

Outside the park the children had trouble stuffing the giant pandas and lions their fathers had won them into the cars. They would remember this day for a long time.

"The kids will sleep well tonight," Dorothy Hoyt whispered to her husband as he carefully steered their new Chevrolet into the driveway.

"After all that excitement? I should think so," he agreed.

She touched the back of his neck and whispered in his ear. "Why don't we open that bottle of champagne you got in Chicago? I'll put on something sheer and we can make some excitement of our own. Maybe you could treat me like an amusement park."

"I think I might just be up for that," said Waite.

"And don't forget, darling," said Dorothy.

"Forget what?"

"We haven't christened the Chevrolet yet."

o o o

The Yankees opted for three o'clock lightning in the first game of the Wednesday twin bill with Detroit. In the second inning Koenig sacrificed home a run. Shocker singled one in, Pat Collins knocked in two with a single, and Gehrig hit a solo homer, his thirty-sixth.

Urban Shocker wasn't firing on all cylinders. Bob Fothergill doubled in two unearned runs after an error by Mike Gazella. Gehringer tripled home another pair after a bad throw by Koenig and Harry Heilmann hit a two-run homer in the fifth. That was all Miller Huggins wanted to see from Shocker. He sent in Moore but it was too late. It ended 6-5 Tigers.

In the first inning of the second game Gehrig hit his thirty-seventh off Samuel Braxton Gibson, from King, North Carolina. The Yankees added a run in the fourth and another in the sixth. In the seventh, Ruth, who had just five home runs in his last twenty-seven games, drove a ball to the deepest regions of the park. Heinie Manush took off after it. He ran up the embankment but couldn't reach the Babe's drive.

"That was close," he puffed as the ball hit the top of the railing 480 feet from the plate and bounced back onto the field. Ruth had to settle for a double. Arthur Mann, the sports columnist for the *New York World* called it the longest two-bagger ever.

The Yankees now led 8-2, but when Pipgras tired and gave up two in the ninth Huggins had to call for Moore again. Wilcy made it interesting, giving up two runs of his own before shutting things down for the day.

o o o

Huggins sent Dutch Ruether and his 12-2 record to the hill for Thursday's game. He gave up two runs in the first, another in the third, and another in the fourth. Detroit went with Ownie Carroll, a Holy Cross grad who threw nothing but junk. His garbage was good enough to foil the Yankees. They managed only five hits and lost 6-2. Their lead was down to eleven games. Huggins couldn't help but think about the big lead his team had almost blown last year.

o o o

On Friday August 5 only eight thousand turned out to see the last game of the series. Hoyt and Pat Collins took a while to figure out which of Waite's pitches were working best. Bob Fothergill singled home Charlie Gehringer and Harry Heilmann singled in Heinie Manush in the top of the first, but Hoyt quieted the Detroit bats from then on.

The Yankees answered Detroit's pair with three of their own in the bottom of the first. Ruth doubled to the wall in center, a home run in most

Babe Ruth

parks and in any other part of the Stadium. In the eighth the Babe hit one of his shortest homers of the season, just 315 feet to right. Red Wingo nearly batted it down before it cleared the fence.

"It's a funny game," the Babe told reporters after the Yankees won 5-2. "I hit one three hundred and fifteen feet and get a homer and I hit one four eighty and wind up with a stinkin' double."

○ ○ ○

The White Sox came to town on August the 6th for a rare two-game weekend series. A big crowd streamed through the turnstiles to see Ted Lyons versus Pennock in the first game. Pat Collins was startled to see his name on the lineup card. It was the first time all season Huggins was going with the same catcher two games in a row. Chicago scored twice in the first and the Yankees touched up Lyons for one in the first and two in the second. Then he settled down. Neither Ruth nor Gehrig managed to hit any of Lyons' offerings out of the infield. With two out in the third Ruth bounced meekly back to the box. He hurled the bat almost to the outfield fence.

"The Babe should think about trying to break the hammer throw record the next time the Olympics roll around," wrote Richards Vidmer.

The White Sox notched three in the sixth and Lyons beat the Yanks for the third time, winning his league-leading eighteenth, 6-3.

Urban Shocker struggled on Sunday, giving up ten hits in five innings. When he started shakily in the sixth Huggins sent for Wilcy Moore. Cy allowed only one man to reach base in his four innings of work and the Yanks held on for a 4-3 win.

"The man's got the nerves of a safecracker," Huggins told Charley O'Leary as he retired the side in the ninth. "He strolls in without a care in the world like he's been asked to throw batting practice."

"The way we're usin' Cy, he must think the American League always has two men on base," chuckled O'Leary.

○ ○ ○

It rained all Sunday night and everyone got sent home the next morning. It was going to take a while to drain the field. They'd take the train out to Philadelphia at 6 p.m. Monday and play a single game against the A's on

& THE 1927 YANKEES HAVE THE BEST SUMMER EVER

Tuesday before heading to Washington for four.

The Babe took advantage of the rare Monday afternoon off to do some banking. He grabbed an umbrella and headed to the Bank of Manhattan with Christy Walsh and met with Frank H. Hilton, the bank's vice-president. Ruth signed a $50,000 bond for the trust fund Walsh had set up for him. The Babe, the big kid who'd never grown up, was finally planning for the future - with more than a little prodding from his business manager.

o o o

"You realize we're only gonna be home one day the next month," Mark Koenig told Benny Bengough as they sat beneath the high vaulted glass ceiling in Penn Station waiting to board the Quaker Express. "The thirty-first is the only day we're in New York until the eighth of September."

"Not enough time for me to look for a car," said Benny. "Guess I'll have to hold off a while longer."

"What are you thinking of getting?" asked Mark.

"Since I can't get one any time soon I might just wait and get one of the new Model A's."

"When are they coming out?"

"Ford's testing them now. It's all hush, hush. He's retooled all his factories and he sent out a secret telegram to the dealers that he's started production of an entirely new car with superior design and performance to anything in the low price car field. It's supposed to surpass the Model T in every way."

"And nobody's seen one? I mean besides the silly newspaper cartoon with a car covered in jewels labeled fit for a king. Only five hundred dollars."

"Not on the streets, no. But some photographer from Automotive Daily News snapped a picture of Ford and his son Edsel driving one outside Detroit."

"Are they gonna cost a lot more than the Model T?"

"Not that much apparently. It's supposed to be a down-sized Lincoln. Four-wheel brakes, safety glass windshield, and a two hundred cubic inch, forty horsepower motor."

"How fast will the thing go?"

Babe Ruth

"Sixty, maybe even sixty-five," said Benny. "Not that there's many roads you'd want to try that speed on."

"Same as before, you can have any color you want so long as it's black?"

"No. They're actually gonna make brown, gray, and blue ones."

"You might just have a World Series check by the time they come out."

"That'd be nice. Ford doesn't have installment plans like the others. He doesn't believe in credit."

The whistle of their train's engine screeched and a conductor's pipe wailed. Mark got up and stretched. "I don't have any kinda car right now, so we'd best make sure we don't miss that train."

o o o

At Shibe Park on Tuesday the A's, who'd expected to give the Yanks a good run for their money and perhaps even dominate them, got a bit of revenge. They didn't look much like a team that trailed the league leaders by twenty games when they scored one in the second, another in the third, and three more in the sixth off Dutch Ruether. They piled on one in the seventh and two in the eighth off George Pipgras.

Ty Cobb led the way with three hits and every other Philadelphia batsman had at least one, including Rube Walberg, who gave the Yankees their worst licking of the season. Ruth went hitless for the third straight game. He smashed a ball deep to center in the sixth but Cobb tracked it down with a big grin on his face. There was nothing he loved more than besting the man who people had dared to say might be a better player than he was.

Gehrig led off the ninth with the game well out of reach and hit an inside fastball onto the roof of a house on 20th Street. For a change Ruth was not among the first to shake Lou's hand.

"Lou's a swell guy, but it's kind of sad to watch him push Jidge aside like this," Koenig said to Lazzeri as he grabbed a bat and headed out to the on-deck circle.

"The Babe had a pretty good run," said Tony over his shoulder. "You know what they say, the king is dead, long live the new king."

As the players were coming out of the showers later Doc Powers came in and said, "Some school wants a bunch of balls signed."

"I'll sign 'em myself this time, Doc," said the Babe.

"Oh. Sorry, Jidge. I was talking to Lou."

o o o

After the ugly 8-1 drubbing the Yankees took the Philadelphia, Baltimore & Washington to the nation's capital for a four-game set. The Babe ended his hitless streak early, driving home Combs with a single off Tom Zachary in the first. With Combs and Koenig aboard his next time up, Ruth creamed one 425 feet to left center off Zachary to gain one on Gehrig.

Sam Rice singled to lead off the bottom of the inning and Bucky Harris hoped to get his squad on the scoreboard. Two strikes down he took a pitch he deemed low and outside.

"Strike three!" called home plate umpire Pants Rowland.

"What?" yelled Harris. "That pitch was a ball ten minutes ago when Zachary threw one there."

"Like I said, strike three," uttered Rowland.

"Ya missed that one, Rowland," called a fan from behind the screen.

"What's a matter, Pants?" bawled another "Couldn't see it through your zipper that time?"

Harris got up in Rowland's face. "There's no damn way that was a strike. If it was, I'da swung."

"You want somebody else managing the rest of the way, Harris? Cuz that's what's gonna happen if you say one more word."

"Just admit that you blew that one," said Harris.

Rowlands pulled off his mask and made a sweeping gesture toward center field. "That was seven words. You're outta the game."

"You pompous ass!" muttered Harris as he stormed off the field and a chorus of boos rained down on Rowland.

"They're all yours, Jack," Harris yelled to first base coach Jack Onslow as he disappeared down the steps to the locker room, kicking everything in his path out of the way.

Sam Rice doubled home Muddy Ruel and Ossie Bluege in the fifth to

Babe Ruth

pull the Senators within a run and predictably Huggins sent Wilcy Moore in to put a stop to things. Harris should have been the first batter he faced but Harris was paying for his outburst, stewing in the clubhouse. His replacement at second base, Stuffy Stewart, who toted a .219 batting average to the plate, struck out. More boos and catcalls from the stands.

"Too bad Harris wasn't still in there, Pants," yelled someone. "Feelin' pretty good about yourself, decidin' the game like this?" Rowland glared in the fan's direction.

Onslow was smart enough not to challenge Rowland any further on ball and strike decisions but when he called Goose Goslin out when it appeared he'd beaten Earle Combs' weak throw home in the ninth Onslow let him have it. He threw his cap to the ground and charged out of the coaching box toward Rowland.

"Not another step, Jack, or I'll fine your ass a week's pay," Pants told him when he got close. Onslow stopped in his tracks. "You're out of the game too."

Another cavalcade of boos showered Rowland. He ignored them.

Gunner Reeves, the Senators' rookie shortstop, took Moore to a 3-2 count in the ninth and Rowlands called him out on a knee-high sinker. The stands erupted. An avalanche of scorecards and straw hats sailed toward Rowland, followed by several pop bottles, which luckily missed, and finally a brief case.

"Must be a banker in the crowd," chuckled Art Fletcher.

Rowland stood his ground as a pile of debris accumulated around him. Then he brushed a candy wrapper off his shoulder and walked leisurely to the steps of the Senators' dugout and into the umpires' dressing room escorted by Police Captain Tommy Doyle. Upset with their team's 4-3 loss, angry fans – many having drained their hip flasks in the early innings - swarmed the dugout and Doyle had to call for reinforcements to hold them back.

"Holy shit," said Dutch Ruether. "You'd think it was Game Seven of the World Series."

Someone yelled, "Rowlands is over here!" from the visiting team's bullpen gate. "He's gettin' away!"

A mass of rowdies headed in that direction but it turned out to be Tommy Connolly, the third base umpire, who hadn't made any close calls. Luckily, they left him alone. Rowlands managed to escape unnoticed through the left field exit to Elm Street and a waiting police car.

o o o

Hod Lisenbee, who was 11-5 and had won all four of his starts against the Yankees, got the ball for Washington on Thursday. He and George Pipgras posted zeroes for the first five innings. In the sixth Goose Goslin lost a fly ball in the sun and Earle Combs scampered home from third but Lisenbee struck out the Babe to end the inning. The Senators scored twice in the bottom of the frame to take the lead. Gehrig tripled and scored to tie it the seventh.

Neither pitcher buckled and it was still 2-2 with one out in the eleventh when Joe Judge sent a ball down the right field line that bounced off the grandstand and out of Ruth's reach. The Babe caught up to the ball and fired it in as Judge rounded second. Koenig, who had two errors already, took the throw and pegged it to third. It sailed into the grandstand. Judge, who had a charley horse from his slide, dragged himself home with the winning run. Lazzeri consoled Koenig after the 3-2 loss.

"You're not gonna be getting a Series check to buy a car if I keep playing like that," Koenig told Bengough on his way from the showers.

"Ask Jidge if he's got a bottle he can spare," said Benny. "You could use a belt or two tonight."

"The hell with that," said Lazzeri, who'd overheard Benny's suggestion. "I'm takin' my buddy to a nice Italian restaurant tonight. I'm gonna get him a nice meal and a tasty bottle a wine and introduce him to a friendly Italian girl. He's gonna forget all about this afternoon."

Mark and Tony went to Gargiulo's in downtown Washington. Predictably, the tables were covered with red and white checkerboard tablecloths. On each was an old wine bottle inside a basket with a small candle burning inside. Paintings of Rome and Naples adorned the walls.

They started with bruschetta with sautéed mushrooms, followed by panzella, a Tuscan bread salad, and then they split a sausage and tomato pizza. They washed it all down with a nice bottle of Chianti. With some encouragement from Tony, Gargiulo introduced Mark to his daughter. Her name was Rosa. She had smooth olive skin, almond-shaped brown eyes, and a beautiful smile. She had a red and white kerchief around her hair and she was lovely. Lovely enough to make Mark forget all about his three errors and even the cigarette girl.

19.

A Speaker on the Floor of the Senate and a Speak Underneath

"No one'll ever hit a ball over that roof."

Herbert Glassman, a former policeman, trucked a thousand gallons of booze across the Maryland border into Washington every week from his distillery in Baltimore. It got distributed from a rental car agency the feds were closing in on. A lot of it went to beer flats where sociable women served booze and the rest went to the capitol's three thousand speakeasies. One of them was underneath the Senate chambers.

Popular with the thirstiest Yankees were Carl Hammel's Lunchroom on Pennsylvania Avenue and the Gaslight Club on Sixteenth Street, which was run by a retired rear admiral who recruited Navy nurses to smuggle rum from Cuba and wait tables. The writers liked the club and the nurses too.

The libations were served in navy mugs. Thirsty patrons entered through a men's washroom where you turned a certain faucet and a door opened to the drinking quarters. During a raid the admiral claimed he'd visited the men's room hundreds of times but knew nothing about the special faucet.

"What? You never wash your hands?" asked a highly sceptical officer.

"Yes, of course. But I guess I just never used that tap," the crusty admiral told him with as straight a face as he could manage.

Nobody liked the Ambassadors Club on K Street that several congressmen frequented. The Yankees thought it was too hoity-toity. It was the same with the Mayflower Club south of Dupont Circle. The Babe had always liked Archibald Gentleman's Club a few blocks down because the waitresses tended not to wear very much. His head was always on a swivel when he drank there. On really hot nights Ruth and his companions rowed out to a dimly-lit houseboat on the Potomac the police hadn't heard about yet.

The HBQ Social club had a dry cleaner on the ground floor, a dance hall on the second floor, a saloon on the third floor, and a casino on the fourth. Officially, the club sold set-ups - glasses of ice or soda water - but if you let your waiter know that you favored something a little more potent – he'd bring you a bottle of wine, or rye, or gin, or brandy from the back room where the good stuff was stored.

The 'club' had a large drain in the floor into which the booze could be poured in the event of a raid, of which there were several. Dugan, Shawkey, and the Babe went to the HBQ after the 3-2 loss. An eager young policeman was taking down the names of everyone who went in when they arrived.

"Ken Tucky," said one man.

"Chuck Wagon," declared the next.

"Rick O'Shea," stated the third.

The cop, who was clearly not the brightest bulb on the force, dutifully recorded the names. The Yankees chuckled and followed suit.

"Babe Lincoln," snorted Ruth.

"Patty O' Furniture," said Dugan.

"Chris P. Bacon," chuckled Shawkey.

They sat at a table near the back so they wouldn't be bothered. They were anyway.

"This is the town where they passed the Prohibition Act," said a tipsy wag at the next table, "and this is one of the joints where they violate it. Sometimes the Senate appoints a standing committee and half of the members aren't able to stand." He laughed so hard at his own joke he nearly spilled his drink.

The man had thin, greying hair and looked to be in his early fifties. He had a fairly high-ranking position in government, but didn't say what it was and neither Ruth, Dugan, nor Shawkey bothered to ask.

"My drinking name is Ferguson," he told them. "At the office I'm known as the son of a bitch in charge. My hero, you should know, is neither Lincoln, nor Caesar, nor Lindbergh. It is Edward Lear, the English artist, illustrator, and poet whose greatest accomplishment was the invention of the limerick. I may not divulge any government secrets, gentlemen, but I do collect and pass on limericks. The raunchier the better."

Ferguson, or whatever his real name was, waited until the Yankees' first round of drinks had arrived and then delivered the first of his favorite verses.

"There was a young lady whose chest

Was acknowledged as one of the best

She had no inhibitions

About competitions

Since she stood out from all of the rest."

His next was,

"There once was a fellow McSweeny

Who spilled some gin onto his weenie.

So just to be couth

He added vermouth

Then slipped his girl a martini."

That made Shawkey think of one of his own. He set his tea cup down for a second.

"I once had a girlfriend named Dora

Who drank like there was no tomorra.

She wasn't pretty as some

But she had a nice bum

And she always came back for some mora."

"I got one," said Dugan.

"There once was a man from O'Hare

Babe Ruth

Who was doing his wife on the stair

When the banister broke

He quickened his stroke

And finished her off in mid-air."

Ferguson was impressed. "Excellent, gentlemen. Here's another.

There was a young girl from Cape Cod

Who thought babies were fashioned by God.

But 'twas not the Almighty

Who hiked up her nightie.

T'was Roger, the lodger, by God."

He set a twenty dollar bill on the table. "One more before I take my leave of you fine fellows.

In Toulouse was a barmaid named Gale

On whose breasts was tattooed the price of ale

But on her behind

For the sake of the blind

Was that same information in Braille."

o o o

Wilcy Moore was given a rare start on Saturday the 13th. He got Sam Rice to ground out in the bottom of the first and then slipped a third strike hook past Bucky Harris. Earl McNeely doubled and Goose Goslin stepped up to the plate. It was no surprise that he was the cleanup batter. Goslin led the Senators with nine home runs. Joe Judge was second with two.

"This is the only guy with any chance to hit one out, Cy," Benny Bengough told him when he went out to the mound after McNeely's double. "Ya wanna put him on and we'll go after Judge. He hasn't hit one since May."

Wilcy considered for a minute. He spat a stream of tobacco juice toward first base and looked at the baseball. "I believe I'll go after him, Googles."

"If you say, so. But be careful."

& THE 1927 YANKEES HAVE THE BEST SUMMER EVER

Goslin hit Wilcy's third pitch into the bleachers and the Senators led 2-0.

After three straight singles tied the match the next inning neither club scored again until the eighth when Firpo Marberry walked in a run. Cedric Durst had taken over for Combs who'd suffered an attack of ptomaine poisoning and could barely stand up. He staggered out to take his position in the sixth and Huggins called him back to the dugout. Combs was too proud to ask for a rest.

Durst bunted one in front of the plate to start the Yankee ninth. Benny Tate, who'd taken over for Muddy Ruel after the eighth, dashed out, grabbed it, and dropped it. Koenig sacrificed Durst to second and Harris yelled in from second base for Firpo to give Ruth a free pass.

After four intentional wide ones to the Babe, Marberry walked Gehrig not so intentionally. Meusel, who was suffering from terrible headaches due to playing the sun field every afternoon and was gobbling aspirins like they were ju jubes, popped out to Harris and it looked as though the Senators still had a chance. For once the Yankees weren't exactly tearing the cover off the ball.

But Lazzeri got around on one of Marberry's fireballs and drilled a hard grounder to the shortstop, Gunner Reeves. The Babe dashed from second and then stopped right in front of the rookie, pretending to avoid being hit by the ball, but really doing his best to obstruct Reeves' view. The ploy worked. The ball went through Gunners' legs. Ruth chased Cedric Durst across the plate, Moore set down the Senators in order in the bottom of the ninth, and the Yanks won it 6-3.

o o o

The Sunday game went ahead even though rain had fallen throughout the night and the field was a quagmire. The visitors started things off with a barrage of hits off Tom Zachary in the top of the first. Ben Paschal opened with a base hit and the Babe singled him home. Gehrig doubled and Ruth trotted in with the second run, then Lazzeri singled to drive in Lou.

The Senators mounted a rally off Waite Hoyt in the bottom of the inning but came away with only one run and the Yankee bats went back to work in the fifth. Collins and Hoyt singled to get things going and Paschal doubled to score Collins. Ruth's sharp single plated Hoyt and Paschal. Once again

Babe Ruth

Washington staged a comeback in the bottom of the inning and once again they managed to push only one run across. Waite Hoyt, now 17-4, won it 6-2. For a change, Wilcy Moore was able to whistle and whittle in the bullpen the whole game.

○ ○ ○

In order to reach Chicago for their game on Tuesday the weary Yanks had to switch from the Congressional to the Pacemaker at midnight. Since their last visit Charles Comiskey had ordered his ball park rebuilt in '26 and a new 75-foot high double-deck grandstand now surrounded the field.

When he did his inspection of the remodelled "Baseball Palace of the World" he looked out to right field. "Nobody is going to hit a ball over those stands," he told the architect.

The architect agreed. "You're right, Mister Comiskey. No one will ever hit a ball over that roof."

○ ○ ○

Tommy Thomas didn't have his good stuff this time out. Wilcy Moore said, "the White Sox were workin' him like a rented mule." The Babe doubled home one of New York's two runs in the first and then threw Ray Flaskamper out at the plate with the bases loaded and two out in the bottom of the inning with a strike to home from left field. A now recovered Earle Combs doubled in one of another pair of Yankee runs in the third.

The White Sox hadn't given Thomas a lick of run support when he headed to the mound for the fifth and he couldn't afford to give up any more runs. Combs and Koenig grounded out to start the inning and Thomas was happy to see Ruth coming up with the bases empty. He knew the Babe had homered only twice in his last fifteen games anyway.

"It's Gehrig I gotta worry about now," Thomas thought to himself.

He did what would normally not have even crossed his mind. He threw a pitch over the plate to Ruth. A loud crack split the air. The crowd gasped as the ball soared high toward right field. It rose and rose and it kept on climbing. His thirty-seventh homer disappeared over the 75-foot high grandstand and landed 520 feet away in a used car lot between a beaten up flivver and a rusty coupe. A shady-looking salesman looked at the ball and then stared up at the towering wall it had flown over in disbelief.

Bert Cole replaced the shell-shocked Thomas and promptly yielded back-to-back doubles off the bats of Gehrig and Meusel, who'd taunted Cole and dared him to throw one at him. When Lazzeri's sacrifice scored the fourth run of the inning Cole had had enough. He threw one right at Dugan's head. Joe hit the dirt. He'd been expecting it.

Stripping down for his shower after the Yankees 8-1 victory, Dugan told a reporter, "It's always the same. Combs walks, Koenig singles, Ruth hits one out of the park. Gehrig triples, Lazzeri doubles, and Dugan goes down in the dirt on his can. "I'm used to it by now, but I thought Meusel was gonna tear Cole's head off when he threw at me."

o o o

After the game some of the players went to Walgreens on the South Side. It wasn't for the milkshakes.

"What? You think they went from twenty stores to five hundred cuzza the damn ice cream?" Ruether asked Shawkey facetiously.

Malted milkshakes had been a boon to the chain when the soda fountains began pouring them in '22, but their popularity wasn't enough to explain the company's rapid expansion. It was the whiskey they kept in the back. The fire inspectors never left without a case of it when they dropped by unannounced.

"Order the butterscotch soda," said Dugan.

"There's no such thing," said Shawkey.

"That's right, Gob. But you don't want a soda, do you?"

"No, I want bourbon," said Bob.

"Then ask for a butterscotch soda," Joe explained patiently.

"Oh. Like the way you order strong tea in a speak."

"Now you've got it."

o o o

On Wednesday Sarge Connally, who'd given the Yankees fits the last time they faced him, blanked them until Gehrig doubled and scored in the fifth to get New York on the board. In the eighth Huggins once again sent

Babe Ruth

Dutch Ruether in to hit for Benny Bengough, who tried his best not to be embarrassed about it. He knew it was nothing personal. Hug was just making the best use of his men's talents. Ruether singled up the middle.

Hug sent Julie Wera in to run for Dutch and Combs doubled him home with the tying run. Ruth came to the plate with the bases loaded, swung hard, and struck out. Wilcy Moore entered in the bottom of the eighth and shut out the White Sox in the eighth, ninth, and tenth.

The Babe came up in the eleventh and watched a ball and a strike go by before sending his thirty-eighth into the left field seats. Cy shut down Chicago again in their half of the eleventh and it was all over, 3-2 New York.

o o o

Back home in New York, Dorothy Hoyt picked up Mattie Pipgras in Waite's Chevrolet and they met Mary Lieb at a diner. Dorothy wore a polka dot dress, which she constantly smoothed even though it didn't need to be. Mattie wore a blue chemile crepe dress and a high side rolling hat. Mary wore a black and white checked gingham dress and, as always, a string of pearls around her neck.

"It was so nice to ride downtown in a car," said Mattie as they ordered sandwiches. "George and I can't afford an automobile so I have to take the subway. It's just awful. All those sweaty bodies jostling one another. And when it's crowded and you have to stand, you have to watch that no one grabs your purse."

"Or your ass," said Mary.

Dorothy and Mattie stared at her, startled.

"Sorry. Your *derrière*. I guess I've been listening to Fred too much. He spends too much time with ball players. The other night at dinner he nonchalantly asked me to pass him the fuckin' salt."

Dorothy folded her napkin on her lap. "Shall we go to the new Montgomery Ward store, girls?"

"Well we're not going to Woolworth's, that's for sure," said Mattie. "Even though they won't jinx themselves by saying it, the boys are bound to get a World Series check, even if it's not the winners' share. I think we can afford to splurge just a little."

"What about Saks Fifth Avenue?" suggested Mary.

"That might be a *bit* too pricey. What about J.C. Penney, or Sears, or Macy's?" said Mary.

"There's nowhere to park at J.C. Penney or Sears. I vote for Macy's," said Dorothy, "I saw some beautiful things in their window the other day."

"Then Macy's it is," said Mary.

o o o

"Did you hear what Lindbergh said the other day?" asked Mattie as they browsed through the shoe department.

"I don't want to hear another word about that man," said Mary. "He may be a fine fellow, but for the past two months he's all anyone's wanted to talk about - where he spoke, what he was wearing, what he had for breakfast, whether he brushed his teeth after he ate, where he takes his laundry, where he buys his socks. It's too much. I wouldn't want to hear any more about Lindbergh if his next flight was to the Moon. And I'm sorry, the man may be brave and a great pilot, but on terra firma he's about as charming and exciting as Gehrig."

"Earle and I wanted to listen to the A and P Gypsies on NBC a week ago Monday," said Dorothy. "They were going to have on Ed Wynn, Rudy Vallee, and Will Rogers. Instead they played a broadcast of some deadly boring testimonial dinner Lindbergh was at."

"I could listen to Rudy Vallee all night," said Mary.

"I tried to get Waite to dance to one of his records but the old stick-in-the-mud wouldn't move out of his chair," said Dorothy.

"I tried to get Fred to go for dance lessons at the studio Fred Astaire and his sister Adele just opened," said Mary, "but he wouldn't hear of it. He said he'd be the laughing stock of the sports department if anybody found out."

"I'm going to try on these red ones," announced Mattie, holding up a pair of bright red pumps.

"You'll never guess what I got the other day," Mary told Dorothy.

"What, the new vacuuming machine you wanted?"

"No. Better. Nan Britton's memoirs. They cost five dollars but I just had to have them."

"You didn't! Where did you find them? I thought The Society for the Prevention of Vice seized the plates from the shop that was printing them."

"They did. But a few copies had already gone out. I got one at Walgreens. The owner keeps them under the counter between the liquor bottles. Harding died so suddenly and he was so admired no one's brave enough to sell the book in the open. Britton's received death threats. Her phone lines were cut and a truck someone thought was carrying the printing plates was set on fire."

"So? Give. What's in them?" asked Dorothy.

"I haven't read all of them," said Mary, "but they're pretty hot stuff. Old Warren was such a regal figure. Who'd have ever suspected what he was up to? But I guess little Nan grew up to be pretty well-proportioned."

"How old was she when it all happened?" asked Dorothy.

"Nan developed a crush on him when she was fourteen. Their families knew one another. Harding was a newspaper editor back then and just getting started in politics. She clipped his portrait from a campaign poster and hung it in her bedroom and she'd peer through the plate-glass window of the Marion Star hoping to catch a glimpse of him. She didn't know that Harding was already having a torrid affair with his best friend's wife."

"Didn't her parents think it was kind of strange that she had a picture of a family friend on her wall?" asked Dorothy.

"I suppose, but her father assumed it was just a schoolgirl crush and she'd outgrow it. When she was twenty, and by then a very curvy gal, she took a secretarial course and wrote to Harding, who was now a senator, to ask if he could help her get started in the business world. He remembered her and took her to see a friend at U.S. Steel who gave her a job."

"What happened then?" asked Dorothy.

While Mattie tried on another pair of shoes, Mary continued.

"She went on the campaign trail with Harding posing as his niece and they met at hotels. They saw one another over the next six years in New York and in Washington, sometimes at apartments Harding borrowed from his friends. She bore his child the year before he became president and named her Elizabeth Ann. Apparently she was conceived on a couch in his Senate office."

"And people say senators don't *produce* anything in Washington," snickered Dorothy.

"Nan was staying in Harding's hotel room during the Republican convention in Chicago in 1920. When the GOP heavyweights asked him if there was any impediment in his personal life that might stand between him and the presidency, they found it a bit odd that he deliberated for ten minutes before telling them there wasn't."

"So what went on after he got elected president?" asked Dorothy.

"At the White House she showed Harding snapshots of their daughter and he'd reach into a drawer and hand her two hundred dollars to help with the baby's care. Then he'd find ways for them to sneak off to private places together away from the prying eyes of the Secret Service. He said he'd take her to a place where they could share kisses in safety. It turned out to be a cloakroom and they had sex there a whole lot of times in a space less than five feet square."

"And no one ever suspected?"

"Nan apparently maintained friendly relations with Harding's wife Daisy the whole time. Daisy'd been Nan's teacher in grammar school and Nan was looked on affectionately as the President's adopted niece. All anyone ever talked about was the scandals cause by Harding's cabinet and here he was putting it to a girl in the closet the whole time. He was lucky he wasn't caught."

"That's right," said Dorothy. "Any carpenter knows that if you screw too hard the whole cabinet could fall apart."

Mary laughed so hard several shoppers turned and stared at her.

"You can never tell with men," said Dorothy. "Most of them are looking for action all the time. Women are always asking Mattie and me how we can be married to ball players when everyone says they have sex with girls in every city when they're on the road."

"To be honest, most of them do, Dorothy," said Mary. "But not Waite and George, at least not from what Fred's told me. Not that he tells me much. Of course the only two you can be sure of are Lou and the Babe, the Babe whenever he can and Lou not on his life."

"I'm no expert on the subject," said Dorothy. "But I imagine it's pretty difficult to have sex while you're writing a letter to your mom."

20.

THE LOSING STREAK

"I've never had farm animals named after me, at least not that I know of."

Ted Lyons had the Yankees' number yet again on Thursday. He had a 4-1 lead after three but the Bronx Bombers gnawed away at him with one and two-base hits and they scored single runs in the fourth, fifth, and eighth to tie the match. Huggins sent for Wilcy Moore who whitewashed the Pale Hose. The Yankees committed an unseemly five errors but redeemed themselves, winning it in the twelfth. It was Moore's fourteenth. His four shutout innings dropped his E.R.A. to a miserly 2.16.

The reporter for the *Herald-Tribune* had a laugh at the Babe's expense. When Ruth watched a pitch go by in the seventh Red Ormsby deemed it strike three. W.B. Hanna wrote that "the Babe looked surprised as he does so very well. His movie training has taught him how to render any emotion."

o o o

On Friday Waite Hoyt allowed one run in each of the first, third, and fourth innings and nothing thereafter. But Ted Blakenship, who'd started the game with an E.R.A. of 5.10, did better, salvaging the last game of the series for Chicago. The Yankees scored a run on three successive hits in the sixth and then nothing else until the ninth when Lou lined a solo shot into the seats that kept him out in front of the Babe in the home run challenge.

It ended up 3-2 White Sox. Most baseball fans were watching the long ball competition closer than the pennant races since the Cubs were now five games up on the Pirates and the Yankees held a fifteen game lead on second-place Washington.

o o o

Babe Ruth

In the opening frame on Saturday at Dunn Field in Cleveland the Babe smacked a ball 480 feet, out of the yard and over the houses on Lexington Avenue to finally catch Gehrig, and the Yankees tacked on two more runs in the second and another in the fourth. But even the three they notched in the ninth didn't come close to erasing the damage done by their pitchers.

Starter Dutch Ruether gave up five runs in four innings and Bob Shawkey, who'd now lost three in a row - tough to do with this club - allowed three in his one inning of work. Myles Thomas got roughed up for six runs in his two innings on the hill and Joe Giard, who'd made only ten appearances all year and none since July 9th, finally got into a game for a meaningless ninth inning. For a change it was the Bronx Bombers that got bombed, 14-8.

○   ○   ○

On Sunday George Pipgras didn't do much better with the Indians than Ruether, Shawkey, and Thomas had the day before. He gave up a pair of runs in the first and another two in the second.

In the fourth the Yankees stormed back to even the score at 4-4, but Pipgras tired in the late innings and this time there'd be no reprieve. Huggins was resting Wilcy Moore to start the next day. Pipgras gave up two runs in the seventh and another in the eighth. The Yankees mounted no more rallies and lost 7-4.

Cy and the Yanks trailed the Tribe 5-1 when the Babe came up to bat against Cleveland starter Joe Shaute in the sixth the next day. Ruth got some revenge when he belted one high over the right field wall to take the lead in the American Home Run Handicap but Shaute shut out New York until the ninth when they scored two futile runs in a 9-4 loss.

"They're lucky they don't have to play the Indians every day. They'd be hanging on by a thread," Richards Vidmer told James Harrison after the game.

"You're right, they're only eleven and nine against Cleveland."

"And that's four straight losses," said Vidmer. "First time all year."

"And it's the first series they've been swept. Maybe the wives need to think twice about spending those World Series checks they've been counting on," said Harrison.

& THE 1927 YANKEES HAVE THE BEST SUMMER EVER

Vidmer bent over his typewriter and began his story.

The Yanks' lead over the Tigers has plummeted to twelve games and the Motor City is where they're headed next. They're hoping not to get run over. The Bengals have won thirteen straight and gained six games on New York the last two weeks. If the Yanks get swept again things might just get interesting. Miller Huggins was seen chewing a nail sandwich after today's loss and Jake Ruppert is holed up in his mansion having worse conniptions than he suffered when the Feds declared his suds illegal.

o o o

"Sacco and Vanzetti are getting the chair today," Pennock told Shawkey as they sat in the lobby of the Book Cadillac in Detroit on Tuesday afternoon.

"That's right," said Shawkey. "You think they did it?"

"Not from what I've read. They weren't anywhere near the place," said Herb. "Say, did you hear what that Italian community club's doing for Tony tomorrow night?"

"No, what?"

"They're giving him a gold watch, diamond cufflinks, and a thousand dollars."

"Kerist almighty! The dagos in Boston gave him a silver tea service, a diamond ring, and a thousand bucks. The guy's gonna soon be hangin' out with Jimmy Walker."

o o o

Waite Hoyt gave up close to a run an inning and the Yankees trailed Detroit 5-1 when they came to bat in the seventh on Wednesday. Koenig, Ruth, and Gehrig each knocked in a run to make it 5-4 but Owen Carroll managed to keep them off the scoreboard in the eighth.

Combs and Koenig singled to start the Yankee ninth.

"Now let's see what Jidge can do," Huggins said to himself. "We need this."

Ruth got ahold of a pitch and hit it high into the air.

"It's another home run in an elevator shaft," Ben Paschal told Mike Gazella.

"The damn thing's gonna bring rain," said Mike.

Babe Ruth

Marty McManus had taken over at short for the Tigers after Jack Taverner slit his index finger groping around inside his ice box. He watched nervously as Ruth's pop up kept climbing. Taverner had lots of time on his hands and he snuck a look at Charlie Gehringer and Jack Warner. It was clear neither wanted any part of it.

"All yours, Marty. Good luck," called Gehringer. "The thing's gonna have ice on it when it comes down."

"Might wanna run in and get a steel bucket to catch it with, Marty," Warner suggested.

"Or a lot more padding for your glove," offered Gehringer.

The ball finally re-entered the stratosphere and McManus, though he stumbled, managed to hold on to it. Ruth was already at first base. He could probably have been at third by now if there hadn't been runners ahead of him. He kicked the dirt in disgust. Now there were two out.

Carroll figured he'd dodged a bullet with Ruth just missing getting a hold of his last pitch. He threw four wide ones to Gehrig. Meusel reached base on a much shorter pop fly that McManus couldn't reach, but Combs had to hold up at third. That brought Lazzeri to the plate. Bases loaded, two out.

"Push 'em up, Tony," called someone from high above first base.

"Colpire la palla lontano, Antonio," came a yell from another part of the crowd.

Tony spit on his hands and screwed his cap on tight. He watched Carroll's first pitch go by wide. Then Carroll curved one over the inside corner. The next pitch was at Tony's ankles.

"Nowhere ta put him, I'm gonna have to give him something," Carroll said to himself.

Lazzeri drove the next pitch over the left field wall and over Cherry Street too. It was one of the longest home runs ever hit at Navin Field.

"Sei il migliore!" yelled someone as Tony rounded the bases with a big smile on his face.

"Ya, Tony, you eesa the besta base a ball player of all times," called someone else.

❦ THE 1927 YANKEES HAVE THE BEST SUMMER EVER

"Ya know Tony's the best player I've ever seen come up," Shawkey told Ruether as they joined the lineup to shake Lazzeri's hand after the 9-5 win. "He's already one of the best infielders in the game, he can steal a base, and if it weren't for Ruth and Gehrig he might be considered the hardest hitter around. When he gets back to New York and his wife sees his diamond ring and his check for a thousand bucks she'll probably give him an extra helping of pasta."

"Or ask him if he wants to go make a bambino."

o o o

Ben Paschal, Mike Gazella, and Cedric Durst sat playing cards in the lobby of the Book Cadillac that night. They'd pushed three large leather chairs together to form a circle around a glass table. Mostly they watched for cute girls.

"What's that noise?" asked Gazella, laying down his cards and looking out the window.

A shrill clanging sound grew closer and louder.

"Fire engines," said Paschal.

They decided to see where they were headed. Two blocks away they saw a building with flames and smoke pouring out of it. Several firemen worked feverously and within a few minutes they had the blaze well under control.

"Coulda had it out a lot sooner," said Gazella.

"How?" asked Durst.

"They coulda sent for Cy."

o o o

Urban Shocker, Joe Dugan, and Dutch Ruether headed to the Tea Room for the evening. A writer they knew named Pete Flanders stepped out of a phone booth in the hallway as they gave the password and went in.

"How's Trix, Pete?" asked Dugan.

"Never better, Joe," said Flanders. "Squiffy on gin half the time, but never better."

Babe Ruth

They sat down and ordered drinks which were served in coffee mugs and began admiring some flappers sitting at a nearby table.

"Did you cover the schoolhouse bombing out here in April, Pete?" asked Ruether.

"I did. I kinda wish I hadn't though."

"Was it as bad as they said?" asked Shocker.

"Worse. It was unbelievable. I never saw anything like it and I hope never to again."

"What exactly happened?" asked Dugan. "It was a crazy guy with dynamite, wasn't it?"

Flanders took a sip of his whiskey and grimaced. This stuff you couldn't drink straight. He asked for some ginger ale then told the story. "It was an elementary school in the village of Bath, near Lansing. The town had a grain elevator, a drugstore, a few houses, and the school. Nothing else. One of the members of the school board was a man name of Andrew Kehoe, a farmer that joined the board just so he could complain about how he had to pay taxes to build the school even though he didn't have any kids. He was a real bastard apparently. He shot a neighbor's dog that was barking at a cat and he shot his own horse because he thought it was lazy. People called him the dynamite farmer cuz he used to blow up stumps and rocks in his fields."

"Sounds like a real nutjob," said Shocker.

"He ran for town clerk and of course he lost. Then he found out the bank was gonna foreclose on his property because he wasn't paying the taxes. So he stole a key to the schoolhouse and packed dynamite into every nook and cranny of it. He detonated it on the last day of school. Killed forty-five people including all thirty-eight children inside. Then he went and saw the superintendent and blew up a bomb he had in his truck. Killed the both of them. He'd shot his wife and burned down his house before he blew up the school."

"That's awful," said Dutch. "I heard it was bad, but I had no idea."

"It could have been even *worse*. They found a short circuit in Kehoe's wiring. It stopped the dynamite from claiming even more lives than it did.

More than five hundred pounds of dynamite and a bunch of sacks of gunpowder were found under a part of the building that was still standing. If the explosion had gone off as the guy'd planned the whole village could have been blown to smithereens."

"You not over it yet, Pete?" asked Urban. "Sounds like you're still kinda shaken up by the whole thing."

"It's lucky I got this stuff," he said, meaning the booze. "The news is all good on that front. The Detroit Chamber of Commerce just announced that the illicit liquor trade now employs fifty thousand people, second only to the automobile industry. We're now known as the City on a Still and we're damn proud of it."

They all laughed and Dugan ordered another round of rye and ginger ale.

"We've got a half a million cases of booze a month comin' across the border from Windsor. Dispatched by my favorite Canadians, the Bronfman brothers, in boats with forged documents that say the stuff's going to the West Indies. Funny thing is the same ship's back for another load two hours later. You'd think the Feds'd catch on that you can't get to the West Indies and back quite that fast."

"Any chance some of them might be lookin' the other way, Pete?" asked Joe.

"Could be. The booze runners are called the Mosquito Fleet. They're armed to the teeth and more than happy to shoot it out with the understaffed U.S. Customs Service. They have to patrol a hundred miles of coastline between Lake Erie and Lake Huron with three boats and twenty men. They might as well be trying to dry up the Great Lakes with a post office blotter."

"It's a shame they're so badly understaffed," said Dugan sarcastically.

"The Federal government makes the law and then they expect the cities and states to enforce it without giving them the manpower."

"Don't they catch *any* of the smugglers?" asked Dutch.

"A few. But when the feds get a company to build them a high-powered motor the smugglers go there the next day and pay them to build them one even faster. People are callin' 'em speedboats. And a motorized cable pulls a pair of sled-mounted containers from some uninhabited island to a waterside house on Grosse Pointe Park every night. I haven't been able to confirm them, but I've even heard reports of a pipeline that leads directly from the Hiram Walker distillery on the Canadian side to some spot over here."

"That's crazy!" said Joe. "Crazy *good*."

"The city's building the Ambassador Bridge so people can walk across to Canada to get a drink and I've driven by factories and seen men parked outside the gates peddling shots of liquor for two bits to men on their break. If Henry Ford ever sees them out there he'll go berserk."

The players had been thinking of going over to chat with the pretty flappers but Flanders was far too interesting.

"And the trucking business is somethin' too," he continued. "Close to two thousand cases a day leave Detroit for Chicago thanks to Al Capone and the Purple Gang. We've got twenty thousand blind pigs, speakeasies, and beer flats. The restaurant business has collapsed in the face of all the untaxed, unrestricted, unregulated competition. Hell, so many waiters, waitresses, busboys, and cooks have fled their low-paying jobs for the speaks and pigs where the drunks are big tippers the AFL's Hotel and Restaurant Employees Union had to shift their organizing efforts to places that don't officially exist!"

"Did ya hear the man?" Dugan asked Shocker. "Drunks like you are supposed to leave big tips. So don't pull a Gehrig and leave a fuckin' penny."

Flanders was on a roll. He could see the Yankees were finding all this fascinating. "An attorney went to see Judge Jeffries in his chambers at the courtroom last week. He was prosecuting a case against a bunch of bootleggers and he had to tell the judge that the evidence had disappeared. The judge asked him where it had been kept and the prosecutor said it was in the police headquarters. The judge said, 'Well that was a lousy place to keep it. Case dismissed.'"

The four laughed so loud that a lot of people heard them over the racket of servers piling cups into the nearby sink.

"Clarence Darrow was in Detroit defending a black man in a controversial murder trial last month and he spent his lunch hours in a speakeasy three doors up from the courthouse. He waited for the verdict in the judge's chambers drinking some of his excellent Scotch."

"Funny stuff, Pete," said Urban. "You havin' another one?"

"Sorry fellas, got to get home and make sure the wife hasn't fallen off the fire escape. See ya next time you're in town. Which I guess will be next year. Good luck in the Series."

"We don't know yet if we're gonna make it there, Pete," said Ruether.

"You boys could have your *mothers* pitch the rest of your games and still win it."

Tiger ace Earl Whitehill had won four of his last five starts and he'd tossed a five-hit shutout in Washington on Saturday. Gehrig led off the second on Thursday by hitting one of his hooks high into the air – a lot higher than most of his hits - and just into the bleachers in right. It was all the Yankees could muster though in the first four innings.

They went to work in the fifth. Koenig, Ruth, Gehrig, and Meusel crossed home to give New York a 5-0 lead and the Squire of Kennet Square, who'd lost three of his last four starts, coasted to an 8-2 win.

"Looks as though Pennock's found it again," Huggins told Charley O'Leary as they sipped stale, lukewarm coffee after the game. "Maybe we'll win the confounded pennant after all."

"Ya. And maybe you won't get an ulcer after all," said Charley.

o o o

Wilcy Moore was having a fine season. On August 26 his record stood at 15-6. On the mound he was great. At bat, he was dreadful. His average was .038 as a result of a grand total of three feeble singles for the year.

Ruth teased him mercilessly about his ineptitude at the plate. Early in the year he'd bet Moore fifteen dollars, at twenty-to-one odds, that he wouldn't get more than three hits the whole season. Moore'd accepted.

The Tiger starter Lil Stoner had given way to Sam Gibson in the seventh when the Yankees scored four runs, three on a base-clearing triple to center, to tie the game 6-6. Moore replaced Pipgras in the seventh and was in line for the win after his teammates scored another two in the eighth.

Babe Ruth

Huggins left him in to bat in the eighth, confident that he could hold the two-run advantage.

Gibson got two strikes on Wilcy and then threw a curve over the outside corner. Wilcy swung mightily at it and dribbled the ball toward third base. It was hit, if that was the right word, so weakly that it got caught up in the infield grass. Moore trotted to first with his fourth safety of the year. He'd raised his average to .056. Everybody had a good laugh, no one more than the Babe.

"This has always been an easy park for me to hit in," Moore deadpanned after the game.

Ruth pulled out his wallet and handed him three one hundred dollar bills. "Way to go, slugger. What are you gonna do with all that money? You're one of the movie set, so I know you won't be spendin' it on booze and broads."

"I need two mules for my farm in Oklahoma and I've just decided I'm gonna call one Babe and the other one Ruth."

The Babe was touched. "I've never had *farm animals* named after me," he boomed, "at least not that I know of."

o o o

It was the Tigers who'd been run over, not the Yankees and it was starting to look as though the only thing that could stop the Yankees was another amendment to the U.S. Constitution.

That night the Babe stayed in his room at The Book Cadillac. He had Marshall Hunt up for beer and cigars. They played two-handed euchre for a while and then Ruth told Hunt he needed to make a phone call. Marshall wondered which of the women he knew in Detroit he was going to invite over. He figured they wouldn't be playing cards much longer. He thought of the time when an angry husband had chased the Babe through the halls of a Detroit hotel brandishing a revolver after finding Ruth in his wife's room.

"I miss you, Claire," Hunt heard the Babe say after the operator had put him through to New York. "We have three games in St. Louis, then we're home for two days, and then we're away for another week. Pardon? Friday, September ninth? Lemme check."

& **THE 1927 YANKEES HAVE THE BEST SUMMER EVER**

Ruth set down the phone and started looking around for a schedule. "I've got one," Hunt told him. He reached for his suit coat and pulled a card out of the inside pocket. "Here, Babe."

"Thanks, Marsh," said Ruth, returning to the phone.

"Ya, we're … oh, it's you Julia. Why did your mom need to know if I'll be in New York September ninth?" He listened. "It's *you* that needs to know. Why, sweetheart?"

The Babe listened for a while. "So your school's having a parent-child baseball game as an orientation activity that morning and the kids can have an uncle or aunt or friend of the family play if they don't have a parent who can … and you want me to come? Why can't your mom play? She's in pretty good shape."

He listened and then broke out laughing. "No. I guess it would be pretty hard to run the bases in five-inch heels. Sure, sweetie, tell the school I'd love to play."

Babe Ruth
& the 1927 YANKEES have
the BEST SUMMER EVER

21.

GETTING LUCKY IN ATLANTIC CITY

"I've been looking forward to this for a long, long time."

Since their cars were at the back of the train to St. Louis no other passengers would pass through them. That allowed any players who wanted to stay cool to walk around in their underwear. The windows had curtains of the same velvet maroon as the seats over each of which hung a small lamp. Some of the men played mah-jongg to pass the time. A few looked out the windows at the verdant, rolling hills and the thickets of elm and birch trees.

"You ever notice it's the same comin' out of every city?" Shawkey asked Hoyt.

"What do you mean?" asked Waite.

"Well, when the train leaves the station you see rail yards, then the backs of the downtown buildings - which are nowhere near as clean and fancy as the fronts. Then there are the delivery bays at the backs of stores. Then you cross a bridge or two, go through neighborhoods and see schools and backyards with clothes on the lines, then you pass smoke stacks and warehouses and factories, and then suddenly the paved streets give way to dirt roads and you're out into the fields and the barns and the hay wagons and kids fishing off bridges."

Hoyt looked at Shawkey and then back out the window. He sighed. "Ya know, Gob, come to think about it, you're right. It is pretty much the same every time."

Ruth and Gehrig were playing contract bridge with Walsh and Hunt. The Babe sipped the railway's best whiskey, Gehrig drank ginger ale. The more Ruth drank, the more outrageously he bet. He knew it drove Gehrig crazy.

Babe Ruth

Finally, red in the face, Lou threw in his cards. He stood up and said, "Add up the score, I'm through," and stormed off. The other three waited until he'd left the car and then burst out laughing.

The game now over, the Babe went and sat down beside Urban Shocker. As usual, he was sleeping sitting up in his seat, propped up against the window. As Ruth thought about going to the smoking car for a cigar, Shocker began to slump over. Still fast asleep, he slumped more and was almost horizontal. He began to choke.

"Rubber Belly! Wake up!" yelled the Babe. "You're choking."

Ruth grabbed Urban by the shoulders and hoisted him upright again. Shocker coughed and sputtered and finally caught his breath.

"You know you can't sleep lying down," said the Babe.

"It's gettin' bad, Jidge. Some kinda defective valve in my heart. Don't tell anyone, but the doctor says every time I take the mound I'm risking my life."

Ruth didn't know what to say. There was nothing *to* say. The only medicine he'd studied was female anatomy, but he knew people didn't get new hearts.

o   o   o

Back on the field for the first game on Saturday Koenig fielded flawlessly and banged three hits including a long double down the third base line to lead the way. His teammates did rather well too, scoring three in the third, two in the fourth, one in the fifth, three in the sixth, one in the eighth, and a superfluous four in the ninth, which included Ruth's 435-foot missile into the busy street beyond right field. The score ended up 15-4 New York.

When the team got back to the Mayfair Bob Shawkey asked Waite Hoyt if the hotel had a pay phone.

"Of course it does," said Hoyt. "It's just inside the other entrance. Why? Do you have to call the Tiger Lady?"

"Ya. That's it. I gotta call Marie," Shawkey said over his shoulder as he headed off to find the phone booth.

o   o   o

It didn't take long for the Yankees to get to 2-9 Ernie Wingard on Sunday. With Combs on in the first inning, the Babe drilled his forty-second homer into the right field seats and the Hugmen added a pair in the second and one in the third.

The Browns actually showed signs of life for a change. They jumped on Dutch Ruether for four runs in the third and when they started knocking Dutch around again in the fourth Huggins had seen enough. He sent Shocker in. His spitter was working today and he gave up only one more run the rest of the way. The Yankees scored two more on Wingard's replacement, Elam Vangilder, in the fifth and another two in the ninth. Most of the disheartened St. Louis fans had left the premises long before the visitors ended it 10-6. They'd only waited around to see if Ruth would hit another round tripper.

o   o   o

Gehrig became the fourth major leaguer to belt more than forty homers in a season when he hit his forty-first in a five-run third inning outburst on Monday and pulled within one of Ruth. It was Ladies Day, but there were few women in the small crowd. It was well known that rats scurried throughout Sportsman's Park. Pennock sailed to an 8-3 win.

The Babe showed he could help his team with the glove on a day when his bat was silent. He went 0-4 but in the fourth inning he gobbled up Harry Rice's fly ball down the left field line with the bases loaded and in the fifth he picked Bing Miller's low liner off the parched brown grass and then speared Oscar Melillo's high liner in front of the left field wall. In the sixth he sprinted deep into left center and robbed Leo Dixon of a sure double.

o   o   o

The team headed back to New York for a break from their arduous road trip and the Red Sox came to town for two games. On Wednesday, August 31st Lazzeri hit one over the fence with Ruth and Meusel on base in the third and belted another into the right field seats the next inning.

The fans were cheering for the Babe to hit one when he came up for the last time and he didn't disappoint. He smashed a Tony Welzer curveball to the very last row of the right field bleachers. His 495-foot blast came within inches of exiting the Stadium.

"How could that thing not go out?" he muttered as he trotted around

Babe Ruth

the bases. "Any other park and that thing would have been on a trolley car uptown."

"That's forty-three for Ruth now," James Harrison pointed out to Richards Vidmer up in the press box.

"He still needs seventeen to reach sixty and only a month left," said Vidmer. "No one's ever hit *that* many in a month. Not even the Babe."

o o o

The September 1st game against Boston was rained out and the Yankees went back on the road again, a shorter trip this time, to the City of Brotherly Love. On the train Pennock read a column from the *Daily News* to Shocker and Hoyt.

"Listen to this pile of drivel, boys."

"What's it about?" asked Waite.

"They're breaking us up."

"What? The ball club?" asked Shocker.

"That's right. Apparently we're too strong and we're bad for business."

"What do they say's gonna happen?" asked Hoyt.

Pennock read aloud. "Gehrig is going to be traded to the Tigers. He and the Babe are too powerful a combination to have on one team."

"Is that so?" said Waite. "Anybody else or just Lou?"

"Oh, no. Seems Joe's being traded to the White Sox for Willie Kamm."

"He's not gonna like that," said Urban.

"And Tony's going somewhere too, but this fellow doesn't know where."

"They gonna break up the pitching staff too?" asked Waite.

"There's no mention of that."

"Well, I take that as a personal insult," grunted Hoyt.

"Did the guy talk to Barrows or Ruppert about all these moves?" asked Shocker.

"He did. The Colonel was quoted as saying, 'When I bought the Yankees and they were in last place, did anyone give me any players? No. Well maybe a couple of lemons, but no one of any use. And now they expect me to give up Gehrig or Lazzeri? Over my dead body! The others can build their clubs the same way I have.'"

Gehrig ran up the aisle at full tilt and nearly landed in Pennock's lap.

"What the heck?" cried Herb.

"Is it true, Herb?" Lou demanded.

Pennock tried to piece his badly torn newspaper back together. "Is what true?"

"Benny just told me he heard I'm gettin' traded ta da Tigers."

Herb smiled, the others laughed.

"No, Lou. You are not going to Detroit."

"How do ya know?"

"Because the Colonel told everybody who'd listen that he's not parting with any of his players. Not you or anyone else."

"Are you sure, Herb?"

"I'm quite sure. Now relax."

"My mom'd be heart-broken if I hadda play somewhere else."

"Well the next time you write her a letter - probably in the next five minutes or so - you can tell her that you're staying put in the Bronx."

o o o

In the first inning of the first game in Philadelphia Ruth hit one deep to centerfield. Ty Cobb turned his back to second base and got ready to play a rebound off the fence. The ball kept on going and fell into the seats.

"I could hit them out any time I want if I swung like that ape instead of the way you're supposed to," muttered Cobb.

As Cobb fumed, Gehrig sent one over the rooftops of some cottages beyond right field. It was Lou's forty-second circuit blast of the year, as some of the writers were starting to call home runs. Ruth and Gehrig were hitting so many, the scribes were scrambling to find new names for them.

"You can bet there'll be more of that nonsense about breaking up the Yankees," Hoyt told Pennock as he got up and ladled himself a drink from the water bucket.

Babe Ruth

In the second inning Ruth blasted a ball high into the afternoon sky over right field. The fielder backed up and backed up some more. His back was right up against the wall when he caught the mile-high sacrifice fly. Combs walked home from third. He could have stopped to tie his shoes.

Connie Mack pulled Rube Walberg after the Yanks had pummelled him with seven hits in two innings. His replacement was battered for thirteen hits in his seven innings. Mack took the beatings in stride but Ty Cobb was livid. While he managed just one hit and his average fell slightly to .354 Gehrig had four to lift his average to .386. Koenig had four as well, which pushed him to .294, but he committed a two-run error in the ninth that cost Herb Pennock a shutout.

Ruth showered and dressed as fast as he could. It helped that he hadn't worn underwear since being teased about wearing the same pair for a week when he joined the Red Sox. He hopped into a cab and headed to the Kensington section of town. William Casey, the assistant pastor of the Ascension Parish, who also was the unofficial pastor of the A's, had told Ruth about a problem the parish had run into. They'd gone $6,500 in debt building a top quality field for their baseball team. They needed to hold a fund-raiser.

"Say no more, Father. Tell me where and when and I'll be there," said the Babe.

"We're staging an exhibition game," Father Casey told him. "If you could just play a couple of innings it would be a huge draw."

"Nothing doin', Father," said Ruth.

"But I thought you told me you'd ..."

"I'll play the whole game."

An Ascension uniform was made specially for Ruth and placed in a store window near the church as a promotion. Word spread fast that he'd be playing and all seven thousand tickets were sold in two days. Another several thousand people stood on housetops and factory roofs, sat on window ledges or clung to tree branches to catch a glimpse of the world's most famous player in their very own neighborhood.

The Babe played first base and batted cleanup against the Lit Brothers, a department store team that was one of the best amateur nines in the country. Ruth flied out to left in his first at bat against a tricky and determined pitcher named Gransbach. His next time up, with Ascension trailing 2-0, he got ahold of one of Gransbach's slow curves and hit a rising line drive so far over the right field fence that no one could tell where it would come down.

A man and his son sat on the roof of their house across the street. They were too far away to see much. They could recognize the Babe but nobody else and there was no way they could see the ball. Except for now.

"Pa, I can see the ball now and it's coming right at us!"

"Saints preserve us, it is!"

They ducked and the boy's father crossed himself. By the time they turned around to look, the ball had disappeared out of sight.

"That ball has *left* the parish," Father Casey beamed to the man sitting next to him.

Ruth scored Ascension's only other run when he hit a fly ball so high that the centerfielder got dizzy and fell down trying to catch it. The Babe laughed so hard he had trouble running around the bases.

Ascension lost, but nobody was disappointed. Between innings Ruth had signed five dozen baseballs which the parish sold for five dollars each and he signed hundreds of others for free. After the game the Babe hit fungos over the left field fence to kids waiting along a railroad track. He was mobbed when he tried to leave the field. When he finally made it to the car Father Casey had waiting for him, Casey asked the Babe how he could repay him.

"Are you kidding me, Father?" was all Ruth said.

o o o

After the beating the Yankees had dished out to the A's on Friday, it was a much different story at Shibe Park on Saturday.

"I guess we used 'em all up yesterday," Koenig told Combs after trudging back to the dugout weighed down by an 0-4 collar.

"Apparently," said Earle, who'd gone 0-4 as well.

Cy Moore started and gave up only five hits, but Robert Moses Grove was firing bullets, with the occasional fade away curve thrown in for good measure.

Art Fletcher let Bill McGowan have it after every called third strike.

Finally McGowan took off his mask and walked out to Fletcher's coaching box.

"Listen, Art, Grove's pitches are tough to call. I'm giving it my very best effort."

"It's not your effort that I'm questioning, Bill. It's your eyesight."

"Well you can question it all you want, Art. From the clubhouse. You're out of here."

The Yanks lost 1-0. It was the first time they'd been shut out all year.

"Not exactly the season you'd planned on, is it Connie?" James Harrison asked Mack after the game ended.

"I thought there was a good chance we'd be in second and now that we've passed the Tigers that's just where we are. But seventeen games behind? No. I would never have imagined that. The Yankees are having an incredible year."

o o o

Urban Shocker's wife Irene, Dorothy Hoyt, and Marie Shawkey had met the week before to talk about what they should do when their husbands finally had a day off in Philadelphia on Sunday, September the 4th.

"Let's get them to meet us at the train station on Saturday after the game and we'll head straight to Atlantic City," said Dorothy. "We'll see a couple of shows and then do the Steel Pier and the boardwalk on Sunday. They can take a train to Boston Sunday night."

"That's a *great* idea," said Irene.

"That'd be a hoot," said Marie. "The boys would love it and one thing's for sure."

"What's that, Marie?" asked Dorothy.

& THE 1927 YANKEES HAVE THE BEST SUMMER EVER

"We won't have any trouble getting a drink in Atlantic City."

o o o

The game took less than an hour and a half to play so Shocker, Hoyt, and Shawkey actually got to the train station before their wives arrived from New York. They got their shoes shined and talked about what they wanted to do in Atlantic City.

"Well, since we've been home one night in the last month I'd like to spend some time in the hotel room with the little woman when we get there," said Urban.

"And I imagine you'll want to do some … catching up with the Tiger Lady when we get to the hotel," Waite teased Bob.

"Are you kiddin'? I'm gonna jump her in the dining car as soon as our train leaves the station. We knock over somebody's soup, tough luck."

"All right, after we've renewed acquaintances with the wives what'll we do?" asked Waite.

"You boys forget about the bathing suit competition they hold to keep the tourists around after Labor Day?" asked Shocker.

"Ya, it was the National Beauty Pageant when they started it five years ago. Now they call it the Miss America Pageant," said Shawkey.

"They should ask the Babe to be a judge," said Hoyt.

"Ya, sure, Waite," said Shawkey. "We all know what Jidge'd want to rate the girls on."

o o o

The women arrived by cab. They were all attractive women and they stood out in the crowd on the busy sidewalk. Dorothy wore a fringe ribbon hat and a Basque dress and Irene wore a pink organdelle dress and a stylish nacre feather trim hat. Marie had on a silk Georgette crepe dress that cost fifteen dollars and a fancy hat that had set her husband back another six dollars, though he didn't know it yet. She wasn't concerned. She had a treat in store for him that would make him forget all about how much she'd spent.

The couples kissed, hugged, and boarded the train to Atlantic City. Bob told Marie he needed to 'talk to her' in the room as soon as they got to the hotel.

"Where are we staying, girls?" asked Waite as they were getting off the train at Atlantic City.

"Since we have only the one night you boys decided to splurge," said Dorothy. "I booked us rooms at the Marlborough-Blenheim."

Shawkey whistled. "The Marlborough-Blenheim, well ain't we the rich swells?"

"There's hot and cold running salt water and a private bath in each room," Dorothy informed them.

"You might need to give me a bath tonight, baby," Urban told Irene. "I musta forgotten to take a shower after the game, I feel kinda dirty."

"It's your mind that's dirty," Irene told him. "I suppose I could scrub your back though."

While they were signing in at the front desk Shawkey saw a phone booth.

"I gotta make a call," he said, hurrying toward it.

"Who ya gotta call this time, Gob?" asked Hoyt. "Marie's right here."

"I ... I ... I gotta call a guy back home. He's getting me some new golf clubs."

o o o

An hour later Urban was hanging up his suit jacket in the closet of their room when he thought he heard the bathroom door open.

"Are you finished your bath already? You just went in ..."

He stopped in mid-sentence. Irene stepped into the room wearing nothing but a towel and high heels.

"I've been looking forward to this for a long, long time, Urban," she breathed. She dropped the towel to the floor.

A floor below Dorothy Hoyt was asking Waite if he'd unhook the back of her dress so she could change for dinner.

"We're not going to spend the money to eat dinner in the hotel's dining room are we?" Waite asked. "It'll be nothing but stuffy old rich people and it'll cost a small fortune."

"No, Waite. I thought we'd eat along the boardwalk instead."

"Good idea. When did we say we'd meet the others?"

"Not for an hour, dear," said Dorothy. She looked into his eyes and started to undo his belt buckle.

Waite inhaled a deep breath and said, "Why, Dorothy, I didn't know you felt that way about me."

"I do, I do. And I'd really like you to feel your way about me too," she said as she undid her brassiere.

Three doors down Marie Shawkey told Bob to lie down on the bed. She took two small ropes out of her purse.

"What are you planning to do with those?" Bob asked, wide-eyed.

"Quiet, big boy," said Marie as she tied his wrists to the bedposts. He pretended to struggle.

She pulled the ribbon from her hair and let her long curls fall to her shoulders. She slowly unzipped her dress, revealing her shapely figure squeezed into a tight-fitting corset. She wore high heels and black stockings held up by garters with pink ribbons.

"I read about this in a naughty French novel called Les Liaisons Dangereuses while you and your pals were on the road taking showers together."

"You're looking pretty dangerous right now, Marie. Should I be scared?"

"Yes. Very scared," she whispered as she brushed her husband's hairy chest with a tiny whip.

They met in the lobby at seven and the women winked at one another. The men had big smiles on their faces. The group had juicy hamburgers, greasy French fries, and cold beer at a hot dog stand on the boardwalk.

"Hell, I thought Chicago was something," said Waite. "You can get a drink anywhere down here. And you don't have to sneak around and give a password or drink out of a damn tea cup."

"And the whiskey's the good stuff," said Bob. "Canadian Club."

"And not laced with God know's what," said Urban.

"Raree! Raree! Right around the corner," yelled a man wearing a Panama hat.

Babe Ruth

"No thanks, fella," said Bob. "We've got a *real* show to catch."

"Look out, Bob!" yelled Marie.

He leapt out of the way as a couple on a bicycle-built-for-two swerved to avoid running into him.

The three couples headed to the Apollo and then to the Globe. They saw Harry Houdini, W.C. Fields, and then Rudy Vallee and his Connecticut Yankees. They danced to young Guy Lombardo and his Royal Canadians and finished off the night by taking in Mae West's risqué 3 a.m. show.

Everyone look tired but happy as they ate breakfast on the veranda overlooking the ocean the next morning. They had Eggs Benedict and champagne with their orange juice. Hoyt missed most of the meal. He was too busy snapping pictures of the beach and the people on it with his new Kodak Box Brownie camera.

"Bob kept me up 'til dawn," Marie whispered to Irene.

"You mean you kept *him* up," teased Irene.

"That Houdini can get out of anything," said Bob.

"He sure can, and that Fields is a funny guy," said Waite.

"He sure can juggle," said Urban.

"Ya, I hear he never spills a drink," chuckled Bob.

"I suppose you boys liked Mae West and her half naked strumpets," said Marie.

"Hey, we didn't complain when the three of ya were droolin' over Rudy Vallee," said Shawkey.

"I really wanted to see Al Jolson. Maybe he's in Hollywood making another speaking picture," said Irene.

Marie was about to say something when a Western Union messenger boy scurried past them. "Telegram for Robert Shawkey. Telegram for Mister Robert Shawkey," he called out.

"Right here, son," said Bob.

"How does anyone know we're here?" asked Marie.

"I called New York when we arrived," he explained as he handed the messenger boy a quarter. He tore open the envelope and a big smile spread across his face as he read the wire.

"What is it, Gob?" asked Urban. "Somebody die and leave you his fastball?"

"Very funny, smart ass. No, it's nothing like that." He set down the telegram and grinned. "When you boys go to check out you'll find your rooms have been paid for."

Hoyt came back to the table and set his camera down beside his plate. "Whad'ya mean, Bob? Who's paying for our rooms?"

"I am," said Shawkey.

"Why would ya go and do somethin' like that?" asked Urban.

"I just found out I made a killing on the market yesterday."

Marie grabbed his arm. "You did? How, Bob?"

"I got a tip from a fellow on the train to St. Louis about a stock and I called New York and got my bookie to put two grand on the company the guy told me about."

"*That's* why you were in such a tizzy to find a phone booth at the Mayfair," said Waite.

"If you don't mind my asking you in front of everyone else, *darling*, where on *Earth* did you get two thousand dollars?" asked Marie.

"I bought on margin. Like everybody else does."

"Didn't Hug tell us that buying on margin was a fool's game?" asked Hoyt.

"He did. And normally I wouldn't have done it. But the fellow said it was a sure thing and I went ahead. I made a ton a dough."

Marie was relieved. "Well I guess you won't faint then when I tell you how much I paid for the hat and dress I had on yesterday."

Dorothy and Irene burst out laughing.

"So what's on the agenda for today?" asked Waite.

Babe Ruth

"Yes, what else have you gals cooked up for us?" asked Urban.

Dorothy was proud of the meticulous planning she'd done. "We're going to see the General Motors Exhibition and the High-Diving Horse and the boxing kangaroos at the Steel Pier this morning. Then we'll go for a ride along the Boardwalk on rolling chairs and then go swimming in the ocean this afternoon."

"Sounds great," said Urban. "I can't wait to see the High-Diving Horse."

"I hear it's amazing," said Bob.

"The General Motors Exhibition is supposed to be really something too," said Waite. "It's got all kinds of new technology."

"And, while we girls check out the kiosks you boys can play midway games or have drinks on the hotel veranda and watch the Miss America contestants strut their stuff," said Irene.

"Which will probably put you in the mood for some more alone time in our rooms before we catch our trains," said Marie.

"I can play midway games in Ohio," said Urban. "I'm for the booze and the babes on the beach."

"And a nap in the room after is probably a wise idea," said Waite.

They all laughed when Bob said, "Forget that, I can sleep on the train."

22.

THE BABE CATCHES FIRE

"I will bet you a shiny Buffalo nickel that is a major league record."

The first game of the Labor Day double header in Boston was the wildest game of the year. The last available seat was sold well before the first pitch and thousands were turned away. A few hundred people were allowed to ring the outfield, which called for special ground rules, and others perched on fences, posts, and nearby rooftops.

It was clear the multitude had not turned up to cheer on their last place team who now sat an embarrassing forty-nine games behind their guests. They'd come to bear witness to the home run derby that was captivating America now that not all of the talk was about Lindbergh.

The Red Sox banged George Pipgras around for three runs in the first. The Yankees bounced back with four of their own off Red Ruffing in the third, two on Gehrig's forty-fourth home run. They got to Ruffing for two more in the fourth, but Boston stormed back with another four before Huggins could get Pipgras off the mound. Joe Giard and Bob Shawkey, who'd slept the whole way to Boston, held the Red Sox to a single run over the next five innings but they still held an 8-6 lead after eight.

The New Yorkers nudged two across to tie things up and Huggins wasted no time sending in Moore. Cy did his job, holding the Red Sox off the scoreboard for the next seven innings before finally giving way to Hoyt. The Yankees finally plated three runs in the top of the seventeenth and most of the crowd headed for the exits. They'd been jammed in like sardines for four and a half hours.

"Gave you a few to play with, Schoolboy," Earle Combs told Waite as he jogged to center. Earle was smiling. He had five hits to show for his ten at bats. It wasn't quite enough.

After failing to score in any of the last eleven innings the Red Sox tied the marathon with three runs of their own. Hal Wiltse shut out the Yankees in the top of the eighteenth, Jack Tobin and Wally Shaner hit back to back doubles the bottom of the eighteenth, and the marathon was over just like that.

"Hurray!" shouted Tobin as he crossed the plate. "Only forty-*eight* back."

Urban Shocker, still grinning about the trip to Atlantic City, held the Red Sox to three singles in the second game, which started two hours later than it was expected to. Earle Combs was the hero, driving in four runs with his sixth and seventh hits of the day. Dick Nallin called things after fifty-five minutes with darkness closing like a curtain and New York up 5-0.

o o o

There was a hint of fall in the air as the two teams went back at it for two the next day.

"Let's hope neither of these games goes eighteen fucking innings," grumbled Meusel. He was one of the seven Yankee regulars who'd played all twenty-three innings the day before.

Many of the enthusiasts who'd sat through six hours of play on Monday without seeing the Babe hit one out returned to work. The much smaller weekday crowd was in for a treat.

Gehrig pulled back into the long ball lead in the fifth inning with his forty-fifth. It didn't take the Babe long to reply. Combs led off the sixth with a single and Koenig followed with a double, so there were runners on the corners when Ruth strode to the plate. Welzer threw strictly outside to the Babe. It had only been a week since he'd come within inches of sending one of Welzer's inside deliveries clear out of Yankee Stadium.

A strong wind blew from left to right field. Welzer gazed at the ball nestled in his glove. "Two on base. He's looking to beat the stuffing out of this thing," he said to himself. "I'm gonna cross him up with a change of pace."

The slow one got a sliver of the corner. For a change Ruth decided not to pull it. He put all his might into his swing and hit the ball farther to left centerfield than anyone had ever done at Fenway. It cleared the high board fence and landed 505 feet from the plate, electrifying the small crowd.

With a runner on first the next inning Welzer ran the count to 3-0. The Babe looked into the dugout. Huggins nodded - the green light signal. Ruth was the only player Huggins allowed to swing away on a 3-0 count, partly because he got so many of them.

Welzer tried a hook. Ruth went back to pulling the ball and hit one a modest 400 feet into the right field bleachers, his forty-sixth. He was back in the lead. Pennock cruised to a 14-2 win in a little under two hours. They'd start the second game a lot earlier today.

The Boston skipper sent Jack the Terrier Russell to the mound for the second game and he had the Yankees tied up in knots. He led 5-0 after eight.

The Babe led off the ninth and hit Russell's second delivery 475 feet into the stands in center field, a bit farther and to the right of where his last clout had landed two hours earlier.

Gehrig followed with a drive to the deepest part of the field. It landed just short of the fence and Lou chugged around for a triple. Meusel drove him in to pull New York within three but Tony Lazzeri struck out, Julie Wera, grounded out, and Pat Collins popped out to end things 5-2 Boston.

Ruth's three belts put him seven behind his pace of 1921. He still needed thirteen more and he had only twenty-two games left. Even *he* didn't hit them that often.

o o o

After the second double header in two days some of the Yankees needed to quench their thirst. They'd only play one game on Thursday before heading home to New York. The Babe went drinking with some old buddies from his years in Boston. Dugan, Shawkey, and Meusel headed to one of the many speaks on Huntington Avenue. The owner, a squat, slope-shouldered man, sat down at their table and bought them a drink.

"How many policemen are you paying every week?" Dugan asked.

"A hundred or so I suppose. Most of the force is on the take."

"And the police chief lets all this go on?"

Babe Ruth

"Sure does. There are four speakeasies on the same block as the police headquarters. Hell, our mayor, James Curley, has the opening notes of How Dry I Am playing on his car horn."

"How can you afford to pay off so many coppers?" asked Bob.

The manager pointed upwards. "We rent rooms upstairs to hookers. They pay us twenty percent of what they take in and they get to eat and drink for free so long as they're friendly to the customers without scaring proper ladies out of the joint. Not that the real proper ones come in here."

o o o

On Wednesday, September 7th the Yankees and Red Sox played for the last time. Deacon McFayden was glad the bases were empty when Ruth came up to bat in the first after Combs and Koenig had lined out.

"Nothing over the plate, nothing over the plate," he chanted to himself as he cleaned his glasses.

His second pitch was not over the plate, not even close, but it was soon over the left field wall, right next to the clock.

McFayden was happy to limit Ruth to a single his next time up, also with the bases empty. The Babe didn't score and neither did the rest of the Yankees until the sixth inning when they knocked the Deacon out of the game with six runs. They needed them. The Red Sox had scored five off Myles Thomas and another three off Joe Giard in the fourth. It was no wonder Hug kept turning to Wilcy Moore. His crew plated three more in the seventh on Slim Harriss, who had the unlucky task of facing the Babe in the eighth.

The score was knotted at 10-10. Ruth already had three hits and was looking for a fourth. Like his predecessor, Slim had no plans to throw Ruth anything near the strike zone. His third pitch was well outside. The Babe stepped into it and belted it to left center to win the game 12-10.

James Harrison jumped out of his chair and leaned forward out through the press box window to watch it. "About seventy feet farther than the one he hit in the first and beside the flagpole not the clock this time," he told Richards Vidmer.

"That's his forty-ninth," said Vidmer. "And his fifth in two days. I will bet you a shiny Buffalo nickel that is a major league record."

◦ ◦ ◦

"Last train ride together of the year unless we get into the Series," Hoyt told Shocker as they boarded the Mayflower for home.

"Sixteen games up on the A's and twenty-two on Washington and Detroit. I like our chances," said Urban.

"The National's a real dog fight," said Waite. "The Pirates are a half a game up on the Giants and the Cardinals are just two back."

"Who would you rather face?" asked Urban. "If we get in," he quickly added, not wanting to jinx things.

"St. Louis," said Hoyt. "They got Frisch for Hornsby over the winter but besides him the only really good hitter they got is Bottomley. They won it on pitching last year. Waner's little brother's hitting up a storm in Pittsburgh and Traynor's being Traynor, but neither the Pirates or the Cards are gonna beat New York. The Giants are loaded."

"I'd sure like another crack at the Cards after what happened last year," said Shocker.

"Let's hope," said Hoyt. "The Browns are coming to town. If we can't beat *them* we're in trouble."

"You're startin' tomorrow, aren't you?"

"So Hug says."

"Well get us off on the right foot, Schoolboy."

"I've won eighteen once and nineteen twice. Sure would be nice to win twenty."

◦ ◦ ◦

Neither Ruth nor Gehrig homered in the first game against St. Louis back at the Stadium. The Yankees managed only four hits and scored only two runs off Sad Sam Jones and one of them was unearned on Spooks Gerber's thirty-eighth error of the year. It ended up being the difference. Hoyt gave up just three hits and only one run of any kind and finally won his twentieth, 2-1.

Babe Ruth

Waite was in the shower when Eddie Bennett yelled through the steam that the owner wanted to see him in his office. Hoyt dressed quickly, checked the gauge on the back of the Chevrolet to make sure he had enough gasoline, and drove through heavy traffic to the brewery. He was ushered into Ruppert's opulent office by a good-looking secretary who looked anxious to go home.

The Colonel drew something from a folder on his desk and handed it to Waite. "Here you go, Mister Hoyt. A deal is a deal and you have certainly earned it with your fine work this year. Miller Huggins told me in April that he thought you would be more serious this season. You have been and it has paid off handsomely for you."

Waite looked at the check for a thousand dollars and thought about how happy Dorothy would be. "Now I won't have to worry about the check for the new radio bouncing," he muttered to himself.

"What was that, Mister Hoyt?"

"Nothing. I'm just glad to help the team. Thanks. I sure need … I mean I sure appreciate it."

o o o

"So Ruppert came through after all," said Dorothy when Waite showed her the check. She gave him a peck on the cheek. "I just knew you were going to win twenty this time."

"I was a little worried when I lost those games in Chicago and Boston, but I figured I had lots of time and with the hitting we got this year I knew I had a pretty good shot at twenty."

"So when are you taking me, darling?" Dorothy purred.

"To bed to celebrate?"

"No, silly man. Shopping."

o o o

"This means so much to her," Claire told the Babe when he arrived at Julia's school for the Parent-Child game the next morning. "The other kids have been making a fuss over her ever since she told them you'd promised to play."

Ruth was glad it was softball they'd be playing, there was a lot less chance of someone getting hurt. Julia played second base for the students' team. She had a grin a mile wide but seemed to pay almost as much attention to the cute boy playing shortstop as she did to her special friend of the family. The Babe hit easy groundballs to him his first three times up and made a point of yelling "Nice play" each time the boy threw him out.

When Ruth came up a fourth time he looked up at Claire who was watching proudly from the tiny stands. She nodded just as Miller Huggins might have. Ruth winked and hit the ball on a gentle arc. It flew over the field and crashed through a window of the school library.

"Sorry about the window," the Babe told the principal after the game. "I'll buy the school some sports equipment."

"That would be great, Babe. I might just leave it the way it is though. The kids'd get a kick out of having a reminder of your visit."

o o o

That afternoon was Tony Lazzeri Day at the Stadium. Koenig took a whiff of the air as he and Lazzeri played long catch before the game. "Do you smell garlic?" he asked. "A lot of your folks are here today."

"Thatsa sooo funny, you musta be soma kinda comedian," Tony retorted, firing the ball at Koenig's head.

"Don't you dare say a word," Tony told Mark as the president of the Tony Lazzeri Fan Club draped a huge floral horseshoe over his hero's shoulders.

"I won't if you take me to dinner with that pot of silver dollars they just gave you."

In spite of all the cries of 'Push 'Em Up' and 'You heetta the ball, Tony' it was the Babe, not Lazzeri who led the way, driving in four of New York's nine runs with two bullet-like singles and a towering sacrifice fly. Tony went hitless, striking out twice, once with the bases loaded. Urban Shocker gave up three runs in the fourth but that was all the Browns could manage. Shocker went the distance. Wilcy Moore had his fourth day off in a row.

"Gonna get rusty, Cy," said Hoyt as they sat together in the bullpen. Waite was smiling. He and Dorothy *had* celebrated in bed after she'd bought some things she'd seen at Macy's.

o o o

Babe Ruth

Huggins decided to give his well-rested relief ace the ball on Saturday. The Browns' starter, Tennessee-born Lefty Stewart, had lost all of his starts against New York. Of course the same could be said of all the other St. Louis starters too. This time Stewart's hooks absolutely baffled the Yanks, but the Browns fared no better against Moore.

It was scoreless in the eighth when Melillo and Gerber grounded out to start the inning. But Lefty Stewart singled and when O'Rourke hit a hard grounder right at Moore he couldn't handle it. Cy looked rattled. Pat Collins noticed and motioned to Miller Huggins. Hug called time and went to the mound.

Before he could get a word out Cy said, "Ya oughta not feel bad if ya wanna take me out, Skip. I know I ain't a starter." He handed Huggins the ball.

Hug smiled and stroked his chin. "Well here's the thing of it, Cy, the fella I'd normally bring in at this juncture is already here on the mound. So why don't we just pretend I'm bringing you in now." He handed the ball back to Cy, patted him on the ass, and trotted back to the dugout. Cy chuckled and then got Rice to pop out to end the inning.

Meusel doubled in the eighth and Lazzeri sacrificed him to third. Mike Gazella, who was in for Dugan for a fifth straight game, lofted a fly to deep center and Meusel jogged home with the winning run.

After Cy retired the Browns in the ninth he told Huggins, "I was pretty fresh out there, just comin' in for the last four outs the way I did."

"Twenty-one straight over the Browns," Richards Vidmer pointed out after the game.

"Think they can make it a season sweep tomorrow?" asked James Harrison.

"They just tied the all-time record with that win," said Vidmer. "Some numbers fanatic at the paper looked it up for me. The Cubs beat the Braves twenty-one out of twenty-two in O Nine."

"You gotta figure the Browns are due," said Harrison. "Maybe they should skip batting practice tomorrow morning and go to church instead."

o o o

"You're playing aren't you, Joe?" Lazzeri asked Dugan the next morning.

"Ya, I guess. Why?"

"It's your day, isn't it?"

"Ya, but it's not a big deal like your days are."

The Yankees combined for just five hits off Milt Gaston. Happily two of them were by Joe Dugan, who was back in the lineup just in time for Joe Dugan Day. Hundreds of tipsy Elks from White Plains Lodge No. 535 were there to cheer on their favorite son. Their president presented Joe with a solid gold card case that was studded with small diamonds and rubies.

The Elks' bus ride to the Bronx had been boisterous because they'd sipped from flasks and beers they'd hidden in the box that held their other gifts for Joe. The ride back promised to be even rowdier. Joe's hits made them happy but they cheered louder when Ruth bashed number fifty high into the right field bleachers in the fourth.

Dugan shook his head as the Babe returned to the dugout. "You just gotta be the big story every time, don't you?"

"Sorry 'bout that, couldn't help myself."

George Sisler and Ken Williams got six of the Browns' eleven hits, eight of which were off Herb Pennock who lasted only three innings before giving way to George Pipgras. Pennock had the distinction of being the only Yankee to lose to St. Louis all year.

When Ruth galloped in from right at the end of the game he was swamped. It seemed like every kid in New York was trying to jump onto his big round shoulders. It looked as though he was about to go down under the weight of the massive throng as he struggled to make it into the dugout. New York's finest came to the rescue and helped him duck into the clubhouse. He'd loved every second of it.

Up in the press box Richards Vidmer said, "It sure looks as though the Babe's won the kids back."

"And apparently the Browns *did* go to church," said James Harrison.

The first game against Cleveland on Tuesday was all tied up until the sixth when George Pipgras gave up a pair of runs. He was still muttering

Babe Ruth

to himself about a pitch he'd left out over the plate that Joe Sewell had hit to the left field wall for a run-scoring double when the Babe grabbed Black Betsy and headed to the on-deck circle. Mark Koenig lined a single to left center.

The Babe looked in at Pipgras and said, "Don't worry, keed, I'll get ya a couple more."

Willis Hudin, who'd been painting the black the whole game, wasn't going to put one that close to the plate for Ruth, not when he had a lead and an outside shot at a twenty win season. His first pitch was down and away. The Babe ripped it into the right field seats. The crowd let out a huge cheer and several now out-of-season straw boaters sailed across the field.

"Damn it!" yelled Hudin.

Pipgras tipped his cap to the Babe and he smiled back as he rounded first on his fiftieth home run trot of the year. The one time he'd hightailed it around the bags for an inside-the-park job.

In the ninth Earle Combs drilled a ball over the left field fence. When he got back to the dugout he sat down beside Hoyt. He pointed toward the Cleveland dugout and told Waite, "That was my fifth. You realize if was playing for *those* guys I'd be leading the club in homers."

"Well keep swinging for the fences, Earle. You're only forty-six back of the lead on *our* club and you've still got more than two weeks left."

Pipgras held on for a 5-3 win and it said a lot about the Yankees' offense that Pipgras was now 8-3 in spite of an E.R.A. of 4.62.

o o o

Hoyt got the start for the afternoon matinee. He gave up ten hits but spread them out nicely, two in the same inning only once, in the ninth. The Indians led 2-1 when Ruth led off the fourth and creamed one of Joe Saute's offerings into the right field bleachers to start a four-run uprising.

The Yankees triumphed 5-3, as they had in the opener. What made this win, their ninety-eighth, special was that it clinched the American League pennant.

"The New York Times would like to know your secret to leading this team to the pennant," said John Kieran as reporters huddled around Huggins.

& THE 1927 YANKEES HAVE THE BEST SUMMER EVER

"You can tell them I did not pitch one scoreless inning. I did not advance a solitary runner with a sacrifice bunt. I never once cleared the bases with a line drive off the wall and I did not hit a single ball into the seats. All I do is write the boys' names on the lineup card and let them play. It's not a tough job. I haven't misspelled one name yet," said Huggins tongue-in-cheek, though Kieran was writing down every word he said.

James Harrison butted in. "Don't you dare believe a word of that nonsense he's feeding you. Miller is the heart and soul of this club."

Earle Combs overheard him as he headed to the showers, "You can say that again. We couldn't have done it without Hug."

To celebrate clinching the pennant the Babe rented a suite at The Plaza, New York's swankiest hotel, at Fifth Avenue and 57th Street. At nineteen stories tall it towered above the buildings around it. A regular room cost $2.50 a night but the Babe was paying considerably more than that. People said if you didn't have a good time at one of the Babe's parties you probably didn't have a good time anywhere.

o o o

When the Yankees got to the suite they were met at the door by a valet who ushered them inside.

"Good ta see ya, boys, help yourselves," bellowed Ruth. He wore a tuxedo and had a big cigar on the go. "The girls'll be here soon. Get yourselves somethin' to eat. You may need some stamina later," he chuckled.

The Babe had thought of everything. He'd even had a speakeasy send over a full bar complete with a chromium foot rail. Four long tables were laid out in the dining room. A chef stood behind them. He pointed out each dish.

"Gentlemen, we have smoked salmon, potato skins with broccoli and cheese, broiled mussels with paprika aioli, pancetta bruschetta, sautéed mushrooms, pickled quail eggs, oysters with presecco mignonette, baked ricotta, smoked salmon with caviar on slices of cucumber, and Serrano ham with Membrillo Crostina."

"Holy shit," said Mark Koenig. "I mean holy cow."

"There's everything *but* cow here," said Benny Bengough.

Babe Ruth

"I had all this stuff for dinner last night," Joe Dugan told Dutch Ruether.

"Me too," said Benny.

o o o

The girls came in around 9:30. They had cropped haircuts and they wore bold makeup. Their strings of beads were steel-cut and their sleeveless dresses were shorter than the players had ever seen. Most had their stockings rolled below their knees and wore gold-painted pumps with straps.

"There was already lotsa great food, but that's one nice-lookin' bunch of tomatoes!" exclaimed Benny.

"Which one are you going after, Jidge?" Benny asked Ruth. "Or maybe I say which two or three?"

"Ya, Jidge, you got some real hot numbers here," said Joe.

"This beauty right here," said the Babe, grinning as Claire stepped out of the kitchen. Her skin-tight midnight blue dress showed off her hourglass figure. Ruth put his arm around her waist. Claire was smiling too. Joe turned beet red and Benny nearly choked on his bruschetta.

o o o

Huggins came out of his office and looked around the dressing room the next morning. "It's pretty quiet in here, boys. I don't care how hard you went at it last night, all the regulars are playing. Nobody's getting stale before the Series."

Luke Sewell smashed a double to drive in Homer Summa in the ninth inning and spoil Dutch Ruether's shutout but his mates had scored a pair in the third and another in the fourth and it was mercifully over in an hour and a half.

Most of the revellers went home to nurse their hangovers. The Babe waded into a throng of kids who'd waited outside the clubhouse. He happily signed autographs and ruffled a few kids' hair. Then he hopped into his Pierce Arrow and went to visit a Catholic hospital. The ubiquitous Marshall Hunt just happened to be there.

o o o

& THE 1927 YANKEES HAVE THE BEST SUMMER EVER

The Babe was robbed in the seventh inning of Thursday's contest when Homer Summa raced up the embankment to the right field fence and jumped high into the air to snag the ball before it could fall into the seats. Summa had to chase another of Ruth's belts and Johnny Gill bounced off the fence and dropped yet another of the Babe's long ones. But apart from that, Yankee nemesis George Uhle slid one curve after another curve over the corners and around the New York bats and won it 3-2. Gehrig struck out in the fourth. He missed strike three by a foot.

"Poor Lou," Combs whispered to Herb Pennock. "He hasn't homered in ten games."

Babe Ruth & the 1927 YANKEES have the BEST SUMMER EVER

23.

WHAT'S WRONG WITH GEHRIG?

"We couldn't have caught that club with a speedboat and a net."

The White Sox came into town for four games on the weekend leading the second division but a dismal thirty-two games back of the Yankees. It could have been worse. The Red Sox were an even fifty back of the front runners now. Comiskey's crew would be even further behind by the time they left the Big Apple.

The Yanks led 2-0 when Ruth came to bat with one out and the bases empty in the third. He lined his fifty-third into the middle of what was once again being referred to as Ruthville. The crowd went berserk and another lucky fan got a prized souvenir.

Starter Wilcy Moore had come into the game hitting, if hitting was the appropriate term, .046. He'd gone 0-4 in April, 1-11 in May, 0-12 in June, 2-15 in July with a memorable two-hit performance on the 8th, 1-15 in August, and he was 0-6 so far in September.

As Ruth finished his handshakes and sat down beside Moore, Cy said, "Huh. You watch and see. I'm goin' ta hit one into the bleachers fore this here game's over. Up 'til now I've spent all my energy pitchin'. But now that we've won the pennant, I'm goin' out to knock a few homers of my own."

Ruth roared and then bellowed, "If you hit so much as one I'll buy you the best box of cigars in New York."

Benny Bengough flied out to begin the next inning. Big Cy spat a stream of tobacco juice and looked into the dugout as he strode confidently to the plate. Ruth pointed to the right field fence.

"That's right, Jidge, that's right where it's goin," he yelled in.

"Son of a gun," said the Babe when Moore belted an outside fastball into the seats. The crowd cheered as Wilcy jogged ever so slowly around the bases, beaming like a beacon the whole way. Every player on the Yankee bench was holding his sides laughing.

"That don't count," yelled Ruth. "You had your damn eyes closed."

"I had no such thing, Jidge. Coronas'll be fine."

He had his eyes open his next at bat too when he stroked a clean single that raised his average to a gaudy .072. Slugger Moore allowed just two hits and won his eighteenth. It was the Yankees' hundredth win.

"Are you surprised New York's already won a hundred games and there are still two weeks left in the season?" James Harrison asked Chicago skipper Ray Schalk.

Schalk spit out a mouthful of sunflower seed shells. "Nope," he said. "I'm surprised they've *lost* any. We couldn't have caught that club with a speedboat and a net."

Urban Shocker and Red Faber were the starters for the first of the two Saturday games on the 17th.

"Batters'll be lucky to hit the ball fifty feet with the two of them loading it up every pitch," Meusel said to Ruth while they took batting practice.

"Laces'll be soggy as all get out after an inning or so," said the Babe.

Shocker's soggy slow ones were working. He gave up just six hits. Faber's damp deliveries weren't so effective. Lazzeri ripped three singles to lift his average to .309 and Ruth easily stole his sixth base. The Yanks won it 3-2.

Between games four men came out to home plate and presented Earle Combs with a gold watch to commemorate his outstanding work as a leadoff hitter and outfielder. He was the star of the second half of the twin bill. His three hits included his sixth home run.

Unfortunately Combs' day was tainted when his unlucky thirteenth error of the season allowed White Sox starter Sarge Connolly to scamper home with Chicago's only run of the second game, spoiling Herb Pennock's shutout. The Yanks won it 8-1.

& THE 1927 YANKEES HAVE THE BEST SUMMER EVER

o o o

It was no surprise in the second inning of the first game on Sunday when Jockey Falk pelted a two-bagger off George Pipgras. He'd hit forty-three doubles in '26. Willie Kamm followed with his thirteenth triple of the year and the White Sox had a 1-0 lead. But Koenig's double in the third scored Combs and three innings later Lazzeri singled home Gehrig. After his second inning hiccup Pipgras blanked the White Sox the rest of the way.

The second of the Sunday games, the fourth of the weekend, featured a duel between the American League's twenty-one game winners, Ted Lyons and Waite Hoyt.

"Too bad the league says we aren't allowed to fraternize," Waite said to Lyons as they passed one another on their way to the bullpens to warm up.

"Landis would have a stroke if he saw me even givin' you the time a day," said Lyons.

"We might be talking about throwing the game when we were really talking about the build on the blonde sitting in row four."

"Ya. She's something, ain't she?"

Lyons was not at his best. The Babe singled home a run in the Yankees' three-run third inning and then swatted his fifty-fourth, a 425-foot clout, into the right field seats with Koenig on base. Hoyt had his best stuff. Kamm doubled home Falk in the fourth but that was the only blemish for Waite who won his twenty-second to take the league lead.

o o o

The mercury hovered in the mid-fifties as George Moriarty sent Sam Gibson to the mound on Wednesday. Huggins went with Dutch Ruether who was 13-5. His secret $2,500 bonus for winning fifteen had seemed like a certainty when he won his twelfth on July 30th. Then he'd gone 0-3 in August and lost his first start in September. He'd won number thirteen a week ago but now there wasn't much time left, just ten days. He had to beat the Tigers today.

"Where are all the reporters?" Pat Collins asked Lazzeri before the game.

"They're all in Chicago for the fight," said Tony.

Babe Ruth

Lazzeri made a wild throw, Gehrig dropped one that was right on target, Combs misplayed a short hopper in center, and Koenig matched them all with three errors, the second time he'd booted three in one game. All six Detroit runs were unearned. Ruether could hardly believe his bad luck.

"We'd better not play like this in the Series or it'll be over quick," fumed Huggins when Koenig committed his third gaffe. Mark wasn't any better at the plate. He went 0-5.

The Yankees' only run came in the ninth. The Babe, who had two hits and a perfect day in the field including a running jab of a long drive by Taverner, stepped in to one of Gibson's few poorly located fastballs and launched it high into the right field seats. He still needed five more for sixty with seven games left on the schedule, a tall order even for the Maharajah of Maul.

o o o

New York held a 6-4 lead at the end of eight after roughing up rookie Ownie Carroll, the Detroit starter on Thursday. He hadn't faced hitters like Murderers' Row when he was racking up a 50-2 record for Holy Cross. Wilcy Moore got another start for New York and he was far from sharp. He gave up five runs over the first eight innings and another three in the Tiger ninth before Hug gave him the hook and sent in Pipgras. He put a stop to the stampede of base runners and the Yankees came to bat in the bottom of the ninth down one run.

Combs, who'd smacked three consecutive triples, drove another one deep to lead off the ninth. Koenig followed with a hard grounder up the middle. Charlie Gehringer hustled after it and made a nice catch. He wheeled and threw off balance to first. His throw was wide and Lu Blue couldn't handle it. Koenig raced past him and headed to second. He just made it.

"Come on, Jidge," Mark yelled in to the Babe as he dusted himself off. He pointed over his shoulder to the right field seats. "Put one up there and we can call it a day."

"Gotcha, keed," yelled Ruth as he stepped to the plate.

o o o

A nine-year-old boy in the front row along the first base line yelled louder than Koenig or anyone else in the Stadium. "Come on, Babe, you can do

& THE 1927 YANKEES HAVE THE BEST SUMMER EVER

it!" He'd been dying for his hero to hit one but the Detroit pitchers hadn't thrown him anything even close to the strike zone.

Ken Holloway's second pitch was down, but not as far outside as he'd planned. The Babe took one of his patented uppercut swings.

Koenig recognized the sound. He'd heard that crisp, resonating crack many times. He started sprinting toward third and then slowed down. "I don't think there's much doubt about that one," he thought to himself.

The ball climbed and climbed and then rose some more. Harry Heilmann, the Tiger right fielder, took one glance skyward and saw there was no chance of catching the ball unless he could run sixty rows up inside of two seconds. It slammed into an empty seat in the sixth row from the top of the towering bleachers in right taking a chip out of it. Heilmann tucked his glove under his arm and jogged off. Most of the other Tigers were already half way to the dugout.

The boy didn't see it land. As soon as it had left the Babe's bat he'd jumped over the railing and sprinted toward Ruth. He caught up to his hero half way to third base.

Ruth was still carrying Black Betsy. He knew there'd be pandemonium after his game-ending blast. People were already pouring onto the field and he'd have to charge like Red Grange to make it around the bases and into the dugout. He didn't want anybody claiming his bat as a souvenir; he needed it for the Series. The boy grabbed onto the bat and held on for dear life. With his other hand he patted Ruth on the back. "Way ta go, Babe, I knew you'd hit one for me."

o o o

"Gehrig broke Ruth's record today with those two ribbies," James Harrison told Richards Vidmer after order had been restored. "He's got a hundred and seventy-two now, one more than the Babe had in 'Twenty-One."

"Sure. But who do you think is gonna get the headlines again?" Vidmer asked rhetorically.

"Gehrig told me the other day he could stand on his head and spit nickels and people would still only talk about the Babe," said Harrison.

Babe Ruth

"Well I'm sorry but Gehrig's a lousy interview," said Vidmer. "He talks in short, dull sentences in that flat Brooklyn accent of his."

"At least he's still talking to us. He's pretty steamed at some of our colleagues."

"He is?"

"Ya. One of them asked him why he hadn't homered in nineteen games and sweet Lou told him to go fuck himself."

o o o

That night Shawkey, Dugan, Meusel, and the Babe sat in Ruth's suite huddled around his new radio. He'd told them it would be just beer and boxing, no broads. Across the country an estimated fifty million other Americans were huddled around their radios. Graham McNamee was at Soldier Field in Chicago broadcasting the rematch between Jack Dempsey, the Manassas Mauler, and Gene Tunney, the Fighting Marine.

"This beer ain't bad. Where d'ya get it?" asked Shawkey.

"From the ice cream parlor 'round the corner," Ruth told him.

"Who's gonna win this time?" Dugan asked Meusel, who had been quietly sipping his beer.

"Dempsey," said Meusel.

"Why's that, Bob?" asked Joe.

"He'd had a long layoff before their first fight and he didn't know Tunney's style," said Meusel. "He'll be better this time."

"Ya, but Tunney's pretty fast and he's mighty clever," said Joe. "And he's never been knocked off his feet. My money's on him."

"And Dempsey's thirty-two now, pretty old for a fighter," said Shawkey.

"We know who you're for, Jidge," said Joe.

"If you're guessing Dempsey, you're damn right. He looked pretty good against Sharkey and I never could stand Tunney with his dancing around the ring and his Shakespeare plays."

"Quiet," said Shawkey, turning up the dial on the huge radio. "It's starting."

& **THE 1927 YANKEES HAVE THE BEST SUMMER EVER**

"There are several notable personages in attendance here this evening," intoned McNamee. "I see Walter Chrysler, who has just come from breaking ground in downtown New York for what will be the world's tallest building. Al Jolson, Douglas Fairbanks, Charlie Chaplin, Harold Lloyd, and Gloria Swanson have flown in from Hollywood for the occasion. Florenz Ziegfeld and baseball's Ty Cobb, who has been in a scrap or two himself, are with us and I am told that there are nine senators, ten state governors, and several city mayors here as well. I understand Chicago entrepreneur Al Capone bought a hundred seats for the bout at forty dollars each. I spoke to Mister Tunney earlier and he was thrilled that Sommerset Maugham has come to see the fight."

"Who the fuck is Summer Set and why would Tunney care that his mom is there?" asked the Babe.

o o o

The bout and McNamee's commentary began. "Tunney's footwork is without parallel in the fight game. He is like a skilled matador taming an angry bull. He jabs away at Dempsey and then dances out of the older man's reach time and again."

Dempsey fans were getting almost as frustrated as their hero when, fifty seconds into the seventh round, Dempsey tagged Tunney with a left hook to the chin.

"The former champ drives his left fist into the side of Tunney's head," exclaimed McNamee. "Tunney careens off the ropes. He's going down, ladies and gentlemen. The champion is going down! Wait. Dempsey hits Tunney again, and again, and yet again."

Screams and shouts from the enormous crowd drowned out McNamee's voice and the thud made by Tunney when he hit the canvas. When the radio audience heard McNamee again he was saying, "Dempsey stands over his opponent with his fists at his sides. Referee Dave Barry, who was a last minute replacement to officiate tonight's bout, is telling him to go to a neutral corner. The Illinois Boxing Commission has ruled that in the event of a knockdown the referee will not commence his countdown until the fighter has retired to the farthest neutral corner. I'm reading Dempsey's lips for you and he has just told the referee that he is staying where he is.

Babe Ruth

Barry is now shoving Dempsey toward the corner. Tunney is sitting on the mat while this drama is enacted before our eyes. Barry returns to him. The count should likely be at five or six by now but Barry is starting, of course, at one."

"What the fuck is this horseshit?" snarled Meusel. "The fuckin' ref's costing Jack the fight."

McNamee continued. "The count has just reached three and the groggy champion is looking up at Barry. Four, five, six, seven, eight, nine. He's getting up, ladies and gentlemen! The champion is getting up on his feet!"

"I can't fuckin' believe this," bawled Ruth.

McNamee described Tunney's slow recovery. "Tunney is cleverly backpedalling, avoiding any more blows in hopes that he can survive the round. Dempsey keeps on going after him. Tunney backpedals more, deftly side-stepping Dempsey's punches. Wait. Dempsey has dropped his gloves to his side. He's challenging Tunney. Stand and fight he's beseeching him. Tunney will do no such thing. Standing still is not his style and Dempsey should be well aware of that. He is clearly not prepared to fight the kind of fight the former champ wants."

A mostly-recovered Tunney out-skilled Dempsey the rest of the way. Dempsey managed nothing more than the occasional glancing blow and Tunney outpointed him in almost every round. The ten-round decision in Tunney's favour was expected and unanimous.

"Rotten, crooked, no good bastard referee just cost me a hundred bucks," grunted Meusel.

"Cheer up, red ass," said the Babe, "the fucker just cost me a grand. I don't feel that bad though. Capone's out fifty times that."

George Pipgras was at his best ever on Saturday. The Tigers got only three kittenish singles. Pipgras won it 6-0, his third straight complete game victory. He could hardly wait to get home to celebrate his turn-around with Mattie. She'd tried her best to hide how anxious she'd been for George to do better, but he'd seen it. She'd been walking on egg shells around him for weeks, making small talk about everything and anything but baseball.

o o o

& THE 1927 YANKEES HAVE THE BEST SUMMER EVER

Miller Huggins was sitting with his feet up in his office after the game, thinking how lucky he was that Pipgras was giving him the luxury of resting his other starters for the Series, when the telephone on his desk rang. He listened and called out to Ruth who was still in his uniform.

"Jidge. Long distance for you from Hollywood, some producer fellow."

The Babe elbowed Ben Paschal out of his way and hurried to the phone. "Ted, Ted Wilde? How's things out there? You keepin' them cuties in line?" He listened some more. Wilde wanted him for another picture - just a cameo role this time - that was being shot in New York.

"Harold Lloyd? I love his pictures. The guy's a riot," Ruth bellowed into the phone, thinking he had to talk loud because of the distance.

Wilde explained that Lloyd's character, Harold Swift, whose nickname is Speedy, falls for a girl after they spend a day together and go on the Barrel of Love ride at Coney Island. He loses his job as a soda jerk because he's always bugging customers for news of the Yankee games and especially of how Babe Ruth is doing.

He gets a job driving a taxi and gets in trouble again for asking his fares if they know the Yankee score and whether the Babe has hit one out. He can't afford to lose this job if he wants to have enough money to marry his new sweetheart. Speedy's thrilled when his hero steps into his cab and tells him he needs to get him to Yankee Stadium in fifteen minutes.

"You, of course, play yourself," Wilde told Ruth, "it'll only be a couple of mornings of work and we'll pay you a thousand dollars."

"Sounds like fun, Ted. I'm all yours," said the Babe.

o o o

He was anxious to tell Claire about his new movie role. It was nice to have someone to share things with. But before heading to her place he needed to pick out something special he'd decided to get for Julia. As he reached the door of her apartment, carrying a box that seemed to be whimpering, the landlord spotted him. "Quiet, little fella," the Babe whispered to the box.

Claire opened the door and Ruth stepped inside. "Is Julia home?" he asked.

"She's in her room," Claire told him. She looked at the box, which was being quiet for the moment. Ruth smiled. "Julia, the Babe's here and he has another present for you."

Julia ran into the room. Her eyes fixed on the box. "What is it?" she asked excitedly.

Ruth handed her the box. When Julia opened it, a Pomeranian puppy stuck its head out. He licked Julia's face.

"A puppy! He's so *cute*. I love him!" she exclaimed. Then her face dropped. "But Mommy said we couldn't *have* a dog."

There was a loud knock. As Claire opened the door, Ruth stepped out of the way, behind it. The landlord, a small man wearing a t-shirt, blue dungarees, and suspenders, came in. He couldn't see the Babe.

"Hello, Claire," he said. "I'm pretty sure I just saw a man come to your door with what sounded like a dog. They're not allowed."

"My boyfriend didn't know," said Claire.

"The actor fella?"

"No. I'm seeing someone else now."

"Another actor?"

"No. But he's had a lot of big hits," Claire giggled.

"Well, I don't care *how* big he …"

Ruth stepped out from behind the door and stuck out his hand. A look of disbelief came over the landlord's unshaven face.

"Name's George. You can call me Babe. Everybody else does."

"Claire. You should have said …"

"How d'ya like a couple a World Series tickets and some signed baseballs?" asked Ruth. "The girl sure seems to like the puppy."

"Well, I don't imagine folks'll say much if they know it's you that gave it to her," said the landlord.

"We'll keep him as quiet as we can," offered Claire.

The landlord ignored her. "Are the Yanks ever gonna lose a game?" he asked the Babe. "Ever since you started cloutin' homers every game, the

& THE 1927 YANKEES HAVE THE BEST SUMMER EVER

rest of the league hasn't had a prayer. You're closing in on sixty, right? How many parks have you hit balls out of this month?"

"A few, I guess. That's what folks wanna see. Can't let 'em down."

"Well you surely aren't. You're all anybody's talking about these days. Say, I gotta go fix somebody's sink. Great seein' ya, Babe."

Once the landlord had left, Claire turned to Ruth. "I heard from Ty Cobb again," she told him.

"What did the louse want this time?" the Babe groaned.

"He said he had two tickets to a new Broadway show and asked if I'd go with him."

"What did you tell him?" Ruth asked nervously.

"I told him to take a friend. If he has one."

The Babe doubled over in laughter as Julia chased her new puppy all around the apartment.

o o o

Fifteen game-winner George Whitehill started for Detroit in the last game of the series on Sunday and kept the Yankee bats in check. Earle Combs managed three singles which matched the production of all his teammates. Gehrig struck out his last three times up. Waite Hoyt, going for his twenty-third win in what he expected would be his last start of the season, gave up eight hits and watched as his mates, to the consternation of Miller Huggins, made three errors behind him, including Koenig's forty-third. He knew he was lucky not to have cost his team a lot of games. The Tigers won it 6-1. No homer for the Babe. He had four games left and he was still four short of the record.

Huggins called Gehrig into his office after the game. Hug picked up his pipe and then set it down again. "What's happened to you, Lou? You aren't the same player. One for twenty-two your last five games and no homers in three weeks? It's lucky the Babe's been hitting them like he has. Your fielding's awful too. You're such a horse. None of us can figure out what's wrong with you."

"The dawcter says it's a swellin' of the neck resultin' from an improperly

Babe Ruth

functioning thyroid gland," said Lou.

"What exactly does all that mean?"

"It's a goiter, Skip."

"You're kidding. I had no idea, nobody's noticed. Not even Doc Woods." He got up and went to examine Lou's massive neck muscles.

"It's not me, Hug."

"What did you say?"

"I said it's not me. It's my mom."

"Oh. It's your *mother* that has the goiter."

"I'm so worried I can't see straight, Hug," said Lou, starting to choke up. "She's sufferin' somethin' awful. It's lookin' mawr and mawr like she's gonna have to have an awperation."

24.

CAN HE REALLY DO IT?

"It's been accused of a lotta things, but never of being too noisy."

Gehrig hit his first homer in three weeks in the fourth on Tuesday when the A's came to town for a single make-up game. He was a distant ten blasts behind the Babe though. Lou received a polite round of applause. He kept his head down and headed straight to the bench.

His homer had given New York a one-run lead. Connie Mack decided he had lost just about enough games to this team. He brought in his ace Lefty Grove, but the fireballer kept getting his pitches up and the Yankees kept laying off them. With the bases loaded Grove had no choice but to go after Ruth and he hung his head when the Babe lined the ball into the middle of the bleachers in right center. The stands erupted in a tumultuous roar. Fifty-seven now and three games left.

○ ○ ○

The Senators came to town for the last series of the regular season. There hadn't been any doubt as to who would win the pennant for several weeks. The only drama left was whether Ruth would top his own record and be the first - and maybe the last - to hit sixty.

Hilda and Gladys were at the game. They waved Ruth over to the stands. "We thought you might be up for some *action*, tonight, Babe," said Hilda.

"We know how much you like threesomes and we've got some new tricks up our garters," Hilda giggled.

"Sorry, gals, I'm stayin' in nights," said Ruth.

"You are?" asked Hilda, startled.

"That ain't like you, Babe," said Gladys.

Babe Ruth

"I'm concentratin' on breaking my homer record," said Ruth. "Gotta save my energy."

"All right, then," said Gladys, disappointed. "Call us when you're ready for some fun."

Ruth headed in to get his glove.

Claire was sitting three rows up. She smiled and called Eddie Bennett over. She handed him a small box. "Could you please give this to the Babe, Eddie?"

"This is from that brown-haired beauty of yours," Eddie told Ruth.

The Babe opened it and smiled. There was a note printed in lovely italic letters that said,

Cobb phoned last night.

I told him he should never call me again.

Hit one for the kids, Babe.

I'll see you tonight, darling,

Love Claire

The note was wrapped around a bag of chewing tobacco. Ruth grinned. He knew Claire was mimicking the ending of *Babe Comes Home*. The note was attached to the bag with a pink garter.

The Babe took care of business early. In the first inning Hod Lisenbee was two strikes ahead in the count and tried to sneak a bender past him for strike three. Number fifty-eight landed a few rows into the right field seats. Ruth hit one hard to right center his next time up. It looked sure to go out but it caromed off the railing and back onto the field instead and he had to settle for a triple.

The Yankees loaded the bases in the fifth. Bucky Harris signalled for Paul Hopkins who had just been called up from the New Haven Pilots. He'd been racking up strikeouts and running up scoreless innings in the minors all summer. Fans looked at him and then down at their scorecards and tried in vain to figure out who this guy was.

"They really oughta think about putting numbers on their sleeves or somethin'," one fan said to another.

As he finished his warm-up pitches Hopkins looked to see who was coming out of the Yankee dugout to bat next.

"I wonder what my E.R.A. will be if I give up four runs before I get anybody out," he thought to himself.

The first major league hitter he would face would be Babe Ruth. With the bases loaded.

He had to wait a minute. The Babe handed ash-blond Big Bertha back to little Ray Kelly and asked him to get Black Betsy.

"Not Beautiful Bella, Babe?" asked Ray.

Ruth pulled some sunflower seeds out of his pocket, stuffed them in his mouth, and said, "Nope. I'm goin' with Betsy."

Hopkins murmured on the mound. "It don't matter, it don't matter," he tried to persuade himself. "The way I bin' throwin' the last few weeks, I can get *anybody* out, even him."

He threw two sharp hooks and two monster shots landed high up in the seats just foul, one to right, the other to left.

"All right, that's two strikes at least. I bin' saving my best curve for last," Hopkins told himself.

It broke perfectly, over the outside corner. Ruth hesitated, unsure whether it was a hook or a change of pace. Then he put everything he had into his swing.

The crowd fell dead silent.

Marshall Hunt recounted what happened next in his column in the *Daily News*.

> There was a moment of hushed expectancy as the count became three and two on the captain of the home run industry. Then there was that ominous sound of a heavy instrument, struck with vast force, meeting a pitched ball from the right arm of Master Hopkins. There was a shriek as the white pellet whistled its course into the right field bleachers and as the mammoth character legged his way around the bases, pursuing his three comrades, there was a symphony of rejoicing from the clients such as these sagging ears have not heard in many a year.

Babe Ruth

In his five seasons playing at Yankee Stadium the Babe had hit a grand total of one grand slam home run. Now he'd hit two in two days. In his last at bat Ruth clouted another long fly. Rookie Red Barnes was already playing deeper than he ever had. He corralled it with his back against the fence.

"The Babe could well have had numbers 58, 59, 60, and 61 all in one afternoon's work," wrote Frank Graham in the *New York Sun* that night. "Not in all his spectacular years has the Babe had a greater day than this."

Hod Lisenbee, in his street clothes, went to the Yankee clubhouse to get the Babe to autograph the ball he'd hit for number fifty-eight. Ruth obliged. When Lisenbee thanked him and left, Ruth asked, "Who in the hell was that?"

o o o

Ruth took Claire to dinner at Sardi's new restaurant that night. She wore a black dress trimmed with French lace and a turban hat with an ostrich feather. Sardi's had opened on 44th Street in March. The Babe didn't like the French décor and he thought the portions were much too small. He didn't recognize a lot of the dishes the waiters took to people's tables but he got excited when they set fire to some of them.

Claire wasn't too impressed with the food either but she liked the twenty-five dollar bottle of Pinot Noir the Babe bought for her. He drank beer from Germany like he had at his old man's bar as a little kid. The people at the next table were talking about a play called Dracula they were going to see after they ate. They said an actor named Bela Lugosi was playing Dracula. The Babe thought that sounded like a girl's name.

o o o

He stayed at Claire's apartment that night. After Julia had gone to bed they had a couple of night caps and made love.

"Be quiet," whispered Claire.

"Me? You're makin' more noise than I am."

"You'll wake everyone up."

"You already did that when you panted a minute ago."

"I did not."

"You did so. Can I put it back in?"

"Yes, but quietly."

"My tool has been accused of a lotta things, Claire, but never of being too noisy."

That got them giggling so hard under the covers they could hardly finish.

o o o

Claire woke up and looked at the clock. It was 3:15. At first she wasn't sure what had woken her. Then she realized that the Babe was tossing and turning and groaning. She could tell he was having a bad dream.

"Let go a me," he called out. "Lemme go! I didn't steal nuthin'. And I ain't goin' back to that school."

o o o

Claire finally woke him up.

"You were having another nightmare, George."

The Babe rubbed his eyes. He realized that even though a cool breeze blew through the wide open window he was sweating like a pig.

"Jeez, Claire, it was terrible. I was in an alley and there was garbage everywhere, and rats runnin' all over the place, and this big truant officer was chasing me. And then a nasty-lookin' cop snatched the pie I was carrying and hit me with his nightstick. And when I fell down and started ta bleed he started kicking me. And my father was looking at me through the door of the bar and laughing his guts out."

o o o

In the Yankee clubhouse before the game on Saturday Ruth was trying to get himself geared up to break his own home run record. He looked up at the hazy sky. It was a muggy day, in the low 80's, with not even a slight breeze.

"Jeez, I just realized. I'm tied with myself," he told Tony Lazzeri. "Guess I'll hit one today."

"I'll bet you ten bucks you don't," Lazzeri challenged him.

"You're on, ya little dago. Now I'm definitely gonna hit one."

o o o

Babe Ruth

It was all tied up in the eighth, 2-2. Ruth had walked twice, for which the Washington pitcher Tom Zachary had been booed mightily. He'd also scored both Yankee runs with a pair of singles to boost his batting average to .356. Koenig slashed a triple to left field to lead off the eighth and the Babe came to the plate.

"The prick's already dinged me for two this year," Zachary thought to himself as he grabbed the rosin bag. "He isn't gonna set the fuckin' record off me." He kicked dirt over half of the rubber so he could move a bit closer to the plate. Ruth watched him do it and grinned.

Zachary's first pitch was a sizzling fastball with great speed and lousy location, right down the middle. Ruth had clearly been expecting Zachary to start him off with a sharp hook. He watched it whiz by.

"Strike one," yelled Bill Dinneen.

The next pitch was another fastball, high and outside this time.

"Nope," grunted Dinneen, clicking his indicator to register ball one.

Zachary's next pitch was a wicked curve, as good as Zachary thought he'd ever thrown. It was low and away.

"Ba …" Dinneen started to say.

Ruth started his swing. The pitch was much too low for a normal swing so the Babe was going to golf it out the park.

"Oh no," Zachary muttered to himself, "not far enough out."

Ruth pulled it hard and on a rope. The ball climbed and climbed and the fans stood and watched it.

"Stay fair, stay fair," a little boy exhorted the ball.

He got his wish. It landed in the second row of seats a foot inside the foul line. Ruth smiled and tossed Black Betsy toward Eddie Bennett who had been waving his arms and willing the baseball to clear the fence. It didn't need any encouragement. Number sixty landed in a dense forest of outstretched hands. A dozen explosions of flash powder wafted from the line of photographers who'd knelt in wait on either side of the dugout.

Zachary threw his glove to the ground as the Babe jogged around the bases grinning from ear to ear, touching each bag firmly and carefully. In

& THE 1927 YANKEES HAVE THE BEST SUMMER EVER

the dugout, his teammates banged their bats on the floor.

When he trotted out to his position for the start of the ninth, the citizens of Ruthville greeted him with a thunderous round of applause. The Babe waved, stood at attention, and then returned their adulation with a crisp military salute.

"Sixty," the Babe announced in the clubhouse after. "Let's see some son of a bitch try to top that!"

o o o

Arthur Mann of the *New York Evening World* went to Ruth's locker as he was getting into his street clothes.

"Did you think you were going to break your record this year, Babe?"

"Not at the start. The first time I believed I really had a chance was when I socked three in two games in Boston early this month and went ahead of Lou. We had the pennant pretty well clinched and I could afford to do a little hitting for myself. That was when I got busy."

"Do you think you'll ever top sixty?" asked Mann.

"Maybe next year I'll get off to a better start and hit seventy. I don't know and I don't care, but if I don't, I know who will." He pointed to Gehrig. "Wait until that bozo there gets wading into them again and they may forget a guy named Ruth ever lived."

As it had turned out, the Babe'd had the field all to himself in the closing weeks of the season. Mysteriously, Gehrig was no longer a factor. Fans knew nothing about his mom's goiter or the effect it was having on him.

Lou had entered the September 7 game batting .389, with 45 homers and 161 runs batted in. He was on a pace to drive in 186 runs. He didn't. Not even close. Some speculated that in spite of his awesome strength and conditioning he was tired from playing every inning of every game including all the double headers. But he'd played every game in '26 and he'd driven in runs in every one of the Yankee blowouts in September. Besides, he took a lot better care of himself than Ruth and the Babe was playing every game as well as the exhibition games on the off days.

Babe Ruth

Others thought the pressure of the Home Run Derby had gotten to him. But Lou was just as happy to see Ruth succeed as himself. He never expected to beat him at his own game, he didn't have a swing tailor-made for hitting home runs like the Babe did. In the remaining twenty-two games of the '27 season Gehrig had hit just .275, with only two home runs, two doubles, and two triples.

Up in the press box Paul Gallico was busy writing his piece for the *Daily News*.

> *There has never been a more determined athlete than George Herman Ruth. With a new record in sight he was bound to make it. He is one of the few utterly dependable stories in sports. When a crisis arises he never fails to supply the yarn. A child of destiny is George Herman. He moves in his own orbit like a far off planet.*

The next day, in the last game of the regular season, Lou Gehrig belted his forty-seventh in the first inning, a three-run shot that propelled the Yankees to their one hundred and tenth victory.

The Babe's bat was silent for a change. "I'm saving 'em for the Pirates, fellas," he told reporters after the game.

o o o

"Gehrig's hundred and seventy-five runs batted in was pretty impressive considering sixty of the times he came to bat Ruth had just cleared the bases with a home run," Richards Vidmer told James Harrison over a beer.

"You're right. I hadn't thought of that," said Harrison.

"And with a hundred and seventeen extra base hits and the Babe not eligible because he's already won the award, it's no wonder Gehrig was voted Most Valuable Player."

"He's not sure if he's going to play in the Series," said Harrison. "His mother's scheduled for surgery. I talked to him yesterday and he said his mother means more to him than any ball game ever invented."

Vidmer looked back at his notes. "Of the eight American Leaguers to drive in a hundred runs four were Yankees - they scored a hundred and thirty more runs than the next highest scoring team. No team had as many triples, homers, or walks and no team matched them in batting average, on-base percentage, or slugging average. Lazzeri's eighteen long balls would have led any other team. With this club they seem like almost a footnote. One out of every four homers in the league was hit by guys named Ruth and Gehrig."

"A writer from Detroit, a statistics buff, summed it up best the other day," said Harrison. "The guy said the American League set a record this year. It was the first time ever that seven of the eight clubs finished in the second division."

Babe Ruth
& the 1927 YANKEES have the BEST SUMMER EVER

25.

POUNDING THEM OUT IN PITTSBURGH

"If they ain't nervous, they ain't human."

A thousand fans cheered the Yankees as they strode to their Pullman cars at Penn Station. Their train, the Iron City Flyer, was due to leave at 10:30. Hoyt, Meusel, Lazzeri, and Gehrig moved through the mob completely unnoticed. Hundreds of kids swarmed the Babe, who wore a brand new linen blend cap. Station police struggled to clear a path for him. A red cap carried his bag and got a five dollar reward. Ruth shook as many outstretched hands as he could. This was the kind of railway greeting he'd been used before his collapse in '25. He told his admirers he thought he would crash a few in the Series.

When they got to Pittsburgh the Yankees checked into the Roosevelt Hotel at 6th and Penn. It had just opened for business, perhaps a bit too hastily. They carried their grips through the large Tudor-style lobby that featured paneled oak walls, polished marble floors, and a twenty-foot tall portrait of Teddy Roosevelt above an enormous fireplace.

o o o

In the morning a reporter sat across from the Babe at breakfast. He figured Ruth ate enough to feed the whole Pirate infield and the batboys too. When the Babe finished, the reporter shoved a picture at him.

"These are the Waner brothers, the Pirates' biggest stars. What do you think of them?"

Ruth took a close look at the photo. "Big? Hell if I was that little I'd be afraid a gettin' hurt."

"How are you figuring to do in the Series after having such a great season, Babe?"

Babe Ruth

"I better have a pretty damn good Series. Else the sixty I hit aren't gonna mean a thing. A lotta people in New York are countin' on us. Me especially. It's been four years now since we won 'em a championship."

o o o

The Yankee lineup may have been Murderers' Row but the Pirates were no slouches. Six of their eight position players had batted over .300. Pie Traynor, whom everyone agreed was one of the best third baseman ever, was coming off a .342 season. The right fielder, 24-year-old, five-foot eight, Paul Waner, a.k.a. 'Big Poison', had led the league with forty-two doubles, 237 hits, and a .380 batting average in his second year in the majors. Hitting wasn't his only forte. People said he could match the Babe drink for drink. His five-foot nine brother, centerfielder Lloyd Waner, 'Little Poison', had batted .355, with 233 hits in his rookie season.

Miller Huggins told his men to take longer than usual shifts in the batting cage during batting practice the day before the first game. He knew the Pirates would be watching. He told Waite Hoyt to take it easy. "Just throw medium speed fastballs right down the middle," he told Hoyt.

Benny Bengough was catching. He kept looking up to where the Pirates were sitting as the Yankee regulars pounded one ball after another over the fences. Ruth and Gehrig each hit at least a dozen into the double-decked bleachers in right field, the Babe five in a row at one point. Most of the Pirates were well aware of Ruth's power but few of them had seen Gehrig before. Bengough noticed their looks of amazement and disbelief when Lou rocketed one over the center field fence. No National Leaguer had ever done that. Then Meusel and Lazzeri drilled a few into the seats.

"Jesus, they sure are big," Lloyd Waner said to his brother.

"The hell with that stuff," said Donie Bush, shooing his players into their clubhouse. "We'll show 'em we've got a few hitters ourselves."

The Babe put his bat away and sat on the bench.

"I sure kissed that last one," he said to anyone who was listening.

"Look out!" yelled Koenig.

On his last pitch before yielding the cage to Joe Dugan, Lazzeri had lined the ball right at Hoyt. He fell to the ground clutching his left leg. He'd been hit just below the kneecap.

"Sorry, Waite," yelled Tony.

Doc Powers ran out to Hoyt. Luckily he wasn't hurt and would be able to start Game One.

"You had better be careful out there tomorrow," Pie Traynor told Ray Kremer, who was going to be the Pirates' starter the next day.

"Maybe I better wear shin pads," said Kremer.

"Well you sure as hell better not forget your cup."

A smartly-dressed young woman emerged from around the corner of the Yankee dugout. She had a notepad in her hand.

"Hello, Mister Ruth," she said.

"Hi ya, miss," said the Babe, a little startled by her sudden appearance.

"Do you remember me?"

Ruth hoped this was not another girl pursuing a paternity suit. He looked her up and down. "I think I do. Didn't you interview me one time?"

"That's right," she said. "It was in Elmira."

"Sure, I remember. You asked me if I really liked children hanging off me all the time."

"And you said you loved it."

"Well I still do."

"My editor saw a picture of you in one of the other papers eating breakfast and he wants me to have breakfast with you and write a story about it."

"He does, does he?"

"Would you mind?"

"Not at all. How's tomorrow suit you?"

"That would be great, Mister Ruth. What time?"

"I eat breakfast at ten o'clock."

"All right. I'll be there. Don't forget."

Babe Ruth

"The Babe forget breakfast?" chuckled Dugan. "Not very likely."

"I met Mister Huggins too that time in Elmira," said the perky reporter.

"Here he is now, missy. Hug, here's a young lady that knows you."

"Glad to see you," said Huggins.

Ruth moved over so Huggins could sit between them.

"They oughta get a picture of *that*," said Bengough, "a rose between a thorn and a gorilla." Right on cue a photographer appeared out of nowhere and snapped the picture.

"This park is the place where I always hit the best," Huggins told anyone who was listening. "I bet I hit four hundred in this park."

"You must have got horse collars everywhere else to get your average down to two thirty-one," snickered Urban Shocker.

"What's all that hammering?" asked Bengough.

"They got some carpenters putting in temporary seats," Huggins told him.

"Where's Eddie?" asked Combs. "Hey Eddie, grab the bats, it's starting to rain a bit."

"Yah, and where's my new glove?" asked Ruth.

"I got it, Babe," said Gehrig.

"What do you think of the hotel?" Cedric Durst asked Lou.

"I like it fine," Gehrig told him.

"Me too," said Koenig, "but I wish they'd cleaned up when they finished building it. I found a step ladder, a set of electrician's tools, and a dirty undershirt in my room."

"Hey Hug, you got our passes yet?" asked Koenig. "I met a gal that said she'd like to come see me play."

"She won't be able to see your baby blues from the stands," teased Dugan.

"They'll be ready in my room before dinner," said Huggins.

"What room are you in?" asked the Babe.

"Seventy-one, Jidge."

"I asked for your room number not your age," chuckled Ruth. "Say, who's shorter, boys? Their manager or ours?"

"Believe it or not, Hug's an inch taller than Bush," said Combs.

"Holy crap," said Ruth. "When's the last time you were taller than somebody, Hug? Outside a the time you went and talked to that kindergarten class."

Even Lou got that one.

o o o

Up in the press box before Game One Frank Graham asked Ring Lardner, who was covering the Series for the *Evening World*, if he thought the Pirates had been intimidated by the batting practice display.

"I don't know if I'd go so far as to write that the Pirates are scared," he told Graham, "but if they aren't nervous, they ain't human."

Photographers had the Babe shake hands with Huggins, Gehrig, Jake Ruppert, Commissioner Landis, Donie Bush, Pirate owner Barney Dreyfuss, and Jimmy Walker. When they finally had their fill Ruth walked around shaking hands with himself. A brass band in red coats marched around the field to entertain the forty thousand fans before Game One.

When the Babe came up to bat in the first inning the Pirates' bench jockeys went to work.

"Hey, look fellas, it's the big Baboon," yelled one.

"The Sultan of Sweat," yelled another.

"The Colossus of Clap," yelled a third.

"You gonna suck any peckers with those nigger lips a yours?" yelled yet another Pirate.

Ruth seethed but he was used to it after all these years. He'd expected it.

"We'll see if your bats are as big as your mouths," he yelled. "I hear you all got tiny dicks."

o o o

From high above, Graham McNamee described the action for millions gathered around the radios they'd bought on instalments. McNamee had read a lot about baseball and attended several games since Opening Day.

Babe Ruth

He still mixed up players' names and positions though. He still called pinch hitters pitch hitters and he still couldn't fathom the infield fly rule. He was often busy describing in great detail a fan's apparel and subsequently missed outs and base hits. He put players on bases they didn't occupy and more than once said the Giants were in the lead.

Early in the game he announced that both third basemen were left-handed, which neither was. In the third inning he informed his listeners that Tony Lazzeri was on third base. Then he had him at second and then he was back at third. The next time Lazzeri batted he thought it was still Gehrig at the plate and he said the pitcher got a fastball over just in time. He never explained what it was in time for.

"The Bambino blazes a vicious drive to right. It reaches the fielder so quickly that he's able to limit Ruth to one base. A popcorn box is blowing across the outfield. Smoke can be seen rising from the steel mills in the distance. Wait. I'm sorry. Gehrig lines a ball to center that scoots under Paul Waner's glove. Ruth, who still runs very well, especially for such a big man, scores all the way from first. Gehrig is driving his tree trunk legs hard and he ends up with a hit of three bases. Lou is feeling better now, as his mother's surgery went well. He is even playing top-notch first base, scooping low throws out of the dirt, gobbling up hard hit groundballs, and knocking down line drives."

McNamee was right. Gehrig robbed George Grantham of a double in the fourth with a running stab behind first and again in the eighth when he snagged a seething ground ball Grantham had shot down the line.

Waite Hoyt took the mound with a 5-3 lead into the eighth. He got Paul Waner to hit a lazy fly ball to left but Glenn Wright singled to right and Traynor followed with a single up the middle.

"Get Moore," yelled Huggins to Mike Gazella as he headed to the mound to pull Hoyt. Gazella jogged out to the bullpen and soon into the game strode Wilcy, just as casually as he had thirty-eight times during the regular season.

Grantham grounded out to Gehrig but sent Wright to third. He scored a minute later when Joe Harris singled to center. The Pirates were within a run of tying Game One. The catcher, Earl Smith, stepped to the plate.

& THE 1927 YANKEES HAVE THE BEST SUMMER EVER

His average had fallen seventy-five points in '27 and he'd gone 0-3 against Hoyt. He was glad to see anyone but him on the mound. The only problem was that he'd never seen sinkers like Moore threw.

"You can do it, Cy," yelled Gehrig.

"This guy's all yours," shouted Dugan.

He was. Smith hit a weak grounder to Gehrig and Lou stepped on the bag for the third out.

In the ninth the Pirates' pitcher Johnny Miljus was due to bat. Donie Bush ignored loud calls from the stands for him to send up Kiki Cuyler. After batting .343 in 1,700 at bats over the last three seasons, the popular Cuyler had found himself in Bush's doghouse. He'd played in only half of Pittsburgh's games. Bush sent 160-pound reserve outfielder Fred Brickell up to hit instead.

"Why the fuck isn't he using Cuyler?" Pie Traynor muttered.

"Brickell's only had six hits all year," mumbled Ray Kremer.

Brickell grounded meekly to the mound and Wilcy Moore threw him out.

"Ya shoulda used Cuyler!" yelled a leather-lunged fan.

Lloyd Waner lined out to Combs in center and Clyde Barnhart, who was playing in Cuyler's former spot, tapped a harmless grounder to Moore. The Yankees won, 5-4.

Wilcy's teammates swarmed him. "Shucks, weren't nothin', boys. That's one in the barn."

o o o

George Pipgras had spent the game in the bullpen. When he got to the clubhouse Miller Huggins called him into his office.

George was nervous, though he couldn't think of anything that he'd done wrong. He prayed Hug wasn't going to tell him this would be his last season with the club. "What's the matter, Skip?" he asked.

Huggins lit his pipe and smiled. "Nothing, George, nothing at all." He picked up a page of statistics from his desk. Pipgras picked at a thread on his uniform.

Babe Ruth

"You had a couple of pretty fine starts in September, George. A four-hitter against the White Sox and a three-hitter against the Tigers which are a hard-hitting club."

"Thanks, Hug. What ..."

"You're starting tomorrow, George. You've earned it."

"Really? You aren't joshing?"

"I wouldn't pull your leg about a thing like that. You're my starter."

"That's great. I won't let you down, Skip."

"I don't expect you will."

George wasn't sure he'd be able to sleep that night. He did, but he'd spent the twenty-five cents to make a long-distance call and given Mattie the good news. She didn't sleep a wink.

o o o

Joe Dugan arrived in a lousy mood for Game Two.

"Fucking thieves," muttered Joe. "If I get my hands on them, I'll wring their necks. Gutless bastards."

"They should really have thought about putting locks on the doors before they opened the place," said his roommate, Waite Hoyt.

"What happened, Joe?" asked Koenig.

"Some creeps must have snuck into our room last night. We had our pants over the backs of chairs and when we went to put them on this morning we realized our billfolds weren't in them."

"Maybe the Roosevelt'll reimburse you," suggested Ruether.

"They sure as hell better," fumed Dugan.

o o o

There were a few catcalls about why Cuyler still wasn't in the Pittsburgh lineup as Pipgras took his final warm-up pitches. Little Poison led off the first for the Pirates. The crowd roared when he hit Pipgras' first pitch over Bob Meusel's head to the big blue *Players' Tobacco* sign. He jogged home a minute later when Clyde Barnhart hit a sacrifice fly to the Babe in right.

Mattie Pipgras and several of the other wives were huddled around the radio in the Pennocks' apartment. She groaned.

"Don't worry, Mattie," Dorothy Hoyt consoled her. "He'll be fine."

He was. Pipgras shut out the Pirates for the next seven innings. The Yanks scored two runs on four straight hits in the third and it stayed 2-1 until the eighth. Apparently five o'clock lightning worked in National League parks too, but it was far from a normal display of Yankee power. They scored three runs on three singles, two walks, a fielder's choice, a wild pitch, and a hit batter. Ruth and Gehrig grounded out to end the inning or the game would have been a rout.

Pipgras blazed fastballs by the Pirates all afternoon. Their speed seemed all the greater given how methodically he worked. Up in the press box Ring Lardner leaned over to James Harrison. "Say, I haven't covered many games this year but does he always take this much time? Hell, he could boil an egg and get a shave and a haircut between throws. And what is with him fidgeting with the cap, rubbing the ball, hitching up his trousers, tossing the rosin bag, and screwing his cap on right again. Hell he does everything but undress and get examined for life insurance out there."

"Well I can tell you one thing," said Harrison. "It's driving the Pirates crazy."

"Sometime today, Pipgras," Bush yelled at him.

"Come on, Pipgras, the hotel's gonna give away my room," hollered Pie Traynor.

McNamee described his style. "The six foot one pride of Ida, Iowa is finally prepared to make the pitch. He turns his back to the batsman, then comes 'round to deliver the ball, and all of his corn-nurtured one hundred and ninety-some-odd pounds are packed into his delivery."

Pipgras took his sweet time, broke a few Pittsburgh bats, and limited them to one more run in the eighth for a 6-2 win.

In the clubhouse Ruth grabbed the young hurler's hand and shook it. "You showed them a real fastball today and they didn't like it one bit. Great work, keed. Allowing just seven hits in your first World Series game is something you should be proud of. I was just as happy as you are right now when I won my first series game with the Red Sox."

Babe Ruth

"Thanks, Babe," gushed Pipgras.

o o o

Back in New York the other wives crowded around Mattie and told her how wonderfully her man had pitched. She had never been prouder of him.

"Maybe I'll sleep tonight," she laughed.

"You should try," Marie Shawkey told her. "You may not get much sleep when George gets home."

26.

CAN THEY BE THE FIRST?

"And ta think, a year ago this time my alarm clock was a rooster."

Among the swells who paid a whopping six dollars for box seats for Game Three at Yankee Stadium were Charlie Chaplin and Harold Lloyd.

"We finished the picture, Babe," yelled Lloyd. "I saw your rushes, they looked good."

"Come on out to my place again if you're ever back in Tinseltown, Sport," yelled Chaplin.

"I didn't know Chaplin was English," said Joe Dugan.

"Sure he is. *Everybody* knows that," said the Babe.

o o o

"Are you worried about all the talk that the Pirates murder left-handed pitching?" James Harrison asked Herb Pennock before he went out to take his warm up pitches.

"We'll see," was all Pennock said.

Specs Meadows was the Pirate starter. When he'd been signed by the Cardinals' scout after winning twenty-one games for the Durham Bulls in '13 Miller Huggins, then still managing St. Louis, had thought the scout was crazy for signing a player who wore glasses. But Specs had impressed Hug with his speed and control.

The Yankees got to Specs for two runs in the bottom of the first. Combs singled and Koenig hit a comebacker to the mound that took a strange hop over Meadows' head. Then Ruth hit one of his trademark mile-high pop ups. Gehrig, who'd been at his mother's bedside at St. Vincent's hospital since returning from Pittsburgh, drove a ball to the wall in center for a triple. Combs and Koenig scored easily and Lou tried to as well. He was out at the plate by ten feet.

"I wish I had your legs, Jidge," he told the Babe when he returned to the dugout.

"Sometimes I wish I had your *arms*," said Ruth.

Meadows restricted the Yankees to their two runs until the time for five o'clock lightning rolled around in the seventh. Pennock singled, Combs singled, and Koenig doubled. Bush sent in Mike Cvengros, "the Slavic southpaw".

"Holy shit," said Dugan. "His nose is the size of a goddam cauliflower! It's bigger than the Babe's."

Ruth had been struggling with Meadows' slow ones the whole game. After the count reached two-and-two Cvengros fired a fastball over the inside corner. He shouldn't have. The resulting sharp, loud crack had been a familiar sound at Yankee Stadium in the past few weeks. Ruth propelled the ball into the back rows of the right field bleachers. They erupted in a deafening wall of noise. As the Babe trotted the bases after his three-run homer he wasn't sure he'd ever heard louder cheering. He noticed that in spite of their ecstatic expressions, a lot of people were covering their ears because of the din.

Pennock's benders broke exactly the way he wanted. He retired the first twenty-two batters in succession - with some help from Lazzeri, Dugan, and Koenig, each of whom made terrific plays. In the Yankee dugout you could hear a pin drop. Nobody said a word about Pennock's perfect game. In the wives' section of the stands no one dared to even look at Esther.

Pie Traynor finally broke up the perfect game in the eighth and scored on Clyde Barnhart's double for Pittsburgh's only run.

"*Finally!*" breathed Esther after Traynor's hit. "Now maybe you girls will talk to me."

They all laughed. Dorothy Hoyt gave her a big hug.

All of the players not on the field were on the dugout steps as Pennock pitched the ninth.

"Come on, Herb, let's have him," urged Miller Huggins between vicious chews on his fingernails that were probably unwarranted with an 8-1 lead.

"Who's that hitting for the Polish guy?" asked Cedric Durst.

"Heinie Groh," said Art Fletcher. "Used ta be a pretty good hitter back in the day."

"Ya, but why isn't Bush usin' Cuyler?" asked Hoyt. "Hug sure wouldn't let one of his best hitters sit out the whole damn Series just cuz he was mad at him."

"Easy does it, Herb," called Pat Collins.

"Take him yourself, Herb," urged Mike Gazella.

Groh hit a little pop up to Pennock and flung his bat in disgust.

"That's the ticket," yelled Durst.

It was Lloyd Waner's turn to try to keep the Pirates from falling into a deep hole.

"Now the little guy," hollered Ben Paschal.

"You got him, Herb," yelled Huggins.

"Make him hit it, Herb," shouted Gazella.

"Lay it in there," Julie Wera called out.

Little Poison hit a Texas Leaguer to center. Combs raced in but couldn't reach it. He corralled it and held Waner to a single.

"Way ta trap it, Earle," yelled Paschal.

Hal Rhyne, the second baseman, stepped into the batter's box. He'd replaced George 'Boots' Grantham, who'd earned his unkind nickname after committing fifty-five errors with the '23 Cubs, even though Grantham had outhit Rhyne by thirty points during the season and had two hits in Game Two. Bush wanted his right-handed bat against Pennock.

The strategy appeared to have worked when Rhyne drove a pitch deep to center. Combs, who'd just had to run so far in for Waner's blooper, now had to run even farther back.

"Attaboy!" chorused several of Combs' teammates when he finally hauled it down at the fence.

Babe Ruth

Paul Waner took a vicious swing at Pennock's first pitch and popped out to Lazzeri. Game Three was over. Three zip Yanks.

The Babe had been swarmed after the final out and he was the last to join the lineup as the two teams squeezed through the passageway that led to the two dressing rooms. He towered over most of the Pirates as his cleats clicked against the cement floor. A group of reporters waited outside the clubhouses.

"One more game'll end it, fellas," he called to them.

None of the Pirates said anything. They silently shuffled into their dressing room, heads down. Ring Lardner could hardly believe it. He turned to James Harrison. "Can you imagine the Cardinals or the Giants keeping quiet after he said something like that? They'd have raised bloody murder and called Ruth every name in the book. The Pirates are beat. And what's worse, they know it."

In the locker room Ruth whistled *Bye-Bye Blackbird*. The other players joined in.

"Stick a fork in 'em," he bellowed, "those boys are done."

o o o

Ford Frick caught up to Jake Ruppert on his way to dinner after the game.

"That was your kind of game, wasn't it?" said Frick.

"It certainly was. The boys got a big lead and there was no doubt they would win," said Ruppert.

"It's going to cost you a lot of money if your squad wins it four straight, two hundred thousand for each home game you don't need."

"I don't care one bit about that. It would break my heart if they lost the next game. I would rather have the honor of owning a team that can beat a National League champion in four straight than all the money in the world."

"No American League team's ever won the Series four straight," said Frick.

"You won't be able to say that much longer, Mister Frick."

George Pipgras didn't get to celebrate his big win with Mattie. Not yet anyway. Ruppert and Barrow had decided that to keep the players' minds on playing baseball instead of going for groceries and taking out the garbage they should stay in a hotel. Mark Roth booked rooms at the Plaza.

"This is where the Vanderbilts stay," Herb Pennock told Benny Bengough as a white-gloved doorman ushered them into the opulent foyer.

"Scott and Zelda Fitzgerald stay here too," said Benny.

"They do?" asked Joe Dugan excitedly.

"Ya, Joe," said Benny. "Maybe she'll come to your room and give you a bath."

o o o

After dinner at a steakhouse the movie set headed to see *Wings*, which was being called a cinematic sensation and possibly one of the best films ever. They had a surprise addition to their group, the Babe. They weren't all *that* surprised though.

"Bow's a Brooklyn girl. She talks a lot like Buster," Ruth told the others as they were led into the theater ahead of everyone else. They'd dutifully stood on line outside, but the Babe's presence had created a mob scene.

"Maybe she'll come home for a visit some time and you can introduce her to us," said Paschal.

"I'd sure like to get her autograph," said Combs.

"I'll ask her to sign your dick, Earle," said Ruth. "Course it's so small she'll have to initial it instead." He roared at this own joke and several people looked around to see what had happened.

"I read that it cost Paramount two million to make this picture," Pennock said as they took their seats near the back. "They hired five thousand extras and built sixty airplanes."

"I heard a double got killed and a stuntman got his neck broken," said Paschal.

The huge audience gasped at the realistic aerial dog fights. Some had been shot with a camera inside the cockpit and, as intended, they provided the sensation of sitting at the pilot's shoulders. Another one was mounted on the outside to let the audience see the pilot's reactions.

Babe Ruth

A Sopwith Camel plunged earthward after being strafed by an enemy plane. Black smoke streamed from it. The Babe's eyes widened to the size of quarters and a big smile overtook his broad mouth when Clara Bow's breath-taking face stretched across the thirty-foot tall screen. From the ground below she watched as the plane carrying her sweetheart crashed into the ground in a fiery burst of flames that reflected in Bow's beautiful eyes. Tears streaked down her perfectly-formed cheekbones.

"That was a pretty amazing crash," said Gehrig.

"It sure was," said Paschal.

"I wonder if the Pirates are gonna crash and burn like that tomorrow," said Combs.

o o o

"The Colonel really wants us to take them four straight," Miller Huggins told his charges before Game Four.

"Well then, let's go out and do it for him, boys," said Ruth, pounding his fist into his glove.

"After the luxury hotels he put us up in all year, it'd be a nice way to thank him," said Dugan. "We lived like Rockefellers," quipped Wilcy.

"Let's not forget the clean uniforms every game," added Lazzeri.

"And he never made Earle pay for that ball he let the alligator swipe in Florida," Herb Pennock pointed out.

Given his terrific work throughout the season, it was only fitting that Huggins gave the ball to Wilcy Moore. He didn't let his manager down.

Lloyd Waner drove one of Cy's sinkers into the ground to short to lead off the game. Koenig gathered it up and threw to Gehrig. The ball smacked into Lou's glove when Little Poison was a step from the bag.

"Safe!" yelled first base umpire Ernie Quigley.

"What?" screamed Huggins from the dugout steps.

He was about to race out and confront Quigley when Art Fletcher said, "Let it go, Hug, we all mess up once in a while. The umps can't stop our bats. It's not worth getting thrown out over."

& **THE 1927 YANKEES HAVE THE BEST SUMMER EVER**

Fletcher didn't feel quite so forgiving when Waner came around to score on Glenn Wright's two-out single to give Pittsburgh the early lead, but three straight singles to lead off the bottom of the first tied things up. Things quieted down and Moore and his opponent, Carmen 'Bunker' Hill, Pittsburgh's biggest winner with twenty-two, put up zeroes in the second, third, and fourth.

Earle Combs led off the Yankee fifth with a bloop single in front of Lloyd Waner. Hill struck out Koenig and then worked carefully to Ruth. Not carefully enough. The Babe smashed one high among the throng in right field and the Stadium overflowed with unbridled joy.

Moore's drop balls were still confounding the Pirates in the seventh when their catcher Earl Smith led off with a dribbler in front of the mound that Pat Collins pounced on and then dropped. Fred Brickell batted for Hill and grounded one to second. Lazzeri fumbled it and the go-ahead run came to the plate. Lloyd Waner wasn't likely to hit one out. Bush ordered him to bunt and his sacrifice moved the runners to second and third. Clyde Barnhart, still in for the sulking Cuyler, singled to center and Paul Waner hit a sacrifice fly to center and the game was tied.

Bush sent Johnny Miljus in to pitch. His major league career had begun in 1915 with the Pittsburgh Rebels of the Federal League. He hadn't given up a run in his four innings of work in Game One.

The fifty-seven thousand fans let out a roar in the bottom of the ninth when the Babe came to the plate after Combs had worked Miljus for a walk and Koenig had reached on a sacrifice bunt attempt that Pie Traynor muffed.

"Fuck!" yelled Bush, throwing his cap at the bat rack. "He makes that play a thousand times out of a thousand."

"Go! Go!" the Yankee bench yelled at Combs and Koenig a minute later when Miljus uncharacteristically let go a wild one with a 0-1 count on the Babe. Earle scurried to third and Mark raced to second.

"They shouldn't have gone," Huggins muttered to himself. "Now they're gonna walk the Babe."

Donie Bush waved to Miljus. "Put him on, put him on."

Babe Ruth

A murderous chorus of boos rained down from the stands.

"Chicken shit Pirates!" yelled someone.

"Gutless so and so's!" bellowed someone else.

The Babe tossed away his bat and spat tobacco juice after the intentional walk. "You can throw balls, but you ain't got any," Ruth called out to Miljus as he trotted to first. Miljis was hardly out of trouble with Ruth's home run partner coming up, but Lou took three mighty swings and missed with each of them. Meusel came to the plate and returned to the dugout three minutes and three not so mighty futile swings later.

"They're gonna be naming streets after Johnny back in Pittsburgh if he can strike out Lazzeri too," Paul Waner yelled to his brother across the outfield.

"Just like last year," Huggins whispered to Herb Pennock. "It's all up to Lazzeri."

"If he hits one the dagos'll go ape shit and Mussolini'll pin a medal on him," Dugan called in to the dugout from the on-deck circle.

"Free shaves, free haircuts, and free spaghetti for life," said Pennock.

"Tonee!" yelled someone at the top of his lungs.

Lazzeri spit on his hands and crossed himself. He drilled the first pitch into the left field stands.

Charlie Moran, the third base umpire, raced down the line and stared after the ball.

"Foul!" he yelled as the ball curved to its left.

"Fuck! Just like last year," Tony muttered to himself.

"Noooooo!" yelled Bush as Miljus' next pitch, a rising four-seam fastball glanced off the catcher's outstretched mitt and rolled to the backstop. Combs threw his cap in the air and dashed across the plate.

"Kind of a crummy way for it to end," said Dugan as they reached the clubhouse. "Too bad Tony couldn't have been the hero. But the main thing is ... we won!"

& **THE 1927 YANKEES HAVE THE BEST SUMMER EVER**

Miller Huggins climbed up on a bench so he could be seen and heard above the chatter. "I'm real proud of you boys. Some of you cavorted more than I would have liked, but come game time you were all ready to go and you always gave it your best effort. You deserve this."

"After that season, we just had to win it all, Hug," said Hoyt. "We had no choice."

Marshall Hunt came into the room. The Babe, who already had a cigar in his mouth, shook up a bottle of champagne and doused him with it.

"Thanks a lot, Babe," he sputtered. "Fellas, I just talked to Ruppert, the winner's share is five thousand, five hundred and ninety-two bucks."

A couple of the players whistled.

"I've never seen that much money in my life," said Julie Wera. "Wait'll I show my check to the fellas back at the meat-packing plant."

"The wives are gonna be very happy," said Shawkey.

Wilcy Moore yelled. "All that money. And ta think, a year ago this time my alarm clock was a rooster."

Wilcy ended up with a sparkling 0.68 E.R.A. for the Series. Koenig led the Yanks with a .500 batting average but the Babe had been the hero with the only two home runs in the four games and seven RBI's to go along with a .400 average. Most important in his mind was that he hadn't let down the kids who adored him again.

Babe Ruth
& the 1927 YANKEES have the BEST SUMMER EVER

27.

TIME TO CELEBRATE

"It would give me some standing in my class if I could tell them I'd gone to bed with a national hero."

To celebrate winning the World Championship the Babe and Claire, the Pennocks, Shawkeys, and Hoyts went for dinner at Larry Fay's El Fey Club on West 45th Street that night. Texas Guinan met them at the door. "Hello, suckers!" she bellowed.

When they were seated, Jimmy Walker came over to their table. He was dressed to the nines as always and as usual had a curvy showgirl on his arm.

"It was good to see ya at the game today, Jimmy," the Babe told the mayor. "Glad you could tear yourself away from city business."

Jimmy chuckled. "That was some series you fellows had. Especially you, Babe. You made New Yorkers very proud." He looked at Ruth and then eyed Claire up and down. She was wearing a backless gold lamé dress. "So *this* is the woman that persuaded Babe Ruth to stay home at night. I can see how."

"Ain't she a peach?" asked Ruth, giving Claire a hug.

"That's quite the necklace Claire is wearing," Marie whispered to Esther.

"I heard it cost the Babe a big chunk of *his* World Series check," Esther whispered back.

When Walker had moved on to another table Dorothy looked at the menu. "Isn't this place a bit pricey?" she asked. "Twenty-five dollars for champagne?"

Waite said, "We're celebrating tonight, hun. With the Series check I can pay off the Chevrolet."

Babe Ruth

"And we can go ahead and christen it," giggled Dorothy.

Everyone laughed when Waite told her, "It can be our struggle buggy."

Joe said, "I was thinkin' of buying some new wheels with my Series check, but I think I'm gonna take my beautiful wife somewhere instead. Maybe a slow cruise to the Tropics." Dot beamed.

The Babe had been whispering with Claire. He turned to the others. "Everything's on me tonight, folks. Christy Walsh gave me a check for a thousand bucks for writing those pieces on the Series."

"They were good, Jidge," said Waite. "I had no idea you knew so many big words."

"I been studying. That's what I've been doin' with Claire instead a goin' out nights."

"Spooning's more like it, I imagine," said Waite. They all laughed.

They started with salads. Their pretty waitress explained that the menu now included three new choices, the Cobb salad that the Brown Derby had recently created, the Green Goddess salad from San Francisco, and the Caesar salad that a chef named Caesar Cardini had served to Hollywood celebrities when they'd visited his restaurant in Tijuana.

They ordered steaks and the men salivated over them as well as the scantily-clad young girls that shimmied provocatively right next to their table.

"Ain't they a sight for sore eyes, boys?" shouted Guinan.

Marie elbowed Bob hard in the ribs. "Eyes back in your head, lover boy."

o   o   o

The couples had a tough time deciding which show to see. They'd all seen *Wings* and thought they might take in a burlesque show instead of a picture show given that it was a special occasion. Billy Minsky's review, which had advertised low gags and long legs, had been shut down, just like Mae West's Sex show. *Irish Justice* had been raided too. The judge demanded that its cast perform the show in his court room so he could decide how lascivious it was and one of the dancers bared her breasts, kicked up one of her long legs toward him and said, "How 'bout meetin' me at midnight,

Judgie?" He had not been amused.

"I think you boys have seen enough shimmying, shaking, and coochy-coochy dancing for one night," said Marie.

"I guess the Padlocks of 1927 is out of the question then," said Bob.

"What about George M. Cohan's new production, The Merry Malones?" asked Waite. "It's playing at the Erlanger. It's a song-and-dance show, but I hear it's got a good story."

"Why not the Ziegfeld Follies show that opened while we were on the road?" asked Herb. "Irving Berlin wrote all the music."

"Is that the one that has Eddie Cantor made up to look like a colored fella?" asked the Babe.

"That's the one," said Herb. "Claire Luce is in it too. She's the doll who starred in No Foolin' last year."

Esther gave him a dirty look.

Herb grinned. "I mean she's the young actress who starred in No Foolin'."

o o o

The theater was so jam-packed they had to sit in two separate sections, but the Follies were amazing. At one point an ostrich carried Claire Luce, dressed in a nearly transparent outfit, through a jungle full of flamingos, tigers, and cobras. The sexy star had a huge tiger she had clearly worked long and hard to train literally eating out of her hand. Then he licked her all over and rubbed his head up and down her legs.

Waite elbowed Urban. "Do you think *you* could do that?"

"Sure. If they'd get the damn *tiger* out of there."

Hoyt laughed so loud the entire orchestra turned around to look.

o o o

Two weeks after the Series ended Miller Huggins dropped in on George and Mattie Pipgras on his way to a dance hall he was buying to convert into a roller skating arena. After Mattie offered him coffee and he declined he took out his pipe and lit it.

"You heard from any of the other fellas, Skip?" George asked.

Babe Ruth

"Well, Dugan's getting his knee looked at again. Pennock's raising his hounds and silver foxes. Koenig and Lazzeri are back home in San Francisco. Pat Collins is in Kansas City seein' about getting in on a bowling alley. Cy bought his two mules and they won't do a thing they're told, just like the guy they're named after. And Bengough's headed down South to play some jazz. What have you been up to, George?"

"My uncle got me a job selling Duesenbergs. A pal of his just opened a dealership. My uncle says they're top of the line, one of the fastest, most powerful cars around. Tom Mix has one and so did Rudolph Valentino. I'm gonna see if the Babe's interested. I make a ton of commission on every one I sell. Say, you wouldn't be …"

Huggins held up his hands. "No thanks. Anything Jidge can afford is way out of my league. You doing anything for fun?"

"Mattie and I were thinking of getting a BMW and goin' for a spin around the country."

"Doesn't BMW only sell motorcycles in the States?" Huggins asked.

"That's what I'm talking about, a motorcycle."

"I'm afraid I can't let you do that, George. They're far too dangerous."

"What do you mean?"

"I've got some news for you," he said.

"Should I leave you two men alone?" asked Mattie, who looked terrific in a new dress she'd bought at Macy's.

"No. You should stay and hear this."

She flattened her dress along her sides and sat down.

"What is it, Hug?" asked George nervously.

"Shawkey's heading home to Slippery Rock to open a golf course after he and the Tiger Lady have a second honeymoon in Paris. Ruether's so mad he didn't win fifteen and get his big bonus he's packing it in and heading out west, and I don't see Shocker pitching much at all, so you're going to be in the starting rotation next year."

Mattie put her hand over her mouth. Tears began to well up in her eyes.

"That's swell, Hug," said Pipgras. "I won't let you down."

"I have some other news but you can't breathe a word of this to anyone. Understand?"

"Yes. What is it?"

"When I told Barrow that you were going to be one of the starters in '28 he said he'd have to double your salary."

"Oh my goodness," said Mattie. "Forget about a gosh-darned motorcycle, we can get a new car. I won't need to ride the subway anymore!"

o o o

Across town the Hoyts and the Pennocks met for lunch to plan a trip together.

"How about a cruise?" Dorothy suggested eagerly.

"I don't know, Dorothy," said Esther. "Getting waited on hand-and-foot? I was really looking forward to cooking and cleaning house all winter."

They both laughed until Herb held up a hand. "All right, you two. Enough already. We know you've been planning a cruise ever since we pulled fifteen games ahead of the Senators."

"Just tell us where it is you want to go," said Waite.

"We were thinking about the Caribbean," said Dorothy.

"Isn't it hot there most of the time?" asked Waite.

"I suppose so," admitted Dorothy. "What's wrong with that?"

"You didn't have to bake like a French fried potato in St. Louis this summer like I did. How about somewhere cooler?"

"What about the Mediterranean?"

"Still too hot."

"What about Alaska?" suggested Herb.

"Fine, I suppose. But we'd have to leave pretty soon," said Dorothy. "It'll be freezing up there in December."

"An Alaskan cruise it is," said Esther.

Babe Ruth

"Oh, but wait a minute," said Dorothy. "That means we'll have to shop for new clothes, deck wear and the like."

"Oh no. You're right," giggled Esther.

The men groaned. "Where can I get a beer?" asked Herb.

"You don't drink, hun," said Esther.

"You're gonna drive me to it," chuckled Herb.

They headed their separate ways, Herb and Esther to pick up the new car they'd ordered and Waite and Dorothy to christen theirs.

o o o

It was still morning in San Francisco. Tony and Maye dropped by Mark Koenig's bachelor apartment to see if he was eating properly. A conservatively-dressed nineteen-year old with long brown hair, smoldering green eyes, and a slender but curvy figure rose from a living room chair to greet them. Tony's eyes widened.

"This is my fiancé, Katherine Tremaine," said Mark.

While Katherine and Maye made coffee in Mark's tiny kitchen he and Tony talked in the living room.

"Where d'ya meet *her*?" Tony asked.

"I used to deliver things my mom sewed. Katherine - she was Kitty back then - was just a little kid. She used to follow me around all the time. When I got back to Frisco she'd just come back from college. She was all grown up."

"She's a bella donna," said Tony. "Maye can introduce her to the other wives when we get back to New York."

"Finding Katherine was a heck of a way to end a great season," said Mark.

"It was a great season, wasn't it?"

"It might just have been the best season a team'll ever have."

o o o

The third Madison Square Gardens had been built on 8th Avenue, between 49th and 50th Streets, in 250 days by boxing promoter Tex Rickard at a whopping cost of nearly five million dollars. The Babe stood on a stage that had been set up in the middle of it. He wore a grey pin-striped suit, a pink shirt, and a pink tie with thin grey stripes. His huge nostrils flared as he towered above the small man who was introducing him. The announcer, who had a splash of grey around his temples and a pencil-thin moustache, stood close enough to get a whiff of Ruth's expensive cologne.

In a reedy, high-pitched voice he said into the microphone, "Good evening. It is my great honor - and might I add ... *thrill* - to introduce to you the Sultan of Swat, the King of Clout, the Bambino, George Herman Babe Ruth!"

By the time the announcer got as far as 'Herman' the audience began to shower Ruth with wave upon wave of deafening applause. The Babe waved his hat in the air and nodded his head. Then he just stood still, basking in the adoration, tears in his big brown eyes. He blushed and waved his hat again.

The emcee was stunned when Ruth jumped off the platform and waded into the crowd. "Babe, where are you ...?" His words tailed off, there was no chance Ruth could hear him. He supposed that the Babe had seen a great-looking woman in the audience and wanted to arrange a meeting when there weren't so many people around.

Sure enough Ruth walked up the aisle to a shapely brunette. He eyed her up and down, taking in her curves. She batted her eyelashes and was about to say something when the Babe left her behind and continued into the crowd. A few rows behind the beauty, a boy in a newsboy cap who looked to be about ten stood on a chair so he could see over the adults standing up in front of him. He was mouthing, "You're the greatest, Babe."

The boy's eyes grew to the size of donuts when he realized his hero was looking right at him and then - impossibly - coming right to him. Ruth turned sideways and bent down a little. "Climb aboard, son."

The boy didn't hesitate for an instant. He clambered up onto the Babe's back. Ruth winked at the lad's father and piggy-backed the boy to the stage. The emcee chuckled as the Babe returned to the stage with the kid.

"Thank you, my fellow New Yorkers," said Ruth, even though not a soul could hear him.

Babe Ruth

After another five minutes of clapping and cheering, Babe nodded again and then carried the boy back to his dad, who looked almost as thrilled as his son.

The Babe shouted in his ear, "Bring your boy to Yankee Stadium tomorrow. He can play ball with me and my favorite little girl."

"Thanks, Babe!" yelled the kid.

"I think he could miss one day of school," said his father. "We'll be there."

o o o

Marshall Hunt had been at the Gardens of course. On his way out he was stopped by a pretty teenage girl. She wore a high school sweater and a pleated skirt. Her ash blonde hair was in a ponytail.

"Excuse me, sir, I hear Babe Ruth is a friend of yours."

"Yes, he is. Why do you ask?"

"Do you think you could fix me up with him?"

Hunt was a bit taken aback. "Why would a young girl like you want to get mixed up with a fellow his age?"

"It would give me some standing in my class if I could tell them I'd gone to bed with a national hero."

o o o

Ruth picked up Julia and Claire to take them to Yankee Stadium the next morning. They hadn't gotten very when Julia realized that she'd forgotten to pick up her ball glove from the front hall table. Back they went. It was already getting hot and the Babe rolled down his window while he and Claire waited for her daughter to run up to the apartment and fetch her glove.

He decided he might as well get out and stretch his legs, even though there was plenty of room in his Pierce Arrow. He walked a little ways down the block and looked down a side street. The kids he'd seen playing stickball a few weeks ago were starting up another game.

This time, he heard the big kid holding the stick say, "I want to be the Babe."

"I wanna be Babe Ruth," said the other boy.

& **THE 1927 YANKEES HAVE THE BEST SUMMER EVER**

"You can be Gehrig again."

"I don't want to be Gehrig. He's boring."

As Julia reappeared, this time with her glove, Ruth smiled.

o o o

Claire sat in the stands in the near empty park. A few groundskeepers and seat painters were its only other inhabitants. The Babe hit soft, easy grounders to Julia and the boy from the Madison Square Gardens event. Claire was soon joined by Marshall Hunt. He offered her a swig from his flask and she declined. Then she changed her mind and took a nip.

"That was *some* year the Babe had," said Hunt. "And people had been saying he was over the hill. Rubbish. I give a lot of the credit to you though, Claire. Because of you he stopped running all over town looking for … well, you know, and he and the team ended up having a season for the ages. Christy Walsh tells me your boyfriend's getting more endorsements than he ever was. And people are saying the Babe is the best player ever again."

"We both know that there's only one thing the Babe really cares about."

"I know. He just wanted the kids to love him again." Hunt motioned down to the diamond. "And it sure looks like they do."

The Babe had hit a roller to Julia. She'd fielded it and thrown it in to the Babe. He let the ball hit him square in the chest and then dropped to the ground like a felled tree. Julia and the boy looked at each other, giggled, and dropped their gloves. They ran in and jumped on top of the Babe. He had a smile as wide as the ocean.

Babe Ruth
& the 1927 YANKEES have
the BEST SUMMER EVER

EPILOGUE

George Pipgras did join the starting rotation in '28. He led not only the club but the entire league in starts and wins. That earned him an even bigger raise, a whopping $5,000. Mattie did a lot of shopping with Katherine Koenig.

Earle Combs patrolled center field in Yankee Stadium for the next eight years and batted over .300 in each one.

Urban Shocker pitched only two innings in '28. He died of complications resulting from a degenerative heart valve before the season was over.

Miller Huggins, the manager of six pennant winners and three World Championship teams, died two years later.

Lou Gehrig became the Iron Horse, playing in 2,130 consecutive games at first base. He never bettered the 47 homers he belted in the Home Run Derby of 1927. He died of Amyotrophic Lateral Sclerosis at the age of 39.

Jumpin' Joe Dugan played 94 games in '28. Then his trick knee gave out for good. He really did Dorothy on a cruise to Hawaii.

Waite Hoyt won 23 games in '28 and later performed in vaudeville with Jack Benny and George Burns. He continued practicing as a part-time mortician.

Marie "the Tiger Lady" Shawkey never did murder Bob. He died on New Year's Eve, 1980 at the ripe old age of 90.

Tony Lazzeri was baseball's best second baseman for the next ten years. He never suffered an epileptic fit during a game.

Herb Pennock pitched another seven years and endured many more of Lazzeri's practical jokes before returning to Kennet Square, Pennsylvania to raise his silver foxes.

Babe Ruth

 The Bambino went on to smash another 303 home runs. When Major League Baseball held its first All-Star game in 1933, Ruth predictably hit the first homer. At the age of 36 he batted .373. The Babe still has baseball's highest career Slugging Average, an incredible .690. He was one of the original players inducted into the Hall of Fame - along with his arch-rival Ty Cobb, who retired at the end of the next season and died years later, bitter and alone.

 The Babe married Claire Hodgson and adopted Julia nine months after he belted number 60.

Babe Ruth & the 1927 YANKEES have the BEST SUMMER EVER

OUT OF THE PARK